WRESTLING
WITH
GABRIEL

WRESTLING
WITH
GABRIEL

A Novel

David Lynn

Carnegie Mellon University Press
Pittsburgh 2002

Book Design: Andrea Georgiana
Cover Design: James Mojonnier

Library of Congress Control Number: 2002101289
ISBN 088748378X

10 9 8 7 6 5 4 3 2 1

They are all we have, you see,
all we have to fight of
illness and death.
You don't have anything
if you don't have the stories.

— from Ceremony
Leslie Marmon Silko

This is entirely a work of fiction.

For Aaron, Elizabeth, and Wendy, always.

PART I

Prologue: A Story

Gabriel bangs again at Juanita's front door but knows already it's no good. The gray weathered wood creaks. Another blow may splinter it. Frustrated, angry, he slams the heel of his palm against the plastic doorbell, cracking it like a child's toy. He glances quickly over his shoulder, but there's no one on the street. Windows closed, doors bolted, lights out, the small house waits for a new tenant. Might be it's been months empty. Except three days ago he caught Juanita staggering up the walk on spike heels with a sack of groceries. He held the bag for her while she fumbled with keys. "Leroy around?" he asked. She stepped inside the door and tugged the sack from him. Shook her head. "Thanks," she said, already shutting the door on him with her shoulder. "When's he back?" "Try Thursday," she said.

"Shit," he says out loud. These people—never dependable. There's no counting on them. He doesn't suppose Juanita lied. Probably just forgot. Or didn't think. Maybe she'd already got a new place and didn't remember to mention it. Maybe Leroy spooked again and yanked her somewhere new with no warning.

Gabriel turns and stands on the stoop, hands in his pockets. "Shit," he says again. All day he's been looking to this and now there's nothing. All day hauling paunches on the kill floor he'll be thinking about cool, sweet air in the night and now, after sweating in that stench and heat for eight hours, the chill blows right through him and he shivers.

Even with Grey on the nightshift at another packing plant, the only thing he can keep in the house without being hassled by her and the Party is some beer. And he doesn't want beer. That won't cut it tonight, not after all the thinking and planning.

The house where Tammy Jean has a room is painted pink, was painted pink. In the streetlight the peeling strips of paint are dark along the edges with a hint of something garish, like fruit rotting from the inside. He raps on the screen door.

"What you want?" cries a woman from back in the kitchen. Tammy Jean leans out her window above the porch. "You looking for me?"

He backs away from the door so he can see her. Her head's wrapped in a green towel. Her large breasts billow over the sill in her bathrobe. "You know where Juanita and Leroy moved?" he calls.

"I know about Juanita. Who the hell knows about Leroy?"

"Yeah, well, I need to find him."

She snorts. "I bet you do. Go on and toss me up one a them rocks."

Gabriel picks a small stone out of the alley and tosses it up underhand. Tammy Jean claps it between her hands and retreats into her room. In a moment she's flinging the stone in a little arc towards the street. A scrap of newspaper's fastened with a rubber band. Across it she's scrawled an address in crayon, no, lipstick. "Maybe you shouldn't tell her you heard it from me," Tammy Jean cries with a rough caw of a laugh and slams the window.

Gabriel jams the scrap of paper into his pocket. 29th Street is only half a mile, but he's impatient and annoyed. The

International Socialist Alliance assigned him here better than two years ago, but he's never had time or inclination to explore the city in any systematic fashion. So he cruises right past 29th the first time because the sign is down. Loops around in a liquor store lot and discovers on the second pass that the street is one-way at this end. "Goddamn mother," he growls. He wrenches the wheel, hits the gas, his tires squeal as they bounce over the edge of the curb.

He's sweating and a headache has swooped out of nowhere. Only one of the street lamps along this block is shining. Half the houses sag vacant, their lots strewn with debris—tires, oil cans, beer cans—tangled weeds uncut this summer or last. Gabriel cruises slowly, looking for a number. He's not sure if it's this block or the next one down. A boy, maybe fourteen, is sitting on the curb, bouncing a basketball between his feet in the darkness. Gabriel pulls over and pushes the passenger door open. "Hey—You know the numbers along here?"

The boy keeps bouncing the ball, shakes his head.

"Shit, man." Gabriel tries not to shout. "You know a Juanita Harris or a Leroy Johnson?—they just moved around here somewhere."

The boy catches the ball but looks away down the street. "You got some change? I sure could use somethin' cold."

Gabriel digs in his pocket and comes up with a quarter and some pennies. He tosses them at the cement. Kneeling, the boy sweeps them together and picks them up daintily one after the other into his palm. "Leroy's house up there, third one, leftside."

Lights are on inside, but the closed-in front porch is dark. No number he can see. Why the fuck can't anyone put fucking numbers up?

Tugging the screen door open, he steps up into the porch. Inside, it's dark and musty, smelling of dog, though he doesn't see or hear any dog. Some kind of tools clutter up against the walls. He presses a doorbell. No ring or buzzer he can make out, so he pounds on the heavy front door. Nothing. He pounds again.

"Just hold on—I'm coming." The door swings open with a blast of light and MTV noise. Standing in front of him she's pretty, sixteen probably, what with the bad perfume and the swelling chest. Behind her on the floor sits a younger girl in front of the tv. "What you want?" she demands, shutting the door to a crack between them.

"This 4847? I'm looking for 4847."

"That ain't here—I don't know where that is. Maybe next block."

Gabriel is patting his thigh with one hand. Rage gathers, swelling in his chest. It shoots hot currents through his legs and crotch and arms, stokes his headache. "Look," he says with magnificent calm, "what about Juanita Harris? Or Leroy Johnson—you know them?"

"I don't know no Juanita. Leroy's my daddy—Leroy Jackson—and he's a big mean sonofabitch. You better get out a here."

"Yeah," he says sourly and turns away. He pushes open the porch door and stares out into the night. It's early but quiet. A streak of light spills out past him and he knows the girl's watching him. What's she so damn curious about? Sounding not scared or angry but full of herself, strutting her old man and her own cockiness.

He isn't going to find any stuff tonight. There's no time to keep looking. He's supposed to be putting up some political friends from out of town. Any minute now they'll be showing up at his house. Gabriel takes a deep breath of the cool night air. It doesn't help. It leaves him panting.

"What you doing?—Go on and get the hell out," says the girl. "You go on."

Gabriel swings round. "Shut up," he snaps. "Shut the fuck up." The door's still open a crack. The girl's scared now. She's frozen, eyes dark pools. Annoyed at her helplessness, he slams his hand against the door, just to scare her good.

She tries to shut it against him and, because she tries, he kicks at it. Kicks it again, this time with the sole of his boot. The door crashes open as the girl falls aside. Before she can run, he catches her by the wrist. "Come here," he growls. Her sister is caught in the middle of the floor, unsure whether to help or flee. "Go hide in your bedroom," he yells at her.

Panting but otherwise silent, the girl is writhing, tugging, slapping at him with her free hand. He drags her out onto the porch. "Stop—don't hurt me, mister," she whimpers at last, too scared to cry out.

He catches her free hand and bends it behind her. "I'm not," he says into her hair, breathing her smell—it's potent with fear, drowning the rank perfume. He's controlling his rage and proud of it. He tugs her close, runs his hands over her ass, squeezing, up round to her breasts. He reaches into her shirt to push the bra up. She's standing still, whimpering, trembling. "Oh man," he murmurs as he bends to suck one breast, then the other. "Oh man." He pulls at the front of her sweat pants, trying to loosen the cord. He's pushing at the pants, shoving them down over her hips.

"No—please no," she cries and starts to struggle, pulling up at the pants, twisting away from him. She flails an arm and scratches his ear.

"Jesus. Bitch." He tugs her forward and trips her. Together they fall, she crumpling under. Her head strikes something hard on the floor, a car battery. Swooning, she's stunned. He's got to have this if there's nothing else to have. And he's pushing at her pants again. She rolls from side to side but doesn't really struggle anymore. As he rears back to work himself free, he pries her legs apart with his knees. He's hard, brilliantly hard, triumphant. Again he sucks her breasts, works up, holds her head in his hands. She's awake but staring past him into the night, her eyes blinking as she chews at her lips. He's watching her eyes. They explode wide as he grinds his hips against her. No need for his hands. He'll find home, digging, thrusting, driving. She's open to him.

A car brakes heavily in front of the house. Gabriel hesitates. A radio squawks. He's pulling back now, rising. Colored lights flash through cracks in the porch door. Quick, measured steps. Someone raps hard.

Gabriel's fumbling, tripping on his own pants.

"Daddy!" the girl shrieks as if she's been playing possum. She darts to the door, pushing free into the street, only her shirt dark-bright against the flashing lights. The cop falls back as she rushes past him.

Gabriel's pants and underwear grab like tangled sails as he yanks at them with one hand. Banging into the house with his shoulder, he stumbles towards the back, searching for another way out. The sister huddles on the couch cradling a phone, digging away into the cushions with terrified eyes. Gabriel rushes past into the kitchen, but the back door's sealed with plywood. He lunges into a bedroom.

"All right—hold it. No way you'll get through a window like that anyway. You're under arrest, asshole." The cop catches him by the arm and jerks him around. He steps back and looks Gabriel up and down with a grin as he takes out his cuffs. "And a pretty sight you are too." Gabriel's still trying to tug his pants back up over his dwindling cock. The cop grabs one wrist, twists it daintily and with absolute assurance as he wraps the cuff on.

Another Story

"Sara, hi—yeah it's me. You heard Marta and Gene are coming in? Yeah, for the Rural Women's program. They're staying here. Look, I'm running over to cash our paychecks and pick up some food. Grey's working the midnight shift again. Keep an eye out for them, okay? If they show up in the next half-hour or so, tell them the door's open. Drop by later if you want."

Gabriel picks up his keys and hurries down the steps. His car's an ancient Falcon beat all to hell, but it runs well enough. He's already worked a full shift today hauling paunches on the line, attended a protest for seventeen Latino workers busted in the packing plant last week by INS, and afterwards shared a pitcher of beer in Los Caballeros to celebrate the big turnout. Forcing himself into a quick pace helps him keep focused on what will surely be a long night still ahead. Gene and Marta will want to hear the latest.

For March the night is chilly, but he keeps the window rolled down to shock himself awake. The engine thrums at a red light—he's been putting off a new muffler. Suddenly a shadow darts out from over by a bar. It rushes into the street, flashes across his headlights. She slaps at the passenger window, startling him as if he's half-asleep, watching from a great distance. "Hey, Mister, come on, let me in— please." She's panting, pleading.

Gabriel's arms hang heavy on the wheel. He hesitates. This kind of attack, the tight green dress very low and very short, are signals he knows how to read. The heavy rouge on her cheeks, now that he peers more closely through the glass, may be covering darker bruises. All the energy that'll be soaked into talking with her, discovering whether's she's got a pimp on her tail, ferrying her to a social-worker friend of his, just that instant's thought exhausts him—and then he shrugs it away and pushes the door open. "Get in," he says and waits while she settles next to him. "How long you been doing this scene?"

She's gulping air. "Just drive, okay? My boyfriend's gone off after me again and he'll kill me sure this time if he can."

Nodding as he acts, Gabriel shifts gears and the car jerks quickly away from the light. "Where you heading? Got any friend to hide you? I wouldn't bother with the cops."

For a long moment she doesn't stir. Maybe she hasn't heard. She gives a little hiccup of a laugh and gnaws at a ragged nail. She's younger than he first guessed. Eighteen, maybe twenty. "Yeah, cops sure be happy to help me out." She hiccups again. "Look, man, just give me a ride home, okay?—ain't no other place for me."

"Anything you say." He's staring straight ahead, trying to calm her, reassure her. After another half-block he tries again. "Listen, you ever hear about the women's crisis center? Woman who runs it—she's this friend of mine. They can put you up for a night or two, maybe give you some help."

"Unh-unh. No way. That's all nice and good, but I got to get back to my place, okay? 29th Street. Back the other way."

Unsurprised, Gabriel swings left at the corner. It would be easy to give in, but she's so damn stubborn and he can be stubborn too. "No reason to run scared of this guy. Lots of women have figured out they don't have to put up with that shit anymore."

"What're you, a preacher? It's my life and I know how to take care of myself from any damn asshole."

She's pointing to a bungalow and he draws to the curb. Without a word she climbs out of the car, slams the door, stands still. Turns back and leans in his window. "I got this bad feeling, man. It's stupid, you know, but I'm scared. Just come up to the porch with me, okay? Just make sure he ain't already inside."

Glancing at his watch (Gene and Marta may not think to knock next door at Sara Oliver's), Gabriel gets out. Together they climb the steps. The street is dark, the house is dark, everything is very quiet. If the boyfriend's somehow beat them here, he's hiding. Her nervousness is catching and Gabriel's gut grows tight and hollow as a drum. He tugs the porch door open. Inside it's even darker.

She's hanging back to dig for keys in her shoulder bag. "I think it's cool," she says too loudly, as if to scare away ghosts. "I'm just checking round. Then you take off." She pushes the front door open, standing for an instant peering ahead into the dark, and finally hurries inside. Her elbow shoves at the door, closing it on the crack.

Gabriel's straining to hear as well as see. She's rustling about inside. A click and faint light pokes through. Almost at the same instant a car pulls up in the street. It's big, powerful—the vibrations rattle through the floor. What if this is the boyfriend? "Jesus," he mutters under his breath.

Footsteps trot on the gravel. Gritting his teeth, he figures he'll talk to the guy, make it loud, give her time to slip out the back. "Stupid shit," he mutters, feeling foolish and vulnerable hanging out alone like this. What if the guy has a knife, a gun?

A fist pounds on the door frame. Gabriel, scarcely breathing, stands still. Another fierce rap—"Police," a voice barks. In the echo, the porch door is ripped open. A dark figure, pistol drawn, is silhouetted by flashing colored lights and a single blinding search beam aimed at the house. Gabriel raises a hand to shield his eyes and steps aside. Could she have called 911? Could the cops arrive this quick?

For a single perfect instant everything's frozen. The cop's staring, a statue. Between breaths, still all but blinded by the light, Gabriel is struck by the incredible silence.

The patrol car's radio breaks the stillness with a sharp squawk. The cop holsters his gun. Gabriel, shielding his eyes, turns to glance behind him, surprised that the woman hasn't appeared. She must still be terrified. Suddenly, his arm is grabbed. He's smacked up against the heavy front door, banging it open.

"Hey, no—we thought the guy was already inside," he says, astonished, furious, in pain—his lip is split and bleeding. "Maybe he's still in there."

"Sure he is. Just shut the fuck up." The cop jams him hard in the back and through the door. All Gabriel has time to notice is a single table lamp glowing in the corner. There's no sign of the woman he drove here, no sign of anyone. "Move," the cop orders. He shoves his prisoner toward a bedroom in back.

"Cut it out," Gabriel shouts, anger drowning out his initial bewilderment. Bumping into a mattress on the floor, he struggles to spin and face his adversary, but the cop has him again by one arm, twisting it expertly even as he tugs out the cuffs. The flash of pain bends Gabriel over and the rush of blood in turn makes him dizzy. He's afraid he'll vomit or pass out. "Not me," he manages to whisper. One cuff on, he's yanked straight again. His other wrist is pincered and cuffed behind him.

"Okay," says the cop. His blue eyes are small and jovial. Acne has long ago ravaged his face. "Let's see what we got." He unbuckles Gabriel's belt and unzips him. "Christ, I hate even touching fuckers like you," he says with cheerful disgust. Jerking the pants down, he pushes Gabriel in the chest so that he topples back across the mattress. "Hey, Stan—he's in here."

On cue another cop enters. Gabriel doesn't glance at him. He's sprawled in shadow, half on the floor, half on the mattress, trying to work his pants up to cover himself. With his hands pinioned behind it's almost impossible.

"Must have been trying to get out the back," the new cop says. "Jesus. You'd think he'd at least want to get his pants up."

Chapter I

At 2:15 Monday afternoon, after morning arraignment and a percentage of $30,000 bail was raised, the police released Gabriel Salter. Released him: a guard let go of his arm and Gabriel staggered forward like a drunk six paces into the noise and chaos (shrieking children, bleary relatives, impatient lawyers) of the city jail's waiting room. Angry welts and bruises distorted his face. One eye was swollen shut. It was hard to tell as he stumbled towards us whether he was grinning in relief or grimacing in acute pain. His wife Grey, fierce in her worry, leapt to catch him. Simon Yoo helped settle Gabriel onto a chair to catch his breath.

His head hung forward, chin nearly touching his chest as he panted. Grey squatted next to him, whispering in his ear, hawkish and fierce, stroking his hand. Her long black hair brushed his battered cheek. From where I stood leaning against a bulletin board it was hard to tell whether Gabriel was taking in what she said or not. He gave no sign.

At last he gathered himself, wagged his head gently back and forth to test how wobbly he'd be. With an effort he looked up and stared directly at me. The one visible eye was unexpectedly sharp. What surprised me was his lack of surprise. He even managed a faint smile as he winced with pain.

Grey had been poised to catch her husband because of what we'd discovered at the earlier arraignment, though the lawyer had warned us beforehand. Grey's own immediate dismay—Gabriel's injuries were worse than she'd expected—were quickly displaced by fury. Not only the eye but the whole left side of his face was swollen above a cracked jaw. A large swatch of his scalp had been shaved around a seam of purple stitches closing a long gash. Two days old, the bruises were already yellowing. To the original rape charges against him had been added several counts of assault for attempting to snatch a policeman's revolver (from an empty holster) and wrestling wildly with two officers in the jail's elevator.

"Let's get him out of this place," Simon said to Grey as if Gabriel couldn't hear. Gently but firmly, they each took an arm and raised him to his feet. He seemed stronger now, more certain, and he strode steadily out of the jailhouse into the bright March afternoon. Grey helped Gabriel into the back of Simon's car and slid in beside him. I jogged around the corner to the Dodge I'd rented at the airport and gunned it through a changing yellow light. They hadn't waited for me—I didn't expect them to—but I caught them turning at the next block and followed them to the north side of town.

By the time I walked in the front door of the spartan two-story frame house, Gabriel had been arrayed on a ragged sea-green couch in the front room. His hair was matted with sweat. Although he was dozing, the business at hand was for Simon to snap a dozen photos of Gabe's wounds from different angles. A naked overhead bulb and a standing lamp tilted close to the couch illuminated the welts and abrasions.

Simon moved quickly, efficiently, snapping off shots as if he'd apprenticed with a wedding photographer. (He was striving for the close-up drama of the posed face. Were he a shooter sent along by my paper, he'd be circling further back, aiming for context, for the unposed, for the casually glimpsed horror.) As soon as he finished the roll Simon shifted the lamp away and Grey settled protectively next to Gabriel. She placed a wet cloth on his forehead and stroked his neck awkwardly with her fingers—she was wary of touching his face.

I'd only met Grey for the first time that morning after arriving on the red-eye from Baltimore. She greeted me at their door with a grim face. But as the connection came clear a certain flickering surprise, an unexpected recognition, crossed her face briefly. I assumed she knew who I was—the Salters, even Gabriel, were always big on family history. I'd certainly heard about her, though not as much as I might have; the family discovered she was living with Gabriel just about the same time three years earlier that Hilary, Gabriel's older sister, was divorcing me.

Her name was Grey Navarro, and as I learned later she was Laguna—not Cherokee as I'd assumed when told she was Indian. Apparently there'd never been any question of changing her name to Salter. There was a question of whether she and Gabriel had ever bothered with a wedding. It was hard to imagine him participating in any formal ceremony, especially one sanctioned by the state. Common-law traditions offered greater appeal.

I watched as Grey moved about their house with a powerful grace—that of a dancer who's neither feminine nor masculine. There was nothing particularly feminine about her at all, as if such a category were a confining irrelevance. Sharp, almost crudely chiseled cheekbones framed her dark eyes under a hawkish brow. Her fine hair fell to the small of her back, gathered by a turquoise barrette. The only contrast to the severity was her birthmark, striking as a brilliant flaw, a silver-dollar-sized dab of crimson that rode high on her right cheek, just brushing the corner of her eye.

Although she'd quickly come to accept my presence, Grey's concern for Gabriel that afternoon swept up all her attention. Simon Yoo certainly didn't bother making me welcome. As far as he was concerned I could stand and observe by the door for the purpose of reporting to Gabriel's mother, but that entitled me to no special notice. Annoyed, bored, professionally curious about what Gabriel was accused of doing and what had been done to him, I decided to hang around a little while longer, as if witness must be borne or a vigil endured so that I could report in all good faith that my (former) brother-in-law, rather the worse for wear, had been delivered home safely.

As afternoon wore to early evening, three or four friends who'd helped raise bail drifted in to check on Gabriel, to pay quiet sympathy and declare the first blossomings of outrage. They stood in doorways or sat on the floor. An African American woman, Sara Oliver, silent but imposing, appropriated Grey's stool and sat next to Gabriel, holding his hand in her lap. But given Gabriel's political ministry this struck me as rather a paltry turnout. Others were probably waiting to hear more about what actually happened. The story in yesterday's Sunday Register (I'd lifted one that morning from a trash bin at the airport) had taken its lead, naturally enough, from the police blotter: 15-year-old girl brutally attacked. Local man, Gabriel Salter, meatpacker and socialist, charged.

I assumed Gabriel's other acquaintances couldn't believe he'd do such a thing, but. . . . Maybe that's why Simon Yoo was moving so swiftly. As Iowa chapter head or director or whatever (they preferred to downplay such titles) of the International Socialist Alliance, Simon stayed on the phone at the kitchen table, never for more than five minutes with the same call, jotting notes furiously on a yellow pad. His wire-rimmed spectacles were pushed up on his brow as he wrote. His dark hair was trimmed very short. At a distance his voice sounded perpetually hoarse, and he spoke in direct, impatient monosyllables. Every half-hour or so Simon would step out on the porch for a few quick tugs at a cigarette.

At five o'clock I rose to leave, my bad knee stiff already. Gabriel hadn't opened the eye he could for some time. His breath was shallow but steady. I waved a hand at Grey but said nothing. She gave no sign at all that she noticed. A reporter has to be patient, but I'd pretty well reached my limit. New developments seemed unlikely and I was spent. I'd arrived in Iowa at six in the morning—in fact there'd been precious little sleep since Hilary woke me two nights earlier. But as I reached the front door Gabriel called out, "Jason."

Limping across the room, I stood at Grey's shoulder. Gabriel was smiling at me, though faintly. I felt a distant but familiar twinge. Battered as he was, the smile revived something of the waifishness of his pale skin and sharp, thin features. That smile had always been the secret of his charm. It made the recipient special, the center of the universe for an instant, someone in on a precious secret. And although Gabriel was capable of self-mockery, he seemed to bank on the effect.

He tried to raise himself on an elbow then fell back. "You haven't even said hello and now you're sneaking away without a goodbye?" he said.

"Your mother asked me to check things out. She wants to make sure you're okay."

"You can tell her I'm better than I look," he said. He laughed (and winced again). "No, you better not tell her how I look. Do I look as bad as I think?"

"If you think pretty bad."

He shrugged and turned his head on the greying bed pillow.

Grey's lips were pressed thin. "It's their turn to look bad," she said. "Wait until Simon's pictures get around. They'll tell the story."

"Part of it anyway," I murmured. "So, what the hell happened, Gabe?"

He pressed his head back and closed his eyes. "There's this elevator in the jail, the one that carries you from intake to the cells. It's famous all over town. They call it the Wonderland Express. People step on feeling just fine and step off in a different state of being. If you're poor or Black or Latino in this city, you know about the Express." He coughed and reached for a glass of water on the floor next to him. Simon had emerged from the kitchen with his yellow pad and was taking notes.

"These two goons loaded me on and stopped the thing between floors. For interrogation, they said. This boy wants to help our wetbacks, one says to the other. I hear he loves nigger ass, says the other. And boy, did they interrogate me. Twenty-three stitches it took to close this eye."

"What about you going for a gun?"

"Yeah," he said with a laugh that twisted hard into the cough again. He took another sip of water. "I may be stupid, Jason, but I'm not blind. There wasn't any gun in any holster.

"Anyway, they throw me naked in a cell for the night, no blanket, no toilet, no heat, nothing. How's that for a story your paper can run?"

He was looking at me expectantly. They all were. Their deliberate misconception first embarrassed then irritated me. "Yeah, well, I'm sorry—but like I said, I'm out here because your folks asked. Not on business." His story sickened but didn't shock me. These things happened and not only in Iowa. Besides, he hadn't answered the question. Did he know that? Tired, I decided to let it go for the time being.

"Amazing they can still make you jump after all these years," Gabriel murmured. I knew what he meant. "But I'm glad to see you, Jason. I'm glad you're here."

For some reason that caught me by surprise too. He didn't look at me again. The pain had reasserted itself. It rolled in surges across his face. Grey left to fetch more pain killers.

I slipped away and drove to the motel I'd checked into that morning.

"I am almost sorry my wife dragged you into this. You don't deserve to be haunted by us for the rest of your life." There was an echo on the line and Joseph Salter sounded very far away. He might have been in India as much as on the Cherokee reservation in Arkansas. Yet even with the lousy connection it was good to hear his voice. Thirty years of various exiles had only faintly marred his Hungarian inflections.

"I'm an old friend of the family, Joseph. Whatever went wrong with Hilary and me, well that's recent history. Tell Marianne that everything's fine—Gabriel's home, a little scuffed up, but okay. I'll report back when I know more."

"Is everything fine?" Joseph asked carefully.

I hesitated. "I still don't know what this is all about. Gabe's in trouble, no doubt there—he's been charged with attempted rape. But you don't have to report any of that to Marianne, at least not yet."

"If only I could come up there too," he said bitterly. "But how can I leave her, the condition she's in? She'd worry herself sick. A nurse—I suppose I could arrange for one from the village." I heard him sigh. "But Marianne would work herself frantic if I left. It would only make everything worse."

It was true that his wife would whip herself into a real state if Joseph came out by himself, though as far as I knew her condition, as he called it, was no worse than it had been for ten years. She was a recluse more than an invalid. But since they'd moved to Arkansas Joseph had faithfully accepted her complaints without question.

"That's the last thing you need," I said. "And you've got your classes to worry about, not to mention running the school. Maybe later you'll be able to get away. Hilary can help work it out if it comes to that. In the meantime, I'll find out what I can and keep you up to date."

Joseph capitulated with another sigh. "I wish I could be there with you for this, Jason."

Not for the first time in my life I wished he could too.

I timed it just about right. I figured I could shower, grab a steak across the street—what did you come to the Midwest for?—and be back in my room for the call I expected from my ex-wife. Joseph would report to Marianne, and Marianne in turn would relay the message along with commentary to her daughter in Washington. Hilary, no doubt, would demand firsthand corroboration.

Two nights earlier, late Saturday or early Sunday, it was Hilary who phoned first, waking me at three a.m. "My mother's going to call and ask a big favor," she said. "It's a lot to ask—way too much—but I hope you'll do it."

"Unh-huh," I replied, groggy, not committing to anything. So Hilary recited the story of Gabriel's arrest on Friday, or at least as much of it as her mother had received earlier in the evening from Grey Navarro.

"Lenny's already been on the phone to a friend from law school. Jeremy Stanton. Apparently the best defense lawyer in Iowa. Woke him too, if it makes you feel any better."

"Why the hell doesn't your Lenny fly out there himself?" I demanded, probing a vulnerable spot. "Isn't this his line of work?"

"He can't, damn it, not right this second. He's in the middle of negotiations here, important talks that'll fall apart if he's not on top of them. Besides, he doesn't do criminal work."

I lay on my back in the darkness. Her nostrils would be flared just so, skin stretched white across the bridge of her

nose, hazel eyes squinting. It had been a long time since I'd
managed to pry some good honest anger out of Hilary.

"I get it. He can't, but I can. Hey, I know, writing for a
paper doesn't have the same cachet as being a corporate
lawyer or a Congressional aide de camp." I was trying to
sound jocular.

"Oh, brother—now you're starting with the self-dramatiz-
ing? Don't bother, Jason. Just don't bother. You don't have
to do this at all," she said acidly. "And certainly not for me.
Mother suggested I call. Now I can't believe I did. Anyway,
I'm flying out in the next few days, soon as I find someone to
stay with Hannah. The Congressman's already given me
leave. I'll take care of things in Iowa myself."

The mention of the daughter she'd had with Lenny soured
my brief pleasure in baiting her. The two-year-old girl represented a world of intimacy I was no part of, that had nothing to do with me. Hannah made the point far more com-
pletely than did the husband himself, who as far as I was
concerned was little more than an opportunistic bystander of
our earlier battles.

"Just hold on, okay?" I said with a long sigh. "All you
want is for me to find out what happened and make sure
everything's being handled right, right? Doesn't sound like
you have much confidence in Gabe's compadres in the Party.
Or his wife."

"I don't."

"Okay, so I'll talk to your mother. The timing could be a
whole lot better. But if my editor lets me put a couple of
assignments on hold, I'll fly out there for a day or two."

"Fine," she said. "Thanks." I could hear her teeth grinding.

Marianne Salter did call later that early morning and I
agreed to run out to Iowa. Perhaps because I was tired from
the start, I was acutely aware of how strange my mission

seemed, that I should be the one they asked. But what I said to Joseph after my first day was true enough. However uncertain my status as a former in-law, I'd known the Salters all my life, had grown up with Hilary and much later Gabriel—I was eleven when he was born—in the small college town in Pennsylvania where both our fathers were professors. Our parents were the best of friends. We practically lived in each other's home. For most of my boyhood I'd all but worshiped Joseph Salter, wishing, as secretly as I could manage, that he was my own father.

Gabriel was still a young boy when I went away to college. It was only later, after I'd also been away to the war, and then after Hilary and I surprised everyone by marrying—we'd never officially dated during high school—that I began to know Gabriel at all.

By that time, while I was away, the Salters had moved to Arkansas, abruptly, unexpectedly, during Hilary's senior year in college. This was the great family mystery. To the bewilderment of his colleagues and neighbors, Joseph Salter threw away his tenure, his position as Chair of the music department, forfeited his periodic concerts around the country and in Europe, and went to teach school in the Cherokee Nation. Of all unlikely places. It was short notice. My parents never forgave him.

Arkansas was where Gabriel grew up, surrounded not by the comforts of a quaint college town, but by squalor and dirt and isolation. He made friends with children who looked on the running water and private (on a party line) telephone of the Salters as great privilege. It was wonderful to see how he took to this new world—and how quickly, totally he was accepted into the swirling mob of Cherokee kids. Red skin. The red dust made them indistinguishable, Gabriel no less than the rest, as they tumbled and scooted and played ball.

Even on our first visits to Arkansas as a married couple, Hilary and I spied Gabriel's character not changing so much as evolving. He'd always been a sweet, not to say angelic, kid, what with his fine dark hair, worn long now like his friends, and his delicately carved features, and a smile that could break your heart because he wanted to please, wanted people to be happy.

Grafted on to that sweetness, however, grew a burning anger, an incomprehension at the unfairness of how his friends lived. It gnawed at him that he had choices they didn't. Later the incomprehension disappeared; he comprehended only too well. The fury that other adolescents focus on their parents he directed at the political realities everywhere about him.

By the time he himself went off to college, first on full scholarship to Princeton and then returning by his own request to the university in Fayetteville, Gabriel already possessed a truth that apparently never wavered. With his smile, his passion, his voice, he was a natural leader; everywhere he went new political organizations whirled together like dustclouds in the firmament. Long after it was fashionable to be a socialist, he became a socialist in the most committed way. A real Commie they'd have called him a few years earlier, though Gabriel always insisted in minute detail on the distinctions between the Stalinists in power in Europe and Asia and the Trotskyites or whatever, who would never have done such terrible things. He had his truth, his hope for a revolution gradual or otherwise that would transform the planet into a more equitable place. And, in truth, I never much liked him after that. Unshakable conviction makes me uncomfortable.

Ten o'clock Sunday morning the city room at my paper had been pretty well deserted. I typed out my request for a short leave to Stan Lupinsky, the city editor. I didn't expect Stan to be in before noon. This way I didn't have to see the first flush of surprise on his face. With any luck I might even be out of town by the time he got the message.

It wasn't that I didn't have the days coming. It was just that over the past few months—really the past year or more—I hadn't been doing much with the days on which I was supposed to be filing stories. Just this past Friday, as a matter of painful fact, Stan had taken the trouble for another stern but supportive chat with me in his office. Two pieces, nothing mammoth, in the next couple of weeks— that's what I needed to produce as a show of good faith.

So as I typed out the message I was also imagining the scene when I returned from Iowa to discover myself fired. Someone new installed at my desk. My belongings stashed in a cardboard box. The image actually cheered me more than I wanted to admit.

When who should come stalking up the newsroom's central aisle two minutes later but Stan Lupinsky, a torn printout of my message flapping in his fist. "Joke, right?" he called from fifteen feet away.

What Stan did best in the world was worry—maybe that was the root of being a good editor too. He was a wonderful worrier. And now his features were twisted in grief and surprise. His tie was already loosened, his white shirt sleeves rolled to the elbow. His dark curly hair had been pushed back from his brow—as if a receding hairline were not a matter of genes but of literally driving his hair back into two tousled wings above his head. "We had a deal," he cried in a gruff wail.

"Family business. I only got the calls last night. Sorry."

Stan wagged his head. Here was a new worry to distract him. "Jesus, what's happened? Somebody die?"

"I won't know for sure 'til I get out there. How about we put our deal on hold a few days?"

"Sure—yeah. I don't know, maybe this'll be the best thing for you. But you better be ready to pump out some copy when you get back. I can't protect you from upstairs forever, and neither can your union." He lingered for a few moments, hoping I'd flesh out the reasons for concern, before stalking back towards his office, one hand absently tugging at his hair.

One other call: I had to let Phyllis Barker, the paper's book review editor, know that I wouldn't be in town the next day. Monday dinner at her place and a film afterward had developed into something of a weekly routine, but I didn't mind the chance to slip away free.

"It's pretty well muddled at this point," I said to Hilary when she called, as expected, on that first night in Iowa. I'd been back twenty minutes from dinner. "I've no idea what actually happened. Except the police were plenty thorough in working Gabriel over. He's sore and bruised—and there's a busted jaw. Anyway, physically he'll be okay in a week or two. Lenny's friend is already talking about suing the cops."

"Jesus," she muttered. "I knew this was going to happen some day. At least he's alive. Who know's what they'll do to him if he goes to prison?"

"What, you think he did it?"

"Rape a little girl?" Her voice was incredulous. "You're kidding. Gabriel do something like that?"

"Before today I hadn't seen Gabe in nearly four years," I snapped. "How well do you know him anymore? He won't breathe a word about his damn ISA or what he does for them. Has there been any other trouble you know about?"

"Not anything like this." She paused and I imagined her shaking her head, tugging at her hair. "What would the Party have to do with a rape charge? He's been arrested before, but always misdemeanor stuff, for protesting and marching. He did once say the FBI had a file—some friend got hold of it. It pegged Gabe as an 'advocate for peace' or something monstrous like that. Shit—you know he's spent his whole life trying to help. He couldn't hurt anyone."

"What about all his fury at how unfair the world is, about capitalist bosses and exploited workers? I always sensed plenty of anger buried away not so deep. Has it ever exploded?"

"What the hell are you cross-examining me for?" Again she hesitated and I remained silent. "No. Honestly no. He's always focused it into organizing workers and writing material for the ISA. This isn't him—what they're saying."

There was a long silence. I sensed that she wanted me to agree, to make a personal pledge of faith in Gabriel. But I didn't know what happened and I'm not given to credos.

She sighed. "You are going to figure out what happened?" she said, reading my thoughts.

"I've got some leave coming. Hell of a busman's holiday, but I'll hang around here for a few days. You know, poke into things. You still planning to fly out?"

Again silence, but this time hollow and deep. I sensed her sudden bristling and realized what I'd asked. Our talk up until then had seemed both serious and casual—more or less natural. It wasn't that I'd forgotten, but for a moment it didn't seem to matter so much. Now my chest tightened with a rush of anger and regret. In no little part I was annoyed it should still matter that Hilary didn't want to lay eyes on me.

She sighed again. "I feel like I should, especially if the police are going ahead with these crazy charges. Though you'll probably be back in Baltimore." Her voice sounded more hopeful.

It wasn't much before noon when I rapped on a pane at Gabe's house, but the door was locked and there was no sign of life. I glanced in the alley. Their car was gone too.

As a matter of habit I'd already begun to take notes, and on the third page of my pad I'd jotted the address of the local ISA headquarters. I found it—Trailblaze Books—along a strip of package liquor stores and abandoned gas stations. Outwardly it was simply a progressive bookstore: a one-story cinder block hut, deep in back, its plate-glass window facing the street.

Propped in the windows as I approached were the predictable titles—dog-eared Lenin and dusty Che; Emma Goldman and Winnie Mandela; pamphlets, brochures, copies of the weekly Worker. Baltimore has similar places of course. In the natural course of my duties I stumbled across these same fragments of socialist causes. But what stopped me short that morning were the bright yellow flyers taped across the window. Simon Yoo had moved quickly. Some lab had already printed the pictures he'd taken the day before. And here were photocopied sheets, three identical yellow ones side by side, blown-up shots of Gabriel's battered face, his eyes swollen shut in the grainy black-on-yellow copies. Block capitals declared he'd been framed by the police and savagely beaten; a protest rally was announced for Friday afternoon.

As I walked into the bookstore, Simon glanced up from a solitary metal desk in the rear of the shop. He was holding a phone to his ear again. He shot me a single glance through his wire-rimmed glasses and then returned to the legal pad before him. He was wearing a neat grey t-shirt and blue work pants. Although he wasn't much taller than five-seven, the shirt revealed his tautly muscled shoulders and arms. I was both fascinated and repelled by his ability to combine in a glance such ferocious intensity along with contempt and indifference.

Two staff members, a young man and woman in their twenties—they might have been working at a clothing store in the local mall—took their cue from Simon. Once they saw him recognize me, they attended to stocking shelves and checking lists. Hands in my pockets, I wandered from table to rack, not really knowing what I was looking for, other than

Gabriel and Grey. I leafed through a recent Worker, picked up an anthology of Trotsky's essays published by the ISA.

After a few moments, Grey emerged from behind a partition. As she reached for a packet lying on a box of books she happened to look up. If she was surprised to see me she didn't show it. I walked towards her without waiting for an invitation. Behind the partition I discovered Gabriel slumped in a desk chair, his face hot and flushed, his eyes closed. I questioned Grey with a glance.

"He insisted," she said with a shrug. "He's a very stubborn man." I caught a hint of annoyance in her tone, but whether with him or me I couldn't make out.

Today Grey's long black hair was woven in a heavy braid. A leather knot tied it off at the end. My eyes kept returning to it as the braid tossed and swayed with a life of its own. "Yesterday you asked what happened—I knew what you were after," she said. "Read this and you'll know. It's what we might expect from them—but worse. Worse. We won't let it go." From a high stack of colored paper she handed me another photocopied sheet, this one bright orange. Like an insignia or logo, a smaller version of battered Gabriel appeared in the upper corner.

"You all know how to move quickly," I said without looking up.

On March 4th Gabriel Salter, a hardworking meat packer, was framed up by the police and arrested. Once in their custody, he was severely beaten. His jaw was cracked. Dozens of stitches were required to close the wounds to his face and head. His body is covered with bruises from being kicked.

Gabriel Salter was singled out for harassment and intimidation because of his commitment to uniting workers at the Consolidated Packing plant. He stood up to bosses who will do anything to speed up the line, to slash wages, to cut costs. Workers are maimed every day and tossed aside. Bosses regularly pit one group against another, African Americans are set against Vietnamese, Latinos against Whites. Divided, workers pose no threat—and provide entertainment besides!

Gabriel Salter did everything he could to defeat these abuses. He brought workers together. He demanded adequate medical treatment. He worked within the rules to make meat-packing safer and fairer. And the bosses didn't like it —they fear the power of workers uniting. So in league with local police thugs they trumped up wild charges against Gabriel Salter. They roughed him up. They'll try and throw him in prison. Anything to break the spirit of the workers at Consolidated.

DON'T LET THEM! SPEAK OUT! JOIN THE COALITION IN SUPPORT OF GABRIEL SALTER! BY DEMANDING HIS RIGHTS WE DEMAND RIGHTS FOR ALL WORKERS!

I turned the sheet over, but the other side was blank. I handed it back to Grey. Simon had drifted over. He was toying with an unlit cigarette. "Who wrote this—you?" I asked him.

He shrugged. "What does it matter?"

"Nothing at all—it's powerful stuff. Except you've forgotten a few things, haven't you?" Simon gave no sign of surprise or interest. Suddenly angry, I wanted to shake him up, to see him wince or fall back—something. Yet I was also painfully aware that I was supposed to be on Gabriel's side. And that was the instant I first felt torn between being an old family friend and trying to discover the truth about what happened Friday night. As much as I hoped to discover that Gabriel hadn't attacked anyone, I now wanted to know what had happened.

"Aren't you ignoring this little problem of a girl being attacked?" I asked Simon quietly, not wanting to wake Gabriel.

"There was no attack." Simon tried to sound matter-of-fact, but couldn't quite disguise a flash of contempt. At his side Grey said nothing, but her eyes narrowed dangerously and her lips were pressed thin.

"No attack? Nothing attempted?" Surprised by the boldness of their claim, I perched on the edge of a table. "This is what Gabe says? The cops arrest him at the girl's house. What's he doing there? You're saying there was no attack at all?"

"The whole thing was a set-up, start to finish," Simon said. He tucked the cigarette in his shirt pocket and pulled his wire frames from behind each ear, exhaled on the lenses and wiped them on a large bandanna.

In the face of all this stern certainty, I was startled to notice Grey's dark eyes soften, slowly dropping away into deep pools, of worry, yes—but deeper and darker than that too. After a moment she turned her head away. Oddly, I felt she'd done this deliberately, that she intended me to see. Caught by surprise, I didn't know what to make of it. I had no key to translate.

"You have known Gabriel how many years?" she asked suddenly, fiercely, turning back to me. "Should I read a list of everything he has done, all the sacrifices he has made, all the people he has helped?—No, I don't have to. Can you imagine him trying to rape a young woman? Him hurt someone younger, weaker? Can you even imagine it? Not Gabriel. We will prove it too." Her voice was low and husky, and she spoke as if trying to stretch the words to fit her meaning.

Balanced on the table edge, I nodded ever so slightly and tried not to squirm. I couldn't for a moment deny that

Gabriel Salter was as gentle a boy as I'd ever known. Yet it was also true that I hadn't much liked the man he'd become, so certain of his truths, so hostile to any others.

Saints, I'd always suspected, wouldn't as a rule be easy to get along with. A pleasant disposition isn't what distinguishes them—faith in an idea beyond all temptation and attack, that's what separates a saint. I had, more than once, used the word in describing my brother-in-law. And yes, barring some crisis of character, some catastrophe that had secretly scarred his very synapses (as though I'd been able to read their original warp and weft), it was indeed unthinkable that Gabriel Salter could perform such a crime.

That privately acknowledged, I felt no sudden impulse to rush over to him, rouse him with a shake, and pledge my belief along with his other admirers. Yet, oddly, I did want to reassure Grey. A quick touch of the hand or a nod, a meaningless few words. For her unguarded gaze a few moments before had shaken me. I felt I'd caught a quick but true glimpse of her and—this was unsettling because so improbable—that somehow I recognized her. Though I didn't quite know what the recognition amounted to.

How could I recognize her?—she lay outside my ken. I already knew her well enough to know that I'd never known anyone like her before. And why was she privileging me with such a secret glimpse of herself, her fears and worries?

Simon Yoo stood next to us, watchful and unwavering. No trace of impatience, though he must have keenly desired to slip outside for that cigarette.

"This thing that never happened. What time didn't it occur?" I asked.

Simon flapped his arms against his sides with studied exasperation. "What time did they beat his face in?" he demanded.

"We think they arrested him about nine o'clock on Friday," Grey said, as if she'd reconciled herself to repeating this story many times to come. "They didn't let him make his call to us until the next morning, after he'd been to the emergency room and spent the night naked and freezing in a cell. You can ask the lawyer your wife hired. We're insisting that everything be open and public."

"She's not my wife anymore," I said with some exasperation of my own.

Just down the block from Trailblaze Books I was sitting in my rented car, feeling out of place and uncertain of a next step. What was my role? I'd promised the Salters to make sure Gabriel was more or less safe and that Jeremy Stanton, Lenny's friend, had the legal angle under control. Whatever machinations the ISA might generate, Gabriel was out of jail for the moment and had a good attorney. But I'd also promised to find out what happened Friday night, and that was only growing less clear. Did I owe the Salters any more than I'd already done? I knew the answer was no. Yet simply by flying to Iowa in their behalf I'd affirmed my ancient ties.

But if I was hanging around a little while longer it was also to scratch my own itch. The police arrested Gabriel at the home of a fifteen-year-old girl and charged him with rape. Now Simon claimed it was all a conspiracy and that no rape ever happened. I wasn't intrigued so much as irritated.

As a first independent step I decided to find my way downtown and chat with the reporter who covered the story for the Register. Cadging some professional courtesy might give me a leg up. And I realized that I couldn't help but think of this in terms of a story of my own, something I could shape and make sense of, once I had the facts, once I got the right angle.

Maybe Brian Phillips of the Register sensed something of that too, as if this reporter from out of town were in fact a competitor trying to take advantage—I couldn't get much out of him. Standing near a rotating globe in the polished grey stone lobby of the newspaper, I'd called Phillips upstairs in the newsroom. Reluctantly, he suggested I meet him for coffee in the canteen.

He was a kid with a journalism degree two or three years behind him and plenty of ambition. Tall, thin, wearing suspenders and a bow tie, his blond hair deliberately mussed, he all but hummed with impatience to move on to better things.

If he was cautious about the Salter story, Phillips was happy to talk about himself. He'd landed a first job at a small suburban paper in New Jersey owned by the same chain and had already climbed a significant rung to the Register. It was a safe bet he'd soon be trolling for a flagship paper somewhere else. He made no effort to hide his quick appraisal—he was a professional after all—that I was too much older to be hot, that I'd have made it by now if I was, that however good my paper's reputation, I clearly was out of the hunt. Disliking him was almost self-indulgent.

"Most of what I know you saw in the Sunday paper," Phillips said, squeezing a lemon into his iced tea. "I'm doing a follow-up later this week, but I've got deadline tomorrow on another piece. Feature. You know what it's like."

"Yeah, I know what it's like." I smiled ingratiatingly. "But I'm burning vacation days on this, Brian, and you could give me a hand. Like I said, my meter's not running. I'm off-duty. It's just that I used to know the guy's folks."

"You sure they really want to know?" he asked with a grin.

"They'll know later—better it comes from me."

"If you say so. But what can I tell you? I spoke to the girl's old man—there's no seeing her—and he's just nuts about what happened. Says he's going to knock Salter's teeth in and make sure he's put away forever. Talk to him yourself. I'll give you the number."

"Sounds like fun. I assume the cops took the girl to an emergency room right away?"

"Broadlawns. But the staff's not allowed to give much

away."

"Yeah, I know that drill too. Listen, thanks—if I come up with anything I'll pass it on."

"Do that."

Emergency rooms, like highway strips of fast food and bargain shopping, exude a generic interchangeableness. Walk in one and you might be anywhere in the country. Fluorescent lighting and cloying antiseptic odors disguise any distinctions between night and day. As the sliding door opened before me and I strode into Broadlawns Hospital, I experienced the discomfort and impatience that all such institutions conjure for me with their smells and tensions and memories gone sour.

Late afternoon mid-week is one of those flat periods when an ER can be catching its breath while the rest of the hospital teems with life. At the admitting desk I asked whether anyone on this same shift—evenings, 3:00 to 11:00 more or less, are also nearly universal—had been on duty Friday. The woman pointed with her pen towards a nurse's station around the corner.

Ruth Wadkins, R.N., a cheerful, adamantine woman in her fifties faced me squarely and skeptically. "I was here," she said. "But I'm not going to tell you anything about a patient. If you're a reporter you should know that."

"That's fine—I'm not looking for anything specific. Just some background."

"Can't help you," she said.

"Maybe I could speak to the doctor who was on duty that night."

"She won't give you anything either." A prim scowl was growing on Nurse Wadkins's face. It made her look older, her frosted perm stiffer.

"Maybe not—you're probably right. But let me tell my editor I tried. It's my job."

Huffy now, all business, she didn't look at me. But she called to a young woman sitting on a stool down the hall and reading a clipboard. "Dr. Harris? Could I trouble you for a moment, please?"

The woman rose wearily. She wore a lab jacket over a set of blue scrubs, stethoscope draped across her shoulders. With short hair and gold-framed glasses, she looked hardly old enough to be out of college let alone med school. I took several steps towards her to beat Nurse Wadkins to any punch. "Dr. Harris? Hi, my name is Jason Currant. I'm a reporter."

"Let's see some i.d.," she said sharply but quietly, thrusting her hand at me.

I handed her a card.

"Baltimore?" The queerness, the unexpectedness made her smile. She slipped the card into her coat pocket. "What story could we have to interest Baltimore? I don't suppose you're covering the International Pork Expo?—that wouldn't bring you to our E.R. unless pork doesn't agree with you." Her diction was clipped and precise, t's crossed, s's sibilant, like a schoolteacher's. I suspected it was a manner originally used to hide shyness. "Are you nauseated?" she asked with a smile.

"To be honest, I was out here on some family business and came across a story I thought might have wider interest. You have a minute?"

"Why don't you tell me what you're after, then I'll say whether I've got a minute."

I nodded, hands in my pockets. I wanted to put her at ease. "You were on duty Friday around nine or ten?"

She lifted her head.

"A girl was brought in here. Police say she was raped. They've charged a guy who's an activist—one of those types who's always campaigning to help the little guy, or girl, as the case may be."

"And that makes you think he wouldn't hurt her?" she

said harshly under her breath. "You should spend time in a place like this." She hesitated. "Come over here." She marched me down the corridor, past a series of tables and booths, to the last examining cubicle. She didn't draw the curtains. We stood facing each other.

"Do you remember the girl?"

"Do you know how many cases like that we get a week? A day?"

"She's about fifteen, African American. I don't know much more."

"That age she's more young woman than she is girl," Dr. Harris said acidly. But almost against her will she was pondering it. "Friday? The guy was older—twenties or thirties—and White, yes?" she said with distaste. "I remember. She talked about him while I was performing the exam. We have a protocol and I filled out a report for the police. There's not much I can tell you—or that I'm allowed to."

"I don't need her name or anything specific. And I wouldn't use it anyway. That's not what I'm after."

"What are you after?"

"Whether something actually happened."

She looked at me incredulously and gave a short derisive laugh. "You figure because he's an activist, because he's White, it wouldn't happen. You got some gall giving this to me."

"Did something happen?"

"Yes, something happened," she snapped, glancing up to see whether anyone had overheard. She lowered her voice, speaking sharply, intensely up into my face. "I won't tell you anything about whether she was raped. Let a jury figure that out. But I can tell you that young woman was scared when she came in here. She was trembling with it so hard she could hardly speak. Had a lump on her head size of a golf ball. Swelling under an eye where someone hit her. So yes, Mr. Currant, something happened. It wasn't pretty and it wasn't nice and it wasn't all that unusual around here. Except now we've got a reporter from christsake

Baltimore poking around because some White-assed activist's got himself in trouble."

She was first to move, ripping one edge of a curtain further aside as if it had been sealing us away from the world. She stalked along the corridor with never another glance at me. Which was fine, just fine, at that moment.

I drove furiously back to the motel and packed my bag. Recalling my chat with the doctor, my stomach knotted with shame and anguish. The echo of her s's—White-assed, activist's, himself, the rising emphatic stress on self—still hummed, not even sound anymore but pure physical vibration in my inner-ear.

I turned my head aside to dodge the memory just as I'd quailed before her harsh gaze in the cubicle. Sitting on the edge of the bed, I experienced a moment of clearest certainty. Like watching the evening heavens from ship deck for the first time, when the familiar bears and dippers and hunters we've projected for millennia seem to ratify our stares with an eerie clarity, a realized architecture that's three-dimensional.

The girl—the young woman—had been attacked; Gabriel was arrested in her house. These were the bare bones of a constellation. The figure stood clear. I couldn't fathom Gabriel's motive—could there be anything so coherent as motive? That suggested something more or less thinkable, if not rational. Could frantic lust be called motive? Could the motive have been anything else?

Why didn't I fly away clear and free?

Maybe because motive was too grand a word, and something in me wanted to try and fathom the simple why.

Maybe because, though I hadn't much wanted to rush out to Iowa in the first place and was, at best, ambivalent about what I owed Hilary and her family, it didn't feel as though I'd completed the task.

Maybe because Gabriel himself seemed oddly vulnerable now, beaten and dazed and led about by Simon Yoo.

Maybe because I was puzzled and annoyed by Grey Navarro. That birthmark, the splotch of crimson touching the corner of her eye, spoke with an eloquence I hadn't yet fathomed either.

Chapter II

Nine o'clock Wednesday morning I drove directly to Trailblaze Books, intending some sort of confrontation. I now clutched one unassailable corner of the truth—a girl had indeed been assaulted—and using that fact as a club I could flail until the rest came clear. Here are facts, I'd announce coolly, calmly, waiting for Grey and Simon and Gabriel to quail, for the walls to crumble and the flood to sweep all confusion away. Something like that.

Even from down the block, however, I could see that the bookstore was already jammed with people gathered in tight shifting eddies and whorls of conversation. Outside, a trio of boys, tough in jean-jackets and cross-trainers, leaned together on the sidewalk, peering at a new flyer posted in the window.

I wedged my way through the door and moved slowly towards the back of the shop. It was very warm. The smell of bodies packed close, of fresh sweat and stale perfume, hung heavy in the air. But an acrid stink—potent, familiar, it puzzled me until I recognized it—it was anger—seeped like smoke through the shop as well, its dry flame flaring and snapping across the tinder of the crowd.

Machinists, meatpackers, farm unionists, several distinct

women's groups, members from the state socialist party, they'd answered the call to protest Gabriel's arrest and beating. They all seemed to know him if not necessarily each other; because of Gabriel they shared a collective sense of intimacy. Whatever initial doubts some of them might have entertained about his innocence by now had disappeared.

This pow-wow, first fruit of Simon Yoo's labors, was an opportunity to share information and plan a full-blown protest campaign. I overheard shards of conversation, most hot with outrage. Simon was fielding questions at a table set up at one side of the room in front of the Mandela bookshelves.

Across the way, Brian Phillips from the Register was standing by the plate-glass window. A black leather bag hiked fashionably on his shoulder, he too was reading the new flyer.

Perhaps a dozen members of the crowd were young and White and well educated, judging from the studied casualness of their clothes and their earnest faces. That many again were black. A handful were Latino, another Asian. Yet I was the one mentally doing the sorting; the knots of conversation shifted and remixed, ignoring such categories. I did notice three or four older women who might have just rushed over from canasta and tea, except for something hard, something tough around their eyes. There was a huddle of older men too, wearing mesh baseball caps from John Deere or the Cubs, their hands stained, gnarled, powerful.

Gabriel was perched on a wobbly chair off to one side, surrounded by an arm's-length magic circle of open territory. He looked hideous. The bruising along his cheek and jaw and rimming his eye had turned comic-book shades of yellow and green and grape. Perhaps for dramatic effect, he'd discarded the bandage from his head. A clotted cornrow of black stitches stood out on the shaved scalp above his temple. Yet Gabe belonged clearly to the living for the first time since I'd arrived in Iowa.

Alone at his side, the heavily serene woman who'd visited the house after his release, Sara Oliver, sat on the floor, knees tucked under her. Gabriel was chatting amiably with her and others who could overhear from a step or two away. Alert, a smile of dead seriousness flickering on his lips, he was willing to talk about his ordeal as if despite all evidence it had occurred to someone else.

Everyone in the bookstore was aware of him yet deferential. Our attention seemed almost irresistibly drawn to Gabriel, though he did nothing expressly to attract it. This, I sensed, was more than a momentary celebrity due his gaudy wounds or the notoriety of his arrest. What was long ago merely Gabriel's boyish charm had matured, had been translated into a tangible presence. There was no doubt of the focus of energy in the crowded bookstore. A gentle thrum of desire, it tugged at the throat, made you want him to notice. Perhaps it explained why all these people assembled on such short notice. He seemed aware of this quality too, but was off-hand about it, again as if it had nothing to do with him or was a slightly embarrassing condition.

I picked up one of the new flyers, two bright red pages stapled together, the logo of Gabriel's swollen mask again strategically notched in the corner. Here at last was their version of the story. I scanned the statement. It might have been crafted, I saw without any satisfaction, not only in response to my conversation with Simon and Grey the afternoon before, but to what I'd discovered in Broadlawns Hospital. The stiff, third-person play-by-play was followed by a chronological chart, noting how long Gabriel had been at a bar near his meat-packing plant, the time he returned home and called a friend—8:45, because Sara Oliver had looked at the clock—the time, roughly ten minutes later— when he was approached by a woman in the street begging for help:

> In the next eight minutes Gabriel Salter was framed and arrested. While he stopped at a traffic

light on his way to the grocery store, a woman ran up to his car. She claimed someone was threatening her and pleaded with him to take her home a few blocks away. Once there, she urged him to wait on the front porch while she searched the house to make sure it was safe. After she went inside Salter never saw her again. Less than a minute later, a policeman charged onto that front porch. He grabbed Salter, pushed him into a back bedroom, handcuffed him, and pulled his pants down. "Let's see what we have here," he said.

My jaw tightened, my bad leg tightened and, knowing what lay ahead for Gabe in the jail's elevator, I tasted a musky whiff of fear at being trapped, helpless and alone. I knew something about that.

Warily, sensing someone's gaze, I glanced up and discovered Grey Navarro standing next to the partition in the back of the shop, studying my reaction to this story. Her scrutiny bothered me because I found it so hard to read her in turn.

"Can you believe they'd print this garbage?" Brian Phillips, nudging my elbow, spoke in something louder than a whisper. He snorted. "This is the most ludicrous piece of fiction I've ever seen. A mystery woman no less. You ought to tell your friends to get real."

I shrugged. I hadn't much liked Phillips the day before, but now I thoroughly detested him, his arrogance, his youth, his transparent ambition, his goddamn shoulder bag. And yet—who could deny it? It was ludicrous all right. A mystery woman no less.

What I found particularly galling wasn't the manifest thinness of the story but that it sounded so pat. The pieces slipped into place with such effortless precision, an oriental box of a tale. Why hadn't I heard a word of this before? Why hadn't Grey or Gabriel himself groaned some hint of it? If I was to be on their side (was I? suddenly I wondered why I thought of it that way, since what I'd assumed I was after was simply the truth, for relay to Hilary and Joseph and for my own satisfaction), why was I privy to nothing but these sheets photocopied for public consumption? As recounted here the story was already shaped by political design. Whose version was this in fact—Gabriel's, Simon's? Did Grey herself buy the notion of a mystery woman used to entrap Gabriel?

I tugged out my own notepad and edged through the crowd towards Simon. "You're saying this was all a police set-up from the start?" I called loudly as if it were a news conference.

Still sitting at the table, he played it straight, revealing not an ounce of irritation. "They've got every reason to silence Gabriel Salter—and to intimidate others working with him," he said. Several of the crowd turned around. One older woman, her mouth collapsing into heavy wrinkles like a dried apple, glared at me.

I had a couple more questions. "This woman who caught him on the street—I assume she's not the same one who claims he attacked her?"

Simon shook his head silently.

"What's the name of the bar she came out of?"

He dug through some notes. "3-Penny Tavern."

"Okay." I jotted it down. I put one more to him. "What makes you—what makes Gabe—think it was a set-up?"

Simon Yoo snorted and glanced knowingly to colleagues on both sides. "Why else lure him to the house? Why use a woman who's disappeared? Why beat him nearly to death in the jailhouse?" His voice soared for all to hear. "Gabriel Salter's been causing trouble in this town, and the bosses and the cops don't like that. He's been marching and he's been organizing workers. He's been showing people they don't have to put up with the shit the cops and plant owners and politicians dump on them. They've got every reason in the world to frame him."

"Police have it different." Skeptical, so sure of himself he wasn't bothering to look directly at Simon, Brian Phillips had edged forward, pen cocked to his notepad to tick off details. "They say they caught Salter with his pants down. Young girl attacked and ready to say so. No mystery woman. No frame."

Simon smiled, but it wasn't much of a smile. Behind the wire-rimmed frames, his eyes were hard. "And what they did to him at the jail was an accident? He jumps two cops in the elevator because he wants a gun. Doesn't have eyes to see the holster's empty. But he's going to take on two of them by himself. Maybe he just asked them to beat him nearly to death?" He gestured towards Gabriel. A murmur of anger rustled through the bookshop.

"What happened then, happened then." Phillips didn't back down but he danced the dance, his voice neutral, disinterested. I couldn't help but admire his technique. "But why was Salter at the house in the first place? What's the evidence to back up his story?"

"He's got nothing to prove," Simon Yoo shot back defiantly. This system of yours presumes he's innocent, right? They've got to prove otherwise, and they can't. This isn't just Gabriel's battle. It's all of ours." Now he was addressing the meeting at large again. "And it's not just the International Socialist Alliance, but all working people."

I caught Simon's eye again. "What about the woman— the one you say flagged Salter's car? You trying to track her down?"

He hesitated. "We are trying to find her, yes," he said.

"What you've got to understand is how crazy this all is."

Everyone turned and stared at Gabriel. He was leaning forward in his chair. His face was flushed. He hesitated, about to say more. No one made a sound. And then he slumped back, robbed of words.

"Is this true, Gabe? This the way it happened?" I called, holding the red sheet aloft.

Gabriel looked at me, his eyes weary but clear, and he nodded.

As I slipped through the crowd I half expected to spot Grey
observing and perhaps now dismissing me as an object of
study, but she'd disappeared once more. I was glad to leave
the bookstore. Out on the street a sharp wind had whipped
up, sweeping along low clouds that threatened rain. I
zipped my jacket and hunched into the wind. Trouble was, I
wanted to believe Gabriel even as I doubted his story. That's
when I've always been hardest to convince.

Early-afternoon on a chilly March day, the street was quiet
near Gabriel's house. I wanted to walk the story through.
Map on my lap, I slowly pulled away from the curb again.
Came to Clark, turned right, drove several blocks towards
Harding and turned again. Up on the right I spotted the bar,
hunkered dark and low by itself. Above the door 3-Penny
Tavern was carefully stenciled across a hand-painted sign.

Traffic was heavier along this stretch of Harding, most
heading quickly somewhere else. Little enough reason to
stop.

Pulling over, I carefully checked up the street and down,
and then I slapped my hands against the steering wheel. It
wouldn't work. It was preposterous. No way the police
would arrange an intercept along here. Odds were too long.
Even staging a dozen women along every street Gabriel
might choose, flagging him at a light—catching him at all—
would be improbable at best. Could Gabriel Salter be worth
such conspiracy and bother?

For the sake of professional thoroughness, I hiked up
towards the bar. I figured it would be open—these places are
always open. Tugging the door, I waited for my eyes to
adjust to the gloom, for the acrid stink of old tobacco and
stale beer to settle.

The bar itself was a large horseshoe in the center of the room. Eight or ten tables huddled against the walls. They were deserted. One old man wearing a shapeless grey hat sat heavily on a barstool, a long-neck bottle in front of him. Uninterested in my entrance or existence, he was staring up at a soap opera on the tv overhead. But the bartender, six-tyish, was waiting for me, rag poised in mid-stroke on the counter. "Help you?" he asked.

"Hope so." I nudged aside a stool and stood in front of him.

"What you drinking?"

"Actually I work for a paper—I'd like to ask you some questions."

"And I'd be inclined to answer if you're drinking some-thing from my bar."

I shrugged. "A beer. Whatever's on tap."

"All right then." He nodded with satisfaction and went to draw the beer. Very natty, his plaid shirt was perfectly ironed and buttoned to the throat, sleeves rolled two turns precisely. His hair was silver, cut short and oiled, his mus-tache razor sharp. He set the beer on a napkin in front of me. "What paper you say you work for?"

"Nothing local." I handed him a card. The bartender studied it and set the card on the bar where he tapped at it with two fingers. "I'm doing a story on an incident last Friday," I said.

He stopped me with an upraised palm. "Walter? Walter—you hear? You come hear this," he called loudly. A moment later Walter appeared through a half-door at the back, carrying a broom. He was the bartender's double, a touch heavier perhaps, a shade older. Same apron, same shirt, same perfect mustache. "My brother," the bartender said. "This is our place. Now, what kind of incident hap-pened round here Friday?"

"Over on 29th. Police arrested a guy and charged him with attacking a young woman. You know what I'm talking about?"

"White guy trying to get Leroy Jackson's little girl? Course we heard," Walter said, his voice gruff and half an octave lower than his brother's. "This end of town's small enough. Word like that gets around."

"Who besides me has talked with you so far?"

The brothers glanced at each other. "Why would anyone talk to us?" asked the first.

That stopped me cold for an instant. "No one's been here already?—Not the police, not anyone?"

The two of them just stared.

Simon Yoo claimed his people were looking for the woman—why would they start anyplace other than the 3-Penny Tavern? And wouldn't the police be checking the story out too? No, I realized—not if they were satisfied with the arrest.

"Look, Mister—" the bartender held my card at arm's length, "—Currant. We heard about the little girl getting hurt. We know her daddy, not that he's much to abide. But no one's done any talking to us. Why would they?"

Was I, I wondered, the only mark in town gullible enough to bother checking out Gabriel Salter's story? Even before entering the bar I'd persuaded myself that the kind of set-up Simon Yoo described wasn't possible. Why should the rest of the tale be any more credible? I felt foolish. I took a deep breath.

"Guy they picked up says he stopped at the light outside your door. Says some woman ran out and pounded on the car, screaming about a crazy boyfriend. Says she got him to drive to 29th, supposedly to her place, but she disappeared and the cops grabbed him. No other girl. No attack." I spread my hands palms up, apologetic for passing on such nonsense.

"White guy, right?" asked Walter. I nodded. "This woman Black?" Again I nodded. Walter didn't look at his brother this time. Something under the bar distracted him and he poked at it with his broom. His brother had his hands stuck in his pants pockets under the apron. No scowl, no smile. Nothing.

"Lots of girls around have trouble with their boyfriends, some worse 'n others," he said very slowly. "Maybe Friday night—maybe, I'm saying—it's payday, you know. And there's this buck with too much liquor or whatever in him even before he prances in here. Comes with a boy we know. Could be his girl's already here waiting and she's had a couple too, and she's mighty fine on a Friday night. Now it's busy. Payday, like I say. So Walter and me ain't wasting too much attention. 'Til he swats her one good in the eye. Walter rushes over with his broom—you be surprised what you can do with a stiff handle if you know how—and him and this buck's friend, they hold him back while the chick clears out real fast. Runs smack out into the street. Buck ain't in shape to chase after her anyway. That's the last of it. Nothing else to tell you."

"You know her name?"

He shook his head. "Never seen her in here before. We'd remember, girl look like that."

"How about the boyfriend?"

Walter spoke. "Not him neither. He comes in once in a while, every couple months, but never got his name. No reason to."

I was scribbling notes fast. I looked up at the two of them. "You all know any way to find her. Either of them? Something for me to go on?"

Walter leaned close and whispered in his brother's ear.

"Cause we already are. Cause all we know's what happened in here and I don't see any reason not to say," he responded impatiently and then turned to me. "The other boy comes in here regular. Name's John Martinez. Real picky about the John 'cause he's American now. Works over to the Consolidated plant, the meatpackers."

"Can I see your phone book?"

Walter pulled it out from under the bar and began leafing

towards the M's himself. All three of us bent over the book. Dozens of Martinez, not a single simple John. We remained huddled together, elbows on the counter like three conspirators. "Any suggestions?" I asked.

"You might try down to the plant," said the bartender. "Except I don't suppose they like you newspaper people nosing around. All them packers are real touchy these days, unless you go applying for a job. You ain't that desperate?" He grinned. "Other thing is just to check back in here every couple days—we'll ask around, keep our ears open."

I nodded.

"You tell me," said Walter, dropping his voice still lower into a growl, "something happen to Leroy Jackson's daughter or not?"

I took out a couple of dollars for the beer. "Yeah, I think something happened. I don't know what and I don't know who. That's what I'm after."

Walter nodded along with his brother. "Understand, we don't much care for Leroy. He's been a pain in the ass long's anybody's known him. Always puffing himself up. But we don't fancy helping anyone hurt his little girl."

My first phone call from my motel room was to the police. It was easy enough to get the name of the Public Information Officer, a Sergeant Hathaway, and make an appointment to see him before he got off duty at 4:30.

Next I tried the Consolidated plant and asked how to arrange a tour. Have to speak to the General Manager, I was told. Okay, I said. He'll have to get back to you, the receptionist said. Give me your name and number.

I didn't put much faith in hearing back. But visiting the packers intrigued me. I'd worked in a steel-stamping plant myself for a summer and had visited plenty of other industries on assignment. Never meat-packing. Gabriel worked at Consolidated and so did John Martinez—a visit was part of my digging for answers.

"This is Stan Lupinsky—leave a message and I'll get back." I was delighted—I was relieved—that Stan was away from his desk in Baltimore.

"This business is taking a few days longer than I guessed," I said to the machine. "Don't let them fire me, okay? At least until I see the whites of their eyes." I hesitated. I was tempted to ask Stan to leave a message for Phyllis Barker, but I didn't know what I wanted him to say. The delay lasted a second too long and the automatic system cut me off.

I hadn't said when I'd be coming back because I didn't know. This was the longest stretch in six months I'd gone without seeing Phyllis. It wasn't that I didn't miss her. At least in the sense of being aware that she wasn't around, and that any plans we might have were suspended. I thought about her. But the thoughts seemed abstract, detached. I missed her but didn't long for her. What message could I leave? She might be tempted to fire me too for my unannounced disappearance and my silence.

Instead I was sitting at the small table in my motel room thinking about Grey Navarro, wondering how I could discover, without the mediation of Simon Yoo or even Gabriel Salter, just what she thought. The phone rang.

"This Jason? Hi, Jason, this is Buster from Consolidated. Hear you want to come pay us a visit."

You've got to be kidding, I was tempted to say. "You're the General Manager?" I said instead.

"That's right," he said.

"Yeah—I'd like to take a tour of your facility. See how your plant operates."

"Well, that's fine." Buster's voice was a cartoon of southern good-old-boy mixed with tin-star western. "But I got to know just who you are, Jason. We don't get many tourists. You maybe with the press?"

"College professor. I'm preparing a new lecture course on the meat industry."

"College teacher?" He didn't snort but he might as well have. "Where at?"

"Johns Hopkins."

"That a college?"

"University. In Baltimore."

"And when you thinking of coming over here?"

"Tomorrow, if you'll give me the okay."

"Well I can't just up and do that on my own, Jason. You need your approval from Corporate out in Utah. We got a new policy about this sort of thing. Since the troubles up in Austin and thereabouts we're a lot more selective about visitors. But hell, showing a professor around's okay by me if it's okay out their way."

I ran the same story by a public relations v.p. in Utah who sounded like a public relations v.p., no more, no less, no twang. The project sounded fine to him, but he'd take it upstairs for approval and then they'd talk to Buster directly. Professor Currant should call the plant first thing in the morning.

Police Headquarters, a great grey behemoth built in the '20s as the Public Safety Building, perched heavily above the river and across from the downtown business district. Sergeant Hathaway met me in the reception area and led me to his own cramped office. Harried, brisk, tired, Hathaway looked like a high-school athlete who'd accidentally drifted into his mid-thirties. Wearing plainclothes—tan pants, button-down shirt, no tie—he was tall, powerful in the shoulders, thickening around the gut. A full mustache he'd most likely grown to look older was no longer necessary.

"Just so we know where we stand, I'd like to see some i.d.," he said straight off. "You must be new—I know most of the media types from around here." He fingered my card, nodding, and tucked it into a vinyl notebook. "Yeah, I heard there was someone from out of town poking about."

That didn't surprise me. Phillips, among others, might have passed the word along to earn a brownie point or two. "Then you probably heard I'm interested in the Gabriel Salter situation."

Hathaway nodded, a small nest of worry lines gathering by habit in his brow. "My job is to be helpful and I'll do my best. But I don't get the interest in this one. Calls, letters, even some telegrams started coming in yesterday. You'd think we booked a bishop. Course, most of it's from the loony left and the unions. So why the interest from you? Your paper is straight."

"I knew Salter in another life. Besides, the case is interesting."

He laughed. "Beats me how. He got caught with his pants down, you might say."

"He's got this different story. Are your guys following up? What about this woman who flagged him down in front of the 3-Penny Tavern? You trying to find her?"

Hathaway didn't flinch. I couldn't even tell whether he'd heard this story before. "There's not much I can say about an on-going investigation—except that it is on-going," he said. "Our boys are plenty thorough. If there's anything to Salter's story, they'll turn it up."

"And then there's what happened after he was in custody. Can you tell me anything about that?"

"Sorry, I'd like to clear up some things about that—let's say some misinformation—but I can't for the time being." He smiled sympathetically. He was proficient at this game, mixing plenty of good will with his skepticism, and not giving me a dram worth having. "Anytime a prisoner gets hurt we start an internal investigation. Until that's complete there's nothing I can say. You know the routine—it's got to be the same out east."

"It's the same everywhere," I said. "But we heard in court that he attacked two officers and tried to get a gun. Is that right?"

"That's part of the public record now."

"What about the guys he attacked—are they the arresting officers too? Any chance I can talk to them?"

"That's not part of any public record," Hathaway said with a scolding grin. "Besides, officers have their right to privacy like anybody else. Come back when our internal investigation is over and I'll gladly give you a full briefing. Nothing held back, promise. And I can guarantee that our I.A.D. is professional and fair. You'll see." He put both hands on the arms of his chair, pushed himself up, and held out a hand. "Glad to help you, Mr. Currant."

Hathaway escorted me to the front of the lobby and then disappeared back into the sweep and chaos of the station. As I turned the corner a policewoman in uniform jostled into me, scattering papers she'd been leafing through. "Sorry," I said and bent to help gather them.

Exasperated, she squatted and shoved at the papers. Two sheets drifted farther towards the steps. "You'd think people could watch where they're going," she said and then ducked closer to my ear. "Coffee in five minutes," she murmured in a matter-of-fact tone, nothing furtive. "Jody's around back."

Together we rose, the papers still confused between us until I tilted my share into her arms. Costello, her name-tag read. "Sorry," I repeated and stepped out into the growing dusk.

Rush-hour traffic had thickened while daylight thinned. The wind swept along a spray of dust, a few rags of paper. Behind the Public Safety Building I discovered a Salvation Army Center attached to a large warehouse. Jody's sat at the far end of the block, half the bulbs in its sign long dead.

A couple, man and woman, both heavy and wearing matching grey raincoats, filled one of the booths, forking through pie and ice cream. Behind the counter a girl was topping off ketchup bottles. I flagged her, ordered a coffee, and carried it to one of the booths.

Almost immediately Officer Costello appeared in the door and ordered coffee to go. A couple of inches over five feet, Costello was very round—her face was round, emphasized by a permanent of tight reddish curls, her hips were round, her shoulders and chest round. Yet she carried herself lightly and with assurance. Without a glance my way, she carried her paper cup towards the back. I rose—not too quickly—pointed to the stack of paper cups and emptied my own coffee into one. "That's a nickel," the girl said.

No sign of Costello in the narrow hall beyond the restrooms, and I pushed on through a fire exit. The coffee shop backed onto an asphalt parking lot. She was standing next to a car wedged between two others. Still she wouldn't look directly at me, but she must have known I'd seen her because she climbed inside. Feeling a little foolish with all this secrecy, like kids playing make-believe, I strolled over and tapped on the passenger window. She leaned across and pushed the door open.

"I've never been picked up quite like that before," I said.

"Would you've come if you thought it was a pickup?" she said with an angry frown. "Look, I know who you are and why you're here—what they did to that socialist."

"My, word gets around."

She sighed with impatience. "Good reporters aren't usually smart asses."

"Sorry—this isn't my usual kind of story."

"I'm risking this because I figure you'd want to know about the department. And there's stories you ought to hear. Like, how these guys give new meaning to pig. It's time some kind of word got out." She looked away from me out her side window. "You want a for instance? How about the way they were initiating Black rookies last month? The old boys dressed up in white robes, hoods and all, and scared the living shit out of them. And the way they treat women, cops and staff, groping a feel every chance, ordering us to fetch coffee. They make a point of calling F.O.P. meetings in tit bars. Matter of fact, this friend of mine just won ten grand for sexual harassment. She won't hang around now that she's won. The Chief naturally denies it all."

"Not that I don't find that interesting or a good story on its own, but what's it got to do with Gabriel Salter?"

"Jesus. Don't you see it's all connected? It's all part of the same mind set. The point is, some of them are just out of control. What they pulled on Salter in the elevator isn't new. It's fun they have every weekend when some of the Blacks or Mexicans party too hard with their pay checks. My colleagues say it's blowing off steam, what goes on in the elevator or holding cells. The mistake they made this time—well, usually they're smart enough not to rough up a White boy with friends who can make a fuss."

"So, why did they—were they just careless or stupid?"

She sighed. "Who knows? Maybe he wasn't respectful enough. Maybe he didn't say sir. Maybe he had an attitude."

"Was it the arresting officers?"

"Nope. He was already processed. But one of the guys who did it was Ed Holloway. Cream of the crop. He's already been suspended twice for unnecessary force, once for falsifying an arrest record. A real sweetheart."

"Okay, but I still don't get why they did it. You say they're not that dumb. Did Salter really go for a gun that wasn't there? Did they know who he is?"

"Hold on—you're asking a bunch. Don't underestimate Holloway's dumbness. Salter and an empty holster? Is he that stupid? And yeah, they knew who he was once he was booked. He hasn't been shy about causing trouble in this town."

While she spoke, a guy climbed into the shabby Lincoln on our left and pulled away. Suddenly her car felt naked and exposed. Dusk was fleshing in about us. Costello herself fidgeted in the deep shadows. "I'd kill for a cigarette if I hadn't quit again," she muttered.

"Are you done for the day?"

She shook her head. "This is only a break, and I'm already stretching it. Look, maybe you should go now."

I put my hand on the door. "One last. Was the whole thing a set-up? Were they really out to nail him?"

She turned her head to me and I could make out a grim smile. "You know, that's something I wouldn't necessarily hold against them. Salter makes all these pretty speeches about helping the working people and the poor, but I don't believe it for a second. Why should I? Socialists got their angle like everybody else."

"But do you think it was a set-up?"

She shook her head and stared out the window. "Beats me. They keep that kind of thing quiet. I wouldn't be in on the know. Hey, it's time, okay? Walk away through the far side of the lot."

"Nice meeting you."

She reached across and jerked the door shut.

I was beat. I hadn't eaten since breakfast. A shower, a good meal, a drink—that's what I had in mind. I found my car on the street, turned the key, glanced up and spotted the weak fluorescent light flickering from the windows of A-1 Bail Bonds. Jail Busters—Who You Gonna Call?

For all its strange familiarity, this wasn't a city where I had any place. A wash of loneliness swept up out of nowhere, worse than anything since those first six months after Hilary left. It seeped bone deep, an old foe. I sat still and waited for the ache to settle if not to pass. And rather than driving back to the motel, I found myself heading north to Gabriel's house once again.

I didn't expect to be invited to dinner. I didn't expect anything. Evening had settled heavily. There was no moon. The chill in the air had gradually carved away all hope of spring. It honed itself on the darkness and quickly pierced the jacket I was wearing.

Light from the living room shone through the front door, but I didn't see anyone. The door bell had been painted over and didn't give. I rapped sharply on the glass. Still nothing. The ground along the side of the house was muddy and littered with sticks and matted leaves. Towards the back was a window above my chin and I peered in on tip-toe. The slatted blinds hung slightly awry at the bottom, giving me an inch or so. In a glance I saw Gabriel sitting at a small formica table in the kitchen. Grey perched on a high wooden stool against the wall. Next to her the door to the living room was shut, which was why they hadn't heard me. No sign of dinner. Nor for once any trace of Simon.

I bobbed up on my toes for that one glance, momentum already carrying me on towards the back door. But I stopped, reached to the sill again, drew myself up for another look. They were talking, but all I could hear was a distant murmur. Nothing very intense. Casually domestic. Might have been about the rent.

Wary, I pulled back. Fifteen feet behind me the neighboring house silently peered at my back. From any other angle it wouldn't be easy to spot me there in the darkness. Uneasy but fascinated, feeling like a peeping tom, I peeped again.

Directly across from the window Gabriel was resting his arms heavily on the table, his head drooping. When he spoke he didn't glance at Grey. He looked smaller, weaker than I'd seen him since he was a boy. With no audience to charm or incite he appeared oddly vulnerable. As I watched from the darkness, however, Gabriel became recognizable in new ways. Perhaps because it had been several years since I'd last seen him, I realized with a new clarity just how much a Salter he was. The sharply carved features and the dark brown hair with a hint of red—those he got from his mother. But the expressive lips, the strong, sharp nose, the hazel-grey eyes which even full of mischief held a distant hint of sadness, these were a patrimony from Joseph Salter.

I remembered his father greeting me with that mischievous-sad smile when I burst by mistake into his study. Joseph would draw me forward, sit me on an embroidered footstool (how clear this was for an instant—I could smell the rosin on his bow), play a little Mozart on the cello just for me. Why wasn't he my father, instead of the tall gangly man, theologian and philosopher, who ruled our household?

A shiver swept along my spine from the cold. My fingers ached on the window sill. Suddenly, as I watched, as I envied him his father, it was me sitting there—Gabriel my brother, my own younger self.

Again I dropped back onto my heels and blew on my hands. Identifying with Gabe made me angry with myself. Whatever he had or hadn't done five days earlier, we were different as night and day. Always had been. I didn't want nostalgia and loneliness sweeping me along into an allegiance that made no sense. There was nothing for me here—it was time to go.

"Shit," I muttered into the cold. And reached up for one final glance to see what I'd come to see from the beginning, though I'd only just acknowledged it to myself: Grey sitting on the high stool, feet drawn up to her chest, leaning back against the wall. It was a pose of considerable balance and flexibility, and yet there was something awkward about it as well. My face felt stiff as I grinned. Always this trace of awkwardness with Grey, as if the world itself possessed the wrong proportions to accommodate her limbs.

Her hair was drawn tightly behind her ears. Her features were too harsh, too sharp. At some point her nose had been broken. The crimson birthmark was a vivid flaw on her cheekbone. Earlier, an uncanny shiver fooled me into thinking I recognized her; now she seemed to belong to a different world entirely. Curled on the stool, self-contained, self-sufficient, she aggravated me, she got on my nerves.

Headlights swung between the houses. I flattened myself

against the wall. In the alley a car rocked across deep ruts and beached itself against the back door. The lights died. Without waiting to hear shouts of pursuit—if I'd been spotted at all—I slipped quickly towards the front of the house, veered sharply to the next one over and then another, and hurried down to the street. Panting, I strolled erect but quiet back to my car and pulled away from the curb. I didn't turn on my own headlights for half a block.

When I was a boy, twelve or thirteen, my father, Professor Bradley Currant, drove my mother, my younger sister, and me along with him to a philosophers' conference in Toronto. This was unusual in a number of ways. For one thing, summer gatherings used to be rare for academics. For another, I can't recall a single separate occasion on which my father included us that way. He preferred to keep his worlds sorted into neat compartments. Family holidays were precisely designed to meet family needs. More remarkable: I don't recall from that trip any of the stone-hard silences that would soon govern all relations between my parents, that settled like heavy weights on Beth's chest and my own, making it almost impossible to breathe, that endured what seemed eternally until about the time I was drafted out of college for the war. Mother left her husband for all of two weeks and then returned in despair, from which time their marriage seemed a model of day-to-day efficiency. How I used to wish for some good fiery storms between them, china hurled against brick, terrible names hurled too, not swallowed and nursed in Protestant silence.

What I do remember of that trip, what I remembered late at night in a motel in Iowa, too weary for the moment to undress for sleep: the new Toronto city hall—just completed, not even fully occupied yet. It was the most wonderful building I'd ever seen, so perfect a space ship in design, in its glass and steel, that I half convinced myself it could surely rise swiftly from the concrete square and streak me far away.

And splashing in the hotel pool with a girl named Cynthia. Initially shy and wearing a heavy one-piece suit, she soon was hanging onto the side of the pool next to me, swimming in the deep end next to me. We agreed to see each other later. But how did I get her room number? Did she give it to me or simply her last name? Did I play detective?

In the evening when our family returned after dinner to our rooms—Beth and I had one to ourselves—I called Cynthia's number. Her father answered. I asked to speak with Cynthia.

"What're you doing, calling a young girl this hour?" he demanded. (It couldn't have been later than eight o'clock.) "What kind of animal are you? Don't you ever call here again or I'll have the police after you." And slammed the phone down.

I was twelve or thirteen years old. I was ashamed, baffled, hurt, angry, scared. I didn't, couldn't tell Beth or my parents. What did Beth and I do before bedtime? Watched tv, probably. Maybe my parents went out again. Before long, Beth and I went to sleep.

Next morning I was walking through the hotel lobby on my way to breakfast. From the corner of my eye (this is how I remember it), I noticed a family huddled together, the large, heavy-set man bending low for confirmation then breaking away and stalking rapidly towards me. He lunged and caught me by an arm, spun me round.

"You're Jason," he declared.

I looked up at him and nodded. He was balding, with heavy arms and a powerful chest. Golf shirt neatly ironed, buttoned to the top button. Bright green. All this I was to remember.

"Didn't I tell you not to call my daughter?"

Again I nodded.

"Then how come you did?"

"I never called again," I said.

"She swears you did. After midnight when I was gone. She says she could tell it was your voice and that you scared her. Both my girls were scared bad."

Now I was shaking my head. Astonished, scared too, all I could do was repeat myself. "I never called again." My voice sounded unreal in my own ears.

Surprised that I should deny it, the man glanced back to his wife, to Cynthia and her younger sister. They all still huddled fifteen feet away. He swung around again. "You lie to me and I'll knock you down those steps."

I tried to sound defiant, but tears had already welled in my eyes and I could hardly see him. "Knock me anywhere you like," I said. "I don't know why she's lying. Maybe somebody else called and she got confused. I don't know. But I never called her or anybody."

Cynthia's father looked uncertain of himself for the first time and let go of my arm as I tugged free. "I don't ever want to see you around her again," he said.

I turned and walked quickly down the steps to the restaurant. My parents were there. Beth was already half-way through her cereal. I slipped into my seat and waited for them to say something. I grabbed a roll and tore at it to hide my trembling. However proud I'd felt for defying Cynthia's father, for telling him he could throw me down the stairs but that it was a lie, all of that had vanished or been shoved aside. I waited for Beth to speak, to give me a clue.

Had I done something shameful in the night and couldn't remember? Could I secretly make a phone call and not wake my sister? What would my voice sound like? What terrible things could I say that terrified Cynthia? Was it a trick she was playing on me? What had I done to deserve such a trick?

For the next two days (for much longer than that, if truth be told) I kept playing the scene in my imagination. Our room was dark—I wouldn't have dared turn on the light for fear of waking Beth. But enough light seeped under the door and through the curtains from the street below. I'd curl up softly next to the phone. Perhaps I'd drag it into my bed and under the covers to muffle the sound. I'd call and say those things, terrible, frightening, that some part of me knew, a part over which I had no control and couldn't even remember in the morning.

Never before had I been afraid of going to sleep. And there was no one I could tell. What could I say?—that I was afraid there was a monster inside me? That I'd been caught out once, but who knew what else it had done, I had done, that I couldn't remember?

And I lay on a bed in Iowa, and it was very late and very quiet. I thought of Gabriel. A saint he'd always been, even if saints could be difficult at times. Gabriel, always helping others, always fighting for a better world. I'd never much liked him since he found true faith. Did Gabriel have a monster inside, one he could or couldn't remember, one who'd just been caught for the first time? Or was someone playing him a nasty trick?

Chapter III

"Why are you sticking your nose in it—why do you keep meddling?" Simon Yoo's lips disappeared into a single taut line. "I told you we were looking for her. Be a good boy and leave it to us."

He tapped a cigarette on the formica table, turned it, tapped again. "You've done your favor for Gabriel's family, haven't you? Maybe it's time you returned to your job."

The skin around his jaw and eyes was flawless. Everything about Simon was flawless: the part in his fine black hair and the precise razor cut beneath his temples; the smooth grey t-shirt, khaki pants and military web belt; the sculpted muscles in his biceps and forearms; the delicate hands.

I hooked my hands around a knee and leaned back in my chair. "Maybe you've got someone checking out the story, like you said. Maybe you could share what you've come up with?" I offered Simon my best disingenuous smile, the one I used during difficult interviews. I didn't really expect or intend that he buy it. "Look, I've got a lead. Why on earth shouldn't I follow it up? With any luck Gabriel can make it easier and I'll fly back home."

Simon tapped the cigarette again and closed his heavy-lidded eyes. We waited in silence.

I'd returned to the house in bright morning sunlight, pulling immediately into the alley and up to the back door. Last night's peeping seemed distant and unreal, a dream I'd just as soon forget. Rapping on the screen, I spied Simon sitting alone in the kitchen. I didn't wait for an invitation, but walked in and took the other chair.

Earlier that morning—six-thirty, actually—I'd rolled out of bed with a call from Buster's secretary at the Consolidated plant. My visit had been approved by Corporate after all, and I was to show up anytime mid-morning for a tour.

"I hope you've both had coffee," Gabriel declared as he came down the last two steps from the second floor and swung lightly into the kitchen. He was wearing a white shirt and dark tie. A grey suitcoat was slung over his shoulder. "We could put on another pot, but I've been reading and writing for two hours with a mug at my side."

"Not for me," I said. "What's with the formal gear?" I cast a quick glance behind Gabriel, but there was no sign of Grey. I wasn't sure whether I was disappointed or relieved.

"Got a meeting this morning," Gabriel said.

Simon was shaking his head. "Your brother-in-law says he has a lead on the woman who flagged you down. Says you can help him." His voice was flat, informative, but derision soaked each word.

I was watching and Gabriel didn't flinch. His eyes flashed with curiosity. He seemed full of energy this morning. Hopping up on the edge of the table, he swung his legs back and forth between us—the old Gabriel, quick, impatient. He looked at me expectantly.

"I got the name of someone who works at your plant. A John Martinez. He may know the boyfriend who scared the girl who ran out to your car. Ring a bell?"

"Sounds like a hell of a stretch to me," said Simon.

"Martinez? There're a couple Martinez, at least." Gabriel rocked back and forth, head raised, trying to recall. The tie and collar of his shirt weren't snug to his neck. "John Martinez? Yeah, I think I know the guy. He stays pretty clear of politics, though at least he's not hostile. Works on the fab floor. I think it's with the computer controlling the line, back by the grinders."

Fingers to his lips, rocking slightly, Gabriel was nodding as he pieced it together. "How're you planning to get him a message? They won't let me anywhere near the place—did you hear they canned me because I'm charged with a felony? But I can put you in touch with someone who'll pass a word on to him."

"That's okay. I'm visiting the plant this morning. If he's on this shift I'll find some way to talk with him."

Gabriel frowned. "No way they'll let you in. After all the bad press from the strike up in Austin they don't talk to press anymore. They've got PR people doing that."

"It's already arranged," I said simply. "You'd be surprised what doors open right up when you're a college professor."

They both looked surprised and puzzled. "Remember," Simon said sharply. "You're supposed to be helping."

The smell picked me up almost as soon as I swung past the river and into the southeastern part of the city: musky, pungent, as if I were passing row upon row of heavily laden cattle cars. But there was an added stench of singed hides, of meat and offal gone bad. The stink hung heavy in the air, beyond the power of the breeze to sweep clear.

As I turned off the highway and doubled back onto a service road, I noticed the Los Caballeros bar tucked away in the shadow of the overpass. Two long blocks further on the Consolidated plant appeared. The sprawling lot gave no external clue—other than the smell—of its function. I drove a hundred feet past and pulled into the dusty parking lot by the administration offices.

Plant managers aren't hidden discretely away. They're not that kind of executive. Their job is to keep on top of things. After giving the receptionist my story, I settled on a vinyl seat in a small waiting area. The office immediately across from me was Buster's. Its door stood ajar, an open dare to the rest of the plant.

I scooted over a couple of chairs to get a better angle. Buster was there all right—only a General Manager could get away with that pose—propped back dangerously in his chair, phone to his ear, his boots, expensive black western boots, crossed on the desk in front of him. He was long and lean, hair dark and swept back, mustache drooping across his lip. As I'm sure he intended, he resembled a tv gunslinger, sheriff gone mean. He reminded me—his expression more than his looks—of a certain Major Czeslaw (known throughout our sector of the delta as Chuckles) who'd been fearless, who raced on the promotion fast-track, and who shipped half a company home with tags on their toes.

For all his counterfeit good will on the phone the day before, Buster resolutely took no notice of me now. I wouldn't have wanted to work for the man. I wondered how far Gabriel had pushed him, how far he'd gotten under Buster's skin. How far would Buster go in making a Gabriel Salter pay?

A secretary suddenly appeared. Her face was small and pink, framed by an enormous aura of white hair like spun fiberglass. In her arms she carried a hard-hat and hairnet, a white labcoat, and a set of ear plugs. She set the kit on the chair next to me. "You're Mr. Currant, is that correct?"

"Professor Currant."

"Yes. I'm supposed to ask for some i.d."

"Doesn't Buster want to see for himself?"

"He's a very busy man."

From my wallet I drew the plastic card I still carried from Hopkins. Once in a blue moon this talisman proved useful. My last year at the university I'd received it while teaching in the summer program. A few months later I finally, belatedly, bailed out on a history dissertation. The past five years had taken their toll, I knew, but not enough so that Buster's secretary was likely to comment.

"Mmm-hmm, fine," she said without enthusiasm. "I'll just photocopy this and then Jackie, one of the foremen, will show you around the plant. In the meantime, why don't you put on this safety gear."

As I was slipping the earplugs into a pocket of the labcoat, a short stocky man hurried towards me down the corridor. "You're gonna need those," he announced with dour conviction. His own plugs were slung across his neck like a stethoscope.

"I'm sure you're right," I said. "You Jackie?"

"I been told to show you around." His voice was high pitched and hoarse, as if it had snagged at some critical moment of puberty. "Ready to go? Got your hairnet on under there? Gotta be careful about these things. Every detail counts. That's what I try and tell my people here. Some learn it, some don't. Those the ones don't last long."

I lifted my hand to pledge. "Regulation all the way."

Jackie nodded but didn't smile. He was, with generosity, five-feet-five. Maybe fifty years old, but that was hard to judge. Everything about him seemed of a piece: his compact but powerful build. His perfectly clean and creased uniform. His carefully laced boots. An unblemished hard-hat sat snugly, squarely on his head.

When he was certain all was in order, Jackie led me out of the lobby and into the sun. "You a college teacher?" he shouted into the wind.

"Right. I'm preparing a new class on the meat industry."

"Yeah—we sometimes get whole groups down from the state college. They're real interested 'cause what we do we do better than anybody."

Across the lot we came to a heavy-gauge cyclone fence. Jackie punched a combination into a battered lock-box and pushed the gate open. A handful of workers were scattered about, shifting hoses, ferrying a forklift back and forth. Near the main entrance a huge trailer was plunged into the side of the plant, heaving off the steady roar of a generator. Jackie signaled me to fit my earplugs. He screwed his own into place. "We'll do the fabrication floor first," he shouted and tugged open the heavy metal door.

I waved my assent. Despite the stench and a hazy antici-pation of what lay ahead, I was determined to see this through. Locating John Martinez was one item. And I was also curious to discover where Gabriel worked and the nature of hauling paunches. I had an intimation that visit-ing the plant would tell me something I didn't know. Maybe it would let me inside Gabe's skin or inside his head. Maybe it would help me establish once and for all just how different we were. I wasn't afraid of the industrial slaugh-ter. I'd seen worse.

I followed my guide through a stairwell and dark hall. The odors of raw meat and animal grease saturated the air like humidity at dew point. I felt them on my face and hands. Turning another corner, we came upon a curtain of beef carcasses heaving and swaying from hooks along a track overhead. They were slowly migrating onto the fab floor. A worker spotted us and without a word braced his back into one of the dangling sides of beef. Following Jackie, I ducked quickly through the portal.

A blast of cold air swept over us in the same pulse as the full roar of the plant. Conveyer belts and heavy chains, the thrum of hidden machinery, the whine of highspeed saws, all swirled in a whirlpool that sucked and pummeled the air about us. I wedged the earplugs deeper. Yet the racket was-n't as bad as a foundry I'd visited a few months before. And the sight before me of the beef being split, torn, and sun-dered wasn't alarming. Except for the scale of the opera-tion, I might have wandered into the back of a supermarket.

Jackie pointed at the floor. "Watch where you step," I saw

him shout. Patches of grease made the concrete slick. Pools of water gathered and dribbled in little rivulets. I wished I'd brought a pair of heavier shoes with me or that Buster had provided a pair of the rubber boots that protected workers in the plant up to the knee.

I glanced along the line, peering, trying to guess where the computers might be. I was eager to contact John Martinez, though just how I'd manage it remained a mystery.

I leaned closer to Jackie. "How many shifts you got running now?" I cried.

"Two here in fab," he said. "One in kill. Takes longer to process the meat."

The heavy sides of beef jerked slowly along the overhead tracks. Like freight cars on a siding, they formed a wall at one end of the fab floor. One at a time they switched over onto a new track to begin the run through a long gauntlet of saws and knives. Meat, workers, conveyer belts extended in every direction and at every height, all packed so tightly I couldn't make out how many of these processing lines ran parallel to each other. Three, four, perhaps more.

Jackie brought me up close behind the line. Workers, dozens of them, stood hip to hip in the bedlam, grappling the beef with a furious casualness. Each wielded a prosthetic hook in one hand, snagging and turning the meat. In the other they slashed a sharp blade, delving with short precise strokes. The hanging body opened itself to them, exposing treasures of secret flesh.

Each carcass surged forward, ever lighter, stripped, ragged, soon a pitiful shadow. At each station workers sculpted the cuts before them. Like a professor himself, Jackie was gesturing and cataloging. "Sirloin," he shouted. "New York Strip. Rib cuts."

As we moved along behind them, my guide methodically tapped each worker on the shoulder, a warning to trim the swing of their weapons. Yet I was aware that the message rarely came as a surprise. From the moment Jackie and I had

stepped on the floor, a ripple of attention, like a wind rif-
fling the top of a rough sea, had been passing lightly ahead
of us. The glances checking me out were quick, casual, only
distantly interested. The impatient press of beef allowed little more.

As I passed behind the line a strange illusion welled up:
that these workers packed so closely together possessed a
single blurred identity. No distinctness, no individuality.
High rubber boots, knives and hooks, white coats like the
one I wore but grimed with grease and blood, white hard-
hats like exoskeletal shells. As much a herd as the animals
they were swiftly dismembering. Hip to hip, shoulder to
shoulder in the din, they sliced and ripped and heaved,
scarcely human in motion, in speed, in endurance.

At my elbow the foreman was shouting. I couldn't hear
him.

Gradually, however, the illusion changed utterly, as if my
eyes were now focusing to a different depth of field. Each
time one of the workers turned to whet a blade, each time a
glance shot my way, checking out the intruder, I spied
someone new. The undifferentiated herd collapsed into
startling particularity. Here a heavy woman, with powerful
Slavic arms and a flushed face. There an Asian boy,
Vietnamese perhaps or Laotian, swung a haunch onto a low
platform. Two Latino men lay on their backs under one of
the conveyers, tools spread next to them. A Black woman
slashed her knife through the last tendon on a delicate cut of
beef. As she tugged it free and swivelled to toss it onto the
next belt she glanced at me through safety goggles. A single bead of sweat trembled at the end of her chin. With a
look blending disdain and indifference, she dismissed me
utterly and swung back to the line. Bashful and ashamed, I
turned away too.

All this while, Jackie was chattering with enthusiasm, a
petty demon showing off his dominion. But all I could
make out was the buzz of his voice.

At the far end of the line we swung left and followed one of the long conveyer belts towards a separate area of the floor. "Grinders," Jackie shouted, pointing to the first of a series of enormous steel cauldrons. "Starts real coarse. Each machine grinds to a finer grade." A steady stream of fat and gristle, cartilage and scraps of beef surged into the polished maw of the first huge grinder.

The machines backed against a curtain of heavy plastic flats swinging from ceiling to floor. Jackie pushed one aside and gestured me through. A blast of still colder air struck us. "Extra refrigeration in here for packing and storage," the foreman cried.

The light from overhead fluorescent tubes was eerie, jagged. It reminded me of midnight shifts at other plants where they over-compensated to fool workers or their body-clocks or the night itself. Not far away two men were tying off sausage-shaped logs of ground beef.

This area behind the curtain seemed both a nerve center and destination for the whole complex. Steady caravans of finished meat arrived aboard the conveyers. At a central station workers stowed and sealed the cuts into heavy cardboard cartons which rumbled in turn towards a computer scanner.

"See, each box has its own bar-code," he was still shouting. "That's how we track the product. If the computer goes down, the whole line goes down."

"That happen often?" I called.

He scrunched his neck into his shoulders defensively. "Naw—not much. It happens."

Two men in clean white coats were standing at the computer station as we approached. One minded the computer itself while the other attended to boxes as they rattled through. What if, after all, this wasn't Martinez's shift? What if Gabriel had been wrong about where in the plant he worked? I felt foolish, like a rookie reporter not doing enough homework to get it right, for setting up such a farce.

"Okay if I ask them a couple questions?" I shouted.

Surprised, Jackie frowned and shook his head. "Nobody told me nothing like that," he said.

"You stand right here and listen. How can I come all this way and not ask basic questions?"

"There's nothing they can tell you I can't."

"I'm sure that's true." I nodded reassuringly and placed a hand on the supervisor's arm. "But sometimes one guy thinks of something and not another, or one comes up with a detail another won't. Believe me, I'm not asking for any company secrets. I'm interested in process, nothing more."

Jackie still looked doubtful, but before he could respond again I'd turned to the heavy-set guy running the computer. "How many boxes come through an hour?" I asked.

"Depends." He stared at me steadily. I couldn't tell whether he was taking a cue from Jackie. His skin was pocked. A thick greying ponytail peeked out from under his hairnet. It was knotted tightly by a broken rubber-band at the back of his neck and tucked into his white coat.

"Like what?"

"Like lots of things." He hesitated but I never saw him glance directly at Jackie. "Sometimes they move the line along up over a hundred head an hour. Sometimes it's slower. Sometimes the line goes down and we have to catch up later. Course, the number of boxes through here changes with the kind of orders they got to fill too. All depends."

I was prepared to keep asking questions until I ran out or figured a diversion or it simply became too preposterous to maintain.

"Jackie," called the other guy who'd been fiddling with the scanner. "Come have a look. Fucker's skipping every third carton. I'm having to enter by hand again."

Jackie glanced at me and walked around to the other side of the computer station. "Let's see," he shouted.

"Hundred an hour? Damn impressive," I said loudly.

"Yeah," the heavyset guy said without enthusiasm. "They

slaughter one-fifty on the kill floor, but fab takes longer."

"Naturally," I said. Jackie was bent nearly double over the scanner. I dropped my voice. "Friend of a friend of mine is supposed to work around here—I was told it was on the computer. Maybe you know a John Martinez?"

"You know him?" He sounded less suspicious than bored.

"Like I said, friend of a friend. I'm supposed to say hi."

The guy grinned at that, flashing bad teeth. "Helluva place for a hello. That's him over there." He pointed to a small wiry man just tying off a tube of ground meat across the way.

Jackie twisted deeper under the scanner. I raised my hand in thanks and strode quickly across the floor.

Martinez saw me coming. He hitched the plastic tube onto his hip then swung it over and dropped it heavily on a belt.

"Hi," I called ahead with a friendly wave. Martinez stared, suspicious and cocky, a small bantam. "You John Martinez?"

"I got my papers," he said angrily. "I'm a U.S. citizen."

"I'm sure you are—I'm not here about anything like that. You know Gabriel Salter?"

"I don't got to tell nobody nothing."

"That's right—you don't." I shoved my hands in the pockets of my white coat. "But you heard about the trouble he's in. I'm just trying to find out what really happened Friday night."

Martinez scowled. "Yeah? Well I never seen him. I don't know nothing about any of that."

"But maybe you know someone who did. Can we talk about it later? A minute or two's all I'm asking. And Salter needs any help he can get."

"So? What's that to me?"

"So you decide. I'll be at Los Caballeros after your shift. Say about four. Let me buy you a beer."

"I only let my friends buy me beer."

I sensed, before I saw him, Jackie rush up to my side. "You're not supposed to do that," he shouted crossly as if to a naughty schoolboy. He put his hand on my sleeve. "You're not supposed to go anywhere or talk to anybody without me."

"Sorry, Jackie—you never mentioned that. I was just asking about the fat content on the final grind, but he doesn't know." Martinez had already turned away and straddled another tube of meat, tying it off like a cowboy over a small calf.

"Nothing any of them can tell you I can't," he said again angrily. "You got any more questions?" I shook my head innocently. "Well, it's time to move up to the kill floor any-way —Diane's expecting you."

"Diane?"

"She's foreman on duty up there. You do want to see kill?" He grinned at me.

"Wouldn't miss it."

The plant had grown familiar, the roar sustainable, the stench drawn so deep in my lungs that it was hardly notice-able. I'd accomplished the first part of my mission—though I wondered whether Martinez would show up at the bar— now I'd finally see the hair shirt Gabriel had fashioned for himself in order to be pure, one of the workers of the world.

Leaving fab, we climbed a set of stairs and followed a dark corridor to a separate area of the plant. The complex hadn't seemed so vast when I drove past it earlier. At last we arrived at a foyer next to a couple of office cubicles. Diane—it had to be Diane—was leaning against a doorjamb checking items on a clipboard. She was solidly built but not heavy. Her light brown hair pulled back in a neat bun, pen tucked in the breast pocket of her white coat, she might have been a harried intern in a medical ward. As we approached she began to lift her head but kept her eyes on the clipboard, confirming one last detail. Then she glanced up and smiled.

"Here's our guest for the day," said Jackie. "This here's Professor Currant."

"Glad to have you," she said with a firm handshake. She might have been preparing to administer a battery of physical tests to identify my malady.

"Deliver him back to me when you're done," Jackie said.

"Sure will," she said, tossing the clipboard onto a metal desk and picking up her hard-hat. "Ever been to a packing plant?" she asked as we set off.

"Nope," I said. "How long you been here?"

"Six years—a little over." She stated this as a matter of fact with no particular pride nor any appeal for sympathy.

We turned a corner and came upon another curtain of beef carcasses. This was the headwaters of the river that wound its way to distant stretches of dissolution on the fab floor. Diane fitted her earplugs and signaled to a young man with watery blue eyes. He lunged forward to breach the line, holding back a side of beef with his shoulder. Diane slipped quickly through and I followed.

As I straightened on the other side a wave of steam and massive heat bludgeoned me. Livestock and hot blood and raw leather, the smells twisted through each other like fibers in a single thickly braided rope. Ambushed, I struggled not to gag. Shit and blood and wet hides. In an instant I was tense and sweating hard. The heat, the smells were new yet eerily familiar. It surprised me there were no flies, no rice marsh surrounding us. The refrigerated fab floor had tricked me into dropping my guard.

Diane hesitated tactfully and gazed at something interesting in the distance. Shaken, embarrassed, I stepped to her side and she set off once more with a nod. Before us, a narrow steel staircase plummeted sharply. No hand rail. Diane led the way. I followed. Moisture coated each metal grid. The leather soles of my shoes provided no traction at all. I moved carefully, eyes on the step below.

Half-way down the long descent I nearly toppled into Diane. She was pointing ahead as if a special view of peaks and gorges was not to be missed. Perhaps fifty yards away, across something indeed of a gorge, live cattle were surging forward up a ramp and through a narrow chute. By the time these same cattle had crossed that canyon and were climbing past our heads they'd been slaughtered, tongues lolling, slit throat to tail, last blood spattering like sweat onto the concrete below.

At the bottom the floor was treacherous with slicks of bright red and clotted blood. Diane strode forward onto a ledge all of eight inches wide. I dutifully followed, step by cautious step. Here the carcasses swung towards us in an arc so close I pressed against the wall to dodge clear. At one point, however, their route actually brushed against the wall.

Diane timed it perfectly: as one cow followed another, she darted lightly between. I tried to imitate the dance. A mottled brown-and-white body heaved towards me. As its swing carried it past like an unwieldy pendulum, I hurried forward. I didn't slip or hesitate, but the rhythm was all wrong. An enormous black shape hurtled forward. I raised an arm just as the lolling dead eyes lunged at me. The blow caught me in the arm and chest and drove me back into the cement. I crashed with my shoulder, breath pummeled from my lungs.

The cow's lumbering embrace was heavy and indifferent as a gym dummy, but ripe with warm stench as it jerked clear on its track. Smeared with blood, furious and humiliated, I sucked for air and lurched out of the way of the next one. Still panting, I caught up with Diane at the end of a small metal platform. I stood half a step behind her so she wouldn't see me gasping or the state of my smock. Had she set me up deliberately? Had Buster sent the order? Or was this a trial, a passage they offered any lucky visitor?

High above us now, live cattle were pressing along the chute, mounting each other with eager and desperate urgency. At the crest a platoon of three or four workers were calibrated in their own minuet. One glided past another to bless each cow with a hand to its head as it stumbled forward. A sharp pneumatic blow plunged a blade into the animal's brain. Death came quickly, perhaps even before the slaughterer pulled the weapon clear, but the body twitched wildly as it slumped into a quick descent, jammed forward by the conveyer and the next surging animal.

In a cavity below the line a Black man, wearing compulsory helmet and goggles but stripped to the waist, fastened a metal loop to the leg of each slaughtered animal as it tumbled down the slope and then he hooked the other end to the overhead track. Immediately, the cow jerked into the air, still twitching, its belly exposed. Another worker darted forward to slash and unleash a torrent of blood into swirling pink drains below.

I watched with vague disgust. My collision with the heavy black beast must have been more violent than I'd realized, because I felt as though a mighty blow had struck me in the chest. It felt hollow, my breastbone sore. I was sweating and thirsty in the massive heat.

"Enough?" Diane shouted. "Got any questions?"

Numb, bruised, I shook my head. So much for my toughness, my objective detachment. It was the very familiarity of casual slaughter, of heat and thirst and disgust that unnerved me, that I neither wanted to remember nor to confess.

Diane led me back onto the narrow ledge. This time I moved more quickly, cavalier about the state of my shoes or what I might encounter. At the critical moment I danced between two animals, fending one off with my sleeve.

As the slaughtered cattle swung up from below, each was set on by teams of fierce knives. Slashing rapidly, they vented the hide, unhinging tendons that bound it. Its flaps were quickly clamped to the metal arms of a machine. In one clean jerk the arms reared back, peeling the hide clear of the flesh.

It occurred to me abruptly that the heads of the cattle had already disappeared, detached so quickly I wasn't even sure where that task had been accomplished. But over my own head I discovered them bobbing along a separate track, staring out over the world below. The effect was disconcerting, especially when I glanced down and saw, just beneath my feet, yet another track with skulls stripped of meat, gliding along as bloody masks.

"We use every bit except the eyes and teeth," said Diane, noticing my gaze. "Even the brains are saved. We've got a new Asian market that thinks they're delicacies." She touched my arm. "This one's hauling the paunches," she announced, pointing.

"Okay," I said, reluctantly pulling my stare away from the disturbing skulls. I shivered in the heat. I took a step back. This small cul-de-sac seemed hotter than all the rest of the plant, the air heavy with moisture and steam, with the confused smells of blood and offal. Sweat soaked my shirt and dribbled down my thighs.

A powerfully built man, his broad back to us, clipped tendons in the belly before him and, with a single ripping embrace, tore the stomach and intestines free, his back straining, his legs braced, before dropping the load into a tray. The mass had to weigh a good sixty pounds, but by the time I'd estimated that, he'd already moved on to the next.

This was Gabriel's job—how he'd earned his living for better than two years. And this was what I had come to witness. Not quite so sickened as I wanted to be, I imagined that watching all of this might be some strange expiation for what worse things I'd seen half a world away.

I stared as the man lurched again under the weight of a paunch. I tried to imagine myself under the load, back aching, arms numb with the effort. Hour after hour and day after day, world without end. Gabriel had chosen to work here, whether as some sort of penance of his own or as a noble step towards uniting the workers of the world.

It was unfathomable to me. I could imagine the necessity of such labor for some but not the deliberate choice of it for him. Was there no other way to earn a buck, or was this something he'd sought? Would you simply become used to this as to any other job, or would it extract some kind of private toll? Perhaps laboring here, hauling paunches, had worn at him, twisted and torn him, so that meat was meat and fifteen-year-old girls were owed no special dispensation.

Ashamed, I turned away. As on the night before, peering through Gabriel's kitchen window, I suddenly felt nothing better than a voyeur. Here I was sneaking through the plant under false pretenses, peeping into something private if not shameful. Was I titillated by the casual inferno these people returned to day after day?

I began to resent Diane as she relentlessly tugged me forward. Was she merely doing her job by providing a thorough tour? Or had she also spotted me as a voyeur, one who should pay for his professorial curiosity? Was she trying to force my own mask to slip?

Sweetbreads were another delicacy, bloody as props in a school tragedy before slipping into great bubbling vats of water, witches' cauldrons, only to appear once again, congealed and grayish-white.

Professorial curiosity. I grimaced. I'd abandoned the academy (staff card tucked in my wallet solely for fraudulent use) with nothing much to show for seven years' work, save boxes upon boxes of notecards from a dissertation that fought off all attempts to have shape thrust upon it. A 1919 workers' riot near Jersey City slipped ever farther beyond my grasp. Yet as my wife Hilary insisted with increasing regularly, I'd also been burrowing clear of the world around us. I might as well have stayed in the V.A. hospital. A point she finally added exclamation to by leaving me and soon taking up with a Washington attorney named Lenny.

I took her point, though belatedly. Dazed and bitter, I left the university. The next steps shouldn't have been so easy. I was dream-walking. From some occasional book reviewing I'd done for the money, I had contacts at the Baltimore paper; unfathomably, Stan Lupinsky gave me a shot; I worked hard; I was lucky. During those first couple of years journalism seemed the Lenny in my life: a close fit I'd been searching for all along. I wrote stories like I breathed air. I certainly wasn't removed from the world any longer but immersed in what glamour and considerable grit the city possessed. Yet being a reporter, writing about that world, also allowed me to maintain a certain detachment. With the paradox of being within and without of the stories I covered, I was comfortable.

Quick to the scene, I'd viewed the charred body of the fourteen-year-old who'd doused herself with kerosene and struck a match because her parents wouldn't allow an abortion. Her fleshless jaws were locked open in a cry beyond sound into the void.

I'd interviewed the pasty, bloated man released from St. George's because federal money had dried up and he wasn't deemed dangerous to himself or others. In turn, he'd been shooed away from the Inner Harbor so tourists wouldn't be offended by sight or smell. Ceremoniously, Wally unwrapped the newspaper protecting his bundle on the shattered park bench. He was honoring me, a reporter who'd taken an interest, with a privileged glance at his precious pet. Tenderly he displayed his pal, his decomposing kitten.

But trailing along the kill floor of Consolidated Packing I was feeling buffeted in a way I hadn't—deeper, more dizzying—since being discharged from that V.A. hospital in Virginia, before marriage, before my new life. The experience rocked me. I wanted to escape the ministering clutches of Diane and Jackie. I was well aware of just how far I stood from the day-to-day experience of Gabriel and others in this plant. And yet the protective detachment of my profession was collapsing weakly about me. I felt a fraud.

"Depends on the day, depends who you ask," Diane was saying, "but we process something like 1,200 to 1,250 head." With that she ducked backed through the cordon of hanging carcasses and I followed gratefully into the outer foyer. Jackie was waiting in the door to her cubicle. He tapped the face of his watch but said nothing.

"Thanks for showing me around," I said, holding out my hand to her and forcing a smile. It felt like a grimace.

"Anytime," she said. "Hope it's useful in your classes."

I nodded.

Jackie led me back through the corridors towards the main entrance. Betraying my eagerness, I stepped past him and pushed through the heavy steel doors. The March afternoon sun was dazzling, the air, the breeze—so oppressive when I'd arrived—was fresh, even sweet. As we headed back across the lot to the administration building I was already peeling off my stained coat. But there was no escaping the stench that had rooted not only in my hair and clothes but deep in my nostrils, lungs, imagination.

"You've been a terrific guide," I said to Jackie in the lobby and handed him my helmet. The rest of the gear I dropped onto a chair.

"My boss tells me to do something and I do it best I can," he said.

Over Jackie's shoulder I saw Buster leaning back in a high leather chair, boots propped on the corner of his desk. Three lesser managers in shirt sleeves clustered around a low table in a cabal from which he remained aloof. Buster betrayed no notice as I waved my thanks through the open door.

I emerged gratefully once more into the cool sunlight and hesitated for a moment by the side of my car. I felt stunned, as if I'd been struck soundly in the center of my chest by a tire iron. Half a mile from the plant I passed Los Caballeros. The idea of returning in a couple hours to meet Martinez—if he even showed—made my stomach churn. I drove quickly back towards the more reassuring oppressiveness of the city: exhaust fumes, the roar of traffic and horns and brakes, a different kind of bedlam.

In my room I stripped and shoved the clothes into a bottom drawer. The shower ran long and hot and, when I emerged, I was finally able to drink one, then several glasses of cold water. A heavy splash of bourbon made a final cleansing gesture. And still the faint odors of hides and blood endured like deep tattoos. A hollowness lingered beneath my ribs, bruise from my own revulsion.

At four o'clock I was sitting in Los Caballeros. The day shift at the plant hadn't ended yet and the bar was empty. Its single broad room was brightly lighted and clean, with wooden tables in neat rows. Along one wall stood three pool tables. The bar itself ran the length of the back wall, tended by two women in tight designer jeans. I'd taken a small pitcher of beer and two mugs and settled at the end of one of the trestle tables facing the door.

By four-thirty the bar had begun to fill, but there was no sign of Martinez. Half the pitcher was gone. No one shied clear of me and no one bothered to drift close. At twenty minutes of five I gave myself until the top of the hour.

A couple of minutes later Martinez walked in by himself. He was wearing a blue jacket and a black baseball cap. He neither pretended not to see me nor gave any sign he had. He went directly to the bar, ordered a drink, and then carried it my way. Without unzipping his jacket, he set a tall coke on the table and swung a leg over the bench.

"I only got ten minutes, you know," he said straight out. "I got to get to my other job." He looked older than I'd guessed before. A thin mustache had made his earlier defiance seem like a kid's, but I saw now that his skin was creased, that under his eyes it was bruised with fatigue. A jagged white scar crossed the back of his right hand as he sipped at the coke.

"Get that at Consolidated?" I asked, nodding at the scar.

He shrugged. "Part of the job. People get hurt worse."

I nodded. "What's this other job? You put in a full shift on the grinders and then head somewhere else?"

"I'm a good carpenter. I help a guy out. Sometimes it's

four hours, sometimes eight. Brings in good money."

"You trying to get away from the plant?"

"No," he said, shrugging. "They pay not so bad too. But I need all I can 'cause my mother and my brother are going back to Salvador. They don't want to stay here no more. I'm a U.S. citizen and I'm staying. But this is a terrible place. They like home much better, you know? But man, you're not caring about that."

I tapped my glass on the table. "So what I care about is figuring Gabriel Salter's story. You know him?"

"Sure—I know who he is. Always political. I stay away from that shit. Why you think I leave Salvador? All damn politics. I don't like the cops and FBI and INS. I don't like Salter with the politics. You may be a cop too and I don't like you, but I done nothing."

"I'm not a cop, I'm a reporter. You can believe that or not." Martinez glanced at my card and then flipped it like a joker on the table. I stared straight at him. "What I want to know is, you were at the 3-Penny Tavern Friday night?"

"I never seen Salter there."

"That's right—he wasn't. But you were with some friend who slapped at his girlfriend. Yeah?"

Martinez's eyes narrowed. He straightened his back like a bantam once more, tough and angry. "Who tell you that?"

"The old men, the bartenders." I leaned forward, Martinez's tension a spark to my own.

"What else they told?"

"Just that. Your friend takes a swing at his girl. She runs outside. That the way it happened? Could be she asked Salter to give her a lift."

Martinez drained his glass in two long swallows and then held it in front of him, swirling the ice. "Those old men, they don't know shit. They just telling you stories they make up."

"But you were there. You said so. So what part of the story is made up?"

"Man, the whole thing, it's wrong. Yeah, I'm there with my

friend. You don't gotta know his name. There ain't no girl. Not one. There're two, three girls. We buy them some drinks maybe. But my friend don't hit none of them. It's this dude who's the trouble. Black guy. Says spicks can't be playing with these Black girls. Spicks. Puerto Rico, Salvador—same thing to this dumb fuck, you know? Girls get scared. My friend get angry. Gonna pick that guy apart, you understand? So I drag him out of there. I don't know what the fuck those girls do. Maybe they run away, maybe no."

I tried to break in but Martinez checked me with a look. He pulled his cap off, wiped his forehead with a napkin, reset the cap. "I never seen Salter. Don't know what they done to him. If cops screw him that's bad, but I don't know and he ain't the first." He rose. "Look, man, I gotta go."

I stood too. "Thanks for taking the time," I said and held out my hand. "Can you maybe give me a number for your friend? Could be he noticed something outside the bar."

Martinez scowled and swung away without taking my hand.

By the time I wandered after him into the parking lot, Martinez was already gunning an ancient Pinto, blowing smoke down the access road past the plant.

I was prepared to believe that the two old men at the tavern got it wrong: that they'd seen things and put two and two together and didn't get four, that they'd made up a story of their own. But was Martinez's version any more reliable? What was he protecting his friend from? The INS? Something more?

Were there any leads here or none at all? I still wasn't persuaded that Gabriel Salter's story was anything more than a desperate concoction. But I'd run up against a wall. I'd report what little I'd found to Jeremy Stanton, Gabriel's attorney, and suggest he hire an investigator. Maybe he already had.

No matter of decision: I discovered I was heading for

Gabriel's house again only after I'd turned north on the free-way spur instead of south towards my motel. I pulled into the alley and up to their kitchen door. An old familiar, I knocked and walked in.

Alone in the kitchen at the formica table sat Hilary.

Chapter IV

Hilary's features stiffened, though she did her best to disguise it. I offered a taut smile to her upturned face and said nothing for the moment. I wondered whether my teeth were going to chatter on their own cue, as they had during one of the divorce negotiations, the two of us facing each other hostile and miserable across a narrow table.

I gestured to the other chair and she shrugged. I dragged it out from the kitchen table. And as I sat at an angle, not quite facing her directly, a disorienting flush of familiarity swept along my limbs. This had happened a thousand times, Hilary Salter's face gazing up anxiously at me. It dispelled any threat of the shakes.

"I got away sooner than I expected," she said as hello. "Congressman Bayard was leaving early on his junket to India."

"Who'd you get to stay with Hannah?"

Her eyes crinkled, grateful for the interest. "We've got this terrific cleaning woman. Her husband's a handyman for the Guatemalan embassy. Carmen's agreed to stay at the house while I'm gone. And Hannah adores her."

"That's great." The words sounded flat in my ears.

Three years—better than three years since I'd laid eyes on

Hilary. She'd lost weight, maybe fifteen pounds, which for a small woman meant significant change. The oval symmetry of her face had always reminded me of some medieval madonna, but it had become leaner, tougher. She'd cut her reddish-brown hair short, almost boyish, with the frazzle of a light perm. Businesslike, yet with a flash of style—the carefully chosen gesture of a Congressional aide on the make. Rumor among my colleagues at the paper had a senator trying to woo her away.

She was doing her own inspecting but, perhaps fortunately, she'd developed quite a poker face. It gave precious little away. That was a significant change in itself. From when we were kids my ability to read Hilary had been a mark of our intimacy. In the bad times later on, that skill goaded me with inescapable evidence of her growing weariness.

"Where are they?" I asked.

"Gabe went out to pick up some Chinese for dinner. She's upstairs, I guess."

Hilary didn't quite manage to hide a scowl. She glanced at me and then down at her hands. "Look, Jason—it was really good of you to shlep all the way out here like this, without warning. I'm kind of surprised—Christ, I'm embarrassed—that I even asked you to. Must be a reflex, even after all these years. It's not like you owe me anything."

"You're welcome," I said. "But it's your family as much as you. Funny thing, hearing your Dad's voice on the phone. Caught me by surprise. It's been a long time and I miss him. Gabriel too, though I wouldn't have expected it."

I felt awkward with this woman, yet it also seemed the most natural thing in the world to be sitting here with her. A problem had come up in the family: we were coveyed together to solve it, the practical ones, the responsible ones, the ones who had it together, the ones both families always turned to, the ones who'd managed to screw up their own marriage first-class.

She reached under the table for her bag and pulled out a

pack of cigarettes. I wondered whether Lenny knew she'd started again. Or was she only sneaking them on the side? I was glad to see her hand tremble slightly as she lit up.

"What I'm getting at," she said, and the poker face melted away, laying bare ancient pain and ire, "it's time you tell me what you've found out. Then you go home. I'm here now."

Again a vivid stab of repetition—I watched my own anger leap erect at her stroke. "That's mighty decent of you," I said.

"Oh, shit. Don't play the martyr, Jason. It doesn't become you," she snapped. "Tell me what's going on, what you've found out, okay? Anything to prove how grotesque this whole thing is. Everybody knows Gabe couldn't possibly do such a thing."

"I'm not sure he didn't," I stabbed back at her, using my own doubt as a weapon. Dismay dilated in her eyes, darkening them. She shook her head slightly. Suddenly all the anger drained from me along with all the echoes. I was just sitting at this table with Hilary, the past a long way away.

"I'm not saying he did. I've know Gabriel too many years to believe it. From that point of view you're right—it's impossible. But he and his comrades have come up with this cock-n-bull story about the cops framing him. It takes a whole lot of faith to buy." I spread my hands. "So, I don't know. I've been following some leads."

She stabbed the cigarette into a small bowl. "The objective reporter. The journalist. Aren't you doing a marvelous job." The words were caustic, but her voice was so heavy with concern that they scorched me not at all. Shifting on her seat, she sighed and changed her tone. "We're talking about Gabriel. This isn't someone you don't know. In a thousand years he couldn't hurt someone, not intentionally. Maybe if you take that as a starting point, the rest of your leads will fall into place."

I shrugged unhappily. Her faith in her brother was no

surprise. Unconditional loyalty defined the Salter clan. It was one of the exotic traits Joseph Salter had smuggled along with his cello and little else out of Hungary. As close to the family as I'd grown, as much as they'd once depended on me as a member of their inner councils, no one from outside could ever fully be grafted into that loyalty bred in Salter blood and bone.

At that moment I heard Grey's step, firm, quick, on the stairs. As she entered the kitchen and discovered me, she didn't smile or nod but strode to the sink and spoke over her shoulder while filling the kettle. "I'm making tea. Like some?" Her voice was deep, a little bit gruff. She was wearing jeans and boots, a collarless railroad shirt, its sleeves rolled to the elbow. A silver-and-turquoise quiver gathered her long black hair at her neck. The surplus fell in a thick braid to the middle of her back.

"Sure," I said.

Hilary shook her head. "The biggest shock is what they did to his face," she said, as if continuing an earlier thought. "It's unbelievable. Insane. In Washington, the ACLU would be all over the case. That kind of beating would be enough to get any charges dismissed. And I really think we should see another doctor right away. An emergency room is only going to patch him together. Who knows what long-term damage the cops may have done?"

"He'll be back any minute with the food," said Grey. Her back was stiff as she prepared a teapot for the water, cradling it as if it could warm her hands already.

The tension between the two women was nothing new, I gathered. I was grateful that Grey acted as if I were welcome here—something I hadn't felt since discovering my ex-wife at the table. Perhaps Grey intended her kindness as a deliberate jab at Hilary, knowing the family history. But that made it none the less pleasing. It was her house after all.

"I hear you visited the Consolidated plant," she said as she handed me a hot mug. "Do you see now why we do what we do? Why should people have to live like that or work in those conditions?"

Hilary leaned forward. "Was this one of your leads? Did you find anything that can help Gabriel?"

"I'm not sure about that yet. But it's a pretty hellish way to earn a buck," I acknowledged to Grey with a nod. A hulking black shadow came swinging at me. The hollow spot beneath my breastbone ached anew. I sipped at my tea.

A car with a bad muffler bobbed along the alley; its lights soared through the kitchen window until the engine cut off. A moment later Gabriel appeared with Simon by his side, each carrying a large brown paper bag. Gabriel set his on the table, and he grinned at us, his eyes alight.

"Hey, look at this—it's like I'm a kid again. Big sister and brother come to take care of things. I don't know whether that makes it a crisis or a party." From the twitching at the edge of his grin, I guessed he was delighted by something more than familial reminiscence, but he was content for the moment to tease us.

From a drawer by the sink Grey fetched a handful of wooden chopsticks and dropped them in the middle of the table. She handed me a bowl without a glance and turned away.

Standing against the sink, Gabriel had already torn open a spring roll and was dipping shreds into a patch of hot mustard. Something tough surprised him as he bit into it and he winced. I'd forgotten about his cracked jaw. Despite the pain, despite his yellowing bruises, he looked boyishly happy, almost giddy. "We got news," he mumbled between bites without looking up, as if he didn't trust himself. "Big news. Tell them, Simon."

Simon held a small cereal bowl to his lips and sipped the soup. His glasses steamed. He set the bowl down, removed his glasses, and lay them on a corner of the table. His eyes seemed strangely weak and vulnerable until he'd wiped the lenses and carefully hooked them back in place. From a

cloth shoulder bag he'd set by his chair he tugged out a folded newspaper and handed it to Hilary. "The Party agrees
that this is an outrage they won't ignore. A hundred copies
of this arrived just as we were leaving the bookstore."

He tossed me a separate copy of the Worker. Grey stood
over my shoulder to read. The familiar photo of Gabriel's
bludgeoned face was spread across three columns in the center of the front page. OUTRAGE BY IOWA COPS, ran the
banner head, Justice for Gabriel Salter!

"They're launching—we're launching—a campaign for
justice," Simon continued. "It's going national. Every progressive organization in the country will hear about it." He
took another slow sip of soup. "The defense committee
we've set up here is keeping separate from the Alliance. That
will make the support of unions and peace groups easier.
Not to mention fund raising. We'll need plenty of cash to
pay for the lawyer your sister set you up with, Gabriel. Your
well-meaning liberal." He said it with a slight grimace as if
some bit of curd in his soup had gone bad.

"There's no hushing it up anymore," Gabriel said. His
hazel eyes, impish and intense, revealed no sign of fatigue
despite the bruises still circling them. "This is our opportunity to blow the lid off how the bosses control this town. In
New York, they know what a chance this is." He talked as
though the campaign had little to do with him personally.

Gabriel cocked his head at me. "So, did you really manage
to perjure your way into Consolidated?"

I nodded. "Got the complete tour. I used some old i.d."

"How'd it go?" He was smiling but playing it coy.

"I suppose there are worse places to work, but none I've
seen."

He was nodding sternly, proudly. "That's right. You got it
right." He turned to the others for confirmation. "A job's a
job, but it doesn't have to be inhuman like that. That's the
point. And? Did you find Martinez?"

I was interested in his interest, but didn't know what to

make of it. "He works near where you guessed—at the grinders, not the computer. We had a beer at Los Caballeros after his shift."

The kitchen was very quiet. "And?" Gabriel repeated.

A swift surge of anger and shame swept over me. "And nothing," I said aggressively, watching for Gabriel's reaction, wanting to shake these people out of their complacency, their dreams of grand protest. "He admits he was at the bar. There were some girls. But nothing about any one of them rushing out just when you happened along. Your mystery woman's still a mystery."

Gabriel's face showed friendly commiseration, nothing more. I was aware of a faint smirk on Simon Yoo's lips, mocking me for my failure. Hilary merely looked irritated.

"I thought I'd drop by your attorney—Stanton, right?— and suggest he hire a pro to track the leads down, if he hasn't signed one on already."

"No need, Jason," Hilary snapped with authority. "We're on our way to see Jeremy Stanton in half an hour. I arranged it before leaving Washington. Evenings are the best time to discuss strategy. I'll pass on your suggestion." She hesitated. She smiled. She might have been at a podium doling out public thanks to a conscientious volunteer. "Oh, and you all should know, Jason's leaving. He's got a job in Baltimore to get back to."

"I hope that's still true," I murmured. (I'd give Stan a call from the motel.)

I was touched—I was startled—by the disappointment in Gabriel's eyes. "Not really?" he said. Setting his bowl down, he strode across the room. He held me at arm's length, studying me, shaking his head. And then he flung his other arm around my neck and pulled me closer into a powerful hug. His arms and back were strong from hauling paunches. Yet he held his jaw away from my shoulder, and I was reminded again of how fragile he was.

"You've just come back and now you're leaving again," he

murmured. "Well, I'm grateful for everything you've done. Thanks for your faith, Jason—it means a lot to me."

I hugged him back, torn, almost suffocating. Was this a younger brother I'd lost a long time ago or was I being manipulated? Was I clutching a Jekyll-and-Hyde or some kind of Gandhi? Faith. I had no more faith than any lame agnostic.

He released me, and with a gathering flurry over the next fifteen minutes, the meal was consumed, bowls and utensils heaped in the sink, bags and cartons shoved into a metal wastebasket. Gabriel, Hilary, and Simon hurried out to the car. Detached, I'd settled again on a straight-backed chair and watched as they fled. I figured I'd sit here a while.

A clatter at the sink startled me. With one hand Grey was rearranging a precariously balanced stack of bowls. I'd been so caught in revery that I hadn't noticed her remaining behind. Suddenly I glimpsed—and realized—what she'd reminded me of from the very start: a warrior. Aloof, powerful, separate from the rest, ear attuned to something far in the distance.

"How come you didn't go?" I asked.

She glanced at me. "These are Hilary's arrangements. She can have Gabriel for the evening. Besides, she doesn't really approve of me." Grey leaned against the counter, hands behind her, and allowed herself a hard smile. "I don't think she approves of you either."

"Not any more," I said. "Not for a while."

"Except she will still call you. Come make sure we are taking care of her brother. She's a very impressive woman. I admire her strength."

I paused, trying to read how much irony she intended. "I guess that's right."

Grey tilted her head back. "So now you run back East, once she dismisses you."

"It's not as simple as that." Wounded pride stirred, but then I grinned. "Though she did a pretty good job of giving me the shove tonight, didn't she? But she's right. I've got a job—I still have one—that I'd better get back to. I haven't been the most conscientious employee lately."

She shrugged with apparent indifference. "As a matter of fact, I know very well about your job—I have read your stories from the paper."

I stared at her. "How's that?"

"It's Gabriel—he asks her to send him your clippings, any pieces you write. I think he does it to tease her. She grumbles. But she will always do what he asks. Of course, as you say, lately she hasn't sent many." For Grey this amounted to a torrent of words, and I suspected she had something else on her mind.

"There hasn't been much to see."

Her eyes narrowed and she wasn't smiling. "You write good pieces, powerful stories about people in pain and trouble. This is what I have thought and why I read them when Gabriel finishes. But why do you always stop short?—I do not understand. Always you refuse to go far enough, to show the truth. So often their pain is caused by a system that is unjust. How can you do that?"

I shrugged. "I'm more interested in the person than the pattern. They have a way of simplifying by being too abstract, too general. Makes for terrible copy. I leave that to the columnists."

She leaned forward. She turned her head slightly.

"That's the problem—for you the article alone is enough."

"It's a job," I said. "Maybe a good piece will provoke someone else to change the world. But I don't really have much hope."

She pursed her lips, weighed what I'd said, and set it aside. "I will be sorry for you to go," she said. "It is good for Gabriel to have you here."

Surprised—delighted—that she'd read my work, that she was sorry I was leaving, I didn't know what to say, didn't trust myself to say anything. This woman with her narrow hips and fierce eyes—I had no clue how to translate her. "Yeah—me too," I said finally. "It's strange leaving at this stage. Not knowing which is the right version." As soon as I spoke I regretted it. I didn't mean to betray my lack of faith.

She laughed aloud without humor, strode towards me (I almost flinched), and claimed the other chair. She straddled it front to back. "You don't believe Gabriel."

"It's not that I don't believe him. There are a couple versions of what happened, and I'm not sure how to fit them together. It's not that I don't believe him," I repeated more desperately.

"But you are sure there's a single hidden story, a true one. If only you can discover it."

Again I felt unable to read her. I wanted to ask what she believed but didn't dare. I changed course. "How'd you get involved in all of this?" I asked.

Her eyes arched mockingly. "You don't mean with Gabriel, do you?" (I was shaking my head already.) "Your wife would be the one to wonder that."

"She's not my wife anymore," I insisted as she went on.

"You mean the socialists, the ISA. There was less choice than you think. On the Navajo reservation—I am actually Laguna—if I stay there, my family and my people dictate life to me. By now I'd be married or divorced already. Batch of kids. I'd be poor. I'd be a victim." She grimaced and a shadow seemed to pass quickly across her eyes. "I don't see myself as a victim anymore. Once—" She halted. She glanced at the window with an angry scowl as if to chase away a memory that pursued her. "That's not how I want to live." She paused again and stared out past me to the dark windows and the invisible alley.

"If I want to change these things for my sisters, I have to be outside. But if I leave the reservation and simply become part of your world, is there any better choice? What should I do—college or a job, play the nice White girl? Which no one would let me, even if I try. Or turn tricks? That's how most of the girls wind up if they dare break away free. I don't want someone else's rules. I don't want to fake someone else's role that doesn't belong to me."

She shook her head and turned her eyes on me once more and smiled, but it was a fierce smile and in her eyes I glimpsed a fury back behind everything else. "The Party— the Alliance—it doesn't have those kind of rules," she went on. "Only rules that help us fight for change. Your world's an unfair world to most of us and my only real choice is to fight it." Her head was raised, her nostrils flared.

"And you," she said with a sudden swift shift, "you are a storyteller." I couldn't make out whether she meant it as an indictment or a simple statement of fact.

"I wish that were true," I admitted. "Most of the time, newspapers make for pretty dull reading."

"Someday you should hear storytellers at my home, in our language. You wouldn't even need to understand the words. There's music in the way they speak." She shook her head once sharply from side to side. Her braided hair whipped back and forth. "Do you know, on the reservation storytellers are very powerful—they possess great power. A kind of magic. They are creating a magic place for us, with-out White people and poverty and disease. There's dignity. Better still, there's revenge. Storytellers are often our best warriors."

I was startled again—had she read my mind, how I'd imagined her as warrior? How much more did she read there that already had me feeling guilty?

Her smile softened with a faint mocking. "You should try less hard to find a single answer here. You, all of you in your world, have this shape in your mind of what stories must be. So straight and rigid. And you rip and tear at life to make it fit. It's like a prison, making all stories obey. If you're not careful, you find yourself locked in too."

I leaned back in my chair and stretched. "I don't know," I said. "There's lots about this case I may never understand. But I'm already pretty sure about what they did to Gabriel in that elevator—one story's true there, one's not. I don't believe he was grabbing for any gun."

Willing to risk her wrath, I looked directly at her. "I'm also pretty sure a young girl was hurt and scared bad. That's a fact, every bit as much as the bruises on Gabe's face. I'm not saying he was the one who did it, and I'm not saying he's lying. But claiming the cops set it all up in advance doesn't make sense. It's too far-fetched." I paused. She was staring at me, waiting for more, her lips pressed thin.

"Who knows?" I went on. "Maybe the girl's lying about who did it. Maybe her family set Gabe up to protect someone else. He just showed up at the wrong place, wrong time. But yeah, I do believe there's an answer, even if we never make it out. Though I'd expect Gabe and his lawyer to be trying harder on that score. They could be digging for some evidence or witnesses, instead of all this crap about him not having to prove his innocence."

I figured she might stalk out of the room, might dismiss me too with a contemptuous laugh. Instead, Grey remained pensive and still, and when she gazed at me her eyes were heavy with worry. "We don't say the girl wasn't attacked. But can we save Gabriel by proving she's a liar? Or her family? How will that look? It's one thing if the cops are behind it all, but if they're not?"

She shook her head. "And I'm not convinced about what you say—in this city the cops are capable of anything. Let them prove Gabriel's guilty. We won't attack that girl any more than she has been already. I won't allow it." Her voice flickered with defiance.

"So, tell me what you think," I said.

She looked at me hard. Her dark eyes blazed again. "I don't know what happened. But I know he's not capable of that. Never, never, in the years I've known and lived and worked with him—Gabriel's never hurt anyone. He's hardly raised his voice, let alone his fist. With me . . . ," her voice trailed off.

I rose and pulled on my jacket. "So long," I said.

She glanced up appraisingly for a moment without answering. "I think you will be back," she said. "You haven't finished your story."

The red light was flashing on my phone. Two messages, the front desk reported, one from Stan, one from Phyllis. I was to call each of them as soon as possible. I sat on the edge of my bed. In memory of countless others in the same position, the mattress sagged towards the phone. My back sagged as well. My life in Baltimore seemed increasingly distant, disconnected, unreal. No, I was the one disconnected on this end. I decided Stan and Phyllis could wait until I returned the next day. Anything they'd tell me now either wouldn't be that pressing or would be bad news. They could wait. I could wait.

It wasn't yet nine o'clock, but I felt ragged. Even now the taut, hollow drum hadn't loosened in my chest from my visit to the Consolidated plant. And I couldn't shake the impression of Grey Navarro still sitting a few inches beyond reach, watching and critical, dark, vexing, and forbidden.

I was restless. From my jacket pocket I pulled my notepad and leafed through it, searching for a number. Making this kind of call had been the hardest part of my job from the start. Like diving into a cold pool, I'd learned to resist the anticipation that gave way to dread and reached for the phone automatically.

"Yeah? Jackson here," growled a voice.

"Mr. Jackson? My name's Jason Currant. I'm a reporter."

"It's pretty fucking late to be bothering somebody at home. Who'd you say?"

"A reporter. Jason Currant. I know it's difficult, but I'd like to talk to you about what happened with your daughter the other night."

"Not with my daughter. To my daughter. That's the

whole damn point, mister. But yeah, I'll talk. The truth ought'a get out. No one around here's paying any damn attention. Them commies got everybody intimidated."

"How's that?"

"They been calling the civil rights groups and the unions, saying it's all a lie. Calling it a frame. They even been handing out fliers at my girl's high school. Tried to give her one yesterday. Think of that, man. She come running home. Ain't been back to school today, no way."

Caught unprepared, I fumbled a pen out of the night stand drawer and began scribbling notes. "Mr. Jackson," I interrupted. "This isn't the best way to do it. I was hoping to come by and see you tomorrow morning, maybe before work."

"Just tell me when. I truck out of here anyways. Just so I know you're coming."

"Eight-thirty too early?"

"Bring something to show you are who you say. No reason for me to trust nobody."

The flask of bourbon still sat by the sink in the bathroom. I carried it back to the night stand and lay down in my clothes, hands behind my head.

I was weary but not ready for sleep. Emotionally I'd been stretched so far my sinews popped. Beef carcasses pummeling me. Hilary greeting me at the kitchen table. (Though she'd thanked and dismissed me, there'd been an emotional brush, an acknowledgment between us that I now found oddly reassuring. I smiled with the small triumph.) Grey talking the story through. Grey, who'd accused me of being a storyteller.

I rolled up on an arm. The phone line cracked and crackled. I didn't hear the connection go through. Joseph Salter's hello caught me unawares.

"Joseph," I shouted back. "Joseph—hello. It's Jason."

"Jason," he cried, alarmed and confused. "Has anything happened? Is something wrong? Where are you?— Baltimore or Iowa? Hilary said you were going home."

"Still in Iowa. I'm heading back tomorrow."

"I see." He stumbled, trying to make sense of the situation. "But everything is all right? What about Gabriel and Hilary?"

"They're fine—I saw them only a couple of hours ago."

"I see," Joseph said again, puzzled.

Tell me about your Great-Uncle Shemi, I wanted to shout. Tell me about the time he traveled across the mountains to buy food during the famine. How the villagers hid their money in the axles of his cart to fool bandits. How he met his bride when the wise man invited him in for sabbath dinner. How you never met any of these people, but they were your family in a time before time.

A wind of static flickered across the phone lines. "I shouldn't have bothered you, Joseph," I said lamely. "Just checking in. I promised to, remember?"

"Yes, of course," he said rather doubtfully.

"I've got to run now. Take care of yourself. And give my love to Marianne."

"You too. You too. Many thanks, Jason."

I set the phone in its cradle and wished I hadn't called. I didn't want to hear the tremulousness, the hint of disorientation in his voice. It made me feel sad and alone and afraid.

I imagined calling my own father to admit I was sad and alone and afraid, and I couldn't imagine it. I hadn't spoken to him since Christmas. My mother, whom I called every week or ten days, would no doubt arrange a chat between father and son with the next holiday that seemed appropriate. Easter? Dad would like the resonance in that.

He and I hadn't spoken much since my decision to leave graduate school, dissertation stillborn, not long after Hilary moved to Washington. We'd talked then for three solid days. The first day had been by phone. Then Dad flew to Baltimore.

Never before had he visited me there, not during all the years Hilary and I were married. Two more days we talked, my father talked. I was surprised at the lack of fury—fury I'd been prepared for. But not the baffled look in his eyes, the fundamental failure to understand. Never before had I suspected that I'd enough of my father's attention to be able to disappoint him. Two straight mornings Bradley Currant the eminent professor arrived from his hotel, freshly shaven, mane of white hair brushed for an instant before tumbling into distinguished disarray. Two days and two nights, we went at it, finishing late over whiskey.

If forced to mingle with academics again at one of Phyllis's book parties, I could drop the old man's name and be sure of someone lighting up with enthusiasm. The thing Bradley Currant held most in contempt in the religions he studied—enthusiasm.

Middle of March now. Would Dad even be in Pennsylvania teaching his classes? Or would a colleague cover for him while he was off being lauded in San Francisco or Bellagio? It was enough to lend a conference prestige that he merely attend—no need for him to prepare a talk. He was broadly acknowledged as among an elite handful of philosophers who specialized in New Testament ethics. A man who during the last decade had been graciously declining offers to translate himself to a major university for a salary double what his small college could ever manage. No, but Bradley Currant was committed to his undergraduates. He was also committed, I well knew, to being a big fish in the college pond.

Big fish enough that as Provost thirty-five years earlier, he'd hired a Hungarian Jew fleeing the Soviets without first bothering to consult the music department. Joseph Salter had been the one to suffer the wrath of his new colleagues, their snubs and behind-the-scenes denunciations, until he'd wooed them with Hungarian charm and broken English, with the music of his cello and the music of his stories.

I rubbed my eyes hard. I felt cut loose, an astronaut whose umbilical cord has been severed, spinning slowly away, weightless, out of control, relaxed beyond terror. I felt myself floating free, anchored nowhere. Closing my eyes, I summoned Phyllis, touched my fingers to hers, and discovered myself touching Grey. Startled and not startled, I sat up and blinked into the light. No, I wasn't going to follow that route. Some whiskey, a few deep breaths, and I tried again, lying down, shutting my eyes. And found Gabriel waiting for me.

Chapter V

I sat with a mug and an open notebook in a coffee shop, sketching other possibilities for why Gabriel might have been set up. This on the chance that his story, or some substantial part of it anyway, were true. Some of the basic facts were indisputable, of course. But before interviewing Jackson, I wanted a framework, maybe a couple three frameworks, on which to stretch those facts. As a historian, I'd discovered that having alternatives was the only defense against being swept away by someone else's convictions. If I were going to make sense of what Jackson told me, other than the sense Jackson himself imposed, I had to be ready to supply some plots of my own, or at least ready to maintain a little critical detachment.

Okay, I thought, what if it was the cops? What if they'd really been out to get Gabriel? My pen doodled on the pad. I shook my head. It didn't add up. Entrapping Gabriel, some woman throwing herself at his car, was too cumbersome and left too much to chance. Not least, it was hard to imagine that Gabriel Salter was significant enough to warrant the expense and effort such choreography would demand. Sure, in towns where they were better organized, the ISA strutted around claiming to be a political force. But

generally they were shades shrieking into a gale. Their existence went unnoticed by all but a handful of believers and
disgruntled workers. Yes, Gabriel could probably be a royal
pain in the ass at the plant. Yes, Buster would probably be
glad to get rid of any guy who was educating other workers. But what price was Buster willing to pay?

Okay, say it was Buster and the cops anyway. They'd
have to get Jackson to play along. How? Money? A favor?
Some kind of blackmail? Would there be any visible clues?
I'd have to be alert for anything along that line.

Say it wasn't the cops. I drained my cup. Mid-swallow I
returned to a fledgling notion I'd mentioned to Grey. Say it
was a set-up after all. But not for Gabriel, not in particular
anyway. Say Jackson's family had their own reasons.
Something big to hide. The girl—maybe she's attacked by
someone they want to protect even while they're getting her
to the ER. An uncle or cousin. Maybe Jackson himself?
They wouldn't want to be explaining her cuts and bruises to
a suspicious doctor.

Send an aunt or a cousin out to flag down any sucker willing to stop his car. Couldn't ask for a better chump than
Gabriel, not with some woman spinning a tale of woe and
begging for help. Lure him up to the house, dial 911. Let
the cops do the rest and send the girl to the hospital without
any questions about how she got hurt.

I sat back. I flipped my pen in the air. That would cover
it both ways. However faulty the specifics of my hunch,
Gabriel would have the facts right about what happened to
him—he'd been framed. So would the cops—they answer
the distress call and discover him at the Jackson house.
Though I'd denied it to Grey, I had begun to doubt that any
single story was buried here, but some scenario like this
would do the trick.

Another thing I'd learned as a historian (before trendy
theorists made all narratives suspect): one story always
grows out of another. Locate evidence of a motive (which of

course presumes an underlying story) for the Jackson family to lie, and the jigsaw of Gabriel's testimony and the official police report would snap together neatly. Though there'd surely be disappointment all around.

My bag packed on the seat next to me, I pulled up to a bungalow. Empty dirt lots like a pair of ragged shoulders sat on either side. The street was quiet. Its children were already in school, its workers at work. I was ten minutes late. One-way streets had swung me and spun me and run me against culverts that no through street crossed directly. The map had been little help. Knowing this neighborhood, I discovered, was the only way to navigate it confidently.

The morning was raw and blustery. Trees swayed and rustled with an odd soundlessness. The March wind had a keen edge, colder than the day.

At the top step I halted for a look around before knocking. What had originally been screens or glass for a small mud porch had been replaced by unfinished sheets of plywood stapled roughly into position. I couldn't guess the reason; it would hardly add security. But it created the impression of a house under siege, whether from storms or more personal threats.

I tugged open the aluminum door. Inside, the porch was dim, rank with old leaves and old smoke and fur. I stepped no further until I could be sure that a dog wasn't crouched in some corner. As my eyes adjusted to the gloom, odd tools appeared: a pile of broken two-by-fours, a couple of tires stacked to the side, a car battery parked just next to the front door. The only open space lay between the outer steps and the entrance into the house. Mud and grease caked the floor.

If it happened, it happened right here. It's night. Gabriel comes to this door, knocks, finds a young girl he's never seen before—does he even know whether anyone else is in the house?—drags her down onto a filthy floor hardly larger than a coffin, paws her, beats her, starts to shove himself into her.

Vivid and brutal, the scene swelled before me. I could smell it, could feel it in my chest. I shook my head defensively. No longer abstract, the question came clearer than before. Was it conceivable? Something had happened—the girl wound up in Emergency. Gabriel was arrested right here.

I was sick to death of Gabriel, didn't want to think about him, didn't much like or trust him, felt myself shadowed, bound to him. Could he be such a monster?

The front door jerked open before me. "What the hell you doing?" a large man shouted angrily.

Nearly toppling back down the steps, I clutched at the aluminum door frame. My knee locked. "Sorry," I gasped, grimacing at the pain. "I called last night. My name's Currant."

"Yeah. Well you're late, Currant." Barefoot, a Raiders mesh cap pushed back on his head, Leroy Jackson blocked the doorway. He stood six-two or six-three, and with a considerable belly had to weigh close to three-hundred pounds. "Let's see some of that i.d," he demanded.

I handed him a card.

Jackson half-turned to get some light from the house and held the card at arm's length. "Baltimore? What the fuck-'re you doing from Baltimore? You sure you ain't one of them commie shits?"

"Like I said on the phone, I'm a reporter. I just want to get the story straight. You heard of my paper?"

"Maybe. But I ain't heard of you. How 'bout a driver's license so I know you're who you say." He was enjoying the authority of the famous and the pursued. He held the license up to catch the light. "See, I gotta protect my family, specially my little girl Teresa." He turned towards the house then stopped to look back. "You can end up lying if you want, but you say what I tell you, it's just the plain truth."

In the living room a woman lay stretched out on a couch.

Considerably younger than Jackson, she was wearing a grey
sweatsuit, a comforter on her lap. She'd been watching a
console television—its bright pictures continued to flicker
silently—but now she was observing the two of us. "This
here's my wife Caroline," Jackson said. She smiled shyly.
Above her head, two smallish bearskins were tacked to the
wall.

Jackson pointed me towards one chair and then took his
own place in a huge recliner. He picked up an open can of
beer from a side table. "Want one?" he asked.

I shook my head. From a jacket pocket I pulled my tape
recorder and set it on a low table. "You mind if I record our
conversation?"

"I don't give a shit," Jackson said. "Better you be accurate
than screw it all up, is what I say. The others have all had
one."

"How many people have you spoken to already?"

"Couple reporters from round here. Got a call yesterday
from some guy in Detroit. Does a paper for the Workers
Committee—says they're communists or socialists too.
Whatever. Except they're real ones instead of these fakes,
our local fruitcake assholes. This Detroit guy's out to blow
their cover. Says this will show the truth, a so-called socialist who attacks working-class girls."

"News travels fast," I said, unsurprised that one of the
ISA's rival parties should be quick to cultivate the scandal. I
was jotting notes and glancing around. Three doorways
gave off from this living room. One opened into the
kitchen—I could see the refrigerator. Two others, one across
from me and one at the far end, led to bedrooms. Two mat-
tresses sat stacked on the floor of the far bedroom. Its door
was off the hinges and propped against a wall. But the room
was dark and I couldn't see beyond the bed. I wondered
where Teresa was. Her father had said she wasn't going to
school.

"Can you tell me about Friday night?" I asked.

"Ain't that why you're here?" Squinting, Jackson tipped his beer back, pleased with his wit.

"Where were you when your daughter was attacked?"

"We was at the bar a couple blocks over. Baja's. Where we always go on a Friday night. You know, with friends." He ran a hand across his head and scratched under the cap. "That night we even come home early, maybe six-thirty or so's to make sure the girls have their supper. An older girl's here with them. She comes over when we want. Then we go back to the bar to finish with our friends. Next thing we know, Syvonie—the older girl—she comes rushing in, hollering about our Teresa, how she been raped and's on her way to the hospital. That's when we run on home, but it's all too late." As Jackson spoke, his wife drew her knees up under the comforter.

"Was Gabriel Salter still here with the police when you arrived?"

"Shit, no. Cops know I kill the sucker right then if he's anywhere close. Rip his dick off with my hands. Rip his head off."

"You ever hear of him before?" Head down, I was throwing out questions and scribbling fast.

"Why the fuck would I? I'm an American and I work damn hard for what I got. I got no time for none of that commie union crap."

"Thought you might have noticed his name in the papers." I hesitated and looked up at Jackson. "So what do you think he was doing here? Doesn't it seem strange he'd come to this street, to this house, just to attack your daughter?"

"Drugs," Caroline called out with soft vehemence from the couch.

Jackson glared. She'd stolen his punch line. "You got the word now," he snapped.

"Drugs?" I looked from one to the other, trying to keep the skepticism out of my voice. "How do you figure that?"

Caroline Jackson glanced to her husband for vindication.

"He give it away himself," said Jackson. "Comes to the door and says to Teresa, is Leroy Johnson here. Get it?—Leroy Johnson. That's the giveaway."

"Okay," I said.

"Johnson pushes crack, pushes dope. Horse. Pills too. Everybody this side of town knows it."

"Okay," I said. Something flickered at the edge of my awareness. There, back behind the mattress and tangled sheets, a shadow shifted within the deeper gloom of the bedroom.

Jackson stretched out triumphantly, his shirt riding up across a great expanse of belly, feet splayed before him. "How about getting me a fresh," he said to his wife, holding out the can. She slipped out from under the comforter and padded in white socks to the kitchen.

"I oughta make you pay me for this," Jackson said with sly satisfaction. "Nobody knows this yet, 'cause I just got the facts from a friend myself. Couldn't even tell the cops yesterday cause I didn't know."

"Why'd you see the cops yesterday?"

Jackson waved the question off. "See, I made the connection now. Salter's got his reason to come over here and find Johnson. It's cause Johnson and his woman, Juanita Harris, they been renting a place right across from him. Same block even. Way I hear, people seen 'em talking together in the street, probably arranging scores. This town is small that way—I got friends telling me." He lifted a finger from his new beer can and pointed. "You get what I'm saying?"

"How long ago was this, that Johnson lived across the street from Salter?"

"That's the whole point, man. They move over here, next block up, middle a last week. Not two days before. So Salter drives over to score his drugs. Guess he got the name wrong from somebody. Shows up to the wrong door. Leroy Jackson instead of Leroy Johnson. Hell of a coincidence, ain't it?" He was wagging his head, relishing the privileged information.

"Johnson? That's what he said to your daughter?" The coincidence seemed too contrived, too convenient—ludicrous.

He nodded.

"And did Salter actually ask for crack or dope or anything?"

"Hell no. Teresa don't give him no chance. She tries and slam the door in his face. He figures he can't get no drugs, he do her instead." Jackson's voice dropped to a growl. He kicked the footrest back and leaned forward, both feet on the ground.

I was taking notes furiously. The information was hot all right. As a reporter I had that sense of urgent exhilaration when a story is about to crack, the way a guerrilla must feel, hidden in a blind at the moment of ambush, nostrils flared and heart pounding.

Yet the coincidence, the timing were too flush to be credible. Could they be making up such a tale? Dealer moves from one street to the other. Johnson instead of Jackson. Both Leroys.

Come on, I thought. Gabriel Salter secretly on drugs?—That was about as preposterous as him trying to rape Leroy Jackson's daughter.

About as preposterous as his own version with a mystery woman.

Unlike Gabriel, though, Jackson had to know his story could be checked out. I was shaken and didn't want to reveal it.

"I suppose you've heard Salter's version," I said.

"Course I heard. Load a horseshit." Jackson shifted angrily in his chair.

All innocence, I looked from him to his wife. "He says it was a set-up. That some woman lured him here. Says the cops were waiting."

"Hmph," murmured the woman under her breath.

"Come on, man," Jackson said. "I heard what he say. But there ain't no sign of no other woman. Nobody round here like that, nobody knows her. How she get a key into my house? How she get past my girls without them seeing her? No way out in back." He sat forward, peering at me. His eyes were red-rimmed. The deeply lined skin on his face hung loose. Jackson was older than I'd first guessed, pushing sixty.

"Man, I ain't stupid," he said. "If cops set this up, then my family's in on it, ain't they? You understand? But if the cops want to get Salter, why would I help? I never been in trouble, nothing big. I don't owe them nothing." He waved a hand at his living room. "Look to you like we got paid off, like there's money gushing round here? I got a little business hauling. Got two trucks. Me and my brother-in-law, we do the driving. It pays the bills. Look to you like there's a whole lot more than that? See, man, I don't gamble and I don't do drugs. And I don't take money from no cops." He turned his head to the side and called. "Teresa. You come on out here, you hear?"

"Leroy, you promised," Caroline hissed.

He ignored her. "Come on, Resa. No one gonna hurt you while I'm around."

The shadow hesitated before drifting forward from the bedroom into mass and shape. Timid, pretty, Teresa balanced on one foot, the other wrapped behind, before darting towards her mother, who opened the comforter and wrapped her in a cocoon.

Physically, Teresa was a young woman well beyond the threshold of childhood. Yet wrapped in the comforter, she seemed disembodied, a face with large, deep eyes, eyes that were frightened and a little haughty. Her fear made her seem very young. I could make out no bruises or scrapes. But a tattered gauze bandage had come loose above her ear and was tangled in her hair.

"This here's Teresa," Jackson said. "Maybe you think we faked the whole thing? Maybe you think no one got hurt 'cept Salter? My baby got hurt, man. He banged her head into the floor, into a car battery. You know what else he do to her? You know what he try? You think I'm letting her be hurt just so the cops can frame him? You think I take any pay for that?" His voice twisted on itself, torn between anguish and fury.

"No sir, I wouldn't say that," I said. "But I've got to ask one other thing. Is she sure? Is she absolutely sure it was Gabriel Salter? He swears he never even saw her."

"Swears? Shit—what good's his swearing? She identified him, didn't she?"

I was confused. "You mean the night it happened? I thought they took her right to emergency. The police didn't make her look at him first? That's unethical—it's against every rule."

"Not then," Jackson said, snorting. "Yesterday, at the line-up."

I stared at him, saying nothing.

"Jesus, man, I thought you was a reporter. You ever do this before?"

"I was following a lead somewhere else," I said lamely, picturing the slaughter of one ignorant steer after another. "This was a formal line-up downtown?"

"Ain't that what I said?"

"And Teresa identified him?"

We'd been speaking as if the girl weren't there. But now she sat forward and nodded. "Pointed right at him," said her father. "Picked him out and said that's the one."

Exhaustion crept like frost along my limbs as I drove to the airport. Even though it was midday, I could hardly keep my hands on the wheel. I knew it wasn't lack of sleep. It was tension and doubt draining from me, putting me through a rapid decompression. I wondered, starting to smile and then abandoning the heavy effort, whether it was possible to get the bends coming up for air so fast.

My thoughts circled but didn't alight. As if it were a brainteaser that meant nothing, just a way to kill time, I continued to concoct explanations. Maybe the family was covering for someone after all. Maybe Teresa had been shown Gabriel's photo in advance. But these mental games seemed entirely disconnected from the leaden resentment, the sense of having been toyed with, that gathered now at the back of my tongue. I could taste it like bile.

That taste was in league with simple exhaustion to rob me of caring. The hot billowing rush of anger at Gabriel and Simon, at Grey and Hilary too, I'd felt along with shame in Leroy Jackson's living room had already ebbed; but those feelings left behind a marker as if at a flood tide, a marker high up in the sands.

My thoughts circled. It wasn't that I regretted coming to Iowa. I wished, though, that my mission had been simply to see that Gabriel made bail and found a good lawyer. Why should the Salters ask me to find out what happened, to make sense of things? (Was I capable, I wondered, of attempting anything less?) I was glad for the chance to be in touch with the family again, with Joseph at a distance, with Hilary who thanked and dismissed me, even with Gabriel who attracted me and baffled me and lied to me, whom I felt bound to beyond all reason and furious with beyond all speech.

Why didn't they tell me about the line-up? If not before, when I was on my way to the Consolidated plant, why not after the fact? Didn't it occur to them? Were they too appalled by Teresa tagging Gabriel? Were they distracted by the ISA's decision to make this a grand cause? Could they imagine I wouldn't find out? Well, it was only by chance I did.

What about Hilary? When she bid me shove off, did she know her brother had been fingered by the girl? Or were they keeping her in the dark too?

Waiting for take-off on the small commuter plane to Chicago, my thoughts still circled, waiting to strike. At last as the turbo-props lifted us slowly into the air, I sighed and turned my head, closed my eyes, allowed it. The thoughts swooped, struck, and Grey Navarro's stern face appeared before me. Her features were vivid, sharply hewn, as if seared into my synapses. I didn't want to confront her—I was furious with her too. She'd predicted that I'd return to finish the story. I angrily shook my head in refusal.

My home and my job and the woman I'd been seeing lay ahead. Only a few hours away. Yet never had they seemed so unreal. I couldn't imagine them. Restless, frustrated, I felt I was fleeing from one journey and into fresh exile.

PART II

Prologue: A Story

Branford jams the clutch to the floor. The gears whine and growl as he wrenches the knob into reverse. Leroy's teeth grind too. The way his brother-in-law drives, the way he treats the truck, makes the sweat pop under Leroy's cap. Usually he doesn't have to sit next to him like this; usually he's off in their other truck so he doesn't have to witness Branford's brutal incompetence. But business has been slow, especially since he changed the phone number, and today a mortgage company needed two men and a single truck to haul away old refrigeration cabinets from a grocery gone bust.

In reverse, even at two miles an hour, the truck howls. Leroy's jaw remains clenched tight. He's keeping his gaze out the side window, holding his tongue silent. Branford grunts as the truck weaves unsteadily back through the alley. It flounders towards its mate, a newer, heavier truck in the shed they built behind Leroy's house. The side mirror next to Leroy brushes the driver's mirror of the other truck, scraping both, twisting both out of position.

"Man," Leroy says through his teeth, not even looking at his partner, "you work at it? You do this just to drive me crazy or you just naturally stupid?"

"Don't you start with me, Leroy," Branford growls. "I don't want to hear none a that shit." Switching the engine off, he sits still behind the wheel, doesn't turn, doesn't move. He's tall and lean, all joints and wire. The hair was gone from his crown even before Leroy married his sister, the first wife. But Branford's heavy beard—his pride and joy—turned steel grey only in the last couple of years.

"Fucking Miller time," Leroy says and climbs down heavily. Branford's pulled so close, Leroy has to turn sideways to wedge between the trucks. Once he's by, he slams the door behind him and doesn't wait for Branford to follow.

Trudging along the worn path around to the front porch, his legs are heavy, his back sore. This kind of work is getting too much for a man fifty-seven years old and feeling it. His sons are grown and gone and no help to him at all. He's ready for that first sweet swallow of beer.

He pushes open the front door and is half way across the living room before he hears the shouting and sobbing from the bedroom. Slowing, not quite stopping, he lifts his head. "Shit," he mutters and continues to the kitchen. From the refrigerator he pulls two beers, sets one on the counter for Branford, twists the top off the other, takes a long pull. Sweet. Sighs and belches all in one.

He feels Caroline pad up behind him. "Can't you quit that, the two of you?" he says. "Man shouldn't have to put up with that every day of creation."

"Ain't the same as every day," his wife says angrily. "Resa says she saw him today. Says he come driving up and past while she's walking from school. He's grinning, laughing at her. Even her friends is scared. That's what makes it okay, she say, her stomping in here smoking and swearing, smell of wine on her breath, sassing her mamma."

"God damn," he says, rapping his bottle on the counter. "You call the lawyer?"

She nods. "Course I did. Says the same thing's always—call the cops. With the court order, if they see him near the girls they can take him. Lot a good that does."

"You call 'em anyway?"

"Yeah, I call 'em anyway." She snorts and goes on. "They come 'round in the car, cruise up a block or two, say they awful sorry but nothing they can do unless they see for themselves."

"Damn," he says again, staring out the window over the sink, and tips the bottle hard into his mouth. Sets it down. Turns his head aside. "Teresa," he calls. "Resa? Come on out here." There's no sound but Caroline's breathing, a growl in his own belly, heavy steps on the front porch with Branford about to find his way in at last.

"She scared," Caroline says. "That's what gives her leave to sass and be wild."

"Ain't no cause to be scared of her daddy," he says and leaves the kitchen to peek into the bedroom. It's dark. Teresa doesn't like the lights on. But he makes her out on the edge of the smaller single mattress at the foot of her parents' double. Tanya's by her, sitting on her hands, infected by her older sister's sullen mood.

Leroy lowers himself awkwardly onto the edge of his bed and pats a seat next to him. He's feeling old and helpless, doesn't know what to do when Caroline and Teresa start into each other. Caroline's closer to Resa in age than she is to him anyway. "Come right over here, Resa. Come on, Honey. Ain't nobody in the world going to hurt you by my side."

Teresa doesn't move. She's hunched and sulky, her head tilting to the side as she stares into the dark. The edge of her eye swells liquid and black and defiant. She won't look at her father. He smells the smoke on her and the perfume.

Leroy slaps his palms onto both thighs. "Now, Resa, you sure you saw him? That asshole been frightening you again for sure?"

"What the hell's happening? More trouble?" Branford stands beer in hand, blocking light in the doorway next to Caroline, the woman who's replaced his own sister.

"Yeah, shit, there's been more trouble," Leroy says angrily. "That little fuck Salter's hassling her some more."

"You calling the cops?"

"What for? What the fuck they do?" He's shaking his head, imagining the grin on Salter's face as he drives by his girls, probably thinking about doing Resa again. He's sitting on the edge of his mattress, big hands clenching and unclenching between his legs. Rage gathers deep in his bowels, swooping up through his chest, driving blood to his head, swirling him dizzy. "I ain't playing pussy no more," he says and his voice sounds very far away.

"Leroy?" Caroline sounds far away too and worried. "Don't you do nothing. Judge warned you."

"Judge warned him too. See how good that worked. Salter's still scaring her. Him and his friends getting richer 'n richer from dumb fucks who believe him. Like he's the innocent lamb't got fucked over. Shit." Fury swells his growl, feeling good, him feeling young. It catches in his teeth and feels mighty fine. Leroy heaves himself up off the bed. "You come on, Branford. You giving me a hand, ain't you?"

"Sure, Leroy," Branford says with a shrug and a quick swill of his beer. He starts to hand Caroline the bottle, thinks better, carries it off with him following Leroy through the house and back out to the truck.

Caroline follows too. She calls after him and keeps walking. "Leroy—you gonna do something dumb, I mean real dumb? You gonna get yourself hurt or killed or busted. How's that helping Resa? You tell me that. Tell me that, Leroy."

He hears but doesn't swing round to throw her an answer. She got to know the answer. Scare him good enough, knock him back just a little bit, no cops standing between, he won't come hassling Teresa no more. Who's gonna prove anything? Judge needs proof. Branford'll swear they were on the other side of town. And he's picturing Salter scared, shit-face scared. And he's figuring the feel of it on the back of his hand, the rasp and scrape that leaves Salter's skin on his knuckles.

He climbs into the cab of the new truck this time, him driving, Branford along for the ride. "I guess you know what you're doing," Branford says, sounding not at all sure.

Leroy doesn't answer, pressing his lips together as he rocks the truck out onto the street. At the end of the block sits a police car. Wasn't here when they came by a little while ago. Lot of good it's doing Teresa now. White cop in the passenger seat rolls down the window and Leroy pulls up. He recognizes the cop. Mean dude name of Holloway.

"Quick trip home, Leroy. Where you headed so fast?" the cop calls out with a grin. His jaw is long and wolfish. It's working hard at a chaw of gum.

"Need some air," says Leroy. "All kinda trash been coming into this neighborhood today."

Branford swats him in the leg for saying such a thing.

Holloway grins and wags his head. "Ain't this guy a wit," he says to his partner, White kid Leroy's never seen before. "A howl. The guy's a real howl." Chewing, blowing a little half-bubble and sucking it back, he sticks his head out towards Leroy. "I don't suppose you got any ideas about locating a certain piece of this trash and kicking it around some?"

"Nah," says Leroy. "Why waste my time on trash?"

"Waste of time, huh?" Holloway runs a hand over his jaw. "Seems to me, piece of trash keeps coming back, smelling up the street hassling me, I'd want to throw it away. I'd find a way to get rid of it. Isn't that what you'd do, Officer Newman?" The White kid nods with great seriousness. "That's what I'd do, all right. Course, maybe all you Black boys don't see it the same way. Takes balls. Know what I mean?" Smiling up at the truck ever so innocent. Gum slips forward between his teeth and he pops it.

Leroy's already shoving the gear shift forward. "Yeah, I know what the fuck you mean," he mutters sharply but softly between his teeth as the truck lurches forward.

"Jesus," says Branford. "I don't know which of you's crazier. What's he saying—that you should be doing what you're doing, going after Salter?"

"Sounds that way to me."

"Yeah, well, how 'bout if it's a set up and they're waiting for us?"

"Risk I'll take," Leroy mutters.

"You'll take," Branford says, staring out the window.

The truck rocks on its springs as Leroy turns. He knows the house. Without telling nobody, not even Caroline, eleven March nights in a row he'd slowly cruised by, praying to catch Salter out for a stroll by himself. Cruising by and imagining it—it riled him, got his blood pounding, better than nothing.

They pull to the curb facing the wrong way and leave the engine running. Branford follows his brother-in-law. The windows are all dark in the early dusk. Leroy rips open the screen as if he means to jerk it out of the frame. He pounds his fist on the door. Nothing.

"Come on, Leroy. Nobody here. Let's get off home," says Branford.

Leroy slams the wood again with the meat of his fist. The heavy thud echoes dully. On the sidewalk a mottled cat, hesitating, head alert, skitters away. "Shit," says Leroy.

Branford's first in the truck, ready to roll. He's leaning a fraction forward in his seat to urge them on. Leroy climbs up more slowly, sliding under the steering wheel, his belly pressed against it. He heaves the truck around, up over the far curb, and into the street again, the cab rocking like a trampoline.

Branford's head snaps round. "Which way you heading?"

"He ain't home. So we're going where they hang out. Make sense he be there, counting the money." Both hands on the wheel, he won't look at Branford.

"You asking for bad trouble, man. He ain't gonna be alone there—what you gonna do then?"

"You and me can scare shit out of a dozen of them fairies. I want to scare him so good he never comes near my babies no more, not ever."

"Tell me who's the stupid shit now," Branford murmurs.

Across the street from Trailblaze Books, they pull to the curb again. It's neither night nor day—the sky's still light, but the sun's down and darkness has swelled from below like a rising fog. Both street lamps on this block are broken. The shop is dark except for a single bulb above a display case. But a glow in the back reveals at least a couple of shadows flickering about.

"Let's go," says Leroy. He doesn't ask Branford if he's ready or if he'll stay by him. No need to give him any ideas. They climb down together, wait for a car to pass, and then Leroy jogs flat-footed across the street. Hanging back for a second, chewing on his cheek, Branford shakes his head, mutters something that's whisked away in the breeze, and lopes after his partner, elbows and knees flapping.

"Leroy," Branford calls ahead. "Before you do it, what you gonna do?"

"Nothing," he growls. "I'm just gonna talk to him, maybe scare him some. Ain't doing nothing, unless he starts with me instead of my kids."

His original anger seems a long way off, an echo of itself. The evening is mild. But the sweat of a long day's work hasn't dried and it's got a knife-sharp chill. He knows how easy it would be to turn away. But not with Branford here to see. And he's thinking of Teresa again, and the little-girl look in her eyes, and how she's been looking at boys too, this last year or so, hands on her hips, hip cocked (where's she learn that?), taunting those boys, her chest thrust forward, her lower lip big and pouty. And her pushing at Salter, trying to shove him out of her, and her sitting in the dark at the foot of the bed.

Leroy yanks at the door but it's locked. Raps hard on the glass. A high bookshelf blocks any view of what's going on in back, but he senses shadows moving across the ceiling. He smacks the glass again, presses the buzzer.

At last a dark figure slips out from behind the bookcases. Hard to make out his face, but he's shaking his head, points to a poster board with the shop hours on it.

Leroy comes up close, mouth to the crack. "I ain't here for no goddamn books," he shouts hoarsely. "Get me Salter out here. I gotta talk to him." He pulls back, then leans forward again. "Get me Salter now, man," he shouts.

The dark figure doesn't move for a moment. He seems to be studying Leroy Jackson and the tall lanky man a pace behind him. At last he unlocks the door and steps down onto the pavement, blocking the way. There's enough light in the street to see that behind his glasses he's Chinese or something, small but powerfully built. Leroy's got him by a good hundred pounds, maybe more.

"Guess you couldn't make out what I was signaling," he says with a faint smile. Leroy hates him instantly for that smile. "If you like, I can find you a catalogue, but you'll have to come back tomorrow for any purchases."

"No way you didn't hear me," Leroy says. "What I want is Salter. I want him now."

"Yes, as a matter of fact I did hear you. But no one else is available."

Leroy's chest is tight with fury and he's breathing through his mouth to get enough air. "Listen you little mothafuck— you know who I am? I'm telling Salter to stay away from my kids or I'm going to tear you apart and tear him apart, burn this whole fucking place to the ground."

Salter's friend doesn't move. Relaxed as all the world, he's standing not two feet from Leroy. "I know exactly who you are. Gabriel Salter never bothered your daughter before, and he certainly hasn't been bothering her since. So why don't you go home and tell the cops we'll take care of it in court."

"I'm a liar, am I? I'm working for the pigs?"

Simon Yoo glances at Branford hanging a few steps away, looks Leroy straight in the eye. "We haven't been calling you any names. I don't know why you're doing it and I don't really care. Maybe the cops have something on you. Maybe they just tricked you too. Wouldn't be the first time they pit working people against each other. Like some sick sport for them. Point is, we've got nothing against you."

"Hah!" Leroy's bark of a laugh explodes, but there's nothing merry about his eyes. He shakes his head. "Hah," he says again more deliberately. "Ain't that fucking White? Hear that, Branford? He don't got nothing against me. Fucking saint. Man, you standing there telling me I'm a liar, that I either got bought off by the pigs or I'm too stupid to see they're messing with me. And you ain't got nothing against me. You mothafuck—how about what I got against you?"

Simon's face stiffens.

"Your buddy come to my house," Leroy goes on. "He ain't invited. Not a soul ask him to. He attacks my little girl, tries to shove his dick in my little girl, man. And you got nothing against me? And now I hear about these thousands and thousands you all are getting from folks around the country 'cause the police do what they oughta do. And your Salter's getting rich for trying to rape my little girl."

Simon's fallen back a step, his heels against the doorstep. His skin has flushed dark even in the faint light. "I don't know where you get this thousands and thousands. We've raised barely enough to cover costs of a trial that should never be happening."

"Yeah? Well, I been talking to some real socialists from Detroit. They know something about you all. They sure do. They tell me you milking big bucks out of all the commie suckers in the world. They say, what kind gets rich off raping a working-class girl. Seems like a plenty good question to me." Leroy's voice rolls hoarse.

Simon Yoo's face goes taut with fury of his own. He rises up towards Leroy. "Workers Committee, yeah? They're fakes. They're frauds, phonies." Spit flies out of his mouth. He's shouting too. "FBI pays them to hassle us. They never spent a minute organizing for real. They're crazies and you're stupid enough to believe them." He's breathing hard too.

Leroy's not listening. Something over the Chinese guy's shoulder has caught his attention. "Is that Salter there? He looking at us? Why the fuck don't he come out here his self?" He rips the Raiders cap from his head, pushes Simon Yoo aside, crashes against a newspaper box on the sidewalk, steps in front of the main window for a better view. "You, Salter," he bellows. "You fairie coward. Big man who frightens little girls. Listen to me, you fuck. You hear me. Why don't you pretend you're a man and come out here and talk? Get out here Salter or I'm tearing this place up good and coming to find you too."

As Leroy's shouting, Simon Yoo slips inside, turns a key, and flips off the single bulb above the bookshelves.

Leroy lunges after him, but the door's already locked. He pounds the glass. It rattles and falls silent. Lights go off in the back. "Salter, you fuck," Leroy cries, his voice cracking with the effort. He's shaking now, his heart's pounding, his head's aching fit to burst. He turns to Branford, then suddenly swings back with frustration and anguish and fury and punches with all his weight. The glass dissolves. He doesn't even hear the crash. The blood's pounding in his ears and then it's not pounding.

His arm's hanging in space. Reflex, he rips his fist back through the jagged dark star, tearing his flesh. He knows he's bleeding. He cradles his arm and feels the warmth spill against his belly.

Branford's tugging at Leroy's shirt, trying to pull him away. "Come on, Leroy."

"Fetch me the cutters."

"Got to find you a doctor. Get you away from here before the cops show."

"Yeah, I know. Just get me them cutters first." He's sucking air through his teeth, his voice low and thick with violence.

Shaking his head but hurrying anyway, Branford trots across the street and tugs the chain cutters out from the toolbox. Leroy's still clutching his own arm, pushing back blood against a deep, jagged gash. "Clip that," he growls, nodding his head at a chain that anchors the paperbox to a post. Branford kneels and twists the chain to earn leverage. He wedges the blade through a link and leans his long body into it. For an instant nothing happens. Then the steel shears like braided rope and with a ringing snap the chain jerks free.

Leroy doesn't hesitate either. He lets go his arm and the blood flows down it and patters on the pavement. He bends low, wraps his arms around the paper box, hugging it to his chest.

"Leroy," hisses Branford, "that's crazy. You gonna kill yourself."

With a long groan, Leroy rises. His head's light and clear, very light. Like a dancer, he's careful to keep his feet under him so his balance doesn't go. The steel box tips against his chest. Slowly, ever so slowly, one foot at a time, he turns towards the bookstore. It's a strange feeling, his blood leaking from him, his strength going with it, his head ever lighter. It's a moment of beautiful balance. His anger's suspended, as though he's carrying it before him too. He almost doesn't want to move. But a tick in his knees is growing to a wobble.

Like a top, its spinning slowed, Leroy loses the delicate pivot, the wobble grows, and he leans toward the bookstore window, dances forward, falling forward, all the weight pulling him forward. The glass membrane punctures, crumpling before the heavy metal box. The momentum of Leroy's rush carries the box free of him and into the display cases. They crash and collapse into the darkness. Fragments of glass shower Leroy. He stumbles but catches himself before falling on the glass daggers thrusting up from below. He's not cut again, at least nothing major.

Branford ducks under his brother-in-law's good arm and loops it 'round his own neck. "Come on, boy," he says softly. Leroy sags heavily onto him. "Come on. Hoo, boy."

"I'm bleeding," says Leroy.

"I know." He halts to tug a dirty kerchief from his back pocket. Winding it just below Leroy's elbow, he ties it off hard.

Across the street Branford leans Leroy against the hood of the truck while he opens the side door. He pushes and heaves him up into the passenger seat. Leroy slumps back. Branford climbs up under the wheel. But Leroy's got the key in his pocket. Grimacing as he reaches under the arm, Branford shoves his hand deep into the pants and jerks the keys loose.

At Broadlawns ER, a pretty young doctor bends over the gurney. Blood is dripping from a plastic sack into Leroy's good arm. His bad arm is bandaged in a splint. Doctor's looking mighty stern into his eyes, schoolteacher who's caught the bad boy. "You're lucky you're alive," she says. "You have an accident like that, you get yourself in here double fast."

"Yessum," sighs Leroy, meek and content, his fingers cold, toes cold, sweat on his brow.

Another Story

"Three a.m. and you're not home. Or are you screening your calls? If you're there, pick up, okay?—I need to speak to you, Jason... Shit... Maybe you've got someone there, in which case I'm sorry. And if you're at someone's, I'm sorry too. I've got no right, and it's your business, and I don't care at all if you're with someone. That's the best thing for you. It's what you deserve, God knows...

"Jesus, I don't mean that bitchy as it sounds. Selfish me, it's just that I'm used to having you there when I need you. Nothing new in that is there? Not after, what? twenty-five years? More than that, I guess. So I've got to tell you about some of what's been going on or I'll pitch a screaming fit and they'll call the cops or boot me out of the motel. How about that—me winding up in trouble with the cops too? Nice symmetry, wouldn't that be? And yes, this trip I'm in a motel—I'm back in Iowa, by the way—because I didn't want to impose on Gabriel and Grey again.   Actually, because I couldn't stand staying with them anymore. I don't imagine Grey shedding any tears either, except she's out on some vaudeville circuit drumming up support and media attention and plenty of money for the defense committee.

"Have you called out here even once since you left? Gabe asked about you when I arrived the other day, but what did I know? And he didn't mention you'd been in touch. It just seems odd, that's all. It felt like I had to shoo you away in March, and now you don't show any concern. Maybe you've been keeping track of things long distance? Or do you feel like you did your duty—more like your good deed—three months ago and don't want to be bothered? I know, I know—you'd have every right.

"So much has happened, and nothing's happened. I mean, the trial's still on for next week. You knew that, right?

"One thing I know, by the way, is that you mentioned Gabriel, at least some part of what's happened, to your parents. Your mother sent a note to Dad. Sympathy and good wishes, I guess. Finding the note in the mail box blew him away. First time he's heard from your folks in years, apparently. He's grateful to you for that too.

"I'm rambling, I know. Well, I'm pissed at you for not being there. It's kind of nice to spew all this at your machine. No you and your irony to spoil everything. I only flew back two days ago, just in time for the latest fireworks. My third trip already. The Congressman's getting plenty annoyed, let me tell you, but I don't think he'll can me. Unless, of course, there's political fallout because his A.A.'s brother turns out to be a left-of-left-wing socialist and—God I hope not—a convicted felon. If the Republicans down-state get wind of it, well look out. I've been smudging the truth to the Congressman anyway.

"Why do I feel I have to be here, Jason? It's not like my little brother can't take care of himself. Although, now you mention it, he's done a pretty fine job of landing in the soup this time. Not that Grey or Simon or his other friends with the Alliance have been much help beyond organizing a powerhouse publicity campaign.

"So why aren't I asleep in my nice motel room? Sleep ain't so easy anymore. Too much is going on. I miss Hannah—I

miss my little girl. And last night, no, yes—Friday night—
what's it now? Saturday night? It's Sunday morning, I
guess, nearly two a.m. out here. Anyway, Friday night
Leroy Jackson went on a rampage. Remember him? The
father. Did you hear he claims that Gabe's harassing the
girl? That he's been trailing around after her like some
demon. That he's trying to terrify her out of testifying, or
maybe just for kicks. They went to the judge and got a
restraining order. It's the most bizarre stuff. I feel like Alice
here, with craziness on all sides and everyone acting like it's
business as usual. The socialists say this just proves their
point—that it's been a set up from the start, that this is just
more harassment of Gabriel. While the papers and Jackson
and the cops say it proves what a wild, evil lunatic Gabe is.

"We were all at the bookstore Friday night, them plotting
strategies and planning the next rallies. Me, I was just sitting back and watching and worrying. When Jackson pulls
up to the front of the shop with a bunch of friends, mean
looking, and they start beating on the window and door and
hollering for Gabe to come out, about what they're planning
to do to him.

"So Simon goes out front to try and calm Jackson down. I
don't like Simon and I don't trust him, but he knows how to
handle himself. And he's built like—well, I don't know, but
have you seen his arms? Jackson is all but foaming at the
mouth trying to get at Gabriel and he just sort of brushes
Simon aside.

"Now I'm the one who's thought to call 911 as soon as
Jackson shows up. Dispatcher promises immediate
response. Nothing. Nothing. We're waiting in there, five,
ten minutes—it felt like forever—and nothing. No sign of a
cop, then or later.

"Meanwhile they've roughed up Simon pretty good and
he barely gets back in the shop with his skin. It was hard to
see what was actually going on—we'd turned out the lights.
But I peek around the corner just in time to see Jackson

punch right through the glass door, and a minute later some of his friends start throwing heavy things, trash cans and all, through the front windows. That's when we clear out through the back and up the alley.

"Actually, it wasn't that easy. Grey was furious—she refused to leave. She was stalking back and forth, and I could see her hands trembling, but it's not that she's scared. Oh no. She's ready to take them on single-handed. She's ready for a full-scale war. The only way Gabriel convinced her to go was because there weren't any knives or guns or even a good bat lying around. Bare hands weren't going to count for much against those thugs. That woman makes me nervous.

"We circled around through the alley to my car. And we just stood there without getting in. What a weird moment. Us standing around the car, leaning against it, listening. And we can't hear anything. Just the usual city traffic. How come they're not tearing the place apart, setting it on fire, who knows what?—I couldn't imagine anything definite, just horrible. After a minute or two, Simon and Gabriel and Grey, and then me too, we slip quietly up the block and peek around to see what's happening. And Jackson's gang has cleared out. Gone. Who knows why? Something must have spooked them. Though still no sign of any cops. Everything was quiet. Just all this shattered glass lying on the sidewalk and this gaping black hole where the window'd been. It was creepy.

"They all, Gabe and Grey and Simon, set to cleaning up right off, patching some cardboard or plywood, whatever they could scavenge, over the naked windows. By this time they're charged up like you wouldn't believe, hot with new conspiracy theories and plans of their own. For my part, I'd had enough. I was drained, empty beyond empty. But it wasn't until later that I realized how the whole thing got to me. Back in my room I was running a brush over my head and great wads of hair whisked out in the bristles. My hair was falling out, for christsake. Tension, fear, anger, whatever. I've never had that happen before, not even when I wanted to murder you. Thank God it doesn't show.

"Yesterday, Saturday, I stayed away from them all day. I needed the time off. So here I am tonight not able to sleep. Instead I'm rambling on to your damn machine. I suppose you could have cut it off by now if you got tired of listening. That'd be okay with me. I just needed to talk it through with someone who knows the whole crew of them and knows this crazy situation. But I guess it doesn't even matter if you actually listen. I'm making a lot of sense. Sorry, Jason. I'll quit now. Bye. Thanks. Bye."

"Yeah, hi. It's me. Turn off the machine now if you want to, or don't. It's an hour later. I'm not going to sleep tonight after all. Maybe I'll grab a nap later in the day. But after I hung up before, I realized there was a whole lot I hadn't said that I've got to say to somebody. I know, I know—you're saying, say it to Lenny. Well, I could. It would be fine with him. I didn't tell you, did I, that he came out here with me a month ago? He wanted to help any way he could. And he came up with some good strategic options together with Jeremy Stanton. But it was still a nightmare. Gabe and Simon and Grey, they were smug little assholes. Mocking and taunting and goading Lenny every chance they got. You can imagine how much patience they have for a liberal Washington lawyer. Better for him to be a John Birch Republican. As a real fascist he'd be more or less a noble enemy. Oh, they were polite enough, if you know what I mean. Nothing I could point to if I wanted to confront them. Bastards. Lenny never said a word, but he didn't offer to join me this time either.

"See, here's the problem really. I don't trust them. I assume the defense committee gets its orders from the

ISA—no surprise in that. But it's clear to me now, they're using Gabriel. They're less concerned with getting him off or proving he's innocent than with making this whole thing a political circus.

"These days what Gabe's talking about is all the organizing he can do on the inside. Sometimes he sounds so naive I want to beat on him. Maybe I'm the one who's naive. But I don't want him inside. Prison is prison. God knows what'll happen to him there. Wardens don't like activists any better than cops do.

"What the hell's going on in Grey's head? The woman's a complete mystery to me, a cipher. I'm beginning to hate them all for it. I guess I'm beginning to hate Gabe for it too.

"So you've guessed by now, right? Speaking of, one of the things I wound up hating most was how you could read me. Naturally, I counted on it too. Sort of like counting on you to be around when I called. But you're not waiting by the phone anymore, so maybe you won't have guessed either. Christ, what a load of garbage. Why can't I just ask?

"Yeah, okay. Look, Jason, can you maybe come out here again? I only realized after I hung up an hour ago, that's why I called the first time. The trial's beginning on Thursday and we don't know how it's going to go.

"What you think matters to Gabe. I began to understand that when he insisted I send your stories out here. You're more like an older brother to him than you may realize. That's my guess. Not that he comes out and says or lets on, of course. Maybe just having you around will help. Maybe you'll get him to see what this is all adding up to. Maybe he'll listen to you.

"Just consider it, okay? Let me know. I've got no right to ask and I'm asking anyway. Is it too shitty of me? In some ways, I'm only learning now how much a part of my family you already were long before we got married. Getting divorced hasn't cut you out as much as I hoped it would a year or two ago. Okay, okay, I'm rambling again. What do you expect at this hour? You know what I'm like when I don't get any sleep. Don't even let me know or talk or anything. Just come out anyway, okay?"

Chapter VI

I was still cradling a mug of cold tea in my hands as the tape rewound steadily a second time. The cup had heft and solidity.

I'd returned to my apartment late on a Sunday afternoon from visiting my parents in Pennsylvania to be greeted by the red light pulsing a quick four flashes. I'd punched the button and stood waiting, bag in hand. The first message was from Phyllis, checking in to confirm Monday dinner and a flick. A computer-generated solicitation waited twenty breathless seconds for human response and then disconnected. The machine beeped a third time, someone's breath hitched on the other end, and I knew before she spoke that it was Hilary.

For a single delicious instant after I'd walked in the door I'd been able to savor all the relief of tearing free from my parents after a weekend of noble attentiveness, all the pleasure of knowing fourteen hours still lay before me with no deadlines and no commitments. With leisure I could begin to anticipate returning to my computer early Monday morning and a story on which I'd already done the preliminary tracking. And here Hilary was waiting vigilant on tape to ruin everything. I could resent her for it; I was also eager to hear her voice.

And now I felt an odd mixture of annoyance and exhila-ration.   With delighted outrage I posed for myself the rhetorical question: how dare she call again, how dare she presume after summoning me in March and then dismiss-ing me like the hired help? A wicked pleasure in her dis-comfort fanned a smile to my lips.

Little she reported was news to me. Brian Phillips had continued to write occasional pieces on the case for the Register. I'd glance through them when they arrived in our newsroom's library a couple days late. I knew about the approaching trial, knew about the offended righteousness voiced by police and city officials over the media attention the story was attracting. Not to mention the letters, nation-al and beyond, they were receiving from civil rights leaders, trade unions, even women's groups who'd been persuaded that rape wasn't the issue at all. From time to time I'd stroll through bookstores in Baltimore and discover Gabriel's bat-tered face staring out at me from fliers and petitions. Or he'd be flapping in the breeze, one eye peeking out from under other debris posted on a kiosk.

I leaned back on my couch and rubbed my eyes. I could-n't very well deny my curiosity about the progress of Gabriel's trial. And at some level it seemed I'd been expect-ing this summons: as if the entire weekend in Pennsylvania, talking with my parents and their friends about the Salters, about my father and Joseph Salter, had also been about Gabriel and me, old questions fanned to life by new ones.

So Leroy Jackson attacked the bookstore? No real surprise there. I sighed and stretched and put my hands behind my head. What would Hilary say if she discovered that no little part of the temptation to take her up on the favor was to lay eyes on Grey once more, maybe find another chance to talk with her? Perhaps that would exorcize the spell.

For to my growing vexation, only the rare day had passed since my return without a thought of Grey, of the proud arch of her neck, the flash of her eyes, the birthmark like the scar of a covenant on her cheek.

Not that these memories were pleasant. They were no set of easy fantasies. The image was more compulsive, nagging, even haunting. I could still taste how my anger flared when she narrowed her eyes at me with her warrior's disdain. But I also recalled the eerie sense of recognition I'd felt—and suspected she did too—when we'd catch each other out of the corner of an eye.

For several weeks now I'd toyed with the notion of dropping her a note, even chancing a quick call to get it out of my system. I hadn't, of course. What was there to say? It wasn't that I wanted anything. It was impossible.

Nor was my hesitation simply a matter of being faithful to Gabriel. I didn't yet know that faithfulness was so much a part of the story.

The occasion of my visit to Pennsylvania had been a fete cooked up by old friends and colleagues in the village, a fortieth anniversary celebration for my parents to coincide with my father's semi-retirement. Starting with the fall term, his teaching load would be reduced still further. (I'm not sure he was pleased with the arrangement, but there was delicate pressure from the college now that he'd turned seventy.) Better than a month earlier, one of the instigators, my Aunt Claire, telephoned that my presence was required. Simple as that. No excuses accepted. "There's nothing you can explain to me that I don't know, Jason," Claire announced even as I hesitated. "And probably a great deal I could explain to you if I chose. Which I won't." The lilt and gravel of her Yorkshire girlhood, tamed much of the time, swelled in her voice as she grew peremptory. "Stay with me if you're still childish enough not to sleep under his roof. But you will make it to the Faculty Club by six-thirty."

A month later, obeying orders, I filed a story electronically into Stan Lupinsky's work station and reluctantly switched my terminal off. The last time I'd done so, knowing I'd be neglecting it for more than a few hours, had been on my way to Iowa in March.

In due course, after a drive that managed to beat the early weekend rush to the country, I kissed Aunt Claire hello, kissed my sister Beth who, eight months pregnant, looked distracted and uncomfortable, shook hands with her husband Jerry Stevens and with a few of my father's older colleagues. Drink in hand, I held my breath with them all as Mother led Dad the round-about way through the Faculty Club's garden and French doors and into our very midst. The sight exasperated me. Fortieth anniversary or not, organized by others or not, my mother wasn't allowed to share the sweet surprise. She was in on it instead, safeguarding my father's innocent pleasure.

Surprised he was. On the doorstep, looking up and seeing the crowd rather than a deserted reading room with his precious newspapers, he hesitated. A tall man stooping slightly, with white hair dramatically swept back, his lips compressed into a remarkably thin line, a telltale stab of annoyance he didn't quite manage to hide before forcing a hale and gracious smile. A general cry went up that drowned away any awkwardness. Friends had already rushed forward to squeeze his arm, hand him a glass, kiss Mother's cheek.

But he still didn't get it—that's what I saw as he stood there putting up a good front. My father didn't have a clue what this was all about. Did anyone else spot it? Oh, he was brave. He smiled and wagged his finger at the naughty conspirators as they congratulated him. He'd been honored enough in his long career that he could fake it brilliantly. Only when he realized they were congratulating my mother as well did he put two and two together.

It was at that moment, however, before he caught on, that it struck home that my father had become an old man. The simple truth rocked me. I glimpsed it deep in his eyes: a slight disorientation, a hunted caginess, a fear of being caught out. And having read the first telltale, I could spot it now in the grey hollows of his cheeks, the throat that didn't fill his collar, the thinness of what had been his great shock of prematurely white hair. I remembered the sound of Joseph Salter's voice on the phone three months earlier and was glad to have the scotch in my hand to swallow away the bad taste.

When he discovered me in turn standing by an old upright piano, my father lifted his head ever so slightly in acknowledgment. His blue eyes, sharp now and daring me to see him on any terms but his own, crinkled with welcome. Perhaps Mother had already slipped him the news that Beth and I had arrived to surprise them. He stepped towards me as I stepped towards him. We shook hands warmly for all to witness. I released his grip an instant before he was ready and bent over to kiss my mother.

Eight years younger than Dad, she looked younger even than that, petite and trim, her face unlined but for fine etching along the eyes and at the corners of her mouth. Yet her shortish hair had become nearly as white as his. She bobbed up to kiss me.

"Hello, Dearest," she murmured in my ear. "You're wonderful to come for this. It'll mean the world to him."

"It's not for him," I said softly into her ear. "It's for you."

Later that night, after cocktails at the college, after dinner at the country club, a select few of us lingered over nightcaps in the library of my parents' home. A good boy, I'd returned a few moments before the others and coaxed a fire in the stone hearth—the June night held just enough of a chill to warrant the gesture. My father sat next to the fire, sharing a brandy with Arthur Stillwood, recently retired and president

emeritus of the college. Since I'd last seen him, Stillwood
had allowed his mustache to explode into a thick
Rooseveltian brush. With them sat my brother-in-law Jerry,
developer of protected condo enclaves in Philadelphia.
Across the way in a semi-circle of their own sat Annie
Stillwood, Aunt Claire, Mother, and Beth.

Between the two groups I could listen to either conversation. A link proving the circle but not belonging to it, I
enjoyed sitting apart even while being engulfed by all that
was familiar. This had always been my favorite room.
Bookcases lined the walls, stuffed fully but neatly with a
hodgepodge reflecting my family's casual reading over
decades. (This was not my father's study. His papers and
the small but valuable collection of rare manuscripts were
secreted away on the second floor.)

This library, however, was where my mother practiced her
music and gave flute lessons to local students. We listened
to the hi-fi here. It was where we watched t.v. once my parents relented—the Kennedy-Nixon debate their incentive—
and let us have a small black-and-white set. The library was
also where I first smuggled girls home to the great couch that
stood in a bay window. To ensure privacy I'd twist my belt
around the paired handles on the library doors.

I never used that method with Hilary Salter. Whether it
even occurred to me, I don't remember. But she was in the
house too often in any event, with or without her parents.
Sealing her away in the library would have lacked the late-
night sense of trespass that was as exciting as the explo-
ration of sex itself.

It's hardly surprising that I should find myself thinking of
the Salters as the others chatted in low voices. I'd never
spent any considerable time in this house or this town without them as a central part of my life, of our lives. Joseph
might drop by on his way home. If his cello happened to be
balanced on his hip, he might settle in front of this stone
fireplace and, as a treat that he made seem almost an impo-

sition on us, share a Bach partita, a quick flurry of
Shostakovich, whatever he'd been working through that day.
Sometimes he'd coax Mother's flute out of its case and
together they would sight-read a duet.

Marianne Salter, it's true, rarely ventured out of her own
house, especially once Gabriel was born. Yet she'd speak for
hours by phone with one or the other of my parents; with
friends near and far across the globe for that matter. She was
famous as an invisible but delightful conversationalist.

When time came I left for college on the west coast; without ever returning home for more than a few days, I was
drafted and shipped off, first to Germany and then to
Vietnam. My father wanted to use his old contacts in military intelligence to get me posted more safely, but I declined.
And while I was gone, Joseph shook the earth by rushing off
to Arkansas with Marianne and young Gabriel. (Hilary had
gone to college a year after me.)

I survived. I returned, eventually, leg torn up, but alive.
And all I wanted—all I'd banked on while bored out of my
mind or sweating with fear or sweating with fever—was to
step mid-stride into steps I'd missed along the way. Like so
many others, I was eager to resume my life, erase its ellipsis,
recapture in all innocence what had been lost.

So Hilary and I, having persuaded ourselves via three
years of letters and, later, her visits to the V.A. hospital in
Virginia, astonished family and friends in our own turn. As
far as anyone knew we'd been too close as friends for romantic involvement.

Without warning, a black sadness swooped over me in my
parents' library. A familiar demon, it sucked the breath out
of my chest. I gritted my teeth, furious with myself. I'd let
my guard down. Shouldn't I be able to, there of all places?
But this was precisely the place that rendered me most vulnerable. Sitting in front of the fire, hiding it from the others,
I felt a vertigo, a hint of that weightlessness, that sense of
tearing loose from all anchors that had disoriented me in

Iowa a few months earlier.

"I suppose you've all heard about Gabriel Salter?" I blurted aloud, as if grappling to keep my seat. The other conversations halted. The evening was suddenly late, the silence pronounced. The dying fire popped in the grate. "His trial begins soon—next week." I glanced at the others. They were all watching me. "Unless the defense pulls some rabbit out, well, he'll be proselytizing in a more restricted environment." My voice had grown matter-of-fact, conveying an item all might find interesting.

"Gabriel Salter?" We all glanced at Annie Stillwood. "He was the boy. . . . What on earth's he done?" The president's wife, an abundant woman whose hair had long since lost any trace of grey, looked aggrieved. It was rare that a morsel of gossip escaped her.

Before I could continue with the story, I saw my father nodding. It stopped me cold. I glanced at my mother. She was staring back at me with a reprimand, but I realized she'd already told him—he was in on the news—and that came as an odd shock. It had been years since I'd heard her mention the Salters, any of them besides Hilary, in front of her husband. Her own continuing interest she'd kept a secret. Figuratively or not, she and I would bow our heads together as I quietly passed on family news. That custom had largely ceased too after my divorce.

My father had taken Joseph's departure for the wilderness nearly twenty years earlier as a personal affront, a betrayal before their colleagues for which there could be no forgiveness. By their own choice—he'd insisted on this from the start—the Salters had excised themselves from our community. It was a point of bitter principle with him. Even when Hilary was visiting the village with me, we'd entered into this game of complicity, pretending that she somehow belonged only to our family or to some other entirely than her own.

Why? Had I ever wondered this before? Why did my

father care so much? Why—and this I'd certainly pondered from six thousand miles away when I heard the news, never received a specific answer to my queries to Mother or Hilary, and had come to accept as a fait accompli by the time I arrived home—had Joseph Salter abandoned his life in our village?

"Apparently," this from my father, still nodding and leaning forward now in his chair, "the boy has got himself into some real trouble. They've charged him—is this right, Jason?—with attempting to rape a young woman."

"But is it true? Could Gabriel do such a thing?" demanded Claire, looking first to my father and then to me.

I shrugged, suddenly not wanting to discuss the case and regretting I'd brought it up. "It's not clear. It's hard to believe, of course."

"But how do you know all this?" Beth asked. "Are you talking to Hilary? How is she? How's her baby?"

"He went out there, to Iowa. Didn't you, Jason," my father said eagerly. I saw that the evening's alcohol had kindled his nerves. A faint dab of fever touched his cheeks. His pale blue eyes shone. I felt embarrassed for him.

"Hilary called when this first blew up in March and asked me to go out and have a look around. Just to make sure Gabe wasn't being railroaded. That his lawyer was on top of it. That sort of thing."

"But did Gabriel, of all people, did he attack some young girl?" Aunt Claire demanded again. "I remember him as such a puppy, a mischievous little angel."

There was a long pause. Everyone's eyes were on me. "Hell, I don't know. There's nothing neat about it. That's the thing. There are these two stories, his and theirs. Both are disturbing, both are convincing in their way, both have holes. I honestly don't know."

"Spoken like a philosopher." My father all but chuckled. "It's unlikely the jury will be so evenhanded, I imagine. Still, it's disturbing. Hard to believe." His voice grew wistful, his eyes more brooding. "He was just a little boy. I hardly knew him." He admitted this with a tone of regret, of amazement. "After he was born, that's when things began to change. They were never the same again, now that I think of it. He might as well have left right then." I knew he was no longer speaking of Gabriel.

Mother leaned forward across the circle protectively, as if to ward him off this path. But she said nothing.

My father continued, returning to the story. "I understand he's been involved with some socialist nonsense the past ten years. Politics." He snorted it away with a wave of his hand. "No sillier than his father about politics."

No one spoke. We all sensed that this was dangerous territory. My father was musing silently, and then he spoke again as if to himself. His eyes were bright but the gaze was inward. His white hair was wild. The brandy snifter wagged dangerously in his hand. "Joseph got himself in trouble too over politics. No luxury of a jury trial if they'd caught him. Criminal—there's a concept you can go round the circle with. But now his son is in trouble and they're saying that's all it is—criminal—nothing political about it." His eyes snapped up to mine. "Isn't that right?"

I nodded. He nodded too and looked angry as if he'd drawn a confession from me. "But you run out there. And Joseph? Joseph stays at home? Isn't that right? He doesn't go. He sends you. Home on the reservation. Home on the range. He sends you."

"He didn't send me," I said with exasperation. "Hilary called and asked a favor."

"A favor," my father repeated.

Not long afterwards the company collectively stumbled to its feet. Weariness fell heavily as we rose into it, a net settling across our limbs. I'd left my bag in the car, intending to take Claire up on her offer. Beth and Jerry had already slipped away to the guest room. And my old room, where I'd escaped as a boy into the sloping eaves of the attic, had long since been reclaimed by the detritus of family trunks and boxes and dust. Mother touched my shoulder as I kissed her at the door. "You're staying?" she asked, puzzled.

"Aunt Claire's expecting me," I said, not wanting to admit my own childishness. I hadn't actually stayed in this house since my father visited me in Baltimore and I soon thereafter stoked a small, illegal, but glorious blaze in the alley behind the history department with several boxes of yellowing file cards.

"Don't be silly," she said, teasing but earnest. "How can you not stay here?" Her smile wavered and I saw that she was upset, stretched taut.

"There isn't room," I said.

"Nonsense," she said. "I've got a cot set up for you in my sewing room. Anyway, no self-respecting woman has a sewing room in this day and age. I'm redoing it next week."

"Okay. Sure," I said, trying not to let my reluctance show. I retrieved my bag from the car, but Mother lingered at the foot of the stairs. Only a single lamp shone in the hall above, dimly lighting us. The house was very quiet. I set the bag down and leaned on the banister. "Something up?"

"I wish you hadn't mentioned Gabriel. In front of him, in front of everyone," she said.

"I wish I hadn't either," I admitted. "An evil impulse came over me. But I was surprised you'd told him about it."

She looked up at me. Even in the dim light I could see her eyes glistening. Then she glanced away. "I had to talk to someone, didn't I? There was no one else. Just telling your father the facts as I got them from you helped. And I think he was actually glad to hear. It separated the present from the past." She shook her head and stared away down the dark hallway to the library. "You don't understand, do you?"

I'd a hand on the banister. "No, I don't think I do," I said. A sudden great curiosity struck me, and I turned back and faced her from the first step. "Tell me something. Tell me why they left. Why did Joseph up and run?"

My mother stiffened. She looked older now too as she stared up at me with dismay. Her eyes were very large, deep beyond depth like a dark and brimming sea. She shook her head as if she were scuffing me away physically. "There's nothing I can tell you," she murmured. Then more strongly, "He left because he felt he had to leave. It wasn't the first time they'd done that."

She brushed the past away with a wave of her hand. "What has any of that to do with Gabriel and his troubles? It's him I worry about until this is over. As I've worried about you. Not that I ever thought you'd wind up in prison." She smiled now. "Listen to me, sounding like the voice of doom. Go to bed, Angel. We're both too tired to be making sense at this hour."

College Commencement had taken place the previous weekend, and the village was already settling into its summer torpor. I strolled to the bookstore in the late Saturday morning to buy a paper, to wander through the village with a cup of coffee. The early breeze had dropped away and the day also seemed suited to summer slumber. Only the last fading scent of lilacs and the violent splash of orange and pink from azalea beds bordering some of the clapboard houses insisted that spring hadn't entirely given way to the doldrums as well.

The dust on the path beneath my feet was real. The warmth that was tickling the first beads of sweat between my shoulder blades was real. I knew full well that for the faculty who lighted here and struggled for tenure or drifted on once more, the village became the center of hopes and fears, of gossip and envy, of mortgages and battles with the local school board. For the maintenance staff, whose families had worked for the college for generations, when they weren't laboring in local quarries or on small farms, no place was more real. And yet, and yet, scuff my shoe into the gravel as I might, this seemed like such safe harbor. So snug and tidy and cut off from Baltimore's Mount Pleasant Center for the Homeless, where broken needles collected under benches nailed to the pavement. Where battered women slumped against the walls, and weary AIDS sufferers who had no place else lay themselves down. It was a long way too from the meat-packing plants of Iowa and police station elevators where your face could be casually redistributed. I breathed the warm air deeply. Lilac, distant and fragile. Restlessness gathered in my thighs and throat.

In one of those harsh transitions that come without warning in Pennsylvania, a raw north wind whipped down upon the village during the afternoon, dragging along an overcast that blocked the sun. By habit as much as desire, I'd settled in my parents' library, listening to music on the stereo, an odd book open in my lap. This was so familiar a position that I half expected Hilary or some other friend of my youth to bang on the door and drag me away. I'd have fled willingly. Comfortable, yes, and familiar, the setting still honed my restlessness to a whistle so keen no one else could hear.

In the middle of the afternoon my father knocked on the half-open door. Diffidently, he stepped into the library wearing an English checked cap, a coat over his arm. "Your mother and I are setting out on a walk. Just a couple of miles along the river and back. How about you joining us?" he asked. His attempt to be off-hand only made him clumsy and stern.

Physically, he seemed brittle, as if the give had given out of his limbs. His white hair strayed out like flares of scarecrow straw from under the hat. He was on good behavior, trying to prevent an argument from blowing up between us like the wind itself, out of nothing. I could tell that the invitation was both an effort and yet something he desired. I felt sorry for him. And just the way he held himself upright, the way his lips set one against the other, aroused in me a dull rage. Everything about his character spoke through those signals. I read them as a son reads the intimate script of his father. Even on best behavior he could not hide who he was, a man of authority and certainty and self-absorption. An age-old bitterness welled full and tight in my chest. I regretted it and was helpless in its flood.

"Thanks," I said as lightly as I could manage. "But I'm off to see some old friends before the dinner." My voice was flat, matter-of-fact. If it wasn't particularly friendly, at least I'd managed to hide, tried to hide, any open hostility.

My father's face tightened. His jaw set more firmly. But in his eyes I spied disappointment and—there—a trace of resentment. A thrill streaked along my spine. It marked one small but telling victory in a struggle that traced its way back to, what?

I had no idea. I have no idea. I wanted to go on the walk with my parents and yet it was impossible. I felt haunted by myself, by a younger, resentful, dangerous me who kept out of sight most of the time so that I could pretend to some sort of maturity. Who wanted only to hurt his father and to shame him, to get even for slights real or imagined that had been forgotten long ago. Cause and effect had no role; the fury fed on itself and needed no reason.

My father nodded and lifted his hand and closed the door behind him. I felt ashamed. I also felt set free, the way a boy who secretly masturbates feels free (and ashamed) for a little while of the urges, desires, and hormones that have been blindly whipping him against himself.

Dinner that evening was a smaller affair. Aunt Claire had invited a dozen close friends to her clapboard-and-ginger-bread cottage. Rather than another buffet, two tables had been shoved end-to-end. Elbows blundered intimately, spirits were high, the wine was good, the pot-luck a stunning dance of salmon and curry and sprouts. I even counterfeited interest—a professional skill I usually reserved for interviews—in Jerry's rambling chat about how wealthy African Americans and Hispanics were moving back into Philadelphia from the suburbs where they'd never felt welcome. They were scrambling after pricy condos he was developing in a bad market. Almost despite myself, I grew intrigued, wondering whether there might be similar developments in Baltimore and whether I could sharpen an angle into a story.

When, after midnight, my parents and sister left with the last lingering guests, I stayed behind to give Claire a hand with the dishes. It wasn't an onerous task. Most of the pots and pans had been fetched away by friends who'd contributed to the meal. So I stood at the sink and passed wet plates and glasses and silverware to Claire and her towel.

"Glad you came down?" she asked. When she was tired, the broad vowels of her native Yorkshire came richer and slower. They never disappeared entirely, not even after all the years since she'd emigrated to rural Pennsylvania as a young teacher.

A large woman, powerfully built, in the old days Claire would have been called mannish—was called that and worse in the local high school. Her copper-red hair, worn in heavy curls, appeared untarnishable, as if it would never grey. Twenty-seven years she'd spent teaching algebra before, in one unexpected moment, her health, mental and physical, collapsed under the siege of hostility to an unmarried woman, a foreigner, a math teacher. Disability insurance had allowed her to scrape by after an early retirement in her fifties. Since then, she'd become even more a part of my parents' lives. Where they traveled, she traveled. What she read, they read.

"I'm glad you leaned on me to make the trip," I said.

"It was time we saw you around here again. Once every couple years isn't enough, you know. I'm sure it must be hard, without Hilary, but it's quite time now. Your parents aren't any younger."

"I'm not feeling particularly young myself," I said. "And by the way, you're wrong about Hilary. It's not simply painful memories that have kept me away. There's more to it than that."

Claire slipped a stack of plates into a cupboard with a gentle clink. "Your father, you mean. You don't have Hilary to push between the two of you anymore, is that it? Oh yes, she deflected the tensions and kept him entertained, so you didn't have to deal with him yourself. Don't I know?"

I swung around and stared at her, my soapy hands dripping onto her kitchen floor.

"Don't you look at me like that, Jason Currant. I'm not accusing you of anything terrible, for heaven sake. Maybe you fooled him. I don't know. But you can't blame me for seeing what's so obvious."

Returning to my chores, I plunged my hands into the hot water again and attacked a colander.

"Don't sulk," she said. "It isn't becoming, a man your age."

"Hmph," I said manfully.

When, fifteen minutes later, the last of the wine goblets had been dried and returned to dress parade in the corner cabinet, Claire folded her towel. "Right then," she said glancing about to see if she'd missed anything. She sighed. "I'm absolutely knackered. And," she put her hands on her large hips, "I know better than go to bed. There's been too much excitement this evening. It's harder and harder to coax sleep along. I've learned to be patient with a cup of tea rather than toss about in bed. Care for a cup? I gather you've something on your mind, haven't you? Or is it too late? What, is it already one-thirty?"

Again she'd caught me by surprise, intuiting what I'd intended to keep slyly hidden for the right moment. "Tea would be good," I said.

"Tell me about my father and Joseph Salter," I said over a fresh mug.

"Ah," she murmured. She closed her eyes and opened them. A smile flickered across her lips. "I wondered if we'd ever have this talk. Whether you'd ever care enough or guess enough to want to know. Or perhaps you'd find out enough on your own. Though I didn't think he'd ever tell you, even if you quit being such a stubborn ass and asked him. And," the smile flickered again, betraying a long-secret pride, "there's hardly another soul knows as much as I do."

Only in that moment did I realize I'd always known that to be true. "That's why I'm asking."

"Yes. Well. I must say it's taken you far too long to bother." She glared at me with a math-teacher's reprimand. "What is it you want to know? To tell you everything, we'd be here until dawn."

"The beginning. And the end."

She nodded. "Yes," she said again. "Right," she said. "Did you know that your father and I came here in the same year? 1952 it was. My older brother had made friends with some American engineers during the war, and when I finished my degree and there were no jobs, certainly not for young women, he contacted his friends. One thing led to another. Forty years and here I am." She smiled again, this time to herself as if in amazement.

"Your father was almost ten years older, just short of thirty. He'd served in military intelligence during the war—that much you know—decoding ciphers, that sort of thing. Afterwards, the army paid for his university degree and he finished in record time. When this college hired him, he arrived with quite a name already. One book on the shelves, one in proofs. Your mother was still an undergraduate at the university. Bradley had been one of her tutors while he was finishing. They already had an understanding, of course, though no one was to know until she graduated.

"In the meantime. Well, this was a small place with few single people. Even though I wasn't on the college faculty, Bradley and I were invited to small dinner parties any number of times. We were introduced again and again by obvious and well-meaning faculty wives. There simply was never any sorting out the misunderstanding. Hopeless. Until your mother did finally arrive at the start of the next year. He was very good about it, really. It could have been quite horrible. Instead we became friends." She smoothed the tablecloth.

"It seems as though it all went on that way for years and years," she said, shaking her head, "the dinner parties, our laughing about the misunderstanding, the talks we had. But it was just that first autumn. No more than two or three months at most.

"At the New Year, Bradley flew all the way to Vienna for a conference. He spent days in the air. The conference was by invitation only. All expenses paid. That wouldn't seem so grand today. But it was another signal of your father's prominence—so soon after the war, that sort of thing was very rare. His colleagues here gnawed themselves with envy, though Bradley was ever so careful not to notice. Otherwise, if he noticed, don't you see, staying here any length of time would be impossible." She laughed softly. "Any length of time. Think of that—forty years on for him as well. I remember one of the old boys whispering rather loudly across a dinner table how the great conference wasn't to do with philosophy at all—that it was some secret conclave of Bradley's intelligence pals. Jealous nonsense. In Vienna, however, and staying at the same hotel, was Joseph Salter."

I was content to sit patiently. All night if necessary.
Claire's large mouth with its expressive lips smiled almost
shyly, with a mixture of pride and modesty. Her color was
high, as if the kitchen were still very hot. "It was me he
talked to, then," she said. "It's me he's always been able to
talk to. He knew he could count on me. No gabbing. No
attempt to get anything. I've always been his friend and he's
known that."

"Tell me about Joseph," I said.

"Oh yes, I haven't forgotten," she said. "I'm an elephant,
Jason—that's what the kids used to call me, among other
things. But I never forget." She raised her chin at me defiantly. "How much of this have you ever guessed? Have you
ever even bothered to wonder? You were always too busy
finding ways to take offense with your father, skirmishing
round every corner. And he you. He's to blame too, don't I
know it? The two of you. Life and death struggles over nothing. Deserving each other, you are.

"Now that it's occurring to you for the first time, you're
thinking I was jealous of your mother. But I wasn't. Bradley
told me about her from the beginning. Only me. And it was-
n't the same at all. She belonged to a different realm for him
entirely, a different compartment of his life. No, if it was anyone I was jealous of, it was Joseph. Especially in those years
before I met him.

"I was saying they met in Vienna. The borders hadn't
become so rigid then. As a famous prodigy—a young man
and a Jew no less who survived the war—Joseph was
allowed to travel. He was a good-will ambassador for his
country. So at New Year's in Vienna, 1953 it was now, he was
giving a series of recitals and special musical lectures for children. It's where Bernstein got the idea for his children's concerts—I've always been convinced of that.

"Your father arrived in Vienna on January second. The
conference was set to begin the next day, and he didn't know
a soul. For the evening the concierge suggested a concert at

the great hall just along the road. With the help of a few dollars, he was able to procure a ticket for Doctor Salter. Later, Bradley strolled along with his head full of nothing but the paper he was to present the next afternoon. I'd let him practice delivering it to me before he left, all about the tension between law and morality in the New Testament and how that illuminated issues in a post-war Europe. You see?—I do remember. He wrote with such clarity. And then Joseph Salter comes out on stage and plays his cello and speaks to the children, and along with the rest of them Bradley Currant is absolutely seduced. It's the most charming thing he's ever witnessed. He loses himself. Philosophy—poof— all gone.

"He confessed to me later that he was ashamed of himself, that he'd been near tears, that nothing like that had ever happened before. Beethoven, Shostokovich, Salter." Claire lifted a hand from the table. "I felt embarrassed for him simply that he should make so much of it. We all get carried away. Well, Joseph could be enchanting with a fiddle in his hands and a story to tell. We all discovered that too.

"It so happened, naturally enough, that Joseph was staying in the same hotel. And, naturally enough, your father stumbled into him in the lobby later that same evening. He introduced himself—what an admirer he'd become and so suddenly. They had a drink. They talked. And talked. All in German, which wasn't so easy for either of them, not because they weren't capable—but the war, there was still the bad taste in the mouth. Your father's German was better than Joseph's English.

"Bradley had sense enough at least to deliver his paper as scheduled the next day, in English, with Joseph in the audience. It made a smash too. One of the Vienna papers gave it a column review. Another feather for the young professor's cap. His elder colleagues in Vienna were swept away, to the extent that philosophers are ever swept away. And adding to his legend as an enfant terrible, Bradley attended not so much as a minute of the rest of the conference. He and Joseph were out on the town, walking and drinking and talking, always talking, and him attending Joseph's remaining performances. That was it, really. They'd become friends." Claire paused and looked to see if I'd followed.

"It's not easy recognizing my father in that story," I said with a smile intended to be wry.

"Because you don't know him, do you? You never bothered to find out." Her voice dropped. She backed off. "But you're right—even I wondered as he was telling me the story, can this be the same man? It was as if he were describing someone else. I mean—there's the Bradley Currant everyone sees. Stiff, serious, always wearing a proper shirt with a proper collar, concerned, oh yes, concerned with the big human issues. And yet here he's sitting next to me with this little devilish smile, the naughtiest look. People who don't really know him never glimpse that side."

I grunted and wondered how much of this Bradley Currant was a creature of Claire's imagination. "So what happened? It had to be, what, another three or four years before Joseph arrived here."

Claire nodded and pushed her chair back from the table. "It's not so simple as that," she said with a conspiratorial smile. She rose and washed out our two cups at the sink, dried them, tucked them into a cupboard. She was standing before me, glancing about, at a loss for something else to busy herself with. Her large hands fluttered restlessly against her apron. "I've often wondered," she said aloud but as if to herself, "if any of the rest would have happened if there'd only been the first trip. Probably not. Probably not. I mean, what reason would there be?" She settled again at the small breakfast table. Her eyes suddenly darted searchingly to mine. "Did you never know any of this? Is that possible?"

"Bits and pieces I knew," I said impatiently. "As you describe it, well it sounds familiar. Pieces slip together, bits that were in the air around us when we were kids. So in a way I did, but without understanding, without being able to see the picture in the puzzle." I gazed at her.

"You see," she picked up the thread again doggedly, "as if his life weren't full enough. I mean, he married your mother and brought her back here the following summer. He was writing. He was Chair of his department and then Acting Provost of the college. You and Beth came along in pretty good order. All of that. And still he managed to travel to Europe at least once a year to see Joseph. The post was no good in those days, and neither were the phones. Things were tightening up over there, and Joseph certainly couldn't come to America.

"I don't know how Bradley managed it," she said, wagging her head. "I've never quite understood why your mother allowed it. Either she was a saint or she recognized just how important this was to him. Because it wasn't easy. Travel on that order was very expensive, cut corners how you will on an academic salary.

"But once a year, in the winter or in the summer, Bradley traveled back through Austria and into Hungary. Grey and bleak it must have been in those years, but Joseph made Budapest seem a great heartbeat of music and food, and there was always the talk. He had your father drinking plum brandy. They went hiking or skiing in the mountains. Bradley has never been one to lug a camera around for the sake of snapshots. But one of Joseph's friends must have taken some photos—your father had two or three tucked in his wallet for years. He shared them with me in private. Grainy, black-and-white kodaks, they were. There was one of a group of men in a restaurant cellar."

She leaned forward suddenly eager, patting my wrist with the recollection. "And another, him and Joseph on skis, sunburned and frozen. Joseph had an arm thrown over Bradley's shoulder. I remember that one. It was so awkward—that was it. You know how Bradley is a good six inches taller than Joseph, and Joseph is reaching up, arm looped over Bradley's shoulder. The look on your father's face. I'd never seen him like that—relaxed, and tired, and happy. His mouth is open in the photo—he's just laughed.

"Joseph's face. Well, that was the first time I saw it, in that photo. I began to understand, though the two of them couldn't have seemed more different. Joseph was darker and shorter, with those wonderful sad-happy eyes of his, and the smile that was so—I don't know—wise and wary. He looked the older of them, though he wasn't. Oh yes, and there was that something mischievous about his smile too. Always a little bit of mischief."

I wasn't looking at her. I was staring at the black, black window above the sink, too dark to reveal anything beyond, nor reflecting anything but the little light about us. A distant smoky sadness drifted across my line of vision. My father had never shared those photos with me, never told me tales of wandering through Hungary with Joseph Salter. Why was that? Was I not interested? Was I unreceptive? A cold and angry son from the start? Or had my father chosen for some reason to shut off that part of his life from himself and so from me as well? I wasn't, in that moment, thinking that Joseph Salter should have been my father. It didn't occur to me then that he, in all his tales and storytelling when I was young, had never talked about those travels with my father either.

"Once, towards the end," Claire was reciting again, "they hitched rides on lorries and wagons out deep into the country to the village where Joseph's family had been farmers and traders for hundreds of years, when Hungary was the center of empire and even the Jews had their rightful place. Your father wouldn't talk about that trip in any great detail. It meant too much. I gather the family moved to Budapest, whether by choice or necessity, not long before the war."

"An unlikely pair." My voice sounded harsh. I was surprised at the resentment and envy that washed up into my throat. Suddenly I was exhausted, weary of the subject and of my father's adventures, weary of the stories upon stories that knit my family and the Salters together. Not for the first time these tales seemed a many-stranded knot that bound me and weighed me down. I wanted it recited once and for all so I could then slip away free.

"What brought Joseph here? And why did he leave?" I repeated the questions as a kind of insistent invocation.

But Claire was dogged in her path. She shook me off with her head. "Now you have to listen as I tell it. Otherwise it won't make sense, will it? What you haven't heard is the one prick of anger between them. Without that, don't you see, the rest won't come clear. Anyhow, I've got to tell it the way it's in my head." She paused, brushing away no crumb at all from the table. "Now then. Like most every other intellectual in Hungary during those years, or so I've been told, Joseph was growing political. He was caught up in the excitement—and the danger too, no doubt about it—of making up a new country that would tear free of the Soviets but wouldn't merely ape our meager models either." Claire had closed her eyes and seemed to be reciting from a program. "They were out to create something entirely new and unsullied, run by artists and workers and dreamers. It would be a glorious thing."

She smiled and shrugged. "Well, Joseph all but abandoned his music. He was too busy visiting factories, lecturing to—and listening to—workers and farmers. Serving on committees. And reading mountains of political philosophy and socialist pamphlets late into the night.

"And Bradley had no patience for it. He and Joseph had some terrible quarrels. Joseph, well he could flare hot in an instant and be so—impulsive—that's what it is, when he was angry, when something he held sacred was attacked. And you know your father when he's angry. It's a good thing they weren't telephoning or trusting to letters—it would have been harder to make it up again. He, Bradley, thought practical politics a waste of time and energy. By definition it was corrupt and corrupting. And, of course, he wasn't very good at hiding his attitude that Joseph and his friends were bumbling amateurs. I think he really did have a better sense of the gulf between philosophy and actually organizing a society. Personally, he preferred the purity of the one to the compromises and evasions of the other. And he also sensed that the danger was only too real. The Russians weren't likely to throw up their hands and say, right then, good idea, full speed ahead to you, we'll be off now, thank you very much.

"That's the funny thing—how different they were in important ways. Your father always so tough and demanding of himself and those he cared for, so cynical about the rest of humankind. And Joseph was such a romantic. Especially about the politics and his hopes for a new world. Brothers or not, the two of them couldn't have been more different.

"But Bradley was jealous too. That's how I always saw it. That was the tone of his voice when he'd tell me later, after he'd come home from a visit there, and we would have one of our talks. It didn't matter that he had married your mother, or that Joseph was married all along to Marianne, who welcomed Bradley into their home. But the politics—it was as if something was being stolen away from Bradley. Not so much Joseph's loyalty as some quality of his attention."

Claire smiled again and shook her head. "But really, how many visits could there have been? Three? Maybe four? No more than that, certainly. Because along came '56, and all hell breaking loose. And I'm almost embarrassed to be telling you this next. Because no one except maybe your mother knows. And it really is like bad film noir. This was where Bradley's old M.I. friends did play a part. They got a message to him, whether it was from Joseph himself or simply that Joseph was in trouble, I don't know. But the Russians had gone in. We all knew that. Some Americans wanted to go in too and have it out with the Soviets once and for all, never mind the Hungarians or whatever the excuse. A lot of people died or were locked away or were sent off into exile or camps in the Soviet Union. It all happened very quickly. And Bradley himself disappeared from the college in the middle of term. I suppose he must have come up with something to tell President Stillwood. I stopped by here on the way home from the high school that day and your mother told me. She was rigid with worry, I can tell you, and she wouldn't say another word about it."

"Well, she's never told this story to me or Beth."

Claire bunched her lips. "Even I don't know much—your father never spoke about this trip—except what I could piece together from stray comments, especially from Joseph or from Marianne. She didn't mind talking about it after a drink or on the phone, especially on the phone after a vermouth. Although talking about this topic usually worked her up into proper hysterics and she'd have to hang up or fetch another drink and shift to some other topic, some local gossip.

"Your father made his way to Vienna again," she said as if plucking up the first crumb along a path that would lead us both clear. "But it was far from direct. He had to run first here, then there. Pulled what strings he could, asked plenty of favors, I suppose. Marianne was waiting when he arrived in Vienna—not waiting for him, waiting for Joseph—Joseph was still inside. And Marianne was a wreck. The experience wrecked her. A neighbor, actually some distant cousin of hers, had snitched to the secret police about Joseph's activities. Envy, pay-off, to save her own skin—who knows? But the police themselves hadn't been purged yet, were still divided, and someone inside warned Marianne and someone else helped her get over the border. She'd have been pregnant already with Hilary.

"Joseph was away, just overnight. But there was no time to wait for him, no chance even to pack anything beyond a single bag. When your father arrived in Vienna, Marianne was frozen by it all, numb, unable to do more than look up at him from the hotel window where she was perched in a chair watching for Joseph. She didn't have the energy for putting on airs of hope and determination to convince the hotel staff. Her money was all but gone, she had no idea where her husband was, and she certainly wasn't expecting Bradley Currant to arrive and save the day. Which is what he did."

My weariness had been swept aside by the pace and urgency of the tale. "But what about Joseph? How'd he get out? Don't tell me Dad accomplished that magic too?"

Claire looked up at me. "Ah now, that's one of the mysteries. Neither of them ever would talk about it, would they? And they're the only ones who know. Marianne doesn't. Oh, I don't suppose Bradley put a pistol in his trench coat and slipped across the border to rescue Joseph. But whether his military friends had a hand in it or whether he raised money for a pay-off —and I don't know where he'd have gotten much—or whether Joseph managed it on his own, I've never heard. All I'm sure of is that the only thing Joseph managed to carry out, other than the clothes on his back, was his blessed cello." Claire patted the table.

"So my father appeals to Arthur Stillwood to make a place for a new music professor. The rest I think I know."

"It wasn't as easy as that. I'm sure Arthur would make it out as practically his own idea," said Claire. "But the mechanics of it don't matter much after all these years. It's enough that a place was made."

I rubbed my eyes with the heels of my palms. "I don't remember them arriving. I was too young. It seemed to me that the Salters were in my house from the very start, that they belonged there as much as any of us did."

She was nodding when I looked up again. "That's the way it soon seemed to all of us."

"The other thing I don't remember," I pushed on, "is this bond of brotherhood you talk about between my father and Joseph. You make it sound almost mystical. But who ever saw it?"

"You're right," she said, "and you're wrong. I think it was always there to the end. But it became more difficult. They were very different men, more different here than when an ocean separated them. Do you see? After a while the families settled into life together. And the closer the families, the more difficult it seemed for Bradley and Joseph.

"The dull everyday round. I was part of it too, I'm glad to say. Your mother was never jealous of me." Claire gave a wry smile. "I rather wish she had been. Just a little. But I was adopted as your Aunt Claire, another member of the household—though not quite so ever-present as the Salters.

"I watched your father grow more famous and grow stiffer and older. It made me very sad. And Joseph was even more famous in those early years. Though he didn't go jetting around the world for recitals the way he might have done. He was content to stay with his family here.

"Maybe if the families hadn't been so close, if Joseph had remained in Hungary and Bradley visited him there once a year forever he wouldn't have aged so quickly. Maybe there was some specific falling out. But if so, no one ever mentioned it."

I sat back in my chair, hands behind my head. "Twenty years in this hideaway. You leave that kind of life in central Europe and settle here in this safe haven. The whole thing beats me. Twenty years and suddenly, no warning, no declaration, Joseph pulls up all roots again. He spirits Marianne and Gabriel away to deepest Arkansas. No explanations. Hardly a decent goodbye as far as I can tell." I leaned forward across the small table again. "What went wrong? Maybe if I wasn't mucking through paddies six thousand miles away they'd have let me in on the secret. Was there something specific that happened? Tell me about that, Claire."

She was shaking her head, hands heavy and inert before her. "It's late," she said. Fatigue had settled heavily like dew before a cool dawn. She clearly didn't want to go on talking. Everything about her sagged: her shoulders, the flesh of her face. She sighed and smiled at me. "I'm not so spry a girl as I used to be, young man."

"Who is?" I said. "Look, I'm beat too and I've got to drive home tomorrow. Just tell me this last part and that'll be the end of it. It's taken—how many years?—for my curiosity to get rubbed raw on this tack, and if I don't find out how the story goes, it'll drive me crazy."

"It's too late. Don't you see?" she said. "I don't mean tonight. I mean to know what really happened." She halted. My insistence had sparked her anger. But as if she couldn't let go prematurely either, she took up the trail again. "It's another mystery. Yes, something happened. Your father looked dark as death during those weeks, partly because something happened, partly because—this is my suspicion— whatever happened shouldn't have been enough to chase Joseph away. Was something done to Joseph? Was it something Joseph had done? Whatever the truth, Bradley believed he should have stayed.

"You say you never saw any mark of a special bond between them. Well, that may be true. But I only understood afterwards, don't you see, that simply having Joseph here at this college, in this safe haven as you call it, had become enough for your father, and was essential too. Even if he never showed it, even if things were never the same between them.

"Something did happen—something that seemed terrible—and that was bad enough. So bad Bradley wouldn't even tell me. And how do you think that made me feel? After all these years of listening, of knowing that I would hear, if no one else on earth. That he'd tell me most anything?" Color flared in Claire's cheeks once more. She looked daring, as if she'd just confessed a great and precious secret. "But bad as it was, it was worse that Joseph left. Your father grew grey and silent."

We were silent too for several minutes. At last I rose. Claire lifted her face to me. She looked haggard, as if stricken with that last image of my father she'd conjured for herself. And yet there was still about her eyes a trace of girlish secrets confessed and of her own triumph in them. I kissed her cheek and slipped out into the dark.

The night was very late and dark and cool. Eerily quiet, the village slept as if the last of its citizens had stolen away after the departed students.

The cool air was welcome. I felt overheated by the food and wine, by the washing up, by the talk with Claire. My mind was filled with images of my father and Joseph, images that seemed more like recaptured memories, as if I'd glimpsed them before only to push them away and forget. The image haunting Claire may have been of my father as an old man, grey and silent, but I was imagining him now as he would have been at thirty, at forty, those forty and thirty years ago. Perhaps I was recalling black-and-white photos I'd glimpsed somewhere along the way. But it was more than that too. I felt I was seeing him—if only in my imagination—for the first time as someone of flesh and blood, laughter and pain. Sleeves of a white shirt rolled up, baggy pleated trousers emphasizing his slimness, he waves at me (or to Joseph, to my mother?) in mid-stride from a porch step, waving and smiling urgently into the next frame and the future. Mid-step in the air, between asphalt road and gravel path, it swelled in my throat, the reality of my father as a man my age with a friend like Joseph Salter.

And Joseph too. Not an old man. A man my age, younger. Old for his years, certainly, with experiences that made even Vietnam seem parochial. Here he was, a man of thirty, give or take. Already a famous musician, a political activist. A Jew who'd survived the great horror only to be fleeing one homeland for an unknown Pennsylvania with a wife and baby soon to arrive. Did he have a beard then? Yes, and it was dark and full. That laugh of his, full-throated, unabashed, but with the hint of sadness about his eyes.

I'd had friends here in high school. But they belonged to another time, another life. And I'd come to have friends in war too, though not immediately. During our abbreviated boot camp we were all still too different, too aware of ourselves, too afraid with an abstract fear. Drinking buddies, sure. Guys you told stories to. But for all the sweat and puke and rage, for all the phony camaraderie that the sergeants engineered, usually by getting us to hate them, we curled in and clutched ourselves and waited.

But in choppers, sitting on your helmet against casual rifle fire from the ground, or in muck up to your thighs and up to your groin and up to your throat—I'm not going to talk about that. That's not what this story is about. But that's where you had friends, I had friends. Friends whose names I sometimes knew, sometimes not. Michael and Amos and D.J. Who I loved while the rotors shook us and the bullets pinged through the fuselage. While flares lobbed high over us to light the sky and keep Charlie at bay and only fleshed the darkness deeper about us. I'm not talking about that, but the friends.

No differences existed between us in the night. Fierce. We loved each other fiercely, to keep ourselves alive while our friends bled and we bled, some more than others, and we shit our pants, and we were scared of nothing abstract except the one abstraction that condensed around us in still-warm slabs. I'm not talking about that.

We'd call softly, fiercely, through the night to warn, to probe, to discover whether friends still lived. And in the morning—the morning after six weeks of night—we, at least I, shied away from these friends, bashful, ashamed, betraying them. Like I betrayed Corporal Zinser later. He was Andy, the shmuck we all tormented for being the hickest hick from Kentucky and who pulled me, not dying like I thought but bleeding plenty, towards the chopper and away and away at last forever. Corporal Andy who visited me in the ward before evac and I pretended to sleep the sleep of the dead. I couldn't face him. I couldn't acknowledge what we'd been through or what I owed him or that I'd never see him again. Like I'd betrayed, a lifetime earlier, the first girl I convinced to let me plunge in, come too soon, and slink away into the night after dropping her off on her front porch.

So. Once upon a time, Dad had a friend. In my heart I'd always suspected that he and I were alike, if no way else, in a certain solitude. But he'd had a friend and I'd never guessed. What happened to seal him off again?

I slept late into the morning. When at last I came down to the kitchen my mother was alone on a stool with the Sunday papers, her small tortoise-shell glasses perched low on her nose. As she glanced up at my steps, she self-consciously pulled the glasses off and folded them in a hand.

"Where is everyone?" I asked, dropping my bag by the door and pouring a cup of coffee.

"Your father is in his study, though he may be napping. The festivities took their toll. Beth and Jerry left early for a big wedding—one of his associates."

I nodded.

"You were out late," she said. "Did you go off and see other friends?"

"Claire and I finished the dishes and then stayed up talking."

"Oh? Was she bringing you up to date on village gossip?" Mother smiled brightly. "Give me something good—I feel horribly out of touch. No one's passed anything on to me for ages."

"Nothing good to tell. Just old stories about Joseph Salter —stuff I should have known years ago but never thought to ask."

I wasn't looking directly at her at that instant, but I was aware of my mother's head rising, her smile stiffening. "What kinds of things?" she asked. Glancing at her, I noticed again the network of fine lines at the corners of her eyes.

"Mostly about how Dad and Joseph met in Vienna, and how Joseph came to be hired here. I'd never heard the full story before. That amazes me. You all must have figured we'd pick it up by osmosis. And since she knew so much about all that, I thought maybe Claire had a clue why Joseph left the way he did."

"And did she?"

I shook my head. "The great mystery remains intact. Unless you know something else you've never bothered to share."

"Oh heavens," she said, dismissing it with a wave of her hand. "That old, old history. I gave up asking that question a long time ago."

She slipped off the stool and carried her cup and saucer to the sink. "None of that can matter after all these years. But what's happening to Gabriel—all the trouble he's in—that can matter. That's now and it's terrible. I feel so awful for him. For his parents too. This must be torture for them. I can't imagine it." She scowled and shook her head. "I don't for a minute think Gabriel would ever, ever do something like that. It's impossible." She'd worked herself up into quick vehemence. Her eyes shone. "Tell me, what's going to happen to him?"

I shrugged. "Unless his lawyer comes up with something I haven't heard about, he'll probably go to prison. First offense or not. They've got more cell space out there. In Baltimore judges have to be more discriminating."

"But what about the police beating him? Won't that affect their credibility?"

"Only indirectly. If the judge lets it."

She stared at me angrily, her eyes shining with fresh tears. "Stop it," she cried. "How can you be so matter-of-fact about it? As though it doesn't concern you. This is a boy you know. You've been part of his family."

"You asked, I answered." I was startled by the snap of anger in my own voice. "Since when are you so concerned with Gabriel? He was just a kid when they left town. Did you even know him?"

Wiping her eyes on a dishtowel, she nodded and turned back to me. "That's why, don't you see? He was just a little boy, sweet and full of curiosity. He was special to us because he was the youngest, the last." She opened the refrigerator, pulled out eggs, milk, and cheese. From a cupboard she clanged free a mixing bowl.

"Us?" I said.

"You were already gone to college," she said. "And then the war. My last memories of the family—other than Hilary and you later, of course—are of that mischievous little boy climbing over and through everything in the house. How can I not care what happens to him, for his parents' sake as much as his own?"

Half-an-hour later, after I dutifully consumed the omelette my mother insisted on preparing, I surprised her with a quick kiss goodbye, picked up my bag, and climbed into the car. My father had not come into the kitchen, and I did not try to find him. Perhaps he was still napping in his study. I am sure that for him, as well as for my mother looking on with sorrow and silent accusation, this was yet another escape, a refusal to deal with him, even another small betrayal. But that wasn't it. They'd be wrong. My head was still full of the stories and images of the night before, when I was glimpsing my father as a young man. I didn't want to confuse that with the immediate reality of his old age or with all the history of war between us, feelings that could be scratched to the surface by the merest intake of breath. My escape represented—at least as I intended it—a new gesture towards loyalty rather than another betrayal.

So I left my parents' home and drove towards Baltimore where Hilary's messages were waiting for me as if this were all a choreographed dance, a necessity laid out for us in a pattern we couldn't yet read.

Chapter VII

Early Monday morning, a rainy dawn at the windows and
the skeletal night crew straggling past me into the wet street,
I sat at my desk checking notes. In two hours I'd drive out
to Randy Schmeling's house in Park Crest, an older working-
class suburb. His mother had agreed to a follow-up interview, the last conscientious check in the story I'd been working on for better than two weeks. It was ready to come now,
after this interview. I could feel it. And once I started writing later in the afternoon it would surge and hold me fast
until I could chuck the finished piece onto Stan's desk at
Tuesday deadline. Until then I'd be able to shut out the rest
of the world, the rest of my own feelings, as I hadn't been
able to do lying awake after Hilary's messages most of the
night before.

Randy Schmeling was guilty—of that there was no
doubt—of cramming into an old Dodge with a bunch of his
buddies one Saturday evening before Christmas. They'd driv-
en down to the Block, that several-block area of downtown
Baltimore bright with the neon of nurtured soft-core vice.
Adult bookstores and bars, novelty shops specializing in latex
and lingerie and leather, a couple of small movie emporia. The
district provided a whiff of earnest sin for the sake of conven-

tioneers or boys up for a ball game from dull D.C.

Randy and his friends cruised along to the strip of nicer, certainly more expensive bars beyond the far edge of the Block. They pulled the Dodge snug against the curb and waited, swilling grain alcohol from a plastic 7UP bottle. They were in no hurry. There was plenty to watch. They waited for inspiration to snag and sweep them away.

About one a.m. George Stephoro left Mr. Henry's Bar disappointed and alone, and George provided the inspiration. He was a willowy, dark-haired boy with a gold stud in one ear. Innocuous enough. (During the last two weeks I'd combed through plenty of pictures, mostly of the before-and-after variety. Some would appear with the story.)

Ripe for fun, out of the car poured Randy's friends. With quiet taunts they circled George Stephoro. A baseball bat, maybe two, passed restlessly from hand to hand. George halted. Now he turned back and found his path blocked. He froze. Jibes and taunts. A shove. A punch. Did George say or do anything then? Did he lure the bats on in some way? Did he cry out for help?

They leapt at him. Shattered the hand he raised before his face. Cracked an elbow. Cracked his jaw. Pummeled and thudded and smashed him, again and again after he was already curled limply, eyes wide, in a puddle that stained his new silk shirt.

It took seconds not minutes. Someone in Mr. Henry's called the cops. Cops are everywhere on the Block. At least across the way, if not on this particular strip. Sirens swelled towards them. Randy's friends shoved back into the Dodge and jerked it into one of the dark side streets and away into the night. Only problem was they forgot Randy. Randy was standing, staring at George on the sidewalk when the cops did finally arrive. At least he wasn't holding a bat.

The rest was easy, once the case was clarified by George dying. Manslaughter. A quick conviction. And Randy was ever so loyal. Never would mention his friends by name.

But Randy had an IQ and temperament approaching those of a sheepdog. Did he know what he was in for that night, what they planned to do? Did he understand what made George Stephoro threateningly different? Did he do any more than watch before he started weeping snot the way they found him? Did he deserve to be heading to prison, alone, next week for a very long time?

Mick Jegla, the photographer who came along with me to Park Crest for that follow-up, snagged a terrific shot of Mrs. Humphrey (she'd remarried years ago) protectively hugging her enormous little boy Randy, his doughy breasts and belly sagging in an Orioles sweatshirt. She'd defended him these six months and had rallied the neighbors. Who knows?— maybe the families of some of Randy's friends were among those who marched to the courthouse lugging posters demanding justice or at least leniency.

And George Stephoro's family? They gave my story that certain something extra. For they did nothing. If they couldn't deny that George was dead, they could bury him quickly and quietly and with no fuss at all. Certainly without talking about why he was attacked by Randy and his friends. Stephoro. The family had been in Baltimore two full generations. Owned one of the city's famous Greek restaurants. A Stephoro in that part of the Block? Impossible.

Behind Randy and his lawyer at the courthouse, Mrs. Humphrey and her neighbors had attended the proceedings faithfully, like members of the groom's party. Who sat on the absent George's side behind the Prosecutor? Not his family. No, no, no. But faithful too, day in and day out, half-a-dozen members of Baltimore's gay community—not the same cast every day necessarily—bore witness on George's behalf. They'd adopted him by default and by rage, and they intended to make sure that justice was indeed done.

And justice of a sort was done. Randy had been convicted and sentenced and now, while appeals crawled slowly along, he was about to go to prison. Tears and confusion smudged

Randy's eyes. Mrs. Humphrey crouched dry-eyed and furious on the sofa, a lioness ready to maul anyone who laid a hand on her son.

This was my kind of story. A dollop of moral complexity, a psychological sketch that undermined earlier portraits, even in my own paper, of Randy as a brutal bigot. And as I certainly knew that late Monday afternoon while working it up, this story also offered bits of cagey titillation. Stirred to it by me, my readers could feel both morally penetrating and, not quite so consciously, titillated by George's predilections and by the Block and by the slap and thud of the bats as well.

For whatever reasons, the past three months had witnessed something of a renaissance in my journalistic energies. I'd already pumped out three major stories, features in all but name, not to mention a regular supply of straight city reporting. My duties had become a deep black pool into which I'd plunged like a waking sleep; they'd swallowed me up and protected me from doubts and temptations. Most evenings and weekends found me, if not at my desk, out on the street running down facts or taping interviews. I hadn't been so immersed—or comforted—since reading sixteen hours a day for my Ph.D. exams, head down so as not to notice Hilary growing impatient, growing apart.

Stan made known to me that Editors-Higher-Up were pleased. My outpouring of copy justified their own patience and judgment.

After a good start with Randy Schmeling's story that Monday afternoon, however, I stumbled. I lost my way. The distractions refused to be shut away any longer. Shards of Hilary's voice, bits from her plea on my answering machine kept surfacing. My concentration was shot. In frustration I began throwing scraps of quote and fact and character onto the screen. Later I'd try and wrestle the article into shape.

Even so, and this was what kept me at my desk rather than wandering out for relief into the wet June twilight, I sensed the larger pieces of the story shifting like heavy flotsam just beyond my grasp. I had faith that when the time came, when I was ready, they would fit neatly together, nudged into delicate pattern, carefully paced, and (again I was coldly aware) seasoned by deliberate titillation. That was my job. I was good at it. Have to entertain the readers or you don't get any readers.

Was I myself titillated? I wondered, sitting back in my desk chair. No. Far from it. I felt nothing beyond an eagerness to churn the piece into something solid. If at the start I'd felt either outrage or sympathy for Randy and George, such emotion was all a long way off. That came with the job too. Working up a story set the world at arm's length. Professional detachment shoved reality right out into the rain beyond those smeared newsroom windows. The burnt coffee in my mug only made the bad taste in my mouth taste worse.

And the longer I stared at the screen, the more unreal the whole package became. George Stephoro, whom alive I'd never laid eyes on, drifted quickly beyond reach. Soon Randy followed, his sad, doughy face fading, slipping away into words that themselves dissolved into meaningless flecks on the amber screen. Without cribbing from one of the photos on my desk I couldn't even picture him anymore. Who had done what to whom? Had anything been done by anyone?

"What I don't get—maybe I don't want to get it—is why it continues to matter to you. It's not like you didn't already live up to some ancient family code by chasing out there in March." Phyllis studied a peppered shrimp at the end of her fork. The gesture reminded me (something was always reminding me) that her family owned horse estates in Maryland and Virginia, that despite her M.A. from U.Va. and her professional talents as editor of the Book Section, scratch a little and you found brahmin soil, jodhpurs and hounds. At least that's what my imagination, scratching, found.

"I'm not surprised she asked you. I'm just surprised you're considering it. What on earth more can you do?" Phyllis looked directly at me, a fine crease in her brow. "Aren't you a little afraid that if you look hard enough you'll find out her brother actually did it?"

"Yeah," I said, nodding and chewing a whole shrimp, "yeah. You're right. I don't see how I could do much practical good. Heaven knows what's in it for me." I shrugged defensively. "It's certainly not for her sake, if that's what's bugging you."

Only the short tail of Phyllis's hair swung back and forth as she shook her head. She wore her auburn hair pulled back with a black barrette. It framed her face into a perfect oval. With her high forehead, rounded cheekbones and sharp nose, Phyllis had reminded me from the start of a serving maid, shrewd and vulnerable, caught by some sly Dutch master. Yet I'd come to see that she was tougher than that and lonelier. She pushed her fork against the pile of empty shrimp casings on her plate. She pursed her lips as if jealousy about Hilary were the farthest thing from her mind.

When I'd first mentioned Hilary's message, after arriving late and drenched and carrying the bag of hot spiced shrimp from my favorite shack on the harbor, Phyllis gave me a look. She was busying herself in the kitchen with plates and drinks so that we could be off in time for the film at Hopkins. The look was one I'd been seeing increasingly in recent weeks. It sized me up and found me wanting. It was a long way from the quick glances of promise and playfulness that she'd continued with long after I deserved them. She was protecting herself, and I knew she had every right to. I wanted to reach out and draw her close and kiss her throat reassuringly, to be the man she wanted, to provide comfortable refuge in the years ahead, perhaps even to provide children—we weren't too old for that—but instead I helped tear away the butcher-paper and divvy up the seafood.

"I've never considered your ex a threat. I don't work that way," she said now.

"I know that," I said. I glanced at my watch. We weren't going to make the Kurosawa.

"But this whole thing with her brother. Like I said, I don't get it. It isn't just your marriage. Who hasn't been married before?" (She hadn't.) She gave a half-sigh and caught herself up. This much talk in one stretch was unusual for Phyllis.

"There's been something about your attitude since you came back," she went on, tilting her head as if this were some puzzling element of a novel under review. A solitary, peeled shrimp sat helpless on the plate before her. "I spotted it right off. Something was hanging fire. You know—unresolved. You weren't satisfied. The harder you worked here, the more good stories you've produced, the more you seemed to be someplace else entirely."

My jaw was tight. She was making me uncomfortable. I didn't want to talk about any of this. "I admit it—I've been distracted," I forced myself to say. "It's not that there's some other place I'd rather be. Or with someone else."

"Okay, right. But you going out there let me get some perspective too. More you coming back, really. I could see us in a different way. And what I saw wasn't a rut so much. It was that I'm in this one box for you, one compartment of your life. I don't mind sharing you with work. I'm as ambitious as you. Maybe more—I'm damn proud of our book section."

"Hell, yes—you should be," I wedged in.

"But there's all the rest in your life, other compartments that you don't give me a clue about. The war for one, which you act as if never happened. As if your leg were a long-ago accident or an excuse so you don't have to climb on a horse. Your marriage too. You pretend otherwise, but these memories aren't all distant, buried in the past. They're an alive part you've just sealed away. See, look, the result for me is you're not all here. And I don't feel like being shut out." She finally stabbed at the shrimp. "I've got to protect myself. It's only fair. If you're going to isolate me into one little compartment, I've got to be able to do likewise. Know what I mean?"

"Shutting you out has nothing to do with it." I lied and knew I was lying and felt helpless not to lie. "Where the hell's all this coming from anyway? You've blown it cosmic. All we're talking about is a few days at most. I haven't even made up my mind." That much was true.

"But you want to." She snapped this softly, as if the accusation carried its own proof.

"I don't know if I want to."

"Well. I think it would be a mistake for you to."

"Nope—no way. That's not gonna fly." Stan Lupinsky was perched on the edge of my desk late Tuesday morning, arms folded protectively across his chest. Two dark wings of receding hair rose like a double tangle of thatch above his brow.

"You're not even hearing me out?" I snapped back. My voice boomed louder than I'd intended and heads around the City Room snapped our way.

"Nothing more I need to hear," he said, his tone rising to match mine. "I covered your butt when you ran out there in the spring, but I'm not doing it this time. You've got plenty on your plate here." He leaned forward. His voice grew conspiratorial. "You've been pumping lately, Jason. You're on a roll. Why risk screwing up the rhythm?"

I leaned forward too. "But this could be a terrific story for us. I'm not even asking for leave this time. I'm just suggesting maybe you want to send me out there on assignment."

Stan hesitated and gave a little growl as he cleared his throat. He was shaking his head. "Can't do it. Sorry. You're a City Desk reporter, even if you've been forgetting that every chance. You're not national. You're not features either, except features that make sense to this desk. Speaking of, aren't I supposed see that gay-bashing story? You got it?"

"Yeah, I got it," I said, hoping he'd let it go at that. But I was angry. Angrier because Stan's reaction had taken me by surprise. All I wanted was to float the balloon. But he'd shot it out of the sky, as if I were demanding some unreasonable favor.

"Shit, Stan," I said under my breath, panting with it, hot, surprised at how my own anger had swept up so quickly.

His face was flushed with hurt and surprise and anger too. His lips pressed together in a thin line. "Shit, yourself," he said with a dangerous calm.

"It's a good story," I insisted. I started to sell it along the lines I'd been thinking about since the day before, the voyeurism and moral superiority of my brighter readers. "Look, it's got everything—cops gone bad, an attempted rape that maybe never happened, socialists who see the world black-and-white and maybe this once happen to be right. Either way the public loves it—an innocent man rail-roaded to the pen, or a great hypocrite who rapes defenseless Black girls and gets what's coming to him."

"And who just happens to be your brother-in-law," Stan said with a grimace of disgust. "Talk about ethics right there for starters. And Jesus, you make it sound like we're turning out high-brow porno. Well, porno's not what we do, not as far as I'm concerned. And that aside, it still's got nothing to do with this City Desk. Like I said, it's a no go."

I snorted. "You just don't get it, do you?"

The newsroom had grown oddly quiet. A wide berth spread about this corner. Other reporters slipped furtively out for coffee. And part of me sat there amazed, staring at the two of us, wondering what the hell was going on.

Stan was more than a buddy. He'd been the kind of editor writers don't even know how much they need. When I landed this job, pissing off reporters who'd earned journalism degrees or bucked their way up from crummy suburban papers, Stan pulled me through and pushed me along. When I handed him lousy work, he wouldn't let me get away with it. He'd throw it back on my desk or, if it was salvageable, he'd prune and pare and shape it into something. He covered for me, pulled no more credit for my work than he deserved, made the higher-ups take notice, did me plenty of favors that probably were unreasonable. And if we didn't go out drinking, didn't hang around grilling steaks on each other's grill, that had nothing to do with it.

So why was he choosing this once to hold the line? And why, as much to the point, was I bridling so hard? Part of me sat observantly aloof; no little part was furious with him out of all proportion. Stan was propped on the edge of my desk and I was leaning back in my chair, smiling smugly up at him. I wanted to make him mad out of all proportion too. I wanted to goad him.

It worked. I could tell. He stared at me and his jaw tightened and my nasty little grin slipped like a shiv between his ribs. Except he didn't explode. I wish he had. Instead he pulled back, cold and angry.

"We've wasted enough time. Have that gay-bashing story on my desk by deadline," he said. Picking up a file he'd brought along to my desk, he turned and headed for his office and his other reporters.

The blade I'd wielded severed something between Stan and me. I felt the wound like a distant cold cramp in my own chest. I was sorry. I'd do it all different if I had it to redo. I'd yell and shout and stamp, and I wouldn't smile. Yet I was also feeling cut loose—as I had a couple months earlier in Iowa, as I had even in Pennsylvania over the weekend, ripped clear of all anchors. But now it wasn't so disorienting. I was ready for it. I enjoyed the sharp, painful breaths. Another plan occurred to me.

Earlier that same Tuesday morning, I'd wandered into the large cubicle that was the newspaper's library and, because it hadn't yet arrived there, pursued the Saturday issue of the Register to the mail room in the basement. Sam the sorter looked on with barely concealed exasperation as I fumbled with the bundles he'd been preparing for delivery to the various floors and departments. Each bundle was neatly constructed, larger envelopes on the outside, two heavy rubber bands holding it together. Equally neat, with closely cropped hair and a black tie held in place by a silver clip, white cuffs turned back precisely at the wrist, Sam pushed me aside with disdain and dug out the several packets destined for the library.

To my surprise, I discovered both the Register's weekend editions. Sunday's didn't usually arrive for another day or two. I tugged them both free of the bundle and sat on a corner stool out of Sam's way. From what I could tell with a quick scan, however, neither carried any mention of Leroy Jackson's Friday night assault on the Trailblaze Bookshop.

Disappointed, I carried the papers upstairs to my desk, intending to rifle them more carefully after I'd finished with Randy Schmeling. I tossed them onto the floor. Slick on its coated paper, the Sunday Magazine scooted clear. Its cover was a black-and-white shot of a large clapboard farmhouse, part of a photo-essay inside. A healthy crop of weeds overran the yard. Against the front door of the farmhouse flapped a ragged foreclosure notice. This was a very different Iowa from the one I'd seen. I picked the magazine up. Out of habit I flipped to the contents.

NOT DIRTY, BUT OUT OF CONTROL?, subhead, Are City Cops Brutal, Racist, and Sexist? by Brian Phillips. Not bad, I thought, finding the story's first page and folding the magazine back.

Yes, paragraph four, Phillips mentioned the federal suit brought against the police by Gabriel Salter, "whose trial on attempted rape, set to begin next week, has itself grown into a political cause celebre." The suit charged the police with beating Gabriel and depriving him of his rights the night he was arrested.

Most of the piece, however, covered the complaints of local Blacks and Hispanics about police hostility. Like a good apostle of the New York Times school, Phillips anchored the tale on precise, coolly recounted horror stories. Color photos provided evidence: the house of a family shredded by cops without a warrant who, it turned out, had come to the wrong address anyway; a Chicana who had been strip-searched, supposedly for drugs, not by a female officer as per regulation, but by a herd of groping detectives.

A shaded sidebar on the third page of the story recounted separate grievances by women on the force, including a lawsuit won for harassment. Ten-thousand bucks; the officer split soon after receiving the award. No mention of Officer Costello. I was disappointed but not surprised. Had Phillips spoken to her off the record? Remembering the clumsy secrecy of our meeting in her car, I hoped she hadn't been spotted.

I read the article through twice. Annoyed, dissatisfied, I flung it, pages flapping wildly in the air, against a partition across the aisle. Phillips could write. And the story was plenty smart. That wasn't the problem. He put the pieces together, laid the picture out, kept a reader reading with growing outrage. It was the tone that bugged me. Arrogant. That's what it was. Distanced, objective, dispassionate. This reporter certainly wouldn't allow himself to be compromised by what he reported. A pro. A star. Maybe this would get him nominated for a Pulitzer too. The thought disgusted me because, after all, I'd been chasing that brass ring as well. Anything for another snatch at journalistic glory.

All this crap about a few bad cops, even a whole lot of bad cops, undermining the credibility of the force in general. I snorted. I wanted to take Phillips and shake him until his bones rattled. Superior little prick. What did he know about it? I happened to know. I'd been there. I knew that when the grunts go bad, when they're out of control, something's sour with the whole damned enterprise.

I felt bad for Gabe that a guy like this was covering his story. Phillips was too good at what he did, which made it just about impossible for him to hear Gabriel Salter.

That's when I decided to do my own version.

No, that's not right. That's when a simple, powerful churning in my gut wrenched me into realizing how very much I wanted to return to Iowa. The desire burst through me as though a levee suddenly gave way. I wanted to figure out what the hell happened that night at Leroy Jackson's house. I needed to get back to Iowa and figure out what was going on with Gabriel and what was going on with Grey and, most of all, figure out why it mattered so much to me. Only then did I come up with the rationale of doing my own version. Hadn't Grey herself predicted it?

"You went out there in the spring, didn't you?" Brenda Glascoe put it to me coolly that afternoon after Stan shot me down. Word about my vagaries had spread through the paper just about as widely as I suspected.

"That's right."

"So why not do it that way again? Why ask the paper to foot the bill? Have you already blown all your leave for the year?" The editor of our own Sunday Magazine was a shrewd, prematurely wizened woman with heavy creases in her face and her grey hair cropped very short. She was also small; she might have been perched on a phone book or two as she gazed up at me with bright eyes over the salad she was eating at her desk. I'd been standing in front of her for nearly ten minutes and she hadn't given me the chance to sit.

"No, it's not that. Though having you pick up expenses wouldn't hurt," I said with a winning smile. "And official sanction will get me access."

Glascoe scowled. "I'm not here to finance your hobbies."

My grin retreated. "Hobbies bore me," I said. I'd already laid out the bare bones for her. "The story's hot. You know that or you'd have blown me off by now. And it's perfect for the magazine."

"Because Stan Lupinsky wouldn't bite?" Again she was tough and straight.

"Sure. But also because I think the magazine's a more logical place."

She nodded and wiped her lips with a paper napkin. "I think so too, as a matter of fact." She folded the napkin, set the plate aside, and looked up at me thoughtfully, coolly. "But to be honest, I'm not sure you're worth the hassle. It's one thing if Stan sends you up here—that's not so unusual. But after he's said no. This means stepping on toes. That's not my style."

I stood and waited and kept my face as steady as I could. She was taunting me or testing me, I didn't know which, but I wasn't going to react.

Taking a sip of water, she seemed to consider it further. "I like your work—that much I can tell you. But it's uneven. We never know whether Jason Currant's going to light up the sky or merely fill in the dots, flogged each step by whatever editor's saddled with him."

"That's a bit harsh," I muttered. I'd had about enough of Brenda Glascoe. The blood surged in my cheeks and temples. "I'll let my work speak for itself."

"Have you any choice?" she asked.

Remaining silent, I wondered again whether she was

goading me deliberately or whether this was her style.

Her grey eyes studied me steadily.

"Stan is obviously right. It's not a piece for his crew," she said at last with a sigh. "But I'm interested. I confess it." She was shaking her head, a sad sybil. "Lord help you if this blows up in your face. You explain it to Stan. If he clears it, I'll pay for a week out there. Ten days max. I'll get you names of photo stringers. You'll have to arrange shoots yourself. And keep me up to date—I'll expect a call every day."

"You got it," I said.

"Damn right I do."

What could Stan say? I suppose he could have fired me quick and simple. Leave me to freelance for the magazine. Maybe it would have been better if he had. A clean rupture like that would have meant easier mending later. Instead, with none of the usual worry on his face, just a hard, distant, thin-lipped smile, he nodded to me and turned away. This was another man from the one I'd known so well and I felt sorry. I liked him better when he worried. "I'll get you the other piece before I leave," I called after him.

Once I was rolling I didn't want to stop. I spent the rest of the afternoon and into the evening pounding out the last voyeuristic details of Randy's (and George's) saga. Instead of simply transferring it through the computer, I printed out a hard copy and carried it to Stan's desk. A note, a funny paperweight, some gesture to make peace? After a long moment I simply set the copy down squarely on his blotter and walked away.

The cab waited outside my apartment while I threw a bag together. By ten o'clock I was heading to BWI to catch the red-eye.

Only once I landed at O'Hare for the layover did I pull out my notepad to find Hilary's motel number. For whatever reason, I'd wanted to be clear of Baltimore before calling her. It was only twelve-thirty Central Time and fatigue had-n't yet snared me. Moving forward was too exhilarating. Waking Hilary struck me as fair play.

After half-a-dozen rings, the hello on the line was heavy with sleep.

"Hi," I said calmly and cheerfully.

"Oh, Christ—Jason," she moaned, quickly burying an initial flash of annoyance. I sensed her struggling towards the surface. "Did you get my messages? Why haven't you called?" She paused and, so I imagined, swiped her hair out of her eyes. "Where the hell were you?"

"I'm in Chicago," I said. "I'll be arriving at six a.m."

"Good God. What time is it now?" Her voice faded as she leaned towards the nightstand to switch on a light. "Huh. Feels later than that. You dragged me out of one hell of a deep sleep."

"Sorry. I wanted to let you know I'm coming. And I need to know where to come."

"Oh. Right."

"And I need a place to stay."

Hesitation. She was properly awake now. I sensed suspicion if not open hostility on the other end. "You can worry about that later," she said, attempting to sound indifferent. "This place may not be the most convenient."

By eight-thirty I was on my third cup of coffee and second newspaper in the Winona Motel's cafe. I'd already booked in for the next several nights and called Hilary's room again. For five bucks the desk clerk had smuggled me into a utility room for a quick shower, since my own wouldn't be vacant until noon. Although the hot water was refreshing, fatigue began to condense in my back and joints, and my eyes only felt drier. But I was still high and breathing hard from the quick pace I'd set since my chats with Brenda Glascoe and Stan the day before.

When Hilary appeared at the cafe entrance, she was dressed casually in a denim skirt and embroidered peasant blouse. I hadn't expected a pang this time, but the outfit did it. It, the peasant blouse, made her look younger, less like an earnest government executive and more recognizably the girl I'd grown up with a long time ago. Smiling, she strode towards me briskly. She neither held out a hand—that would have been ludicrous—nor offered a kiss on the cheek, but pulled out a chair to join me. I saw her notice my hair, still damp from the shower. It puzzled her, concerned her, but she tried to hide that. Always quick on the uptake, Hilary.

"You actually came," she said. The fact might have surprised her, but as I'd learned last time out here, she'd developed quite a poker face. I couldn't tell whether she was pleased or not.

"Abracadabra," I said.

The corners of her mouth twitched. "If I had wishes to blow, they'd have blown a long time ago." She caught the waitress's eye and signaled for coffee. "You know, maybe you took my wee-small-hours babble on the phone a little too seriously. I didn't really think you'd come. Not that I'm not glad." She said this last in a rush, with a glance at me then quickly away. "But what I needed the other night was the chance to spill my guts like a little kid. I was exhausted and frustrated and missing my husband and daughter. Your machine, by the way, is a better listener than you ever were."

"Thanks a million."

"Get off it," she said. "I didn't mean it nasty."

"I'm not on it," I said. "Anyway, I didn't come back out here just because you begged. It's been on my mind. Where

I was when you called, by the way, was at my folks' fortieth anniversary and Dad's semi-retirement. Gabriel's troubles came up, not surprisingly."

She nodded. I could see her thinking about the village in Pennsylvania and my parents and how odd it was that she hadn't been at the festivities too. They'd been parents to her as well for a long time. Did her eyes glisten? She blinked to hide it. Casual as all the world. She nodded again. "I'll send them a card. I should have remembered."

"So it's not just for you. Besides, this time I'm on assignment."

She perked up. "You're kidding." Her nose for media exposure tickled. "Your friend Stan put you on it?"

"Nope—this one's for our magazine."

"Jeez," she said. "I'd about given up hope that anyone outside Iowa would notice. Except the lefty brigade, of course. Gabe's pals."

"Bitter are we?"

She glanced darkly at me. "Okay. Let's get this straight right off." Officiousness stiffened her neck. She was going to call the shots. "You're on assignment. Right? So, unless I say otherwise, and I mean explicit, whatever comes out, I'm totally off the record. Right?"

"Sure. No problem." I raised my hands in surrender.

"Bitter?" She grimaced and picked at the pocket in her denim skirt but only came up with a ratty kleenex. She dropped it in the ashtray. "I'm getting there all right. I don't think any of them gives a damn about Gabe going to prison. They're using him as a political marker and loving every second of it. He's better than a pawn. A knight or bishop maybe. And what makes it worse of course—jesus, I wish I had a cigarette—Lenny found out and he's trying to get me to quit again—is how Gabriel's happy as pie to be used. He talks so much about the reality working people have to face. How this is just part of that reality. I think sometimes he's on Mars when it comes to reality." She'd worked herself up and was fidgeting with annoyance.

"Maybe they'll get him off," I said. "Any new evidence or leads come up? What about his mystery woman?"

"No, that's the point, damn it. I'm not sure they want to find any evidence. Jeremy Stanton's frustrated too. He thinks he could win this in a more orthodox way, but Gabe and the Defense Committee are insisting on the full conspiracy angle. The police had a bias—everyone had a bias—it was all a set up. Who knows? Maybe they can earn more political capital by martyring him."

"What about Grey? She's got to be doing everything she can." I'd managed to resist asking about her so far. Now the question seemed natural.

"Grey. Who knows with her too? Maybe she wants to make the sacrifice. I don't get her. I don't get the two of them. And they treat me like they're on good behavior with some alien. They've always assumed I was so damn conventional and disapproving."

"Weren't you?"

"No," she snapped. The waitress hurried over. Hilary waved her away again. "I may have my problems with her, but it's this total commitment to the Alliance that gives me the creeps. It's both of them—it's all of them. They might as well be Moonies."

I acknowledged her point without being drawn.

"They're expecting me this morning," Hilary went on. "A public rally's in the works for Sunday. Oh, and there's a pre-trial hearing this afternoon. You interested?"

"Let's play it by ear," I said.

"Hah!" cried Gabriel with a small whoop as I followed his sister through the screen door. We'd surprised him reading a newspaper at the kitchen table. His dark hair had been cut short and parted raggedly. He was very pale for June, his strong nose sharply defined. Perhaps the paleness was why his hazel eyes seemed larger and ringed by purple shadows. No obvious signs of his injuries remained.

Flinging the paper aside, Gabe leaned back, hands behind his head, grinning at me. For a moment I was the center of the universe. And his eyes crinkled with a teasing mischief. They pierced any play at indifference I could throw up.

"I've asked my sister a dozen times if you'd be showing up again," he said. "Best I could manage from her was a shrug." He turned to Hilary. "How long have you known?"

"Hey, he woke me last night calling from O'Hare," she said.

"Good to see you, Gabe," I said. As in March, the warmth of his welcome surprised me. And the pleasure I felt too, shone on by that grin of his, made me distrust myself.

"Grey! Simon!" he called over his shoulder. But Simon was already standing in the hallway. Light from the kitchen glinted off his spectacles. He actually gave me a nod.

I was listening to movement in the room above. A shuffle. A moment's hesitation. She was finishing something— the page she was reading or a tuck of needlepoint. I grinned secretly at the unlikelihood of that. She crossed the floor purposefully, not hurrying. The rug ended before the stairs and her boots rang a quick staccato all the way down. From the bottom step she ducked past Simon under the low door frame and swung into the kitchen. She raised her head and saw me.

"Look who's returned," said Gabriel.

"Hi," I said to Grey. Anxious as I'd been, the moment was flat. I felt no chill at first sight of her, no sudden rush, not even the sense of distant recognition that had been so unnerving before. My conscience did ease a bit.

"Hello," she said simply. Her broad cheekbones and dark eyes revealed nothing, not surprise, neither pleasure nor disdain. She was wearing jeans and a plaid western shirt with silver snaps instead of buttons. Her braided hair hung down her back.

"The big news," Hilary announced, "is that this time Jason's here on assignment. He's doing the story." She placed a hand on my shoulder. It scorched.

"Are you?" said Gabriel, turning back to me.

"Yeah. Sort of." I slipped out from under Hilary's claim.

"Starting with the hearing this afternoon," she said.

Simon drew his hands out of his pockets and set them on his hips.

"It's what you all haven't managed to get," Hilary said, as if it were her doing, as if she were showing up the entire ISA propaganda campaign. "This is mainstream media—a Sunday magazine that'll be up and down the east coast. In D.C. we kill for that coverage. What do you think, Jason," she said, swinging an arm through mine, "are we talking another Thin Blue Line here or what?"

I felt like a calf being harried toward the pen. "Hold on," I said with a laugh, trying to squirm free. "Let's hope it doesn't come to that—he hasn't been convicted yet."

"What's to wait for?" Simon demanded. "It's a frame. It's harassment. Whether he's convicted in their stooge courts or he isn't. The cops are railroading him. That's the story for anyone who'll listen."

Grey gazed quizzically at me. But she said nothing.

Neither did Gabriel. The smile had gone from his mouth, if not entirely from his eyes. He was watching me, curious but patient.

"What about the cops beating him nearly to oblivion?" demanded Hilary, urging me on. "There's enough right there for a hell of an expose, I'd assume."

I raised my hands defensively. "You just had a big piece in the Register on police brutality. It even mentions Gabe. There's no need for another version. I'm not saying the cops weren't thugs once they had you, Gabe. But it's only part of the picture."

He raised his head and smiled again as if he were trying to reassure me. "I'm not sure I see where you're going with this," he said.

I laughed again. It sounded forced. "Neither do I. I just got back, remember?" I glanced from one to the other of them. "And whatever I write, remember it won't hurt or help with the trial. That'll be finished before I'm in print. For that matter, what happens in the courtroom has to be part of any story. The outcome will determine how I pitch it."

Simon's impatience leaked a dry venom. "The question is, are you writing about what happened or aren't you? You do, and sooner or later you have to choose sides."

"I'm not on any side," I snapped. "Not, anyway, as a reporter. What interests me with this—as a journalist, Gabe, separate from as your friend—are the contradictions." I was off and chattering now, afraid to halt. I was selling the piece again.

"See, we've got these two stories—at least two—and they're both believable, and they're also mutually exclusive. Usually in a case like this you get one story from the prosecution and a denial or alibi from the defense. Not two totally separate tracks. What we've got here is powerful and disturbing. My editor thinks so too. Competing narratives, you know? Very postmodern," I said with another small laugh I hoped would be disarming.

"Crap," said Simon.

Hilary had already pulled clear of me. "That's all fine and good," she said. "But they're still planning to ship my brother off to prison for something he didn't do. Isn't that the story that matters, not all this abstract bullshit?"

Gabe pulled a leg up across his knee and looked at me with disappointment. "I'm sorry you can't believe me, Jason."

"My believing you's not the point either," I said, flailing, loosing my point, wishing my business out here hadn't come up yet. "The last thing in the world I want is for you to go to prison. Let's hope it doesn't come to that—especially for a first offense."

"There you go again, sounding like you believe them."

Anger finally flashed in Gabriel's voice. "All this postmodern garbage. Reminds me of those arguments we used to have, years ago, when I came home from college to scratch up any job I could for a few weeks. The two of you'd be in for a visit, always leaving a couple days later. You never stayed very long, once Dad moved us to Arkansas, did you?" He stood and walked across the kitchen as if he were caged and restless. He kept his back to me for a moment then swung round.

"Remember how we couldn't go for walks anymore because you didn't want to see the way things really were? Not the way I made you look. You remember? The old men who weren't fifty and already burned out with booze. The women bruised and desperate. The kids—you remember what it was like for kids there?

"Hell, Jason, you were still so dark in those days about everything yourself. I figured you didn't want to see any more than you'd already seen in the war. Burrowing away to hide in your dissertation. But that wasn't really it, was it? You were always seeing complexities and different sides and different versions." He was shaking his head in frustration at the recollection. "Competing narratives. Jesus."

I'd already lifted my hands to ward off that whole conversation. Frustrated myself, I was growing angry and impatient. But Gabriel, cutting me off, raised his hand insistently too.

"You never could take seriously that I'd found a politics I could believe in. Something I could act on. Not simply pat myself on the back for feeling guilty about the state of society. You wanted to dismiss it as a boyish infatuation or college naivety. But, damn it, I've stayed true to it. There's no hocus-pocus, nothing mysterious. If you're brave enough and honest enough, you can see how workers and peasants, how almost everyone—if they only knew it—is raked by a system they can't beat.

"Does that sound naive to you? People like you—no

offense, brother—say my party's irrelevant. But I tell you what, at least we're dealing with the real world. Nothing make-believe. Ever see a Republican in a packing plant? Or some Democrat on an assembly line wrestling the guts into a washing machine? The only thing real about their politics is raw power, which they use to keep things just the way they are. Not to mention flicking troublemakers like me out of sight."

Gabriel's passion flashed in his eyes but he kept his voice on a tight leash. The room was quiet, as if an intense crackle of electricity, nearly soundless, had stunned us.

"So tell him," Grey said at last. Off-hand and grim, she was leaning against the door frame.

Hilary looked puzzled. "Tell him what?"

Grey mocked her with a glance. "We got word yesterday after you left. Gabe'll be going away all right, if they convict. They've added a burglary charge."

"What are you talking about? What is she saying? What burglary?" Hilary demanded of her brother.

"They get me on attempted rape," said Gabriel directly to me, "it means I trespassed on private property—the girl's house—to commit a felony. In Iowa that's enough to convict on burglary too. Automatic. And burglary carries a mandatory sentence."

"How long?" Hilary said.

"Twenty-five years," Simon said.

"For a first offense?" I asked Gabriel.

He nodded. "Says a lot about the system, don't you think? Assault a young girl, especially a Black girl—first offense usually means they slap your wrist, give a wink, and let it go. But threaten somebody's holy property and it's mandatory you're slammed away. I love the irony. With me, because they want to stick it good, they're using the one to get me for the other." He tossed it off lightly. But the wryness in his eyes was wicked as a razor.

"Too bad there's no choosing sides," said Grey to me as

she turned away. "Liberals and journalists always have trouble with that. That's the trouble with liberals."

I wanted to catch her by the wrist, to wrench her into a chair and make her listen. But I wasn't sure what I'd say, and anyway, I was tired of speeches.

Her boots climbed the stairs again and crossed to the other side of the house. A door closed but didn't slam.

Gabriel took a deep breath and let it out slowly. "I know Hilary here thinks we've just been playing games. Not taking the danger seriously enough. Maybe that's true." Resuming his seat in the wooden chair, he was calm now, his tone detached, almost scholarly. "Way we see it, the important thing is to snatch any chance they provide, take advantage of situations they're trying to use against us, anything to educate people about how the system is stacked."

He leaned back, tilting the chair against the wall, and closed his eyes. His face was very pale and I recalled the mask that had been left after they beat him. "But twenty-five years," he murmured. "Sure, there's plenty I can do on the inside. More in some ways than out here. Still," and he paused and sighed. "A sentence like that, it doesn't sound like any game to me."

Chapter VIII

I left the house winded and weak, as though I'd been wrestling with Gabriel. He may have been disappointed. But I was furious with him for lecturing me. With them all for putting me on the spot, judging me, spitting me out. By the time I reached the street I was seething with recollected offense. I kicked the front tire of my car. Pulled back, considered, and lashed out with another kick. A proper little tantrum.

Abruptly I froze. Grey, I realized, might be observing all of this from an upper window. I didn't dare glance back. Nonchalant as a browser, I casually climbed into the car and drove away as if nothing had happened. At the first stop-sign I smacked the steering wheel.

Imminent at last, Gabriel's trial had become a vortex sucking energy and concern and time itself in a quickening tide. That vortex, I well knew, would only grow stronger once courtroom testimony began sometime Monday or Tuesday. It would twist and distort the complexity of the case as the jury surged towards a verdict. I imagined Gabriel, this man I cared for almost despite myself, dressed in prison blues, legs and arms manacled, prodded along a gauntlet of gated corridors like arterial valves siphoning the flow in a single direction.

Although I'd resisted pleas for loyalty and alliance, I couldn't shake the sense that I should be doing something, digging for answers, tracking down a lead. Even if that meant the risk of discovering his guilt. Although any story I might write wouldn't appear until well after the trial, something useful might crawl out from under a rock in the meantime.

The pre-trial hearing was scheduled for late afternoon. I had several hours to kill. As I drove away from the house I had not a clue where I was heading. It was a warm June day in the city, and I rolled my window down. No hint of slaughtered cattle stained the breeze, but from a distance drifted the scents of wet earth and young crops.

Competing narratives. That was a sexy angle all right. Brenda Glascoe thought it was hot. No doubt, if it came to that, I'd spin the piece along those lines.

But I didn't really buy it. It wasn't, finally, honest. It was a postmodern copout. I'd never finished my dissertation because of similar resistance to such trendy notions. I'd run smack into the fact, in the person of my advisor, that historians don't much like narratives anymore. Causes are suspect, not to mention any possible effects. One thing doesn't necessarily lead to another, and when you glance back at the first, why it's disappeared altogether. Been relativized out of existence. You can paint a statistical picture. You can piece together the daily life of a village peasant. But stay away from a story. Unless you can demonstrate there's more than one.

All right, here we had more than one. Gabriel Salter, socialist martyr, entrapped by a police conspiracy. Gabriel Salter, druggie and maniac, attacking a young girl on the porch of her own home. Mutually exclusive tales. How unsettling.

But as I cruised slowly through tangled neighborhood streets that afternoon, deliberately losing myself among one-way alleys and improvised cul-de-sacs, I wasn't satisfied with competing tales. Something, scratch the bottom of it, happened that March night. Either Gabriel had tried to force himself into Teresa Jackson or he'd been set up.

Okay, so I didn't really think the police, FBI, and G-Men everywhere had gone to the trouble of framing one minor pain-in-the-ass labor organizer. But I found it mighty hard to imagine Gabriel pawing Teresa in the filth of her front porch either. Yet someone had certainly knocked her around, if the doctor at Broadlawns Hospital was to be believed. No, somewhere there was a hard, nasty little truth. What might be relative was my ability to ferret it out.

It didn't help that both sides stuck to their extreme versions. Neither seemed interested in compromise. Was there no middle ground where the truth could linger? Had it to be either a vicious attack or a Machiavellian conspiracy?

My own desire to know, to follow this through, had flared beyond the scratching of any simple itch. I'd left Gabriel's house angry. I'd grown so angry at the liars—and there were liars—that it gnawed at me. I wanted to unmask them, to hold them up to public scorn. Most of all, I wanted to know what Gabriel Salter was capable of. Either an astonishing and all-but-saintly consistency of virtue or an equally astonishing capacity for savagery and demonic denial.

I managed after all to lose myself. I was disoriented, still somewhere in the northeast quadrant of the city—my wandering hadn't carried me beyond the boundaries of river and ravine and freeway. But I was thoroughly turned around and didn't want to cheat by looking at the small map from the rental agency. As a Pennsylvania boy scout, and again later, when it wasn't play, I'd been trained in what to do when you're lost: start back with small overlapping circles across the territory you've covered, searching without panic for the trail. That was the key. That's what I decided to do.

I used the pay phone in the back of a grimy gas station. Just as someone at police headquarters answered, however, the shriek of a lug wrench forced me to shout for Officer Costello. Whoever answered seemed unsurprised, but the connection I got surprised me. By then the wrench had gone silent.

"This is Sergeant Hathaway. Can I help you?"

I hesitated. The call had been switched to him, but his tone suggested he didn't know why.

"Sorry—must be a misconnection," I said. "I was calling Officer Costello."

I sensed a sudden concentrated alertness on the other end.

"Officer Costello's on sick leave. Who's calling?"

Again I paused. The Public Information Officer didn't know about my first meeting with her, and I wasn't sure, for Costello's sake, whether he should discover I knew her. I decided to break the good news of my return at some later moment.

"We're old buddies, but I've lost her home number. I don't suppose you can let me have it?"

"Sorry. That's against policy."

"No big deal. I was just passing through town and thought I'd say hi." I was about to hang up.

"Hey—you want to leave a message?" Hathaway called as if he didn't want to lose me. "Listen, she's due back today. Tonight actually. She's working that shift for a while."

"Yeah?"

"Yeah. How about leaving your message? Have her get back to you?"

"That's okay. I'll be hard to catch. Maybe I'll try her later."

"Sure," he said.

Funny how, pulling out of that gas station without asking directions, I had a feel for where I was.

Another small circle across my own tracks brought me to 29th Street. I didn't bother calling first. I figured I'd chance dropping by unannounced. At the end of the block a school bus was flashing its lights as half-a-dozen kids climbed down. I checked my watch. It was only two o'clock. For an instant the children were motionless as the bus pulled away with a garish plume of exhaust, and then they scattered with cries, racing and scooting and pitching books to all sides. A young girl, maybe nine or ten, skipped deliberately towards me. She was wearing dark denim pants and a pink blouse, her hair pulled into several short pigtails with blue and red and green ribbons. Her heavy books she carried clutched to her chest as she turned up to the dark bungalow across from my car. At the first step she swung round and shouted at another girl farther down the block. "Evey Wright—you 'member your promise."

"Don't hassle me, girl," Evey responded archly, hand arched on her hip.

Teresa's sister nodded and headed up the steps. I waited until she'd tugged the porch door open.

Armed only with my notepad, I walked up the pavement to Leroy Jackson's house. I didn't imagine I'd discover anything new here, but it was good to touch base. The porch was dark and rank and stifling after the bright summer day outside. As my eyes adjusted it seemed that nothing had shifted since my last visit. There was the car battery next to the door. Had those starter cables lain tangled by it before?

I knocked loudly again and almost at once I heard someone fumbling with the knob. I expected the sister or her mother, maybe Teresa herself, but it was Leroy Jackson who tugged the door open and stood heavily before me.

"Yeah—what do you want?" he said, staring vaguely at me with a sullen hostility but no particular interest. "Who the fuck're you?" His right arm was bandaged heavily from elbow to thumb. It hung in a pillowcase sling from around his neck.

"Mr. Jackson—hello. You may not remember, but I came by in March. I'm a reporter. Jason Currant."

Jackson squinted at me and nodded, though without a great deal more interest. "Oh yeah, I remember all right. Reporter, shit. You're Salter's fucking brother. I heard the story before you hardly got out my door."

"A long time ago I used to be married to his sister, that's all. And I am a reporter—my paper's sent me out on assignment."

"You ever write it up last time? I never saw nothing." Looming before me, he seemed both suspicious and curious.

"Not yet—I'm waiting to see how the trial goes. You got a few minutes?"

"Middle of the day, middle of the fucking week, and I'm here, ain't I? What does that mean to you?" He looked at me hard. "It means I don't got any hauling. Means I got nothing better to do than stay home with the women. This arm don't help none." He scowled. "Do I got a few minutes ain't the question. Question is, do I got any time for you?" He stared at me mean and threatening. Slowly a sly grin broke across his face for having me on.

I held my ground, demonstrating my own stubbornness.

Jackson let out a deep breath that was half sigh, half belch and swung away without shutting the door. "Ain't no skin off my nose," he muttered to no one in particular.

I followed him through into the lesser gloom of the house. The tv flickered silently in the corner. Teresa's sister had already settled on the rug in front of cartoons. No sign of her sister or mother. On the far side, a lamp illuminated Jackson's recliner. Despite an air conditioner thrumming in the window, the house smelled close and musty. Jackson himself seemed aware as he turned restlessly from side to side as if searching for a new berth.

"It's a nice day. We could walk around the block," I suggested.

Jackson rolled his eyes. "Walk around the block," he mimicked me in falsetto. "That's so White I could puke." He looked at his big reclining lounger. He glanced about his own living room and shrugged. "Fuck yes—let's go out for a nice little stroll. I need some air."

On the front walk Jackson stood blinking in the powerful sun. The harsh light exposed him, stripped him bare, and I was startled by the changes in the man. He might have aged ten years since March. His skin hung loose around his jowls; his eyes were all but hidden by dark pouches; despite his still considerable girth, he actually seemed shrunken—not a great deal, just enough for nature to make its point.

"Business usually slow this time of year?" I asked.

"Nah," said Leroy, wiping his left hand across his face again. "It's just bad. Last week I sold one of my trucks. Ain't busy enough to make sense keeping two. Branford, my brother-in-law, he got the old one out running a job now."

He set out slowly along the broken sidewalk. My leg had cramped with all the travel and I couldn't disguise the limp. We must have looked quite a pair.

"After the hassles from Salter and all in the spring, I changed the phone number. But that turned out dumb. Customers ain't been troubling to find out the new one, even folks that know me. Maybe that's the reason. Maybe not. Business is bad." He grimaced as we trudged slowly along. "Man, you still think the cops paid me off to nail Salter? Look at all it's done for my life. I sure am one lucky son of a bitch today."

"Is that why you went after their bookstore?"

He lifted his wounded arm and let it fall back in the sling. He stroked it with his left hand. "Lot a good that did. Your brother's a fucking, running, coward."

"Because he wouldn't fight you?"

"Because he won't let my little girl alone. 'Cause he keeps following and calling and scaring her."

I bent over and picked up a pebble and pressed it between my palms. "You see him do any of that? You believe he's doing it?"

Jackson surprised me by hesitating. "Yeah, I believe it.

Teresa swears." He was shaking his head, working himself up. "Lucky for him I didn't get my hands round his throat. Wouldn't be no trouble of a trial if I did. That's for damn sure."

"You glad it starts Monday?"

"If there's got to be one–yeah, I'm glad. Can't lock him up and be done with soon enough for me." He'd stiffened with agitation.

"So you're still sure he did it. No doubts at all that maybe it's mistaken identity or some, who knows, misunderstanding?"

Jackson wheeled on me, fury in his eyes, but the fidgety agitation hadn't disappeared. I braced myself, afraid he might actually hit me. "You fucking with me? Don't you fuck with me, man. Course he did it. Where'd they catch him? Right there on that porch, in that house, my house, they did. Even if Teresa didn't identify him—and she did— there ain't no doubt about where he was."

Something in his voice, an extra brush of hoarseness, made me switch tack. "How's she doing? Teresa."

He seemed to deflate slightly as he trudged forward again. "Her? She's doing okay. I mean, she's changed by all this. Got to be. Probably won't ever be the same again. She's okay."

He waved his hand before him. "Course, she's growing up too and changing all the time. My other kids, the ones from marriage number one, all of them are boys. Now I got these two little girls and I don't know what to expect." He glanced at me and raised his eyebrows. His tone had become confessional, almost pleading. "See, I don't really know."

He stopped, embarrassed and confused, and then began again as if he couldn't help it. "Her mother ain't worried. Either the two of them are fighting like wildcats, or they're buddies, hanging out together. Secret is, Caroline can't make Resa pay no mind. Maybe I'm old. But Resa's growing wild, and her mother don't really care, except for the sass. It's like she's watching the girl do what she never got the chance." He shrugged.

"Maybe this time I should talk to her," I said as if I were offering something. "You want me to?"

I sensed Jackson about to agree, as if maybe I could do him a favor. Then his mouth puckered into a sad shrewd little grin. "You foxin' with me, man. You foxin' with me." He wagged his head from side to side, not angry but bemused. "Maybe you come talk to her once Salter's locked away. But only if she say. And I doubt that. I really doubt that."

I had one more question. But before I could speak, a blue Camaro, five or six years old and jacked-up on over-size tires, rumbled slowly past us to the curb in front of Jackson's house.

"That's her. That's them," he said, lifting his bandaged arm.

His wife climbed out of the driver's seat, Teresa from the other side. They looked like sisters, like buddies, as Jackson said. Teresa's clothes were tighter and louder than her mother's—especially a skin-tight orange top—but the difference was only in degree. Two more passengers pulled themselves out of the cramped back seat. One was a tall, skinny man about Jackson's age with a beard. The other was a boy, late teens maybe, with a strut to match his good looks, a comb wedged in his hair, his jeans so loose they were slipping off his hips.

"Shit," said Leroy.

"Yeah?" I said.

"That little fuck's her cousin. Too goddamn full of hisself. Old man there's my brother-in-law from marriage number one. He's supposed to be on a job."

"Nice he's friendly with wife number two."

"Hunh," he grunted.

"So, what's the deal on your civil suit?" I asked. "You still after Salter's money?"

"Every cent. Every fucking penny for what I been

through," he growled. "How much you know, anyway? You know about the big bucks they come up with, their lies and all? What right's Salter got to that money? Might as well be stealing it, all the scam it is. All they need is prove he done it, he's a criminal, then our case is a piece of cake. Every cent."

We'd halted again. My hands were stuck in my pockets. "What if it doesn't play out that way? These things are hard to forecast—what if the jury doesn't convict?"

Jackson laughed. "How long you been back in town? Maybe you ain't heard. That ain't happenin'. Salter's dead meat."

I continued to stare out into space because I couldn't bring myself to look directly at him. I didn't want Jackson cluing me in on new evidence yet again, some late development my friends had failed to share.

His good hand patted my shoulder. Undeterred by my silence, his voice crowing at my ignorance, he continued. "Word's come down. Whatever it takes, they give it. All that publicity and the letters and the calls, it's made them cops look bad and it's made them angry. Only way to answer that shit is show they didn't fuck up from the start. Horses's mouth told me. We, Teresa anyway's, been practicing with the prosecutor."

My eyebrows must have jerked up in surprise.

"Hell, yeah—I know that ain't supposed to happen, but they don't call it practice, do they? Know who the prosecutor is? Hottest gun over there, and she's a Black girl. Get that? See how sweet that is? She's going to nail your brother's ass." Jackson laughed again, but it tailed into a sigh. As he trudged towards his bungalow he looked shrunken and worried and a little bit wistful.

Jackson was right. She was hot. That was apparent before the preliminary hearing even got under way. Joyce Kilburn, Assistant County Attorney. Thirty, maybe, her hair short and natural, crisp black linen suit, blue blouse. Her hands flickered through the briefs before her as she waited impatiently for the hearing to begin.

At the next table sat Jeremy Stanton, the city's, probably the state's, most successful liberal lawyer. Forty-fivish, he was tanned and fit, his ginger-curly hair greying at the temples as if for deliberate effect. His suit was nothing he could have bought off the rack in Iowa, a light summer grey, double-breasted, with a secret flick of crimson in the breast pocket. Low on his nose rode a pair of horn-rimmed granny glasses as he glanced through his own sheaf of papers.

The courtroom—two attorneys, court reporter, and me (a couple rows back and to one side)—rose when the judge entered five minutes later. Settling himself at the bench, Judge Theodore Stevens nodded at us without quite looking up. I'd been expecting a white-haired eminence, apostle of all Iowan virtues. Stevens, however, might have split the difference in age between the attorneys before him—forty or so—though already jowly, as if that were an occupational hazard. He wore no glasses; his eyes, heavy lidded, flicked quick and sharp between the papers he'd spread out before him and the advocates who awaited his pleasure.

"Miss Kilburn," he said, lifting his eyes to her, "why don't you proceed by stating your first Motion in Limine."

"Yes. Thank you, Your Honor." She was already standing, a hand resting on her notes. But she referred to them only to confirm what she already knew. "The State asks that, pursuant to Rule 412 of the Rules of Evidence, the Rape Shield Law, evidence of past sexual behavior, if any, of the victim in this case be excluded. Specifically, I believe it's indicated that the victim was on birth control pills. I ask that any such information be excluded." As she finished, she looked directly at the judge, her chin lifted slightly, before she returned to her seat.

"Mr. Stanton," the judge's gaze moved steadily, "is there any resistance to that motion?"

Stanton had risen already. "Yes, Your Honor. It may go

directly to the issue of the young woman's credibility." Stanton remained on his feet, looking expectantly at the judge.

Judge Stevens was taking notes and neither ceased nor looked up. "I'm going to sustain the motion in that regard. I see no reason why the Rape Shield Law should be set aside at this point. Let's have your second motion, Miss Kilburn."

"That the Court exclude testimony regarding what occurred at the City Police Department after the defendant's arrest." She paused here briefly. Her voice had been clear, steady, uninflected. Now she struck quickly, decisively. "Your Honor, the defendant was transported to the city jail for processing. While there he scuffled with police officers other than those involved in this case. Therefore, any evidence offered by the defense regarding this incident is immaterial."

"Mr. Stanton?" the judge said.

Stanton had already surged to his feet once more. "Your Honor, it's crucial that the defense be able to present testimony about what happened after Mr. Salter's arrest. I grant that this is unusual, but this is an unusual case in every respect. We intend to demonstrate that there was clear institutional bias against Mr. Salter. That bias resulted first in his being put into an incriminating position at the Jackson home and then in his subsequent beating in the police department."

Stanton leaned forward earnestly with both hands on the table. "Your Honor, Mr. Salter will claim that as a result of his political activities, the City Police Department deliberately placed him in an incriminating position. That defense must make relevant what would otherwise, in a more ordinary criminal case, be irrelevant. We ask that the jury be allowed to consider the fact that police officers broke Mr. Salter's jaw while he was in custody as evidence clearly pertaining to this case."

For the last couple of minutes Judge Stevens had ceased jotting notes. He listened to Jeremy Stanton, nodding, his lips slightly pursed, his eyes heavy-lidded. He tilted his head now at the prosecutor. "You care to respond?"

Kilburn took her time rising. She toyed with a pen in her hands. Even from where I was sitting I could spy a little smile of bemusement, almost disbelief as she began. "This blind allegation that the police deliberately placed the defendant in an incriminating position is just that—blind. There's no evidence to back it up, at least in any papers the defense has produced so far. But more important, whatever happened at the city jail was at a different time and a different place from the crimes for which we are trying Mr. Salter. To go into any of that would only distract the jury from the serious matters that occurred at the Jackson home."

Judge Stevens was scribbling again. "The motion is sustained."

Kilburn slipped back behind her desk, confident, on a roll. She lifted another sheet of paper for a quick glance. "Recently, Your Honor, the father of the young woman attacked by the defendant was involved in an incident at the Trailblaze Bookshop. Approximately two-thousand dollars worth of damage was done. My office has decided that prosecution is not warranted. Whatever happened or didn't happen at the bookstore is immaterial to the issues before the court."

Stanton stuck doggedly to his line of attack. "What happened at the bookstore, Your Honor, and, more to the point, what didn't happen afterwards—no arrest, no charges— powerfully demonstrates the institutional bias against Gabriel Salter. A jury should be allowed to know that no charges were filed against Leroy Jackson for committing what, in effect, was an act of terrorism against the offices of the Gabriel Salter Defense Committee."

The judge sighed and shook his head. "I agree that it's a unique case, but to introduce all sorts of extraneous matters would only make it more unique. I'm going to treat this as a straight-out criminal case and not permit that sort of evidence to be introduced. Period. Any other matters the State wishes to take up?"

"Just the last motion, Your Honor." Joyce Kilburn lifted another sheet. "The defendant claims that he has received information through the Freedom of Information Act, information collected by the FBI. On the list of defense witnesses are several FBI agents. The State moves that all such information is hearsay, irrelevant, and immaterial."

"Mr. Stanton?"

The defense attorney flapped his arms against his sides in frustration. He was clutching his glasses in one hand. "Again, Your Honor—Mr. Salter has been subject to the most virulent institutional bias. Shouldn't the jury have the right to know that in fact—in plain fact—the FBI believes Gabriel Salter important enough to spend time, energy, and effort tracking his whereabouts?"

The judge was shaking his head. He couldn't conceal his growing annoyance. "I simply can't see the relevance here. This is a criminal case," he said, tapping a pen against his desk with each word. "And I've got to tell you, Mr. Stanton, if we let a jury in the state of Iowa know that your client was investigated by the FBI, well, my guess is that would do him more harm than good. In your client's own interest, I ought to keep that sort of evidence out."

"Thank you, Your Honor," said Joyce Kilburn.

Jeremy Stanton's lips moved too, but I couldn't hear a sound.

I left the courthouse feeling that Gabriel had been mugged again, this time in broad daylight and with his attorney present.

At something past eleven that night I was back in my room. Earlier, Hilary had returned and left a message for me. Together we'd gone for dinner down the street. We both figured it was better than eating alone. That judgment marked no little advance in our relationship.

Yet it had been a fairly silent meal. I reported on the preliminary hearing. Hilary took the news gravely but without surprise. "You were skeptical about the whole conspiracy angle," she said. "Doesn't this about cinch it, that it's true, from the court on down?"

I shrugged.

For much of the meal Hilary seemed absent, thinking no doubt about her daughter and husband in Washington. She was probably still annoyed with me as well for declining the role as Gabriel's advocate in the press. I didn't mind. I was tired. And the situation seemed oddly familiar: the two of us, conspirators of a sort, separate from the rest and yet irritated with each other.

What came to me vividly as I stared across the plastic tablecloth was what good friends Hilary and I once had been. I sipped the grayish coffee while she stabbed at a rubbery meringue. In high school, our friendship had been a source of strength, a special kind of intimacy. Time and again, leaning over bad food in some diner, we'd anticipate each other's next thought, hardly having to speak it aloud, baffling other friends in the same booth. And now, as Hilary backed a dollop of whipped cream off to the side of her plate, I was sorry, maybe for the first time really sorry, that we'd screwed it up by marrying each other. We'd betrayed something more precious.

I could blame her, though I didn't dare. In all the years since, she'd never once admitted it. But even as I was acquiescing, I'd known well enough what her notion was: by marrying me, she could help bring me back to myself. She'd draw me out of the deep black pit into which I'd huddled. By then I'd already been discharged from the hospital, more or less physically healed. Marriage and a graduate degree. A sweet intention of hers, and a lousy idea.

I must have looked pretty morose over my coffee. "It's bad enough without you going morbid. Get a grip," said Hilary. A faint smile flickered across her lips.

Back in my room, I was sketching out plans for a busy day ahead. Earlier, I'd made an appointment to meet with Gabe's lawyer. I left a message for Brian Phillips at the paper. I also wanted to visit the Latin-American Club, not far from the Consolidated plant, to learn more about the immediate history surrounding Gabriel's arrest. The INS raid was one event I still knew nothing about. What about the protests he'd organized? I wanted to see if any more of Gabe's co-workers would talk about him or what had happened. With luck I might even run into John Martinez again.

The last item on the platter was to try Costello on night shift. It might be she could give something more, something new about what the cops did to Gabe. Maybe they were talking about that federal suit he'd filed against them. But really I just felt like touching base with her as well. The way she'd contacted me last time—the silly collision and spray of papers, the secret confab in her car—had lingered in my imagination. And my admiration for her had grown after Phillip's piece appeared. I was sure he couldn't have managed without her aid. In fact, I couldn't help but wonder whether she'd contacted him, whether the whole story, festering since before our own chat, hadn't been her idea.

When I called the central number and asked for Officer Costello this time I was switched immediately to her desk.

"Costello," she said.

"Hi," I said. "This is Jason Currant. Remember me?"

"I remember you." Her voice was brisk, wary. I pictured her glancing around to check whether anyone was watching. "You call earlier today?"

"That's right."

"Yeah, I got the message somebody wouldn't leave a message. They don't like that." Her tone finished with a sharp snap of irritation. "Where you calling from?"

"Winona Motel, near the airport. Look, I'm sorry about the call before—no hassle intended. I'm back in the city on assignment. Covering that same story. I wondered if maybe we could just chat a little bit, informally, you know? See if any developments—"

"Nope. No can do," she was cutting me off. "I'm not talking to nobody. You got any questions, try 'em on Hathaway." She slammed her phone down. I was left sitting on the edge of the bed in my shorts, holding a dead receiver.

Two hours later the phone rang. I fumbled my way out of a deep sleep, pawing towards the shrill sound and orienting myself in stages, first that I wasn't at home and then, after an instant's panic, remembering the motel. "Yeah, hello?" I mumbled.

"This is Costello." Even though her voice was low, it had a forced brightness.

"Okay," I said. I was lying in the dark, blinking, not want-ing to abandon the last fabric of grogginess. Once it was shredded, no matter how tired I was, sleep might never return.

"I been thinking about what you said. Maybe we should do that after all."

"Okay," I repeated. "You sure?" I crawled up onto my knees in a tangle of sheets and switched on the bedside lamp.

"Yeah," she said. "But it's gotta be when I get off."

"Yeah?"

"Yeah. Say five-thirty."

"You're kidding."

"Do I sound like I'm kidding?" she snapped.

"Okay, no sweat. I'm an early riser anyway. Where—same place?"

"No." She lowered her voice. "It needs to be further away from here. There's this coffee shop east on Locust, away from the river. Corner of Fifth. Can't miss it."

"Okay," I sighed, but she'd already hung up on me again.

When I drove away from the motel at a little past five, the sky was a dark steel grey, sitting like a cap on the night that remained fully fleshed among the trees and lampposts. I'd managed to get back to sleep after all, and I felt alert enough in the pre-dawn twilight to grow uneasy about the arrangement. My vague concern only sharpened as I passed through the still largely deserted business district, crossed the river, and drove by police headquarters. Why did Costello have to be so dramatic about staging her rendezvous?

Ahead of me, looming on a slight rise above the landscape, sat the capitol and government buildings commanding this bank of the river. Around them bloomed nothing at all. This was a low-slung wasteland of pawn shops, abandoned buildings, used-car lots with multicolor flags and few cars, all sprawling in a ragged skirt down the hill.

As Costello predicted, turning at Fifth I couldn't miss the place: a small strip of used furniture stalls, a barber, a pool room, and a coffee shop. I rolled down my window. In drifted the stench of the packing plants. The wind had swung out of the southeast. The early shift had started already at the Consolidated Plant less than a mile away.

But Costello hadn't bought coffee here anytime recently. Across the window, CAF..., had once been stenciled before being scraped off. Only a faint shadow remained. What with the grime, the tattered bills for circus and rock concerts, it had been a good while since anyone had brought their custom to this place.

Maybe it was the familiar rot in the air that poked up a good case of the jitters. That happened to me now and then. First time was out in the delta somewhere, where jitters seemed a perfectly natural response. But my clearest memory was actually from the Tokyo hospital. I'd be sitting up in bed, my leg stretched stiff and not quite belonging to me, and then I'd be trembling, shaking hard, amazed at what was happening to a body over which I had no control.

Now, I wasn't really shaking as I sat in my car. But a film of sweat blossomed on my chest and across my upper lip. I snorted at myself in disgust. Costello, after all, was simply being smart. No reason to invite suspicion by meeting openly. That wouldn't help either of us. And she probably didn't realize this greasy spoon had closed down for good.

Still, I didn't like the hour. I didn't like being so alone. At least on patrol there'd always be someone on point and wing, even if obscured by bush or darkness. A soft call, a curse or taunt or lousy joke in whispered reply, were reassuring, if no guarantee of safety.

Fed up with my own sense of melodrama, I climbed out and was surprised to notice that the door was open on the crack. I tried it. The door scraped hard on warped floorboards. I shoved it open with my shoulder and peered in. The only light drifted through patches of dirty glass. The depths of the shop lay hidden in gloom.

"Costello?" I called into the shadows, not too loud, not expecting any answer. I had no intention of entering. I'd wait on the sidewalk or, better still, in my car. It was already past five-thirty. If she ever did show, we could sit in the car and talk, or find some other place for coffee. Coffee I could use.

As I turned back towards the sidewalk, a voice called out. "Hey, Mister Currant. In here."

Now this is one of those inexplicable things. It might have been a joke—I knew instantly that it wasn't even a woman's voice, let alone Costello's. It sounded more like some spoof of a drag queen, a man only half-trying to sound like a woman. But what's unaccountable, especially given the willies already chasing up and down my spine, is that I swung around, stuck my head through the door, peering to discover who was calling me. I was striding through the looking glass of my own free will.

For a long moment, everything inside the shop seemed as it had before—dark, silent, deserted. I almost wondered if I'd imagined the weird summons. Once more I began to turn away.

A claw snatched at my arm. I was so startled, I fell back a step and almost tugged loose. But I was off balance, and my left arm was clutched more firmly, twisted hard, and I was dragged further into the darkness. As I stumbled across the broken floor, the door slammed. I lurched around. Four dark shapes appeared between me and the exit. None was Costello. That much I knew at once.

Perhaps because the sun was rising and more light leaked through the dirty front window, my eyes adjusted quickly. But I couldn't really make out the faces of the men in front of me. Their backs were to the dim light. I could tell they were wearing civvies—a lumberjack shirt, a baseball jacket—but I also knew, by the way they held themselves, by the way they set their feet, what was going on.

"You're cops," I said with as much disinterest as I could muster.

One barked with a laugh.

"Let's pretend for the time being we're not," said another voice, hoarse and full of good cheer, an older man.

"Okay," I said, as if playing the game in good humor as well. "What's going on?"

Just then I spotted a baseball bat leaning next to the door. My mouth went dry even before I recalled, in the next instant, the pictures of George Stephoro. And I remembered Gabriel staggering towards me out of the police holding pen, his face swollen and bruised.

My mouth was parched, but my shirt clung to me, cold with sweat. I'd been afraid before. And fear greeted me like an old comrade, no preliminaries but a swift unfurling through my limbs. I wasn't trembling yet. I didn't want them to see me shake.

"We thought it was time we had a little chat with you," the older voice said.

"Okay," I said. My voice sounded different, no longer disinterested, and there was nothing I could do about it.

"You shouldn't of come out again." Another man spoke. "You got no business here."

"Only doing my job. I'm on assignment this time."

"Who the fuck cares?" said one.

"Assignment for who? Some fuck paper out east for christsake, as if anyone there gives a damn." This was the older one again, his good cheer grown detached and nasty. "You're Salter's brother. That's why you're here."

Before I could deny it, he went on. "Point is, we don't give a fuck. But you shouldn't bother Costello. She don't need to be talking to no more reporters, if you get my drift."

"Look, you know I had nothing to do with that weekend piece. That was local. What's it got to do with me?"

"Listen, fuckhead—it's got to do with you because we say so. Because you're calling Costello. Because whatever reason you're supposed to be here, it's to cause trouble." This from a square-headed kid in the baseball jacket.

"See, we can't do nothing to Phillips, our distinguished local journalist. The one who smeared us in the Sunday paper," said the older man, the leader. "Not that we wouldn't like to shove that story back up his ass. Our bosses, they won't let us visit him. They say whatever he does, he's no real threat. But see, you don't belong. We don't owe you shit. And you can't touch us."

"This is nuts," I said. "What're you planning to do?"

He seemed to muse. "I don't know. We're only bothering to talk so you'll appreciate what's happening. See, we want you to understand. What'll we do? I guess we'll just have to improvise. Play a little White man's jazz."

One of the others snorted.

Baseball Jacket reached down and hefted the bat. He

swiped it once or twice through the air with one hand as if he were hitting fungos.

"Look," I said again. And I had nothing else to say. There was nothing, no one, to appeal to. Certainly not their god or their sympathy or their sense of duty. I held nothing over them. I couldn't touch them.

"What do you want me to do?" I asked.

"Sweat. Sweat good," said one.

"What do you think would do you any good?" asked the lumberjack shirt with philosophical curiosity.

They wanted me to beg. They wanted me to fall on my knees and plead. Maybe that would get them to hold off. Maybe not. I was thinking about it. I wasn't opposed in principle. Intellectually, sure, I was willing. I was plenty scared. If pleading would save me, I was willing.

Except that I couldn't do it. Something in me rebelled. I stood frozen, scared to the quick, yet unable to move or mumble or kneel.

I was concentrating on the baseball bat as if it were a hot iron, when the first blow blind-sided me, fist slamming my ear, pitching me off balance and into the arms of a mate. My weak left knee buckled and distracted me from the radiating warmth around my ear. Worry as much as pain made me clutch at the wounded leg, but from out of the dusk a forearm caught me square in the jaw. I reeled back, stumbled to the floor, and then the four of them gathered in a circle over me as I rested on my knees.

They were businesslike. They were methodical. With a deft chop to my kidney, the bat rolled me, the pain heaving me slowly over onto my back, opening me to them like a crab smashed against the rocks. I groaned as the kidney ache sickened through me.

Now the blows came more steadily, more deliberately. It was a carefully calibrated operation. The bat flicked in with a kind of exclamatory delicacy, articulating itself against my shoulder, into my hip, cracking—I heard the sound even as it seared the breath out of my lungs—two ribs under my left arm. The pain began to surge in waves separate from individual blows. Each wave carried the tide higher.

A work boot gently nudged my head so that I was staring into the darkness above. A short, sharp kick snapped my skull loose. It rattled back against the floor. Blood leaked into my mouth. My ear, my head were ringing with sound and pain.

"Stop," I grunted. "Uncle," I gasped.

Was one of them humming as he worked?

The pain hadn't dug deep enough yet to cut away the root of fear. I was still afraid. But my attention now was on patience, on waiting them out, on enduring.

But they were patient too. They didn't lose interest even when I'd gone limp, when I no longer tried to protect myself—what was left to protect?—and my body only recoiled in reflex to the thudding shots.

My concentration dissolved in the flood. I didn't lose consciousness; I just wasn't paying attention any longer.

I didn't know they weren't going to kill me until they hadn't killed me.

At some point they weren't beating me anymore. I noticed that. They'd left the door open behind them. It was sunny, very bright through the door. I noticed that. Through the door I could see the car I'd rented parked against the curb and facing the wrong way. Some cop had tucked a bright yellow citation under the wiper. I noticed.

I lay on the floor and concentrated on breathing. From moment to moment I could do that. I knew what had happened to me. I knew I had a concussion. I'd had one before. I got it when the medic lurched with me towards the chopper and my head flopped against what?

Little by little, I gathered myself. Didn't want to think about what the separate pieces of my body were up to. Actually climbed to my knees, I think. Anyway made it to the door. See, the idea was I could make it to the car. And I could drive.

Driving wouldn't be so tough. But I knew enough to be smart. I mean, I was planning to find a hospital, sure. What with my ribs. I knew about them. And something about my ear. And I had a concussion. I knew that.

But I was waiting on the sidewalk. Next to the car. The plan was to drive. But I was waiting. No need to rush. I was clutching a bent signpost. A wave of nausea caught me and hurled me and swept blood and acid up out of my gut. My ribs, jesus, the heaving tore my ribs apart. But, oh, afterwards, a moment of calm, me resting my head against the base of the signpost. The signpost was bent and painted green but bubbling with rust from underneath the green paint.

A flame bit into my shoulder. I jerked clear of the hand squeezing me, arm to my face. Had they returned? Yes—a cop. No—white helmet and shades. No eyes. Leaning over me, disgust on his lips, he's rising now and speaking into the radio pinned to his shoulder.

So I'm crawling again towards the car. If I can maybe pull free of this bent green signpost and sidle into the car, maybe he'll think I'm okay and I can get away. Maybe he'll let me go if I pay the citation on the windshield. I'm up on one arm and he's stepped between me and the car and I'm leaning against the bent green signpost. There's a small pool of vomit close to my hand on the pavement.

Emergency squad swoops down. I'd rather drive myself. They roll me onto a stretcher and into the ambulance. Every little bob and jerk flares the pain. Tears are coming. I don't think they were there before. And we're moving, and the motion of the ambulance is swaying me and I'm going to be sick again and I can't hear any siren and I can't hear the chopper blades. Where's the evac? I'd like to sleep, but the medic keeps shaking my arm. Won't let me sleep.

In ER, I remember the doctor. What's just happened, each moment by moment, it's gone fuzzy already and I can't recall and it's gone. But I remember the doctor. Young schoolmarm. I've seen her before. I'm smiling. Her lips press tight together, she's so serious. Needs to smile. Needs to lighten up. She's very handsome and stern, I think. She doesn't remember me, I think.

I'm awake. I think I was asleep. But here's the doctor again or still. She's bending over me. "Know where you are, Mr. Currant?" she says.

I smile. "Broadlawns, right?" I mumble. I'm proud to show I can do it. But my tongue is thick, and my lips are sore, and my jaw feels heavy and stiff, like it's not really mine but a new one I've got to break in. Taste of blood proves it's new. "Broadlawns ER, right?" I say. Have I just said that?

"That's where they brought you," she says. "We've got you in I.C.U. right now, just so we can observe you for a while. You're beat up pretty good, but you're not critical."

"Feels critical." I'm proud because I can smile and joke even if she can't see it.

"Would you like us to notify anyone?" she's saying. "We found your wallet. You want us to call your newspaper in Baltimore?"

I try shaking my head but that's a bad idea. The room blurs and spins and I'm afraid I'm going to vomit but there isn't anything to vomit. I breathe, not too deep, can't breathe deep.

"My wife's at the motel. Winona Motel. You can let her know." I know I've got it wrong before I finish getting it out, but it's too hard to explain, and if Hilary is mad later, so okay.

Nurse is shaking my arm, well, stroking it. I didn't think they made them wear the little hats anymore. Maybe she's a nun or something. I miss the doctor. "Mr. Currant. You've got a concussion, Mr. Currant."

"I know that," I say patiently. I know that because what she's said is already blurring.

"You're registered at the motel in a single, Mr. Currant, and there's no one else by that name."

I'm breathing carefully, considering the economy of explaining, effort versus pay-off. "Her name's Salter," I say. "If she's not there, try her brother. In town. Salter. Gabriel Salter." I'm looking at the old woman's face but the name doesn't register as anything special. Or she's giving nothing away.

Chapter IX

When I woke again I was lost. I had no idea where I was
lying. What I remembered first was fear, and fear swept over
me in a great bruising rush. My teeth began to chatter, but I
wasn't cold. I seemed to be floating, my head riding and dipping like a bobbin on a deep, still pool. My hand crept out
from under the sheet and groped for anchor. It banged
against the cold metal rail of a hospital bed and clutched the
rail tight.

So, I was in a hospital. The idea of hospital was familiar,
almost welcoming, yet memories of hospital also awakened
a gray dread that weighed with suffocating force on my
chest. I thrashed a leg and tried to lift myself, but a grinding
jab in my ribs, hot with pain at each breath, returned me,
slowly, slowly, then with another rush, to the fact of Iowa.

I lay back, panting. My hand still clung to the bed rail.
They'd moved me out of Intensive Care. I knew that because
I was connected to nothing. No monitors. Not even an i.v.
drip.

Another bed blocked the window, but I couldn't tell if the
bed was occupied—I assumed it was—because long white
curtains hanging from tracks in the ceiling draped it protectively like a cocoon. Because I could get no clue from the
window, there was no telling whether it was day or night.

Our lights were dimmed. The door stood on the crack to the corridor where the light was sharper. And I could hear nothing, which in a hospital usually means it's late.

Grey Navarro. Her I recognized. I should have been surprised and wasn't surprised. It seemed natural, it seemed inevitable that she be here. Had she been conjured by dreams I'd already forgotten? She was leaning on the bed rail but not looking at me. How long had she been standing sentry? Her profile was broad and expressionless, reminding me this time not so much of a hawk but a cat, a dangerous dark-eyed cat.

She didn't know I was awake. She was staring across the room and I turned my head to see. The sudden motion set the world spinning and I had to close my eyes again against the vertigo, to let it settle away like sediment swirling in water.

After a steadying moment, I opened my eyes. The other bed was empty and the curtains were drawn clear. The darkness beyond the window wasn't night but a rainy morning. In swirls and gleams the glass reflected the room's dimness. When I swung my head back, more gently, Grey was studying me.

"Hell of a place to wake up," I said. I meant to sound smart-assed, but the words slurred. My tongue was thick and dry. I flopped an arm suggestively at the pitcher on the night stand. Grey poured a glass of water. She started to hand it to me. I fumbled. With a grim smile now, suspicious of my clumsiness, she held the glass to my lips. The water was warm but wonderful. I drank and lifted a hand to help her and emptied the glass.

"You look pretty rough."

It took me an instant to realize she'd spoken. A distant thrumming in the corridor interfered. Her voice negotiated a great distance. She smoothed her hand on my forehead as if checking for fever. Her fingers were cool and dry.

"I feel pretty rough." Having said that, I began an inventory. Until then I hadn't been able to focus or I'd been preoccupied with the concussion or I hadn't really wanted to know. Carefully, I turned my head away again to concentrate. Just that slight movement hurt. My left eye was swollen nearly shut, but I could see enough to tell that the eye itself was functioning. My lips were swollen too and cracked. The water had stung them and reawakened the taste of blood. And my left ear felt hot and enormous.

What the hell was making that noise?—Why would they allow it in a hospital? The pulsing hum from the corridor was annoying, a background buzz I struggled to ignore the way I had the constant roar in the meat-packing plant. But I noticed that Grey seemed indifferent to the sound. Which tipped me (my mind was laboring slowly): the thrumming had to be a private affair between my ears, a constituent of the dizziness and dull headache that wouldn't disappear either.

My arms and legs, my buttocks and my groin all ached from the pummeling. I felt like a slab of tenderized meat. Having seen Gabriel three months earlier, I could imagine some of the welts and bruises. But only the relentless sharp stabs in my side seemed like anything to worry about.

"I don't suppose you've seen the doctor?" I asked.

Grey nodded. "She was leaving the room when I arrived, maybe half an hour ago."

"And?"

"And, you've got a concussion and a couple of cracked ribs. Other than that she says you're basically okay."

I grunted. "She should feel the way I do and say it's okay."

"She thought I was Hilary and she thought Hilary was still married to you." It might have been a good joke, but Grey didn't sound particularly amused.

"Where the hell is Hilary? How come it's you?" I tried to sound impatient.

"When did this happen?" she countered.

"In the morning—five-thirty about," I said. "But what's today? How long have I been here?"

"Friday. You must have lost a little over twenty-four hours." She leaned over and touched my cheek again, gently but no caress either, as though to make sure my wounds weren't a hoax of greasepaint and powder. "So who chewed you over this way?" Her voice was deep.

"Some of Gabe's friends. You know, the ones in uniform. Except they weren't actually in uniform." I tried to grin. "How about it?—You plastering my face all over the billboards too?"

"You deserve what you got any more than Gabriel did?" she asked.

"Nobody deserves this," I said.

For a while neither of us spoke. We were each taking stock.

"They probably tried to contact Hilary yesterday or last night," Grey mused. "But she was with us at the bookstore and with the lawyers too. When they called our house this morning Gabe and Simon were already gone for a breakfast meeting with out-of-town supporters. The hospital wouldn't tell me anything on the phone. Anyway, I don't know where Hilary is. I tried the motel, then decided to come by here myself."

"Thanks," I said. My mouth was dry again. How long had she been here? The early part of our conversation was already blurring, though the present instant seemed sharp enough. What I was blindingly aware of—perhaps I'd never been aware before and, if I had, that was so far away it didn't matter—was Grey, the simple fact of her. Maybe it took the beating so I could see. Stark, with her strong slightly hooked nose and her dark eyes and the hard, thin mouth, a warrior's mouth. The awareness hurt like any other bone-deep bruise. I turned my head away.

"I better be going," she was saying. "I'm supposed to plan a rally for Sunday. When I find Hilary, I'll pass on the news. She'll fetch anything you need."

"Hold on—don't go," I cried, panic seizing me. Being left alone in the hospital terrified me. "I'm okay. A little beat up is all. Just help me check out, all right? You any idea what they did with my car?"

She stopped and looked back at me sharply. "Doctor says you need another couple days. A concussion's nothing to mess with."

"Yeah, I know. But it's not my first time—I can live with it. Get the doctor if you like while I'm dressing."

"No way," she said with a shake of her head. "It's your choice if you want to take the chance. But seems to me you should stay put another day at least. Your motel's got no one to look after you. And the rest of us are too busy for playing nursemaid." She paused only briefly. "It's not like you're doing us any good out there."

Ignoring her, I propped myself on one arm, slowly, carefully, trying to keep my head in line with my body, fighting the dizziness. With one hand I lifted the bed rail and let it drop clear and, slowly, carefully, swung my feet over the side of the bed. They were my feet. I saw the hem of a hospital gown half-way down my bare legs. "My clothes are probably in that closet," I said. "Get them for me, would you?"

My shirt was only lightly wrinkled, with a splotch or two of blood on the collar, not much worse than a shaving accident. A small stain peeked out from the inside thigh of my pants. Probably the remnant of my own vomit. All in all, the clothes looked less shabby than I felt.

Grey was waiting for me impatiently at the nurse's station. I hadn't managed to tie my laces. I'd jammed them in the sides of the shoes. My balance wasn't good, but I could fake it. Next to her stood the doctor. Dr. Harris—that was it—I remembered at the same moment I spied the name tag on her smock. She glanced up at me with a frown from the charts she was reading.

"You know what you're doing, Mr. Currant?" she demanded.

I leaned nonchalantly on the counter. "More or less."

"Doesn't sound like it to me." She was studying the charts again and shaking her head dismissively.

"Thanks—I appreciate the concern. But I'm not a big fan of hospitals. I've spent too much time in them." I was smiling or making a stab at it, but my bad knee would hardly bear my weight and my head was light and dizzy. I admired how well I was able to fake it.

"You want to be macho, fine by me," Dr. Harris said with her clipped precision. "But you're signing a waiver. You won't be my responsibility any more. No coming back with some malpractice trash."

"Promise," I said, raising my palm.

"Sign the forms and let's go, if you still want that lift," said Grey.

By the time we pulled up to the motel in her ancient pick-up, I suspected I'd made a mistake after all. I was seasick from rocking along the highway. Blood pulsed great thuds in my head. I didn't want her to guess.

Despite my knee, which had locked again, and the thrumming still swelling in my ears, I managed to climb down from the high cab. "Thanks a bunch," I cried with a hearty smile and a wave. I don't suppose it was very convincing. I never quite looked up at Grey. Did she say anything? I had to concentrate.

I steered slowly, carefully, through the motel lobby. As I approached my room, I drew the key from my pocket gently—I didn't want to risk dropping it.

Plunging through the door, I staggered towards the bed. I noticed the message light glowing on the phone. Too fast, too fast I fell, the world aflame and spinning. I held on tight.

At first, frightened of consciousness, I didn't open my eyes. But thirst more than curiosity flushed me into the open. I lay on my stomach. Warily, tangling sheets and blanket, I began to roll in slow stages onto my back. I twisted onto my side and agony froze me—I'd forgotten the ribs. I couldn't go back without grinding shards of pain, couldn't go forward, couldn't balance where I was. At last I thrust through a blinding stab and over onto my back. I lay panting, bathed in fresh sweat.

But at least the rocking and the pain didn't trigger a fresh wave of nausea. For that I was grateful. After a few moments I lifted an arm and looked at my watch. Quarter past one. I turned my head to the window. Through the heavy drapes filtered the weak light of a rainy afternoon. This time I'd only slept for a few hours.

As long as I didn't swing it too sharply, my head remained clear. The thrumming had retreated to a distance where I could ignore it. Gradually, I pushed myself up and limped stiffly into the bathroom to use the toilet and fill a glass with water. The journey felt like an achievement, a moral victory. But when I returned to bed I was weak and gasping again, and nausea threatened on the horizon, like a line of squalls above a sea only recently calmed.

I lay on a high bank of pillows. The motel room was very dim but I could see it with an astonishing clarity: the vague physical reality of the tv set, the single peeling strip of veneer on the bureau. I'd never noticed them before, never known how to look. Anticipating what lay ahead, I was afraid to leave because the world would be too bright, too new, terrifying.

Weak as a baby, I stared out into a dim world that had been transformed. Even in the evac hospital on my way to Japan, I hadn't felt I was seeing with new eyes. Oh, I'd been plenty scared then, and furious, furious with a rage that stunned me. Ferocious, it brimmed up out of a cauldron that was deeper and wider than anything I could contain. I didn't know where such rage came from, hadn't known I had it in me. Perhaps rage is something we all carry out of the womb and hide away to protect ourselves; perhaps I'd picked it up like a bug in the swamps. I wanted to holler from my belly. I wanted to smash everything in that ward and in that hospital. I wanted to smash someone, gut someone. The anger surged and fell, surged and fell.

And that's also, the evac hospital, where I discovered I was going to die. Even though the possibility had terrified me night and day while wading through the paddies, I'd never really believed it. I'd be waist deep in muck and watching other men die and scared to the jitters that shook me, and yet dying itself didn't seem real. Shrapnel, nearly severing one leg at the knee, rescued me from the booby-traps and sappers. But in the evac it occurred to me with simplest clarity that I was going to die. Though she may never have known what to blame precisely, Hilary was to deal with the effects of that discovery for a long time to come.

But for all the mighty change in the world around me, I looked out from the other hospitals in Japan and in Virginia with weary indifference. I had my rage and my depression (how I loathe that clinical dismissal of utter, scorched despair), but nothing of any consequence seemed altered. The country was spinning too fast in 1971 to trouble itself with my skepticism.

Without leaving Room 27 of the motel, however, I realized that the world had indeed been transformed, if this time only for me. Those four cops had, quite intentionally, ushered me into a first-hand encounter with my own powerlessness. It was a lesson. Sure, I knew that a stray accident could strike me down at any instant. I knew that sooner or later I'd tumble into the grave of my own momentum. (To this I'd grown grudgingly reconciled.) But four cops had just beaten the shit out of me: it had nothing to do with fate and I was powerless to do anything about it.

Though even that wasn't the point. I was grateful. Yes indeed. Nearly weepy with gratitude. They could have been more thorough. They could have maimed me. They could have killed me. Nothing I did prevented it; there was nothing I could imagine doing for the sake of justice or revenge. I was grateful to them for not killing me.

An illumination, not a conversion. No violent urge seized me to rush from my sick bed and swear allegiance to Gabriel's cause. I wish one had. At least I'd have shared company with other believers. Instead, I lay on my bed and I was shivering. Maybe the jitters had me again. I clutched the mattress to keep my head still, to fight off the dizziness that rocked me. The boat rocked on the sea, cut loose of anchor, floating free and alone once more.

Neither asleep nor quite awake, I noticed a thudding. It had been going on a while. "Yeah—come in," I called to the door, hoping that was it. Maybe Hilary had finally received the news.

The handle jiggled. "Can't," she called. "It's locked."

What does she expect? I wondered, even as I grasped it wasn't Hilary.

"Hold on." I pushed myself up with an arm and sat on the edge of the bed. My head felt incrementally clearer than before. I pushed a hand through my hair and rubbed my eyes.

"You coming?" she called. "You want me to get the manager?"

"Hold on," I repeated angrily. "Jesus," I muttered. Irritably, I padded into the bathroom for a drink of water. I was still wearing my rumpled pants and shirt from the day before. One of my socks had slipped off somewhere along the way. I pulled the door open, saw Grey standing there, nodded, and turned back to the bed. For whatever reason I was both thrilled and annoyed that she'd returned. No— petulant. I wanted to make her feel bad too.

She picked up on that. "Hey, you rather be left alone? Just say so." Her voice was cross. She hadn't passed the threshold.

I made it to the bed. My brain was still bobbing like a buoy inside a shell. "No," I said to the bureau. "Come on in," I said. If she was cross, I was cross. But I was also eager for her to stay.

She didn't seem inclined to do me the favor. But after a moment she closed the door. "You looked pretty lousy when I dropped you off," she was saying. She turned and stood in the middle of the room, arms crossed on her chest. She was wearing loose-fitting blue work pants and a plain white shirt, collar open, sleeves rolled up. Had she worn them in the morning?

"I thought I'd better stop back and make sure you hadn't passed out on the floor or something. We don't need any more distractions before the trial starts."

"Thanks for your concern." I lifted a hand in acknowl- edgment. "But I'm fine. Heaven forbid I should distract anyone."

"Fine then." Her eyes flashed, dark with irritation. I expected her to stalk out of the room. I didn't want her to. But she was facing me squarely, as if remaining were a mat- ter of sheer stubbornness, a battle of wills between us.

Suddenly, the uneasy suspicion smoldered once again that Grey and I had faced each other this way before. Surely we were old adversaries. We belonged to different worlds, but the strangeness, the chasm was precisely what was familiar. My concussion may have been toying with me. But the vivid echo, the harsh echo of recognition was dis- orienting. It flashed so hot I believed she heard it too. And as it faded my strength subsided as well. I was too weak for the struggle.

"You're here," I said with a shrug.

"That's right," she said. "I'm here." Nodding to herself, she dragged a chair over and sat facing me just beyond arm's reach. "How do you feel?"

"I'm sore. Could be worse."

"You look awful." She said it as a matter of fact.

"Thanks." My ribs were aching again, worse with each breath. "You mind if I lie back? Sitting's not all that easy."

Slowly, carefully, I eased myself back onto the bank of pillows.

"You really do look like hell," she said. "The hospital was the place for you."

"Couldn't stay. I have this thing about hospitals."

"Yeah, but who's supposed to take care of you?"

"I take care of me."

"A great job you do." Impatient, Grey was already glancing about the room. She rose and disappeared into the bathroom. When she returned she was carrying a wet washcloth and a towel. I struggled up on an arm.

"You lie still," she ordered.

I didn't rise any further. But propped awkwardly on an arm, I didn't fall back either.

"Okay," she said, "the shirt's got to go." She put a knee on the bed and leaned across. Roughly, she unbuttoned my shirt. To my surprise, none of the buttons tore free. The shirt peeled away, wrinkled and bloody and grey. I shivered.

"Now the pants," she said.

"I can do the pants." For modesty's sake I untangled a sheet and pulled it up. But whichever way I moved, my ribs burned, hotter and hotter. I was gasping. I grunted, I heaved, I rolled. I managed to force the pants down to my thighs. I was sweating again.

"Give it up," she said. She unceremoniously stripped the sheet down to the foot of the bed and, taking each cuff in hand, tugged my pants off in a series of short jerks.

"Careful. That hurts like hell."

I was left in my shorts and didn't have the dexterity to recover the sheet.

"I never pretended to be a nurse. You're only making it worse." With a quick yank, she freed the single sock from my foot and dropped it. "This'll help." Sitting on the side of the bed, she wiped the cloth across my forehead, my nose, my cheeks. She might have been more gentle, but it felt cool and wonderful. I closed my eyes.

"Hold on," she said and went quickly to soak the cloth once more. Returning, she gave me a quick sponging, chest and legs, turning me gently for a few swipes at my back.

And with each rough stroke, Grey Navarro came alive for me. The cloth burned with the simple reality of her. Yes, I'd sensed all along a faint spark of recognition, but it was like spying someone I'd once known across a great gulf.

Here she was, bending close over me. Nothing eerie, nothing mystical. I could feel the breath from her nostrils. As she reached back for the towel, her long braid brushed my chest. I noticed that individual strands of hair had gone gray, filigrees of silver amidst the raven black. Her throat was long, her arms strong. Her chest was flat within the loose white shirt. She wore no perfume. But I could smell her own scent, faint and distant, a smoky sweetness.

She spread the cool cloth over my forehead and eyes. I was shivering as she patted me dry with the towel. At last she pulled the sheet back over me. I sensed her wrestling with a blanket and then it fell like a drape across me too.

"Thanks," I murmured, my eyes still closed under the damp cloth. As I grew warmer my body, part of it, respond-ed to the recollection of her rough swipes. I hoped the blan-ket would conceal just how fully her friction had kindled me. I heard her settle back into the chair, but she didn't speak.

"I got something to tell you," I said.

"Okay," she said, but she sounded suspicious.

"You know how before, a couple months ago, you were

going on about storytellers?"

"I remember." Her voice was low. I was reminded again of other voices, other tongues haunting hers like faint shadows.

"So, here's the thing—you were wrong," I said. "I've been thinking about that, in the hospital and in this room."

"Seems unlikely you can think straight about anything, the shape you're in."

"No, I have been. It's a little ragged maybe. But you were wrong. That's what I understand now. Whether you're talking about old folks on the reservation or about me, since you were generous enough to include me in the fraternity. See, unless we're telling the story they want to hear—or allow us to tell because it doesn't really harm them—we're only speaking to ourselves, which hardly counts."

"Who wants to hear?"

"Them." I pulled the rag off my eyes. "Them that's got the guns and the baseball bats and the badges and the payrolls. They decide."

"No." Her jaw was stiff as she shook her head. "The stories survive. Our memories do. They make us who we are."

"Bullshit," I said fiercely, and suddenly I was near tears, and it was the concussion again. "Stories aren't weapons and storytellers aren't warriors. That's what I'm saying."

She screwed up her mouth scornfully. "After what they did to you, I thought you'd want to make them listen."

I turned my head to her. "What could I say? Where's the proof? Who would care or notice? I might as well go into a closet and shout at the top of my lungs." My head fell back again and my ribs ached. I was thinking of Brian Phillips. He knew the rules and just how far to push them and what angle to take. He'd go far.

She was shaking her head. "We do better than that."

"Do you?" I was panting shallowly as I stared at her. "It's seeming to me that all these damn stories remind the losers of what they've lost. Fucking pipe-dreams of fucking vanished glory."

She looked grim, her dark, dark eyes stern and very deep. The birthmark on her cheek blazed like a signature.

Like a strand of spider's web before a gust of wind, the thread of my outrage suddenly disappeared. "Jesus, Grey," I said softly.

"You always talk so much?" she asked, disgusted rather than angry. "You talk too damn much. Save your words for when you need them."

I knew I was going to say it, and I'd sworn not to say it, and if everything hadn't been thoroughly screwed up before, now it was about to be.

"Yeah," I murmured. It was the best I could manage.

It took an instant to register—she cocked her head—and then I saw she understood. She tensed, her jaw tightened, and far away in her eyes I spied a flicker of something hidden away, a reserve, a fear. She retreated a thousand miles. Then her mouth twitched, surprise melting into amusement, and she was merely a woman sitting next to me. Her face warmed as if a storm had blown past. "You're not up to it," she said. Her lips twitched.

The twitch made me ache. "Probably not," I admitted.

"I don't do quick fucks," she said.

I nodded. We both took a breath and looked at each other.

"Why hasn't Hilary come?" I asked, content to change the subject. I'd declared myself, got it off my chest, and felt relieved if also vanquished.

Grey blinked twice and glanced away. I'd never seen her off balance. "I haven't told her yet."

"Yeah?" I said.

I was aware that neither of us had mentioned Gabriel.

After Grey left, I dozed for a while. And when I woke again in the early evening, I was famished, so hungry that my stomach was actually cramping. My body was waking to the fact that I'd gone two days without feeding it. This gnawing was an unpleasant addition to my other aches and complaints.

The motel coffee shop was possible—I figured I could manage it. But I didn't relish the idea of appearing alone in public looking the way I did. Even if no one said anything sympathetic or asked solicitous questions or let me overhear nasty surmises, I'd be the object of scrutiny. I might even scare a kid or two. Someone suspicious might call the cops. That was an attractive thought.

Instead, I called out for pizza. When it arrived, I swallowed a couple of slices, hardly bothering to chew. But my stomach rebelled with a violent ache, nausea threatening again, and I abandoned the rest. Sipping carefully at a soda, I yearned for a bottle of bourbon, dangerous though that might be.

Several messages from Brenda Glascoe in a sequence of growing impatience were waiting for me when I finally checked with the front desk. Two from Hilary, wondering where I was. One from Phyllis, no message. I called the paper in Baltimore, but it was late night on a Friday and Glascoe was already gone. I left a recorded message in turn. It didn't give much away, no mention of the personal attention that the city cops had paid me, but it reassured her that I was building a good story. It sounded convincing. Pure fiction could be part of my job too.

The rental agency at the airport was still open when I called. I'd been taken ill, I explained, and forced to abandon the car. (Perhaps it was still sitting faithfully outside the coffee shop collecting yellow citations.) The girl had no idea what I was talking about; she'd heard nothing about any car missing its driver. She'd have someone check.

As I lifted the receiver again to call Phyllis, someone knocked sharply at the door and I hung up. I knew who I hoped it would be. I slipped gingerly off the bed and was half-way across the room when Hilary called out, "Jason? Jason, are you in there?" and rapped hard at the door again. Her voice froze me. I didn't think about it, didn't consider, I just froze.

Hilary had been next on the list. I was going to ring her room. But now I tip-toed quietly—and tip-toeing with cracked ribs is no cheap trick—back to the bed. I didn't want her to find me just yet. Not that I didn't feel naughty too, like a kid caught with dope or dirty magazines. I was tempted to hide under the covers.

From the angle of my bed I could see her shadow under the door. I all but held my breath as she rapped one last frustrated time and then stalked off down the corridor.

I'd dozed again with the light on. A soft tapping at the door woke me. I couldn't locate my watch. "Jason." The call was low, hardly more than a dark whisper. Still groggy, I pulled on a robe and rolled heavily onto my feet. The world spun as I lumbered towards the door. I grasped for the handle to catch me.

Grey was standing in the corridor. As I gathered my balance, I realized it was very late. Heavy silence had settled through the motel, broken just then by the rattle of an ice machine far away. Grey slipped by me.

"Come in," I said.

"If I'm disturbing you," she said. She turned, arms hugging herself, still wearing her white shirt and baggy work pants.

"As a matter of fact I was asleep. What do you expect at this hour?" I faked knowing what hour it was.

Tension had ignited between us in a glance. We faced each other impatiently. I suspected she was about to stalk off again, and that was all right by me, just fine. I tried to believe it.

"Look—I don't get you at all. You don't make any sense

to me," she said harshly.

"Likewise."

"No, I mean it. I can't decide who you are. That's why I came back. Couldn't get it out of my head. Are you a coward? Or for sale? Or what? How can you see what you've seen in the war, and write about the stuff you do in Baltimore—homeless people, working people—and now go through all this out here, and not be with us?" She shook her head and her dark braid flew back and forth. "You can't be one of them. That much I think's not possible."

I sighed. "Mind if I sit? I'm not up to prime yet."

"Sorry," she said and almost looked it.

Gently, I lowered myself onto the edge of the bed and ran a hand through my hair. "It's just the way I'm put together. I'm not a believer," I said.

"Of anything?"

"Of anything. Maybe I envy you and Gabriel. Sometimes I do. But the more I see, the less I'm able to believe in anything larger than helping someone hungry be fed or someone else keep a job. Not that I do even that much. I earn my keep titillating people into buying a paper. Anyway, the larger stuff you peddle—the coming revolution—that's not for me."

Grey smoldered with exasperation. "No—you can't slice it that way. Either everything changes or nothing does."

I shrugged.

She scowled. She sighed. "You feeling any better?"

"Sort of. The clearer my head, the sorer my body."

She nodded, not quite listening, not quite looking at me.

"You haven't mentioned anything to Hilary yet, I suppose?" I neglected to mention Hilary hammering at my door.

She turned her eyes directly to me, her exasperation ripe once more. "Look, I haven't seen her since this morning. I'm sorry I didn't mention it then, all right? I don't know where she's been, probably out with Gabriel again. By now they've walked half the city and back."

"At this hour?"

"You know the family. Trouble comes and they huddle. They lock the rest of the world out."

"But not you."

"Oh, not me—if I want in. But I don't do that sort of thing very well. It's too close, too cramped. All the talk." She shook her head again. "By the way, their father—Joseph—he's flying in tomorrow."

The news caught me unawares. "Joseph's coming after all?"

"Like I said, they huddle."

I glanced at her and she was looking at me and as I watched her face changed. Her eyes opened to me and I saw into them and they deepened away. Did she sense now too, at last, that we'd faced off this way before? She seemed vulnerable, not so hard, not so aloof.

"I'm not staying long," she said. "Lie back."

I did as she commanded. Pressing her lips together gravely for unpleasant duty, she lifted one knee on the bed and leaned over me. I didn't need another sponge bath. After dinner I'd floated in the tub through two changes of hot water until I was wrinkled and sleepy. I wasn't about to confess, however.

Grey loosened my robe. I expected her to fetch the wash-cloth. I even glanced towards the bathroom. But her long thin fingers touched my throat, faltered, then traced a line across my breastbone as if they'd reached a decision of their own. Astounded, I lay very still, hardly daring to breathe. There was something awkward to her touch. It was gentle, even tender, but clumsy, as if this didn't come naturally to her.

Slowly she leaned farther over, the tail of her blue-black braid with its fine silver traitors brushing my chest too. Hesitantly, she kissed my chest, tasted it with her tongue. She scraped at my left nipple with her teeth. I closed my eyes and breathed her deep, the sweet and smoky smell that marked her off.

Reaching up, I fumbled with the buttons on her white

shirt. It fell open as she twisted fully to allow my search. Under the shirt she wore nothing. But she shivered violently as I touched her. And far away in her eyes again I spied something, a dread, a longing, a secret that threatened to pull her away.

Her breasts were small, the nipples hard to my touch, as I was to hers. Gently squeezing each breast, I tugged her forward, drawing her face down to mine. Her expression was dark and intense. I spied heat in her eyes but no pretense of dream or swoon. At last, at last, I lifted my fingers to her cheek, tracing its bones, its cool skin and shadows. At last, the crimson shadow. I stroked it with my fingertips. I pulled her head closer and kissed the mark, kissed the crease between her eyes, kissed her dry and slightly parted lips. She closed her eyes. Earlier she'd sworn she didn't do quick fucks. I hoped to hold her to that.

"How are your ribs?" she whispered.

"Sore," I said.

"How sore?"

I lay awake for a long time in the stillness before the early stirrings of dawn. My body had become so thoroughly confused that it no longer navigated by night and day. I felt exhausted, calm, as though I'd been beached high on the sand after a pounding ride without keel or rudder or direction. I'd been blasted to pieces and caressed to wholeness once more. Grey lingered on my lips and tongue, on my fingertips and flesh. Again I took inventory, not to count my wounds but to capture the memory of her touch and seal it away.

Yet, still sore, I also felt I'd torn free of a spell I'd largely woven for myself. Betrayal—heady, coarse, wrenching, unerasable—had cut me loose from ties to them all, from Gabriel and Hilary and Joseph. From Stan and Phyllis and Glascoe too. I didn't know where I'd go in the morning, but my head was clear and my body was healing, and I could light out for the territories with no one's claim to call me back.

Chapter X

I was already waking to the light tapping at the door when it grew sharper and more insistent. "Jason," Hilary called, her voice tense. I lay still, gathering myself.

"Hey, Jason." This was Gabriel. "You in there?"

My stomach clenched tight. I wasn't sure whether to answer. Why had they come? Did they know about last night? Would Grey have confessed?

Someone rapped again still harder, as if they knew I was hiding.

"Yeah. Okay," I shouted back from a long way away. "Hold on a second—I'll be there in a second."

Pulling on my robe, I trudged heavily towards their summons, my body stiffer and sorer from the sleep, my left ribs so tender I could hardly breathe. I opened the door. "Hi," I said.

Hilary stared at me with dismay. Gabriel was shaking his head. Behind them stood Grey. And Joseph. Joseph Salter had come too. Almost before I could register that fact, Hilary took my arm and steered me like an invalid back towards the bed. The others trailed behind. Gabriel flung the curtains back, flooding the room with late morning sunlight. The sliding glass door he shoved open to draw fresh air into the stale sickroom.

"Careful—watch it," I said, sucking with pain, as Hilary nudged me a little too forcefully onto the bed. Her movements were jerky, her skin stretched tight across the bridge of her nose. I knew that stricken look in her eyes, their lids drawn wide. Taking refuge from her, I wedged the pillows into a fresh bank against the headboard. Gingerly, I settled against them.

"What the hell happened?" she demanded.

Inwardly I quailed, but I tried to disguise it with blank incomprehension. What had Grey told them? Had she betrayed our secret? I'd face Hilary out, face them all, until someone launched a proper j'accuse.

"Christ." Gabriel stood back to study me. He was shaking his head again. "I can imagine what happened. It's a weird feeling," he murmured. "Like I'm seeing myself three months back. It's all inside-out."

I stared at him blankly. "Oh," I said. "Yeah," I said, as I realized what he was talking about. "They were more thorough with you. With me they were just making a point."

"A point?" Gabriel looked at me skeptically, but he let it go at that.

I was gazing past him, trying not to be too obvious, trying to read Grey. She'd become a sphinx again, observant but removed, and absolutely unreadable. Her expression belonged to a different alphabet altogether.

"How could this happen to you? When did it happen?" Hilary demanded. "Wasn't there any way to let me know?"

"Remind me what today is," I said.

"Saturday," she said.

I figured it through. "That's right—Saturday. Two days already." I shook my head in amazement. "Let's see— Gabe's friends on the force bushwhacked me Thursday morning. The hospital tried to find you late that day, but you weren't around. In the morning—yesterday—Grey was the one at the house when they called, so she came to the hospital and then ferried me here. I insisted."

"But I came by yesterday and knocked. Did you sleep through it? No wonder, I suppose." A hint of suspicion lurked in her eyes.

"Why are we wasting this time?" Joseph Salter made an impatient gesture from the door. He'd been observing, but now he took charge, speaking as though I were comatose. His voice was musical, not deep but resonant. Despite the warm June day, he was wearing a blue suit that had grown slightly too big for him, billowing in the arms and legs. Yet his grey hair was swept back dramatically. As always his presence was electric, as if he were still performing on European stages, rather than running a small school with a faulty well and no reliable heat.

"How can he stay here?—we cannot leave him like this," he was saying. All Joseph lacked was his baton to direct us all. "We will take him to your house, Gabriel. Hilary, please, you pack his bag." He touched her arm lightly. "Take things from the bathroom. Take it all, why not? He will go with us now. We will settle his bill. If he wants to come back later to a motel, so he can come back." Joseph's eyes were smoldering with outrage. He glanced at me, nodding, bringing me in on the secret, but saying nothing, as if between us a greeting weren't necessary.

Even as Hilary obediently dragged my bag from the closet, however, I sensed a tension flare between Joseph and his son. Gabriel said nothing. He didn't protest the plan. But he turned away, his own shoulders stiff.

Perhaps the source of tension was simply that Joseph should appear on the scene and immediately take charge with such assurance. The friction rather pleased me. The old urge to compete for his affection lingered deep in the bone. Like a tuning fork, it was struck to life by the sight of him and by the sound of his voice.

I gathered a few clothes and shut myself in the bathroom. Biting my lip and holding my breath, reaching, stretching, I gasped as I struggled with a sock. Tears in my eyes from the pain, I couldn't manage it. I sat on the toilet and panted. I stuffed the damn socks into my pocket.

The bag was packed and the family waiting when I emerged. I stepped, sockless, into my shoes. I couldn't bend. Grey watched but, expressionless, didn't move. Hilary didn't immediately notice. And so it was Gabriel who knelt and tied my laces.

Suddenly, even as he kneeled before me, I didn't want to go. I resented them all. Gabriel and Hilary and Grey. Even Joseph. They were dragging me out against my will. I didn't want to be snared into their lives again. I wanted to light out for the damn territories. I'd turn back to the bed, claim I wasn't up to it.

Yes, I began to swing away. My eyes caught Grey just as she raised her head. Her face was stern. She didn't smile, didn't nod, gave no sign at all. She was just a sullen woman, Gabriel's wife, nothing to do with me. And her indifference wrenched me with anguish and fury. I knew the touch of her skin, I knew her smell, I knew the taste of her face, and I hungered for her angrily. My face was hot. How could the others not see? Confused, ashamed, still angry, I snatched up my own bag and limped heavily through the door ahead of them.

Simon Yoo stood staring out from the front porch, hands on his hips, as we drove up. Next to him on the steps sat Mary Sillito and Meg Callahan, one pear-shaped with over-sized overalls and irony-grey hair, the other tall and thin, chain smoking while outdoors. Sara Oliver regally occupied a plastic chair behind them. Even from a distance I could tell that Simon was furious. No doubt he considered whatever happened to me merely an annoying distraction from the business at hand. In two days Gabriel Salter was going on trial.

As Gabriel pulled his ancient Falcon against the curb his face was unguarded. I noticed a thin whitish scar where they'd taken stitches beneath his right temple. It was the only visible trace of his beating in the spring. Yet his skin seemed pale, even sallow. Just in the last couple of months lines had etched themselves into his brow and along the corners of his eyes and mouth.

Gabriel glanced back to make sure I was all right and, duty done, hurried from the car. Grey followed quickly. Hilary and Joseph and I remained in the cramped back seat.

"You okay?" Hilary leaned across her father to check with me. "If you can't manage those steps, I'll move the car around to the kitchen."

"No problem," I said as bravely as I could muster. "The exercise'll do me good—I'll just take it slow."

"How about you, Dad?"

Joseph was staring out the window. "You go on ahead," he said to his daughter. "Jason and I will take it slow together. You know, we will lean on each other as if we were old men."

Relieved, she retrieved my bag from the trunk and hurried up the steps. Heaven forbid she should be left out of the cabal. The Gabriel Salter Defense Committee now was gathered in executive session on the porch.

Joseph made no move to abandon the dirty vinyl backseat, and I was content to remain with him. Given the hot spot in my side, those half-dozen steps up the hill looked daunting. Joseph shifted slightly.

"Your parents—they are well?" he asked. "They sent me a letter in the spring. Your mother did. It was the first I have heard from them in years upon years." He turned to me with a wistful little smile.

"They're okay. As a matter of fact, I was up there a week ago for their fortieth anniversary and for Dad's semi-retirement."

He arched his brow. "Forty years?" he said. "For Marianne and me it is more than that, nearly forty-five. And your father is retiring? This I can't believe. Bradley swore they would carry him out. In a box, he always said."

"My guess is the college had to do a little shoving. But he'll still teach one seminar a year. And this way he'll have more time for his writing."

"Yes, his writing," Joseph said, but his thoughts seemed already to have drifted.

"This mess with Gabriel came up in conversation while I was there," I went on. "No surprise really. Funny thing I realized this time, Joseph—it's as if you left only a little while ago. They still miss you."

"Yes, well, as you can imagine I miss them too."

The two of us sat awkwardly side by side, gazing straight ahead. For once I decided to persevere.

"Do you remember, when we were kids Hilary and I called any of the ancient family histories the olden days? All those stories you loved to tell us about your uncles and grandmothers and cousins upon cousins in a far-away place. Maybe they were all just fairy tales. But what struck me last weekend was how little I knew about the not so olden days. Like how you and Dad met. Or how you wound up in the wilds of Pennsylvania, of all unlikely places. Not to mention packing up and disappearing into Indian territory."

He brushed my hint away. "You are right—this is ancient, ancient history. Nothing interesting to anyone after all these years." But he couldn't dismiss it so casually from his own thoughts. He was staring away beyond the car window.

When he spoke again his voice had grown pensive. "Your father was the closest friend of my life, Jason. Yes, even the only true friend, after we left home."

"Okay. But didn't that change? Even with all the time our families spent together, I don't remember you and Dad with arms around each other."

He lifted his delicately tough musician's hands and articulated them into his lap once more. Without a cello bow they looked oddly forlorn. "Is that what friendship is? Yes.

No. Remember, Jason, you were very young. On the surface, perhaps, my friendship with your father wasn't the same. But underneath, you see, it never changes."

He glanced up. "And your mother—she is well?"

"Sure, fine. As far as I can tell," I said. "But that's another thing I realized—how little I've known her. Who she is other than my mother, I mean. She's so private. Most people fathom that about their parents a lot sooner. I guess I'm a bit slow."

"This is true though," he said in a soft voice and brushed my leg. "Your mother, Eleanor, was always complex—she is deep in her own way. Very quiet. Very private, yes. Bradley never appreciated this, I think. Not in all of forty years."

He gestured with a nod at my swollen eye and the bruises on my face. "Who did this? Is it all madness in this place?"

"Probably some of the same guys who mauled Gabriel in the spring. It's their chance for a little fun. They're not allowed to treat local reporters this way."

"Police are like this everywhere," Joseph said with a firm nod, his jaw set. "Federals in Cherokee territory, you should see. And the Indian sheriffs—they do no better. They are what they are. In Hungary, police did these same things to my friends. If only they had captured me, you can imagine. Police. Judges. I do not trust them. I cannot. And Gabriel they bring to trial on Monday. Isn't this more madness?"

"No question about the cops," I said.

"And what they claim?" Joseph's eyes flared again. "How can anyone think Gabriel—Gabriel—is capable of such a thing? Do you?"

I took a deep breath, a notch too far for the hot spot in my side. Why did the Salters keep demanding these credos? The ribs stabbed me. "No," I gasped. "I don't think Gabe's capable of attacking a young girl." Somehow that seemed not the same as saying he didn't do it.

"Insane, all of it," he repeated. But his fire was waning. Joseph settled more heavily against the car seat, his strength sapped, anger faint but brooding in his eyes.

Most of that afternoon I spent sprawled on the same couch where Gabriel had lain while Simon snapped his photos. I knew I wasn't a pretty sight either, but I didn't feel so bad anymore. I was merely an out-of-town visitor who'd dropped by and was lounging carelessly. Every so often, when she thought of it, Hilary would bring me a cup of tea or freshen a washcloth with cold water. The slightest rub set my skin aflame, but the cool water was soothing.

The day was bright, the porch was bright, the room was light, though I lay in cool shadow in the lee beneath a window. Warm drafts of summer breeze breezed through the screen door and through the room and out the kitchen. Other visitors were drifting through as well, up the front steps to the porch, through to the kitchen and back again. I recognized some of the faces. I didn't pay close attention. Every so often I overheard the tale being recited of who I was and what had happened to me. I wasn't so much a celebrity in my own right as a reminder of Gabriel's earlier beating, as well as of the threats for him that lay ahead.

On the front porch the buzz of conversation never ceased. Snatches of talk wafted by. I wasn't much interested. My attention fluttered in and out of focus. I knew I should be working on a story for Brenda Glascoe. Perhaps I should have Simon snap a shot or two of my face as evidence of what happened while I was on duty—proof I wasn't merely loafing.

I'd spied nothing of Grey in several hours. Not since she left the car to follow Gabriel. Was she hidden in some nook out of my vision? Had she left the house on assignment? Could she pass me by without a word or without me noticing?

More friends and confederates arrived with beer and bottles of wine. Someone propped a small boom-box in a corner. It blared tapes of Guthrie and Dylan, some newer political punk from London. And in the gap between the music and the low chatter and the silence behind it all, I became aware of tension filtering like incense through the air so subtly I hadn't noticed earlier. Now it stained every breath, every sound.

Buckets of chicken appeared. I was happy to snag a drumstick. I was very hungry. I tore at the meat quickly with my hands and teeth.

As daylight finally faded, voices from the porch drifted through the screen door and settled on the floor and clustered in tight fists of conversation. Orange stabs of cigarettes gestured in the growing dusk.

Someone was settling next to me. I resented the intrusion and didn't acknowledge my neighbor.

"This makes no sense to me," a voice said softly. I jerked slightly—Joseph had returned. "A party, with Gabriel to go on trial."

Startled and embarrassed, I whispered sharply. "Didn't Gabe tell you? These are his friends. It's not really a party. At least it didn't begin as one. They're planning the rally for tomorrow. And probably trying to keep spirits up too."

"Rallies. Friends." He was shaking his head impatiently in the shadows. "Who do we know is among them? They are not family and in moments like this you trust only family."

Did he consider me family? I'd always wondered, even when I was married to his daughter. At the moment I probably qualified by default. "How can it hurt at this stage?"

"It can hurt," he said, "and we shouldn't find out how. That we don't need."

"Okay," I said.

It was Gabriel himself who switched on a small table lamp, shooting harsh shadows across the room and illuminating tired faces, weary faces. His own seemed haggard, his eyes lost in dark craters. The light seemed to be a signal for those five or six friends who'd lingered. Loyal and steadfast, Mary Sillito and Meg Callahan were gathering plates and bottles. Not far from them, Sara Oliver, heavy and regal, was wrapping an electric cord around the boom-box.

Gabriel squatted by my shoulder. He rubbed the back of his hand on my knee. His father had disappeared with Hilary into the kitchen. Simon was sitting on the floor, watching and biding his time. No sign of Grey.

"How you feeling?" Gabriel asked. "Up for a short walk?" His fingers picked nervously at a frayed edge of the upholstery. "I need some more air—can't seem to get enough. I suppose that makes sense, given what they're planning for me."

"Air sounds good." I was wide awake.

Without another word, Gabriel slipped away towards the front door. Stiffly, I followed. Once we were out in the cool night air the tightness in my legs and back began to loosen.

"Man," he gasped and stretched. I sensed him drawing in one lungful of air after another. He was already a pace and a half ahead of me.

"Hey, Gabe," I called.

He glanced back, surprised. "Sorry," he said with a grin.

Shoulder to shoulder, we set off again more slowly along the broken sidewalk. Although the sky was clear, no moon appeared and the street lamps along this block had burned out. Nor did light from any houses reach this far. We heard the sounds of the city, cars out on the main roads, televisions indoors. But we were swallowed by a sea of darkness. Only Gabriel's voice survived next to me and I clung to it.

"You were talking to my father," he said. "What was he saying?"

"Nothing much. That he wasn't wild about the party."

"Of course not." Gabriel's voice flashed with resentment. "He'd rather the family hole up together in secret, barricaded against the world."

"Something like that."

"Was he saying anything else?"

"Not really."

"Funny," Gabriel said. "I always thought he told you everything. I was always so jealous of you."

I glanced at him, astonished. "Likewise," I said.

"You have any idea what he was saying to me this afternoon? You know him—you should be able to guess."

I strolled ahead slowly, considering it. We'd fallen into rhythm with each other. "Not a clue," I said at last.

Gabriel punched at a stone with his toe. "He wants me to take off. He doesn't think I should wait for the trial."

My lips were dry. I tried to whistle. No luck. Just a rush of empty wind.

"He figures there's no hope of a fair trial—I'd be better off taking my own chances."

I kicked at a stone myself. "Doesn't he care that people would take it as admitting you're guilty?"

I felt rather than saw Gabriel shake his head. "For him, people believe what they're going to believe. Or what thrills them most. Can't say I entirely disagree."

"But what about the ones you've been preaching to? The workers who just might convert to your cause."

"Their cause. It's their cause," he corrected me. "That's it exactly. I knew you'd see. Even if they believe me now, trust me, it'll be different if I split. How could they not feel like I betrayed them?"

"But the ISA can help you disappear, I assume."

He remained silent.

"You tempted?"

For several paces he didn't answer. "Twenty-five years inside's a long time. It's not like I can expect a judge here to cut me any slack."

"Jesus, Gabe," I murmured.

"It makes sense, that he'd offer this advice." He was musing it through aloud. "What happened in Hungary scarred him so deep. He thought he and his friends were creating this new world of justice and beauty, and then the Stalinists blew it all to hell."

"Some of your socialist pals," I said to goad him.

"Not socialists—Stalinists," he repeated like a weary professor without breaking stride. "And what was worse for him—all the souls willing to collaborate for a share of the loot. That's what he couldn't get over. How few there were to trust. He's never believed in much of anything since then, beyond the family."

"You make him sound like more of an anarchist than you are."

"I'm not an anarchist," Gabriel said with distaste. "If I don't trust this system it doesn't mean a better one's not possible."

We walked silently for a while and I tried to grasp the reality of what felt entirely unreal. "So Joseph ran for his life from Hungary," I said. "That makes sense. Then he bugged out of Pennsylvania. Now he wants you to jump bail and spend the rest of your life on the run? Hey, it's almost a family tradition."

A thought struck me. "What about Hilary? I always assumed I chased her away. Can't blame her, of course. It's no treat being married to a basket case. But maybe it's part of the Salter genetic code. Is she planning to disappear again too?"

"Don't be a shit," Gabriel said without heat.

I felt like a shit. I also wanted to put my arm protectively around his shoulder. Though I wasn't sure he hadn't tried to rape Teresa Jackson and didn't deserve to be locked away. And I recalled my own desire, waking in the middle of the night after Grey had gone, to fly away free and clear. What did I deserve? Gabriel and I kept walking.

When at last we made our way slowly up the alley, we discovered the house eerily open. One naked bulb burned in the kitchen. Upstairs, all seemed dark. Friend and family might have fled into the night, not bothering to fasten the doors behind them.

A small lamp sat glowing on the floor of the living room. Through the screen door I spied a shadow on the front steps. I touched Gabriel's arm. Together we stepped onto the porch and the shadow split into two without moving. Grey and Simon were watching us, waiting patiently, their knees drawn up. A thrill raced through me at the sight of her. It was an effort not to rush across, grab her hand, yank her after me into the night. She neither avoided my gaze nor gave any sign of acknowledgment.

Gabriel lowered himself to the top step and leaned against the rail. "I suppose we need to do some more planning about tomorrow," he said.

Simon nodded, but I couldn't make out his eyes. Weak shards of light reflected off his glasses.

Gabriel reached towards Grey and took her hand. Their fingers locked. Ashamed, angry, I wanted to cover my eyes.

"Where's Hilary?" I demanded. "Did she go back to the motel?"

Again Simon nodded.

"Damn," I said softly.

"Don't worry," Gabriel said. "Stay with us for the time being. We brought your bag, remember? It's already upstairs in the spare room. But you'll have to share with my father. There's a mattress on the floor for you."

I sighed but tried to disguise it. My room at the motel seemed singularly appealing. "Fine," I said. "Thanks."

I sensed them hesitating and turned to go. When I glanced

back from the front room, they were already descending and moving away, dark moths drifting through the trees.

I did not wake late, but Joseph's roll-away bed already lay empty, and the others who'd slept in the house had scattered to the winds. Only Simon Yoo remained, sitting at the kitchen table drinking strong black tea. I wondered whether he'd slept here or slept at all. He seemed freshly shaved. Behind the spectacles his eyes were hard and unreadable.

"Is there more of that?" I asked.

He pointed with his thumb to a cabinet. I found a small packet of teabags but no kettle. I contented myself with hot water from the tap.

"Where is everybody? Gabe gone to fetch the Sunday papers?"

"I'm supposed to bring you along to the rally," he said.

I rubbed my chin with the back of my hand. I hadn't shaved or showered yet. "Yeah?" I said doubtfully. "I'm still feeling pretty lousy—I'm not sure I'm up to those kinds of festivities."

His expression didn't change. "Plenty of time. We don't leave for an hour."

I scowled. He sipped his tea. Was that the faintest of smirks on his lips?

My rebellion extended to keeping Simon waiting an extra twenty minutes while I showered and dressed. As we drove downtown, I considered the angry line of impatience in his brow a sign of my triumph.

The protest, legally sanctioned with all appropriate permits, was scheduled for noon on the steps of the County Courthouse, a massive grey period-piece of classical revival. When we arrived, a dozen or more protesters were already milling about between the courthouse and the county jail. The political symbolism of holding the demonstration here was obvious: between the stolid grandeur of the one and the stark, sour, faceless other. The police had cordoned off the street to siphon any traffic away.

Many of Gabe's friends were already chatting and clutching bundles of printed fliers. Sara Oliver directed traffic among the protesters. Circulating in tandem through the growing crowd, Meg and Mary passed out leaflets and shared news. At the center of a throng on the steps, alert like a hawk, solitary even amidst the others, stood Grey. I knew better than try and draw close.

The late morning was already very hot, the air muggy and still. The sun wasn't baking the steps so much as steaming us all. Thunderstorm weather. I glanced hopefully to the sky for any hint of relief. But it was white and hazy, blinding with light. Thunderheads, if they were to appear at all, would be gathering energy through the rest of the day.

A number of protesters were carrying two or three placards apiece, waiting to distribute them. FREE SALTER! they demanded. STOP POLICE ABUSE. JUSTICE FOR WORKING PEOPLE. Some posters, nailed to wooden crosses, bore the venerable icon of Gabriel's mauled face. The picture had been reproduced so many times that by now it resembled an abstract pen-and-ink blotch. No sign yet of Gabriel himself, nor of Hilary and Joseph.

The sight of that old photo made me queasy. I was also aware that invisibility no longer cloaked me. Some of the protesters were nudging newcomers and pointing. I drifted to the far edge of the sidewalk. I might have ducked away entirely except that I couldn't shake Simon. I kept expecting him to attend to the business of the rally. But he clung faithfully, if to all appearance indifferently, to my side.

As protesters continued to arrive, clustering in loose knots, new faces appearing by the moment, I became aware of the police as well. In groups of two or three, they kept their distance across the street, on the fringe, outside the jail, hustling Sunday strollers along. Furtively, I studied them, wondering who among them had been in on the ambush. It pleased me that even in summer uniform they'd be roasting in this weather.

So where the hell was Gabriel? The rally was scheduled for noon, and twelve-thirty had come and gone. I knew well enough that these events never begin on time, but it worried me he was nowhere in evidence. Had he heeded Joseph's advice?

And the crowd continued to swell, some arriving directly from Sunday church, others wearing clean work clothes. Something—maybe it was his discomfort, his hangdog frown—tugged my attention to a short man, a Latino. He wore a white western-cut shirt. It took me an instant—I knew I'd seen him before—and then I recognized John Martinez. Given the arm's length he'd kept any mention of Gabriel three months earlier, I was amazed to find him here. Nervous, he was trying hard not to glance at the police. Yet stubbornly he held his ground.

Across the street I spotted Brian Phillips. How young he appeared, like a college kid on summer vacation. He hadn't seen or at least recognized me yet. With Simon still in tow, I strolled his way.

"Nice magazine spread on the cops," I said.

Phillips was already smiling with a smear of arrogance as he turned to thank me. Brushing aside a shock of straw-blond hair, he saw my face. "Thanks," he stammered. Then he recognized me. "What the hell happened to you?" he said. "I wondered why you never showed up."

"Just think—this could be you," I said.

His face darkened. "What are you talking about?"

"Some of your local cops arranged a little rendezvous. It was kind of a surprise—I was expecting someone else. Another cop actually. Officer Costello. You know her?"

Stunned, lips pressed tight, his eyes widened. He looked like a frightened boy.

"Yeah, I thought you would," I said. "Anyway, among the

reasons for working me over was that they'd been leashed back from doing the same to you. Count your blessings."

"Jesus," he muttered, licking his lips and glancing nervously at the cops milling across the way.

"Some of them are probably here," I said, "but I can't make out who's who."

"They told you why they were doing it?"

"Sure. Why not? It only stoked their fun. They knew there wasn't a damn thing I could do."

"Shit," he said. His eyes flickered with another idea and a sympathetic sneer curled his lip. "But I'll bet your connection with Salter was plenty part of it too. That's why you're out here again, not because of any piece I did."

"Sure, they liked that too."

"Yeah. Well," he said. He was already edging away. "Glad you're not hurt any worse. Give a ring next week and we'll get together, okay?"

"About the trial," I started to shout, but a squealing blast of feedback drowned me out. The howl rang in my teeth like an electric shock.

Microphone in hand, Grey was bending over the sound system. Around her gathered other members of the Defense Committee. She flicked a switch and again the feedback shrieked towards the impassive jail. Giving up, Grey dropped the microphone and was handed a loudspeaker instead.

"Friends," she said. "Fellow workers." Her voice rang out tinny and unimpassioned. I assumed she was the opening speaker, prepping the crowd for the main act. And that main act was billed as Gabriel Salter. Many in the crowd—and it had grown to two hundred or more—were no doubt here to see him, to hear him, to be exhorted and rocked and swept away by Gabriel's voice. By reputation he was as brilliant a performer as his father once had been. And now, notorious fiend or noble martyr, he'd become even more a celebrity.

"Tomorrow there will be a trial here, in this building,"

Grey was saying. "Gabriel Salter will go before a judge and jury, but he will not be the one on trial. Your city will be on trial. Your city's police force will be on trial here. They have hounded Gabriel Salter, a worker like you. Not a wealthy man. A man who has committed his life to protecting others, men and women, Back and White and Yellow, yes, and Red." She was rising to the occasion. Her voice dipped and swelled. It never quite soared.

In her words, in their rhythm and the way her tongue shaped the sounds, I sensed always the distant shadow of another tongue, another language altogether. She was translating herself from one world to another.

What we'd shared two nights earlier seemed unreal, preposterous, as if my concussion had conjured a vivid fantasy I'd grotesquely confused with reality, a potent fairy tale I'd mistaken as true.

I craned to make out the others standing close by. No Gabriel. Hilary wasn't in evidence either. Nor Joseph. My unease ripened. Where the hell was he? Had he done it already—jumped bail? This rally would be a perfect cover. Did Grey know? Was she the main act after all—and a diversion?

Simon Yoo put his hand on my arm. "Come on," he said. "Where to?"

"Up there. That's where you need to be."

Grey was working the crowd. "Gabriel knows color doesn't matter. It only matters to those who use it as a weapon to gather more wealth and power. Color is used by the bosses. If you're Hispanic, they pit you against the Asians. If you're Black, they whip up fear and distrust so the Whites will hunt you like dogs, because they've been told their own jobs and lives depend on it. That's what Gabriel Salter has worked to expose. The bosses are in on this. The FBI and INS are in on this. Your local police are in on this. They have hounded him. They have framed him for a crime he never committed. It is obscene, what they have done. And they have beaten him nearly to death while he was in their cells."

Simon was pushing me rudely through the crowd and up the steps. I could see Grey ahead and I was content to be steered towards her.

"It is important for us all to see that this is not really about Gabriel Salter. The police are on trial not for what they have done to him alone, but for what they do to so many, many who have no power to protect themselves. Look," she cried and pointed. I twisted around to make out her target, but all about me the crowd was giving way with hungry curiosity. By reading their eyes, I realized her finger was aimed at me.

"Do you see what they have done just three days ago?" she demanded. "Why? This man is a reporter from out of town. He works for a newspaper that props up the dirty system like all the commercial papers. He is no activist. He is no threat to the bosses or the cops or their fascist system. They beat him because they felt like doing this. Like they did to Gabriel Salter three months ago."

Simon released my arm. It was for this purpose he'd clung to me, and to it he now betrayed me. Abandoned, I was set free. A swathe of empty space opened about me, protestors vying for a better view or backing away as if I were contagious. I was feeling queasy again. Hundreds of people stared. They were seeing me and thinking of Gabriel. I was his double, a stand-in for him. My head was throbbing again.

Grey's voice continued to float towards me, but I was no longer hearing her words. The voice sounded angry, yet detached as well—what was I but an empirical example to prove a larger point? My foot slipped and I tottered. Queasy, I lowered myself to the steps. Still a magic circle surrounded me. Everyone kept a distance. No one came to my aid. No one realized I was ailing in the heat and sun. I wondered whether my friends in the police were watching. Did they think I was courting a fresh visit from them or that, perhaps,

I'd failed to learn my lesson?

"You had no right," I said as the screen door slapped behind me. The carefully rehearsed words seemed thin as I finally delivered them. They hardly carried enough force not to float away entirely.

Sitting on the floor of the living room, knees drawn to his chin, Gabriel was holding up a palm to silence me. "Thanks, yes. Thanks, Eleanor. That means a lot to me. Yes. Bye." He hung up.

"That was my mother," I said. That she should call this evening seemed both incredible and somehow inevitable. I noticed Joseph leaning forward on the couch, his face pinched and brooding.

"She phoned to wish me luck," Gabriel said. "That was nice. Your mother was always kind to me." He ran a hand through his hair. "And yeah," he said, "you're right. The rally was another bad decision." He rested his chin against his knees. "I shouldn't have assumed—it's just I thought you wanted to help. Or at least demonstrate what they'd done to you."

"My wanting or not wanting to help isn't the issue." I'd prepared a small but indignant speech for whomever I found in this house. But the words now escaped me. In truth, I was surprised to discover Gabriel still in town, squatting there in the midst of his inner circle. Hilary sat next to her father on the couch. Grey perched on one of the kitchen stools, but I couldn't bring myself to confront her. She seemed now as before, unabashed, even unaware that she'd used me unfairly. On the floor protectively behind Gabriel sat Simon.

After the rally I'd escaped his clutches. He didn't offer much resistance. I'd served his purpose. Woozy, I flagged a cab. It dropped me in the motel's lot. At the front desk, I registered once again and also found the keys to my car waiting for me—the agency had recovered the car and dropped it off.

"When did you decide to use me as your surprise celebrity?" I asked Gabriel grimly.

"I didn't lie to you," he said, looking up at me again. "It wasn't until after we talked last night, when I was out again with Simon and Grey. That's when I realized I couldn't show up today. I just didn't have it in me. Too much on my mind. Too much to decide. I knew Grey could handle it—with your help. You were still asleep when I left this morning."

"Uh-huh," I said. "And where the hell were you?" I turned and accused Hilary.

She bristled. "Sit down already. And don't you take that tone with me. There was no reason for us to be there if Gabe wasn't. He needed us. We went for a drive in the country." She was twisting a ring full of keys in her lap.

"But do you think your father's right?"

"About what?"

I'd propped myself against one of the window sills. I faced Hilary skeptically. "What do you mean, about what? About the advice he's urging on Gabe, that's what."

After an initial blank stare, she turned a troubled glance to her father and then her brother. "What advice?" she demanded.

Joseph wouldn't quite meet her gaze. Gabriel stared at his knees and shook his head. Neither spoke. Simon looked puzzled. I turned to check Grey at last. For once I could read the concern in her face. She looked up at me with a questioning frown.

"Jesus," I muttered under my breath. I shrugged at Gabriel. "Hey, I'm not going to betray your precious secret."

He nodded slightly to himself. Any trace of the puckish waif with a magic smile had long since vanished. Weariness cloaked Gabriel. His dark eyes were ringed with fatigue. "Okay—so you all know. My father wants me to run. To skip bail. Do I have to say any more? You can all imagine the reasons." Again he shrugged.

No one said a word. Simon blinked warily. Grey's eyes narrowed. Her back stiffened. Hilary was openly astounded. She glanced from her father to her brother and back again. She couldn't believe they hadn't confided in her.

"There was no need to say this out loud," Joseph said with soft disgust. His lips were pressed thin. In the dim light his skin was drawn tight as a drum. He didn't look younger so much as ageless, his white hair pulled back, his nose sharp as a blade thrust.

"More secrets," snorted Gabriel. "Why more secrets? From them of all people?" He seemed to be talking only to his father. "I'm sorry," he said to the others. "I should have told you. I meant to. But until I decided—it would only confuse everything."

"Decide, on your own?" Grey asked.

"How could you not tell us? Why only Jason?" demanded Hilary.

Gabriel didn't speak.

"What are you planning to do?" This from Simon, his voice oddly high.

"He must go—that is what he must do," Joseph declared. "How can he stay? For what will he sacrifice twenty-five years of his life? It is nonsense. Better he should go somewhere else. Anywhere. Abroad maybe. That is the only decision."

"No—no way." Grey's voice was flat and hard. She was staring at Gabriel. Not a glance for his father. But the tug of war between them couldn't have been more evident, as if it had been keen all along—even if until this moment she didn't fully grasp the stakes—and I'd never managed to see. "There's no running from this. You've got to fight this one out, Gabe. You've got to fight it to the end and keep on fighting, no matter what."

"This is impossible," Gabriel muttered. Abruptly he rose

and thrust quickly through the screen door and into the dark street. Simon slipped quietly behind him, content to follow watchfully.

"This is all bullshit, Papa," Hilary stormed. "Where do the three of you get off, thinking you can handle this on your own? What, we're supposed to just follow along, happy to support anything you decide?" She flung the ring of keys to the floor. Snatching them up once more, she stalked out. Grey had already disappeared from her stool.

"I am glad your mother called before this uproar," Joseph said, brushing the turmoil aside. "This is what happens on such a night before it finally begins. If it begins."

"You still want him to take off," I said.

"I think he must save his life."

"Like when you escaped from Hungary?"

Joseph stared straight ahead, his lips set stubbornly, and didn't answer.

"You sure it's the same thing?" I asked. "Maybe it is—I don't know." I rubbed a hand over my face. "Should I have skipped to Canada or Sweden when I had the chance? Plenty of times I've thought so. Whatever price I paid would have been better than what I did pay."

We sat silently. He said nothing.

"Know what, Joseph?" I went on finally, "You shouldn't have taken off last time. That's something I'm pretty sure about. You shouldn't have left the college and my folks and everything else behind. Whatever made you do it, it could- n't have been necessary enough."

He turned and studied me, not startled by the leap I'd made, even expecting it, as if his imagination had done the same. "Yes? How could I stay? No one drove me away—it was my choice. And I could not stay. It was impossible." By the time he came to the end, he'd put the question to himself once more and arrived at the same answer.

And as Joseph stared at me, his eyes sad but resolute, I understood with a jolt that he assumed I knew the reason for his last exile.

"Impossible," I echoed.

When I opened the door it was late, well after midnight, and Grey was standing in the motel corridor. Her face was grim. I stepped aside without a word and let the door swing shut behind her. I was awake and still dressed. I'd been sitting in the chair for over an hour.

Hands in my pockets, I faced her. She leaned back against the low bureau. I watched her study me. Her eyes flicked across my face, from one eye to the other, to my mouth, my brow.

"Why should you be so angry with me?" she demanded. "Shouldn't I be angry too?"

My jaw was tight. "You're kidding, right? You set me up that way at the rally, you use me without bothering to see how I feel about it, you destroy—I mean totally—my credibility as a journalist out here, and now you wonder why I'm not tickled."

Only the lamp next to my bed cast any light in the room. Grey's eyes narrowed as she studied me gravely. Her features were cut with shadow.

"I don't care if you are angry," she said with an angry twist of her head. Her long hair, unbraided, startled like a black bird and settled again on her back. "What should that matter to me?"

"You're the one who came here."

She was leaning, rocking against the bureau, rocking on her hands. She might have been listening for a distant sound because her gaze had wandered far from me.

I was tired and sore and impatient for her to go. As a signal, I stepped aside once more, leaving her a clear path. She pushed herself upright.

Only in that instant did it strike me, like one of those kidney blows from the cops, that she was actually about to leave. Suddenly, that was the last thing I wanted. It wasn't that my anger disappeared—anger I could live with. But if she walked out of my motel room she'd be walking away from me.

"Wait—hold on." Catching her arm, I swung her towards me. She jerked free. Tall and haughty, she faced me. "Not yet," I said. "Don't go."

She cocked her head skeptically.

I scoured her in the dim light, her eyes and nose and jaw, a wisp of hair by her ear.

"So, why'd you come this time?"

"I didn't think you were fair, being angry with me." She listened to herself, shook her head and grimaced as if she'd bitten something sour. "No, that's not it. Or only part. Each time I think, if I see him it will make sense, I will under-stand—and then I won't need to see him again. This doesn't make sense to me, Jason, none of it does." Her frustration beat up like a dark flame.

"But."

"But."

I took a deep breath. "What about Gabriel?"

She nodded as if she'd been waiting for this. "Gabriel is my closest friend—he and I understand each other. If he must, he will understand."

I wondered whether he would understand me.

Our hands brushed. Fingers didn't lace: fingertips pressed against fingertips, rising, palms together, our faces serious as if this were a dance of precarious delicacy.

Her breath brushed my cheek. I whispered my breath into the hollow of her throat. Right palm still and always pressed to left palm, slowly, carefully, to the rhythm of this dance we touched each other and kindled each other, left hand and right hand.

"Don't go," I murmured.

"No," she said.

"You are the one who is wrong," she said.

"Huh?" I murmured, dozing.

"You said I was wrong. About storytellers. About how it's only the powerful whose stories are remembered." She rolled over in my arms, solid, warm, snug, to face me in the darkness. "I've been thinking—is this true? No. It isn't true. You are the wrong one.

"When I was young," she went on, settling in, her voice a caress, "and it was dark in our cabin except for an oil lamp—electricity that far out was still ten years away—and I was huddled up under a blanket with my grandmother, she would tell me stories of Corn Woman and Reed Woman, and of droughts and good harvests. Sometimes she and my aunt and other women from the village would tell the stories with colored grain and seeds, mapped out just so on the ground. Old man Faraday watched over them so that each seed was in its place. And spring would come.

"My grandfather, he told stories too, of Coyote and of fighting Japanese from island to island. I remember him coming in, shaking with cold, his skin hard as iron—he'd spend ten hours shingling a roof in the middle of winter because that was the job the boss gave him for the day—and Grandmother rubbing life into his feet before she dared put them in warm water. It was on days like that, after hot tea, Grandfather would sit by the kerosene heater, blanket over his shoulders, and he'd be talking, whether anyone listened or not. I was always ready to listen. He told stories of the war, when being a young man in uniform, even if you were Indian, you were treated as something special. He talked about the Japanese, what they did to prisoners, what things he saw. And how many of those Japanese died and were willing to die for each step of ground, so that sometimes you couldn't tell the difference between stepping on them and stepping on the mud itself. How he and other Indians, they came back and at first there was nothing but celebration and then there was nothing but nothing for them, those that came back."

I shivered once—it sneaked up on me—and I was clenching my teeth against the trembling from another war. Sensing it, understanding, Grey touched my face and calmed me, and she kept on speaking softly.

"Grandfather told the older stories too, old, old tales, of the land before it was fenced, of my family before we were fenced out and fenced in. His own grandfather was a warrior who was never captured, never killed. He disappeared across the water into Mexico but was never far from us. He became one of the spirits of our land. Those were the special tales, the ones Grandfather cared about most. They had nothing to do with him and they were everything he was."

"And you left all that behind."

"Not because I wanted to," she whispered vehemently.

"Then how come?"

She paused. She sighed and her sigh was bitter. "Something happened. I could not stay."

I remembered Joseph using the same words and I wondered at this further mystery.

She lay pensive for a little while and I, no longer sleepy, was content to remain silent and hold her.

She whispered again. "Gabriel's father—you know, even if we disagree on so much—he has learned Cherokee tales and teaches them in the BIA school. I have heard him. He is wonderful with the children."

"He's born for that," I murmured. Joseph had already come to my mind along with his stories and my own boyhood and how I'd loved him. "Helps if you're far enough from the story to be certain how it goes," I said.

Later, cupping her head in my hand, I kissed her. The taste of salt on her lips startled me. "What?" I asked.

She twisted away and now she was the one trying not to tremble. She was shaking her head.

"Tell me."

Her breath caught. "Tomorrow. The trial—it scares me," she admitted, hating her own fear. "What they will do to Gabriel."

"Where is he tonight?"

She shook her head. "I don't know. He wouldn't tell me. No, not wouldn't, couldn't, because he didn't know, only that he will be walking again."

"Will he show tomorrow?"

She shrugged.

I tugged her towards me and kissed her again. With my mouth I pushed her lips apart and felt for the sharp line of her teeth.

"What about this?" I murmured. A surge of defiance swept through me. "This is good. This matters too. I needed for you to come tonight." I felt the full truth of that only as I spoke it.

I felt her nod.

With a stark certainty that frightened me, I grasped how much I wanted her. With her in my arms, I was drinking long swallows of water, cool and clear and light, as though I'd been parched for so long I'd ceased to know my own thirst.

A question, an inspiration hit me like a physical blow. If Gabriel fled, could I clutch Grey to me and never let go? If they sealed him in prison, could I steal her away? This further betrayal had been lurking in my mind. I'd just never been honest or brave enough to confront it.

Chapter XI

Minor deceptions blossomed on both sides. I don't know whether Grey ever actually slept. I must have been dozing lightly. But as she rolled gently out of my arms in the darkness, I woke. She wanted to slip away without disturbing, without alerting me. My own breathing remained steady as I lay with my eyes open towards the wall, feigning sleep.

Even with my back to her, however, I could tell that her movements weren't really stealthy. She had nothing to hide. She was quick and she was quiet. I lay on my side, knees tucked up and arms rounded, still hugging the hollow where she'd lain.

Now that she was leaving, I wanted her to hurry. My mannikin pose was stiffening into an ache.

Noiselessly, she opened the door and disappeared. I flopped an arm over and rolled onto my back, breathing deeply.

Where was she going? To slip into her bed—Gabriel's bed—as if, in the great tradition of dissembling adultery, nothing had happened? Would he be there? Would he care?

What was she thinking? Her heart had been thudding against my cheek; the sound of it sang through my bones. And yet I couldn't know that heart. Any more than I'd been able to fathom Gabriel's.

I reached for my watch and made out that it was almost three-thirty. I was thoroughly awake. More awake, in truth, than in a long while. My eyes were open in the darkness. I was aware of breath in my nostrils. I listened to the hum of the universe about me. Grey had done this and it astonished me.

I stretched my limbs in the big bed and imagined being an adolescent again with time to think about Grey Navarro and only Grey Navarro. To recall the taste of her skin and develop some marvelous excuse for another encounter. But already other thoughts were intruding. Would Joseph, I wondered, win the tug of war? Would Gabe show up at the courthouse in a few hours or skip out? Would the judge and prosecutor continue to tie Jeremy Stanton's defense in knots?

Fifteen minutes later I'd mixed a glass of instant coffee at the bathroom tap and was sitting in my robe, typing notes. I didn't want to disappoint Glascoe.

At seven-thirty, Hilary and I arrived separately at the motel's coffee shop. We nodded more than smiled and strolled side by side to a booth by the windows. We hadn't planned to meet, but it seemed natural to do so, as if we'd reestablished a rhythm that neither called attention to.

By the evidence of her eyes, bruised with fatigue, Hilary hadn't managed much sleep either. She made no apologies this time when she pulled a cigarette out of her bag. Anger crackled as she struck the match, but it wasn't anger directed solely at me. I was grateful.

"So?" I said.

She shook her head and the match at the same time and blew away a quick puff of smoke. "No idea. We'll just have to see."

Flurries of activity in one office or another seemed puny as we walked quickly through the County Courthouse's corridors. We scaled one of the grand marble staircases and spotted a crowd milling about a courtroom door. We pushed our way through.

Half an hour before the trial was scheduled to begin, the courtroom was nearly full and oddly hushed. Two long bench rows provided the only seats for observers. What with the clear division between parties, it might have been a wedding. Clustered forward behind the prosecutor's desk sat Leroy Jackson and his family—his wife and brother-in-law, and several young men in their twenties and thirties, sons from his previous marriage, I guessed. Half-a-dozen family friends formed a further protective ring. At the center sat Teresa Jackson, huddled almost out of sight.

Behind the empty table for the defendant and his lawyer gathered Gabriel's supporters, filling the second row as well and even spilling over into the narrow aisle. Most wore work clothes, many with bleary eyes and unshaven faces that suggested they'd come directly from one night shift or another.

Joseph Salter sat in front, an empty space on the bench separating him from Grey. Her head turned. She didn't smile, but she gazed steadily at me, eyes keen and dark. A secret spasm of joy wrenched my chest.

Joseph, also turning, nodded to Hilary and me with a little wave. His other hand clutched at the wooden rail in front of him. Grim and weary, he was apparently waiting like the rest of us to discover whether Gabriel would appear. Hilary touched my hand and then waded towards the empty spot next to her father.

I was relieved not to be dragged once more to their bosom. A single empty seat at the far end of the second row would do very well. I slipped towards it and settled in as comfortably as possible—I'd covered enough trials to know how grueling the day might become.

Glancing around, I spotted Brian Phillips. He was working earnestly not to notice me. I didn't mind. Nonchalantly as I could manage, I turned to watch for Gabriel.

At nine o'clock, a bailiff escorted the jury to their chairs. They'd been selected on Friday while I was out of commission. One woman was African American. A couple of the men were Latino. The foreman was White and, at a rough guess, in his mid-fifties. Could be he taught woodworking in high school; could be he owned a garage. He wore a white shirt and thick brown tie, no jacket. His pug face seemed squeezed out of shape like soft clay, his mouth a wide gash. A mean mouth.

Joyce Kilburn had already taken her place across from the bench, an assistant by her side. For them nothing seemed amiss, nothing out of the ordinary. Monday morning and a new trial, one out of a continuing stream for the prosecutor's office.

Not far from Kilburn, however, Hilary kept twisting awkwardly every few moments to check the entrance to the courtroom. Her eyes spread wide with worry. The skin stretched taut across the bridge of her nose. Yet I noticed that neither Joseph nor Grey would glance back. They seemed locked in some silent competition to reveal neither faith nor doubt. Behind them like a protective spirit sat Simon Yoo. So Gabriel had not revealed himself either. From what I could guess, he'd taken no leave, said no goodbyes, made no promises. The anxiety from his family radiated towards me in waves that prickled the hairs on my neck.

The courtroom had grown tightly packed. A brace of police officers barred further entrance; they wouldn't allow observers to stand.

My own ambivalence had coalesced into an impatient dread; I didn't know whether I wanted Gabe to appear or not. But the uncertainty had gone on long enough. Joyce Kilburn was eyeing the empty table next to her with concern. She too glanced to the back of the courtroom.

At ten past nine the door to the judge's chambers opened and we all rose. Judge Stevens moved briskly in his black robe to the bench.

So I heard rather than saw the door behind us flung open, startling the guards, and a sudden low cry of voices. Jeremy Stanton was thrusting past the officers—and there, yes, came Gabriel in tow—briefly acknowledging greetings and pats on their backs and arms. They pushed through a low gate and quickly took their places, standing across from the judge. Stevens fingered his gavel.

"A reason for this delay and grand entrance, Mr. Stanton?" he demanded. The judge remained standing and so, necessarily, did we all.

"I apologize," began Stanton. The judge interrupted him by taking his seat at that moment, and so, therefore, did we all. The lawyer spoke once more. "I'm sorry, Your Honor. We were unavoidably detained."

"In my experience, very little is unavoidable," said the judge. For a long moment he stared at the two men before him. "Now then," he said, opening a folder. "In the matter of the State versus Gabriel Salter. Are we ready to do this?"

The two attorneys spoke together. "Yes, Your Honor."

"Mr. Salter, your plea remains unchanged, I assume?"

Gabriel rose. "I'm not guilty."

The judge blinked and turned his head away. "Miss Kilburn?"

"Your Honor, the State would begin by calling Teresa Jackson."

Kilburn was launching us with a jolt. I nodded—I'd been doing this long enough not to be surprised. Teresa's mother kissed her. Her father, massive and balding without his Raider's cap, glared defiantly around the room. Teresa made her way through the gate and took her place on the stand.

As she was being sworn in, it occurred to me that what we were witnessing was not the simple parody of a wedding but a more complex bit of theater. Teresa wore a simple white blouse and a navy blue jumper with straps over her shoulders. Her chest had been flattened away entirely. They'd even gathered her hair into two long pigtails, a yellow ribbon at the end of each. She looked about eleven years old.

Gabriel sat across the way, at an angle to his accuser and attentive. His plain grey suit had come off the rack at Sears. His hair was clipped short, his mustache trimmed. He looked earnest and beleaguered, like a teacher with too many essays to grade. He seemed to be studying Teresa, trying to figure her out.

Joyce Kilburn strode briskly forward. "Would you state your name for the record."

"Teresa Louise Jackson."

"Can you speak up a little bit, or move closer to the microphone, please. Teresa, how old are you today?"

Dutifully, the girl leaned forward. Her breath exploded into the mike. "Sixteen."

"And how old were you on March fourth of this year?"

"Fifteen."

By pacing her through this catechism Kilburn was giving Teresa time to relax and become comfortable with the procedure. So far the girl had given her answers directly to the woman standing before her. She was tense but eager to please, her voice soft and very high, a child's voice.

"Teresa, I'd like to ask you some questions about March fourth."

She nodded.

"Do you remember what day of the week that was?"

She nodded again. "It was Friday."

"Did you go to school that day?"

"I went to my high school, Hoover High School, like always."

"Did you take the bus home that day?"

"Uh-huh, the school bus."

"What did you do after you came home?"

"Me and my little sister, Tanya, we watched tv some. And my dad let us go up to Kandy Korner. Then we come home."

Kilburn paused, nibbling the end of her pen. "What time was it you came home from Kandy Korner, Teresa?"

"Maybe six-thirty or seven o'clock. I'm not for sure."

"Were your parents there?"

"No, Ma'am. They left when we did. Fridays, they always go to this place, this bar around the corner with some friends."

"What did you do when you returned home?"

"Tanya and me watched some more tv."

"Did anything unusual happen?"

Teresa nodded importantly. "This phone call came."

"Did the caller identify himself?"

"No'm. He just asked for somebody, somebody I don't know, and hung up."

"What else happened?"

"Like a little while later, maybe five minutes, there was this knock on the front door."

"Did you go to the door?"

"Uh-huh. And I asked who it was. And the person said something, but I couldn't be sure. I thought he said Dave, which is one of my older brothers. He's sitting over there by my dad."

"Did you open the door?"

Teresa nodded and bit her lip. "But it wasn't my brother."

"Did you recognize the person?"

"No, Ma'am."

"What did he look like?"

"He was pretty tall. And he had a mustache. And a jacket—like a lumberjack one."

"Is that person in the courtroom today?"

"Yes, Ma'am, he is."

"Could you point out where he's seated."

Teresa bit her lip again and then her finger shot out at Gabriel, stiff and absolute, as if she'd been waiting three months for this moment. "That's him, the one on this side, with the mustache."

Joyce Kilburn merely looked at Gabriel. She let Teresa's gesture speak for itself. "Your Honor, may the record show the witness identified the defendant?"

Judge Stevens looked significantly towards the jury. "The record may so show."

"What happened next, Teresa?"

"Well, the person, he asked for 4847, and I said, this ain't that address—You got the wrong number."

"Did he ask you any questions?"

"He asked for Juanita, but I don't know no Juanita. And he asked for a Leroy, and I thought he meant my dad. But I told him to go away."

"What happened then?"

"Well, he kind of was leaving, so I start closing the door. When, like all of a sudden, he come back and kicked it open."

Teresa was no longer looking at Joyce Kilburn. Her eyes were fixed on the wooden rail in front of her. Her voice had all but died away entirely. It broke now with a sob, and she was chewing her lip again.

Kilburn paused, taking her time. She didn't want to rush the girl or upset her any more. "I'm sorry, Teresa. I know this is very difficult. Would you like to take a break?"

The girl shook her head but didn't glance up.

"You're very brave," Kilburn said. "Can you tell us what happened next?"

She snuffled. "He catched me by my arm and says he got a knife. And he's rubbing my chest already."

"What did you do?"

"It was making me sick, I was so scared. To my stomach, you know? I wanted to throw up, but I couldn't. He's telling me, get down on the floor. And then he like trips me—that's when I hit my head so bad—and he crawls down on top of me."

"Did he stop when you were hurt?"

"No'm. He just pulled my pants off. And he got his own pants down and he's, you know, sticking out."

"You mean he had an erection? Is that right? Then what did he do?"

"Yes, that's right. He's rubbing and touching me and spreading my legs. He starts trying to push it up inside me."

Again Kilburn paused, this time not for Teresa's sake but for the jury's. Slowing the pace of testimony so the girl's story could sink in, she stalked back towards her desk to consult a particular sheet of paper. The jurors were certainly rapt. So was the rest of the courtroom. I was sweating from the closely packed bodies about me, from the heat, from the story. Gabriel looked pale, calm, stricken. Kilburn swung decisively to the girl once more. "What happened next, Teresa?"

She looked calmer too and angry. Her jaw was set. "I'm laying there and he's on top of me still trying to do it. And I can't even wiggle no more. I'm just kind of praying and shaking my head and saying no. So right then there's this big pounding on the door. And I think, it's my dad, and he's going to whip this guy good, he'll kill this guy 'cause of what he done. And this guy, the one sitting over there, he's already off me and trying to pull his pants up. That's when I push out the door and seen the police."

"Did you say anything to them?"

"No'm. I was in shock." She pronounced the diagnosis proudly. "I was wearing only my sweatshirt, you know? And it was real cold. So after they chased after the guy, I went back in to get some pants."

"Did you see anything of the police officers or the man who attacked you?"

"Yes." She nodded with certainty. "Back in my parents' room. He was sitting on the bed, hands behind his back. His pants were still kind of down, his thing hanging out and all."

Kilburn did nod this time. She turned away, her lips pursed, and then swung around to her witness once more.

"Thank you for your testimony, Teresa. As I said, you've been very brave. I have no more questions, Your Honor."

"Mr. Stanton." Judge Stevens lingered on each syllable. Teresa was faced by Jeremy Stanton. Her father's daughter, she wore a small smile of scorn, her lower lip thrusting forward.

"Miss Jackson, you say that someone called your house at seven-thirty. Is that correct?"

"I'm not sure on the time," she said.

"Well," said Stanton, "didn't you tell me during your deposition that the call came at seven-thirty p.m.?"

"It could've come at seven-thirty. I don't know. I didn't have no watch."

"Miss Jackson," said Stanton benevolently and without a trace of impatience, "let me read from the transcript of your deposition. I asked you, How do you know the phone call came at seven- thirty? Your answer, Because my tv show, Video Soul, it was on. Did I read that correctly?"

"Yeah, you read that correctly." Teresa glared at him insolently.

"So you were sure that the phone call came at seven-thirty?"

"No, I'm not sure. I was going by the time the show came on. I could've been wrong. The show could've been delayed or something."

Stanton paused, suddenly curious. "Has someone perhaps mentioned to you that if the phone call did happen at seven-thirty it creates a serious problem for the prosecution's case?"

For the first time Teresa appeared flustered. She blinked back a sudden squall of tears and glanced towards Kilburn. The prosecutor maintained a reassuring smile but gave no further sign. "I don't know," the witness said softly.

"Excuse me?" said Stanton as if he hadn't heard.

"No, nobody told me nothing," she said, her head drooping forward.

"Ah. Yes, I see." Stanton gestured with his glasses.

"Now, please, what did the person on the phone say?"

"He asked for somebody. I don't know who."

Stanton nodded as if he'd expected this. "Let's go back to the deposition. On May third you said, Around seven-thirty I hear the phone ring. So I answered and it was this man asking if a Leroy or Juanita was there. There wasn't no Juanita, so I told him that and hung up. That was your testimony earlier. Did I read it correctly?"

"I suppose so."

"Haven't you testified that when a man came to your door a few minutes later—the man who attacked you—you recognized his voice, and that you were sure he was the same man who had just called?"

"I was under pressure," Teresa snapped. "What was I supposed to believe? I still am under pressure."

Stanton smiled sympathetically, attempting to help her through this treacherous puzzle. "We want there to be as little pressure as possible, Miss Jackson. That's why all I'm asking is for you to repeat the facts as you've already sworn to them. Didn't the same person who called you at seven-thirty come to the house and attack you approximately five minutes later?"

She was shaking her head sullenly even before he finished. "Maybe that's what I said, but back then I was still upset, you know, and confused. I don't know who called. It's not like they left a name or nothing."

Stanton spread his arms, the copy of the deposition flapping in one hand. "But the phone call and the person at the door had something else in common, didn't they? They both mentioned Juanita."

Teresa's lower lip thrust out again. "Yeah, I guess."

"Isn't that an amazing coincidence, if they're not the same person? One person calls and asks for Leroy and Juanita and then, five minutes later, someone else knocks on the door and says, is Leroy or Juanita there?"

"I don't know about no incidence, except him trying to do

that to me." She pushed her jaw in Gabriel's direction without looking at him.

Without any dramatic gesture Stanton had drifted gradually towards the jury, and now he spoke to Teresa from the side of their box. "You do understand, Miss Jackson, that if someone was there at your house five minutes or so after seven-thirty, that person could not have been Gabriel Salter?"

"I don't know that. No way." She lifted her chin, adamant.

The jury was listening intently, their eyes shifting back and forth between Stanton and Teresa Jackson. The last question had certainly snared their attention. I had to hand it to Gabe's lawyer. Entangling Teresa in the issue of time, when the phone call occurred, when the attack happened— seven-thirty or a little later was more than an hour before Gabriel's arrest at her house—might strengthen the claim of a grand conspiracy to entrap him.

"Miss Jackson," Stanton moved back towards the witness stand, "how tall are you?"

"Five-four."

"On the night of March fourth, when you were in the Broadlawns Emergency Room, didn't you tell Doctor Harris that your attacker was only a little taller than you, maybe five feet six inches tall?"

"Can't you hear me, or what? I was in shock that night. I didn't want to be talking to her anyhow."

"But you did tell her that your attacker was about five-six?"

"I don't know. I just told her anything. I mean, this guy's at the door and he's trying to rape me and all, and I'm supposed to say, Excuse me, how tall are you?"

"Isn't Mr. Salter much taller than five-six?"

"How would I know?"

"And at the time of your deposition, hadn't you changed your story. On May third you swore without hesitation that the person who attacked you was six feet tall?"

"I suppose."

Stanton began to turn away. Recalling another question,

he swung back towards her. "Does one of your brothers work at Consolidated Meat-Packing?"

"Yeah. Dave works there."

"Your brother ever talk to you about problems at Consolidated?"

"No. Why would he?"

"By any chance does Dave have a girlfriend who fits this description: tall, African American, very thin, eighteen to twenty years old, who might have been around the night of the attack? Who might have seen what happened?"

"Not that I know. Maybe he got a bunch of them fits that. How would I know?"

"Are you trying to protect your brother, Miss Jackson?"

"My brothers can take care of theirselves, 'long with my dad."

A ripple of laughter swelled from the family audience.

"That's all the questions I have," Stanton said. "Thank you, Miss Jackson." Buttoning his jacket, he returned to his seat next to Gabriel. My regard for him had grown. Like a fighter who lacked a knockout punch, he'd scored with a flicking jab. He would surely home in on discrepancies he'd exposed. But after a single round it was too early to know how much damage he'd done.

After lunch Joyce Kilburn steadily built her case. Gradually the contest came to appear less a boxing match than a carnival: it was theatrical, moralistic, and unreal, carefully scripted, with the denouement hardly in doubt.

Tanya took the stand and reaffirmed her sister's story, carefully correcting some of the details. That she'd been coached was obvious. "Did you get any visitors that night?" asked Miss Kilburn.

"Yes," said Tanya. "There was a knock at the door."

"About what time was that?"

"Probably around eight-forty-three," Tanya announced decisively.

A flicker of discomfort crossed Kilburn's face. "A little before nine?"

"Yeah," said Tanya. "That's right."

The 911 dispatcher dutifully described the protocol for handling emergencies. A mousy woman with stiff blonde curls and pink lipstick, she explained how a squad car on regular patrol in the neighborhood could arrive at the scene within two or three minutes, though that could never be guaranteed. And then she played, at Kilburn's behest, the tape of Tanya's call.

"He's raping my sister," Tanya whispered frantically, her voice rigid with fright. "He got her on the porch and he's doing it. You got to do something."

It was devastating. In front of me, Leroy Jackson was twitching with rekindled fury, shooting glares across at Gabriel. A silent sigh deflated Gabe's supporters.

Was Tanya faking it? I wondered as the tape crackled and hissed. Possibly, but if so she deserved an academy award.

The time of the call had been automatically recorded by computer as 8:51. The car dispatched in answer to a Priority One call arrived at the house one minute later. That too was logged. Within the next couple of minutes, Gabriel Salter was arrested inside the Jackson house.

Ernie Rodriguez, the arresting officer, took the stand. Tall, powerfully built, with pocked skin and a mustache, he recited the story by the book. No doubt, no confusion, just the facts of the arrest.

Stanton, cross-examining, wasn't impressed. "Officer Rodriguez," he asked, "when you arrived at the house, did you have any trouble locating Mr. Salter's car?"

"No, sir, I didn't."

"Wasn't the car of this would-be rapist parked right outside the house?"

"Yes."

"Don't you think it's odd that someone bent on a terrible felony would park their car directly in front of the house?"

"I wouldn't know," Rodriguez said with a stolid blankness. "I never tried to commit a felony. And guys who do, they're not always so smart."

Stanton stared with cold contempt. "Officer Rodriguez, did you know about Gabriel Salter or his political activities before the arrest?"

"Never heard of him."

"I see," Stanton nodded. He turned towards the jury and spoke without looking at the witness. "Isn't it true, Officer, that the Chief of Police once suspended you for lying about the details of an arrest?"

Rodriguez's sleepy eyes suddenly hardened with malice. Before he could respond, Joyce Kilburn had risen, her own face glaring with indignation. "Objection, Your Honor. That's an outrageous line of questioning."

"There's nothing outrageous about it, Your Honor." Stanton didn't move away from the witness box. He didn't want to let Rodriguez off the hook. "I've got every right to question an individual's bias, his motives, his prejudice, and his credibility. Our defense is that police officers have lied from the start in this case, and we have a right to pursue that line."

"I understand your defense perfectly well, Mr. Stanton." The judge's eyebrows shrugged up and down as he spoke, a professor putting a presumptuous student in his place. "But if I let you show that Officer Rodriguez was suspended for lying on one occasion, am I going to have to let the prosecution demonstrate that he made a thousand other arrests without any problem? No, I'm sustaining the objection on the grounds of relevancy. What you're after just opens up a Pandora's Box, and I don't want to get into that. As a judge I believe in the old maxim, If in doubt, keep it out."

Stanton turned away. I couldn't see his face, but he was frustrated and willing to show it. Judge Stevens ignored him for a moment. Finally he raised his eyes to the attorney before him.

"You have any problem with my ruling, Mr. Stanton?"

The attorney lifted his head. "As a matter of fact I do, Your Honor. I'm going to use this as an offer-of-proof if an appeal is necessary."

"You do that," Stevens said, his voice dry, his blue eyes firm.

In the late afternoon, my friend Doctor Harris from Broadlawns ER was called by the prosecution. It was the first time I'd seen her without a white jacket and stethoscope around her neck. She was smaller than Joyce Kilburn and dressed with less fashion. Her pink-and-brown-check dress might have come from a church rummage sale. She sat stiffly, more nervous than prim in the witness stand, answering questions as briefly as possible. She described herself as a family physician, and then described the protocol in examining Teresa Jackson the night of the attack: the use of an ultraviolet lamp, the careful combing of the pubic area. And she described her interview with Teresa. Again, the story was straightforward, even rather boring.

This was precisely as Joyce Kilburn intended. She wanted the story repeated over and over again, recognizably the same despite small snags—they added the flavor of truth and character rather than inconsistency. Echoed often enough, it would develop a strategic authenticity. She was determined to keep the lines simple. I noticed she wasn't bringing the Leroy Johnson-Leroy Jackson confusion into her argument. Trying to link Gabriel with other issues—a motive such as drugs, for example—wasn't necessary. By and large the members of the jury were still listening, though their interest had begun to flag.

"Doctor Harris," Kilburn was saying, "what did you notice about Teresa's face?"

"She had an area of swelling just beneath the left eye, and also a much larger area of swelling above the right temple." As always, my doctor was clipped and precise.

"And by the condition of these two injuries, could you tell how long she'd been suffering from them?"

"From the amount of swelling, I assumed they were acute."

"You mean recent?"

"That's right."

"So that, having seen the condition of her clothes, her extreme distress, and the acute bruises on her head, you as a doctor have no doubt that Teresa Jackson was attacked on the night of March fourth."

Stanton was on his feet at once. "Objection. Calls for a conclusion."

The judge shook his head. "Overruled."

"I have no doubt," said Doctor Harris, her face lifted with indignation. "I see it too often. Day in and day out, these girls come in. I'm not saying who did it, but it happened."

"Thank you, Doctor," said Kilburn with satisfaction.

Stanton had never quite taken his chair again. "Doctor Harris," he said, "nothing in your pubic examination of Miss Jackson suggested any kind of sexual assault, did it?"

"We found nothing decisive."

"No semen, no foreign pubic hairs?"

"No."

"So you can't be sure of just what happened, by whom, or even precisely when, isn't that so?"

"Yes, that's true," she admitted with professional candor.

"That's all I have," said Stanton, already turning away.

Kilburn rose but remained behind her desk. "Would you expect to find semen or foreign hairs in every case of attempted rape?"

"No. As a matter of fact that would be quite rare. We only find something in, maybe, five percent of such cases."

"Thank you, Doctor Harris," said Joyce Kilburn. She turned to the judge. "With that, Your Honor, the prosecution will rest."

Like birds waking at a signal, a wave of rustling passed through the courtroom. Relatively few birds remained, however. Many of Gabriel's supporters had drifted away during the course of the day. Not, I assumed, from sudden loss of faith, but because of exhaustion or children to feed or factory shifts to meet.

The prosecution's case had carried nearly to five o'clock, and the judge adjourned the court until Tuesday morning. We rose as he and the jury departed. The two separate parties, of more equal size than in the morning, remained standing, edging towards each other in the aisle but pretending not to, making their way towards the exit in uneasy company.

Someone may have slipped, some elbow may have jabbed an arm or back, but suddenly heavy jostling roiled the pathway. Thrusting past two of his sons, Branford tugging at his arm from behind, Leroy Jackson gathered himself to full menace and shoved a thick finger at Gabriel.

"You, sucker," Jackson shouted, "whatever they do to you ain't enough. Nothing's enough. You remember that. I'll get you myself if you're outside, and I got friends inside be glad to do me the favor." Behind him, his wife Caroline was nodding with a smug smile as if she'd goaded him to this.

This all might have been scripted too. Even if Jackson were capable of carrying out his threat—and I suspected he was—his words sounded wooden, like a lesson imperfectly learned from a bad movie. But the thunderclap of violence was real, striking close.

Gabriel halted. He was staring at Jackson with a smile of his own, puzzled and—he couldn't quite hide it—amused by the melodrama. He shook his head in fatigue and lifted a hand as if to touch Jackson. "I've got nothing against you or your family. If your daughter was attacked, I'm sorry—" He was going to say more, but Jeremy Stanton grasped his arm to lead him away. At the same instant, Simon Yoo slipped past Grey, lunged forward, and caught Jackson by his outstretched wrist.

Off-balance, Jackson was startled by the smaller man. He reared up to use his height and weight to advantage. But Simon, protecting his leverage, gripped the wrist in his powerful hand, the muscles in his arm and throat taut with effort. His face was deadly serious. For an instant the dance was in delicate equipoise. It was hard to make out who was leading. Jackson's sons, Gabriel's friends moved toward each other.

"That's enough. Cut it right now," cried a guard as he and a partner crashed into the central knot of the fray, parting Leroy Jackson and Simon Yoo with astonishing ease. The antagonists were panting. They glared at each other.

"You want, I'll book the lot of you," the guard shouted, glowering to all sides. "One more word, one more step and you spend the night. Hear me? Now go home. Get out of here."

Embarrassed, I raised my hands and stepped clear.

I tried to stay clear, at least for the one night. But I didn't manage. Where else, after all, was I to go? Should I have huddled solitary and noble in my room at the motel? Even if I was concerned only with getting material for the Sunday Magazine, better I should be on the inside. Of course, that wasn't all that concerned me.

I arrived at the house around eight o'clock. The porch was deserted, though the front door stood open. For once the family wasn't gathered together in confab but scattered throughout the house. A brooding tension washed over me as soon as I walked in.

In the living room, Hilary and her father were sitting next to each other on the couch. Joseph, heavy black glasses on his nose, was reading a book. He glanced up at me over the frames and nodded wearily, as if this were a vigil we were all sharing, biding our time. He returned to his reading. Hilary was fumbling with a deck of cards in her lap. Several had tumbled onto the floor in front of her, but she didn't bother to collect them. She was looking up at me too.

"When you didn't show for dinner, I thought maybe you'd gone over to the other side," she said.

"Underdogs make a better story," I said, hands in my pockets. "Tough day for Stanton."

Hilary made a sour face. "Can't really blame him. Whatever you thought before, you've got to admit they're railroading Gabe. The judge isn't even pretending to let Stanton set up a defense."

I shrugged my acquiescence. "What about tomorrow? Is he launching any surprises? A mystery woman or two?"

"If there is a tomorrow," she muttered. Joseph glanced at me again over his glasses.

"Because," I filled in the rest, "if tomorrow Gabe's convicted, they'll revoke bail until sentencing and that'll be the end of it. Right? So he's got that choice again?—now or never."

Father and daughter faced me. Neither spoke.

"What's he going to do?" I asked.

Joseph closed his book, pulled his glasses off, rubbed the bridge of his nose. "What's Gabriel going to do? I don't know. I doubt he knows yet. My opinion, however, doesn't change."

"Opinion," Hilary repeated with impatience but also a more general hopelessness.

"Where is everybody?" I asked.

"Around," she said.

Though I'd no particular plan, I was eager to stumble into Grey. She hadn't been out of my mind for more than a few minutes all day. But I couldn't manage to think about her— about what we were doing, about where we were headed— without the thought tangling with conflicts and problems and betrayals, like a fishing line running afoul of one neighbor after another.

In the kitchen, however, it was Gabriel I discovered by himself at the table. His back was to me, and I halted outside the door. Legal papers sat gathered by his elbow. But he was staring at the window intently. He could have been any of the soldiers in the V.A. ward with me, the ones listening to a delicate music in the distance beyond hearing, beyond anyone else's sharing.

This house had always struck me as spartan and cold. But as I watched Gabriel, I became aware that gloom had seeped through its rooms, filling space vacated by light and hope. June twilight still drifted through the window, yet the kitchen was thick with shadows. Another shadow flickered in the alley. Simon, I gathered, was sticking close to Gabriel, if unobtrusively.

Gabriel sensed me behind him and turned. His face was drawn, his eyes hooded. Yet he smiled with a hint of the old mischief. "Come to join me in my hour of need?"

I had no answer but to pull out a chair. "Stanton did a pretty good job today."

"Yeah, well, so did Kilburn. She's got my boy on the ropes, thanks to how the good judge lays out his rules." Bitterness crept in. It startled me only because bitterness seemed so alien to Gabriel. It was something he'd achieved.

"What about Jackson's scene at the end? He worry you at all?"

"Nothing he does surprises me, not after the bookstore." He dismissed it with a grimace. "I wish I knew where the guy was coming from. He must believe the whole story. But not if he's in on it, right? Maybe he's doing this all for show." Perplexed, Gabriel shook his head.

"There's plenty going on in his head and in that family we're never going to know." I looked at him. "You decide yet whether to grace the court with your presence tomorrow?"

His mouth remained set.

For a little while the two of us were content to share the silence as shadows fleshed themselves dark. Gabriel seemed to drift away again. At last he broke the spell. "I'm curious. How do you see it playing out?"

"What playing out?"

"Everything. If I do or if I don't. Anything you like."

"Come on, Gabe," I cried softly. "What the hell do I know?"

"You got better plans for the evening?"

I could barely make out his hard smile, but I felt his power, his intensity.

"Go on. Don't tell me what I should do. Just how you see it developing from here."

"Okay," I said, raising a palm. "How I see it. Okay." I took a deep breath. "Nothing I can tell you you don't know. The two paths. And neither's pretty. One version is you jumping bail and spending the rest of your life on the run, new name, new everything. Oh, I'm pretty sure your ISA can arrange it easy enough. Maybe on the Coast or in what, Canada or Mexico? Maybe farther. But that's a hell of a life. Not to mention how it wrecks the faith of your supporters.

"The other story's you going inside. You did say there's plenty of work for you—lots of convicts to convert. Still, that doesn't sound appealing to me." I halted lamely. "Told you, I'm no prophet."

He smacked the table with his hand. "But you've already convicted me, damn it. What if the jury doesn't buy their case? Even with all the limitations the judge has imposed, what if only a couple of them listen to me?"

I said nothing.

"I know." He passed a hand across his face. "Whatever you think, Jason, I'm no fool."

"I never thought you a fool."

"But you're still not able to believe me either." He got up, turned away, swung back to me with passion. "Yeah, I was caught on the girl's front porch. Yeah, I believe her too, partly—someone must have attacked her that night. And yeah, my story's preposterous if they don't let you see the bigger picture."

I wasn't sure the big picture made his story any the less preposterous. But Gabriel's anguish rang bone deep. Even in the dim light I spied it in his face. His cheeks were hollow, his brow pale and high, his nose sharp. A physical pain seemed to glimmer in his eyes. His flesh and his youth had been refined away as if by fire. Though he stood very still, I imagined him all but writhing before me.

Was he in torment because of a terrible secret wrenched into the open for all the world to see, thanks to his own inexplicable loss of control?

Or did he despair because a lifetime's commitment, a saint's self-denial, were being mocked, were transformed into something grotesque? And because the faith of others in him was corroding beyond salvage?

I wanted to feel for him. I wanted my sympathy to blossom. But it didn't, it couldn't. I sat where I was, dismay seeping like bile into my mouth. But I felt only that I was stumbling in the dark, my hands outstretched. I wondered whether I was guilty of a deeper failure in myself: did some incapacity of character paralyze me, in suspicion of everything and everyone?

Of course—a giddying blaze of joy and shame recalled the truth in the same instant—I'd certainly rediscovered my feelings when it came to Grey Navarro. Because of her, I could breathe again. I could see so clearly that the light hurt my eyes. It was as if she'd ripped ancient gauze and bandage clear, releasing me into myself. In just the past couple of days I'd awakened to a vividness that was almost cruel.

Yet here with Gabriel, my friend, my brother, I remained cold, unable to feel anything much beyond a general annoyance. Covertly, my fingertips touched my thigh, thrumming the old scar for reassurance.

Glimpsing the next step before me and no way to avoid it, I gritted my teeth and pressed ahead: I'd returned to Iowa bent on determining Gabriel's guilt or innocence. Instead, I was sleeping with his wife. The impression of her lingered in my arms and against my lips. I pictured the fold of skin in the crook of her elbow and my heart winced tight.

The trial earlier in the day had been a series of set-pieces, Teresa playing her role as violated young girl eager for vengeance; Gabriel his as clean-cut martyr poised for public flaying. And I—I'd strutted my part as well: the objective, untainted reporter. The old friend. The dual deception nauseated me; the lie was suffocating. I must have jerked my head with disgust.

"You okay?" Gabriel asked.

I rose, walked to the wall, flipped a switch. The naked bulb in the ceiling scattered the shadows and shut out the world beyond the kitchen.

"I got something," I said returning to my seat, gut churning.

"Yeah?"

I was plunging quickly so there wouldn't be time to think. "See, there's this thing with Grey." I wasn't being fair to her; I'd have to make it up later; perhaps this would set us both free.

"I know." He said it straight, his eyes steady on me.

"What do you mean?"

"She's told me."

A slash of surprise and shame raked me. I remembered to breathe. "She told you."

"Yeah." This was a matter of fact. He seemed almost reassuring. "We have this understanding. Grey and I do. About not lying to each other."

I nodded. I swallowed. When had she spoken? What had she told him? A hot rush of anger soared towards her for betraying something precious.

"It's sweet of you to want to tell me too," Gabriel said. Something jagged lurked in his voice. "I mean, I under-stand. She's a remarkable woman. Not everyone appreci-ates that. It wasn't easy for her, telling me. I'm pretty sure she cares for you a great deal."

"Uh-huh."

I was furious with him for the patronizing good will. But he didn't get it. He didn't see what I was driving at. I wasn't confessing. I was making a declaration.

"Can you tell me something, though?" he asked confidentially as if the question had been nagging at him. "Between us, okay? I know you, Jason. You don't do something like this for the hell of it. Then why? Why my wife? Just for Grey's sake, honestly? Or is it something against me personally? Are you paying back an old family debt?"

I stared at him blankly.

He watched me for a few seconds and then smiled. It was a terrible smile, weary and sad, and angry too, but not angry enough. "Look, I'm not saying it's not Grey. She saw something in you. You saw something too. Maybe both of you needed it to happen. But these things are usually more complicated than that, at least inside families like ours. Don't you think?"

"What the hell are you talking about, Gabe?" My jaw was clenched tight as I tried to gauge what he was after.

"Maybe it's me," he said as a matter of conjecture. "I can't picture anything specific I've done to you, but maybe you resent my politics more than I thought. Or are you getting back at Hilary, indirectly, for leaving you?" He looked at me quizzically. "No," he shook his head, dismissing the equation. "That's not it. You brought that on yourself and you know it."

I turned my head aside. I resented being the one suddenly on trial, though I'd struck the indictment myself.

"Or is this all ancient history?" He studied me. "That's what I've been wondering. It must have been hard for you—marrying into the Salters. Maybe you went away to war and when you came back wounded, marrying Hilary, the rest just got pushed out of sight until you had the chance to do something about it. Especially now that you're not in the family anymore, not legally. Are you doing this as a payback for your old man's sake?"

I said nothing. I stared at him.

Gabriel seemed to need to talk the story through and perhaps not think about his other nightmare for a little while. "It's the one thing I've never forgiven my father, by the way," he said. "Not just for what it did to my mother, but the running away, not having the courage to face up when the truth came out. I hated that.

"Your mother, well she kept it from her husband longer, all those years—I always wondered why, not to mention how. Was it for the sake of the family or the marriage? I don't know. Maybe it was to protect the friendship between the two men. That'd be a riot, wouldn't it? And how could he not see? Did your father not want to know?

"And of course none of us could breathe a word, not even to each other. Our brilliant little game—we'd been caught up too—protecting the secret. A conspiracy no one had to teach us. Most natural thing in the world. You and Hilary were masters. Never so much as a hidden grin, not a wink or a nod I ever spied. She made sure I wouldn't break the code by talking to you about it.

"Did you know—I never found out 'til later—that my mother caught on early in the game? Any wonder she barricaded herself in the house and kept the world at bay? Or maybe that wasn't what started her. Chicken, egg—who knows?" He paused, considering. "He's nursed her all these years since. I'll give him that."

Gabriel walked to the window and leaned back against it. "I learned it on the teat, so to speak.

"But I always figured it was extra hard on you, Jason—your father's son. And you had this special relationship with my old man too. How'd you manage? Lord, I was jealous. And yet I was looking up to you. You were always so solid, the big brother I wanted to have, someone I wanted to be like. Especially since the rest was this big, warm, ever-loving lie.

"And no one ever talked about it. Not even when your old man finally stumbled into the truth. For sure not after mine raced us away in shame to Arkansas." He halted, looking at me earnestly with a half-smile. I spied again the pain in his face.

I was glad to be feeling so little. Oh, there was the satisfaction of a historian in the archives: that rare, ever so rare sense of completion as the last shards of a shattered puzzle slip into place almost by accident, realigning all the others in thrilling pattern. The story comes clear in outline: suddenly it's been inevitable all along.

No, no satisfaction. Feelings—I felt like weeping, not at the story but at my own slowness, my own blindness.

Had I not known? How could I not have known? It was so obvious, so ordinary, so terrible in its little way. And I'd blown it up into a grand mystery, worrying it like a dog with a rank sock. Poor excuse for a historian. I felt dazed with discovery and shame. What a fool I must have appeared to Aunt Claire only ten days earlier, to my poor mother too, and to Hilary for years and years.

My father appeared before me vividly, not as he would have looked when I was a boy, but older, worn, as I'd seen him so recently. And I wanted to put my arm around him and I wanted him to put his arm around me. Together we would support each other in our shared innocence, our astonishing ignorance, stumbling along paths in the darkness.

"Is that it?" Gabriel asked. "You sleeping with Grey to settle a family score?"

I shook my head. "No," I said.

The world seemed odd, out of joint, when I left their house a little while later, as if my concussion had flared anew. Or as if the concussion had been only one stage in a process that was continuing and over which I had no control.

I wandered out the back and into the alley. I didn't want to see Hilary again. I didn't want to encounter Joseph. Just outside the kitchen door, Simon was leaning on Gabriel's car, smoking. His cigarette danced a jagged orange seam. He noticed me but didn't move. Did he know the story too? I wondered. I was very careful driving back to the motel because I couldn't trust my instincts.

I stood in the doorway to my room, keys in hand, and then turned and walked back to my car. The room was suffocating. I was restless. And I didn't want to discover whether Grey would appear. My thoughts were too confused with anger and shame and desire to deal with her if she did. And if she didn't—well, that would likewise be too terrible.

I headed south past the airport. With astonishing abruptness, scudding out from the bright overhead lights of the city, I was lost in dark farmland stretching away with a gentle roll and flattening before me. If I turned left I would meet the Mississippi. If right I'd eventually rise into the mountains. I was tempted, one route or the other. But heading south, there lay open farmland and darkness, the late June night heavy with moisture and warmth and the rich, rank smells of grass and hay, manure and dust.

When I turned at last, it was towards the city once more. I knew that, for now, any destination would only bring me back.

I arrived at the motel well after midnight. Parking my car, I stepped out and spotted the disappearing tail lights of a pickup truck two blocks away. It could have been Grey's. Had she come and waited for me? I considered chasing, but it was too late. Anyway, I didn't know what I'd say. But the thought swept over me that after all I'd made a mistake not being there for her, whatever the risk should she show, whatever the risk should she not. In that moment, neither my shame nor my frustrations nor all the confusion of feelings that had been loosed seemed very important.   What mattered was that I wanted Grey, a deeper need, a more powerful desire, than all the rest.

Chapter XII

Tuesday morning Hilary and I again traveled together to the courthouse. Neither of us spoke as we hurried up the walk, eager and wary of what we might find. I'd lost all sense of what I hoped. We pushed past the guard at the courtroom door. And there, on the other side of the gate and rail, apparently indifferent to the comings and goings of people who could come and go, sat Gabriel alone next to Stanton's still empty chair. The room might have been deserted for all the notice he paid. Yet I sensed in the square of his shoulders an ease, a calm absent in recent days. I was proud of him. And I was grateful that at least this one portion of suspense was so quickly relieved.

Behind Gabriel once again sat Grey. Deliberate or distracted, she seemed unaware of my arrival. Joseph's seat from the day before, however, was empty. I was turning to ask Hilary about it, but she'd already slipped dutifully towards the empty bench as if to hold her father's place. She and I had hardly spoken during breakfast or the ride to the courthouse. She'd been lost in her own thoughts and I, suspecting now that she'd known more all along through our youth and our marriage than she'd let on, didn't want to discover just how much she also knew about current events.

Once it began, the morning session dragged with stunning

deliberateness.   Stanton was laying the foundation for Gabriel's defense with a series of witnesses testifying to the nobility of his character. At this preliminary stage the attorney had no intention of simply reciting a story to compete with the prosecutor's; the jury would do that bit of work themselves once he'd furnished the materials.

I wanted to catch Grey's eye, but I was behind her and she never glanced my way. She too seemed subdued this morning. Now and then she'd murmur something, leaning her head slightly towards Simon at her side. Frustrated, I sat yearning for a recess.

Among the early witnesses appeared a woman I'd noticed at the house and perhaps at the rally, but I'd never caught her name until now: Marta Collins. Small, fine-boned, with wispy blonde hair and a shapeless periwinkle-blue peasant dress that matched her eyes, she taught in the religion department of Mount Vernon College, two hours from the city. Her role in Stanton's campaign was a double one. Although not a member of the ISA, Marta testified that she and her husband Gene shared similar political views with Gabriel Salter and Grey Navarro. Over the past couple of years, the couples had become close friends.

"Do you feel that you know Gabriel Salter fairly well?" asked Stanton.

She leaned towards the microphone. "Yes, I do."

"Based on the considerable time you've spent with him as well as with his wife, have you ever thought of Gabriel as a violent individual? Have you ever been scared of him yourself?"

"No," she answered firmly. "On the contrary—I believe Gabriel to be one of the most gentle and caring men I've ever met. To me, he's a model of someone who, day-in and day-out, is absolutely committed in his beliefs as well as his actions to non-violence of all kinds, especially against women." She smiled as she spoke.

Stanton nodded slowly, letting the jury take the testimony

in. "Have you ever noticed any problems between Gabriel Salter and his wife that would lead you to believe that per- haps he's occasionally violent with her?"

"Absolutely not." Offended, she snapped like a teacher responding to a foolish question from the class. I thought she might slap a ruler on the rail for emphasis. "If anything, Gabriel has always exemplified a man who is tender and able to listen. And he's—well, he's about the most gentle man I know."

I sighed. I couldn't read what the jury made of her testi- mony. But to me the small speeches rang too pat, as if she'd written them out in longhand and carefully revised for class. It soured me with impatience. That Gabriel was a saint in daylight we already knew. So three others had already testi- fied, including an Episcopal priest who'd marched in various protests with him; so swore the young accountant from the IRS who, anything but a socialist herself, had been deeply moved by his speeches on behalf of immigrant workers. Was the jury also growing impatient for a direct engagement of the charges?

But Marta's second purpose came to light only now as Stanton veered into a different line of questioning. She and her husband Gene were the friends planning to stay in Gabriel's house the night of March fourth. That visit had been scheduled a week earlier, she testified; no doubt or confusion about it. She and Gene were coming to the city for a conference and needed a place to stay. Since Grey Navarro was working a night shift, she wouldn't be home until early morning, and Gabriel was supposed to greet them.

"What time did Gabriel Salter expect you?" asked Stanton.

"We couldn't be sure—we thought we might be at the house as early as nine o'clock. As it turned out, we didn't arrive until nearly ten."

"Was he home to welcome you as expected?"

"No."

"That strike you as unusual?"

She nodded, with a frown of her original unease at discovering the house dark. "We had these plans. It wasn't like Gabriel to stand us up, so we wondered what happened."

"And you found out he'd been arrested?"

"Yes, later that night. We'd gone to stay with his neighbor Sara Oliver."

Joyce Kilburn, during cross-examination, refused to fight on the ground laid out by Stanton. She rose briskly to confront the witness.

"Miss Collins, is there anything I could tell you about Gabriel Salter that would make you change your opinion about him?"

Marta hesitated. Showing her nervousness for the first time, she glanced at Stanton. He was already on his feet, swift and businesslike.

"Your Honor, that question is too vague to warrant an answer. How is the witness to guess what anything might mean?"

Judge Stevens hardly paused. He gazed out with his cold blue, heavy lidded eyes at Jeremy Stanton. "Then she'll simply have to answer the best she can. Overruled."

Kilburn looked once more at Marta Collins.

"No," said Marta defiantly.

"I see—whatever facts might appear, whatever evidence may be produced, you're absolutely fixed in your belief in Gabriel Salter's character. Tell me one more thing, Miss Collins. Were you with Gabriel Salter when he was arrested on March fourth at the Jackson home?"

"No, how could I have been?"

"Thank you," said Kilburn already turning away. "Nothing further."

Sara Oliver was next to take the stand, moving with a slow dignity. This morning she wore a round African cap and a caftan in browns and greens and yellows. They emphasized the squareness of her face, the stolid mass of her body. She was an imposing figure.

Yes, she confirmed for Stanton, Gabriel had called her on March fourth. His call came at 8:45 p.m. He was rushing to the market for food and he wanted her to keep an eye out for Gene and Marta in case they arrived. Oh, yes, she could be sure of the time because she'd been asleep—she worked a midnight shift—and when the phone rang she naturally checked the clock.

Joyce Kilburn was more wary of Sara Oliver. All but deferential, she didn't challenge her testimony about time or place. Nevertheless, she put her through the same paces as Marta. "Is there anything I could tell you that would change your opinion of Gabriel Salter."

"There is not."

"Were you with Gabriel Salter at the Jackson home on March fourth?"

"I was not." Sara spoke slowly and simply, with an assurance that hinted at a larger serenity, her dignity an earth mother's. Kilburn's words scathed her not at all, and clearly the prosecutor was glad to be done with Sara Oliver.

I'd covered enough trials to know that the effect of character witnesses, however impressive, was uncertain. But Marta and Sara had also launched Stanton's assault on one flank of the prosecution's case. Marta's testimony attacked the issue of motive: why would Gabriel go off to assault young women when he knew that out-of-town guests were due on his doorstep within a few minutes?

Sara not only confirmed that question; her testimony also recalled a basic confusion in the prosecution's case. Teresa Jackson had originally claimed that her attacker appeared a little past seven-thirty at the start of her favorite tv show. But Gabriel didn't call Sara until eight-forty-five, and the time of his arrest was roughly nine o'clock. Had someone perhaps attacked the girl earlier and she, or her sister Tanya, only called the police more than an hour later—once Gabriel had been lured to the scene?

During the brief morning recess I couldn't get close to

Grey. I didn't feel like invading the family patch and she didn't leave her seat. Despite being surrounded by well-wishers, she seemed entirely alone. In this she mirrored Gabriel, who sat quietly next to Stanton.

After the recess, Stanton called Grey to the stand. Whatever doubts one might have about a wife's credibility, she is the most important of character witnesses. Her loyalty to a man under siege can be moving—and can make a jury believe he's worthy of it. She herself evokes sympathy. And in a case of sexual assault, a wife's testimony bears extra weight. Nevertheless, I shifted on the hard bench and then shifted again. I didn't much want to hear Grey extolling Gabriel's virtues.

As she was sworn in, she looked tense and fierce, a captured hawk. She was flushed, her skin dark. Her hands lay awkwardly in her lap.

Stanton circled out from behind his table and stood midway between Grey and the jury. His manner was relaxed and reassuring. Hands pushed casually in his pockets, shoulders hunched a bit, he nodded to her with a warm but serious smile. "Will you state your name, please, for the record?"

"Grey Navarro," she answered with a slight stammer. Frustrated, she shook her head sharply back and forth once.

"And what's your relationship with Gabriel Salter?"

"I'm Gabriel's wife." Her eyes glittered with defiance.

"Where do you work?"

"On the fab line at City-and-Country Packers. I bone the hams."

Stanton nodded again, perfectly pleased with the preliminaries. "Do you mind if I call you Grey?"

"All right," she said.

"Okay, Grey. Can you tell me a little bit about your background?"

I spotted the dangerous set of her jaw. This was difficult territory. Wrestling with her own pride and privacy, she seemed hardly to draw breath before speaking. "I'm Indian, what they're calling Native American these days. Laguna. I come from just outside the Navajo Reservation in New Mexico. My family has a small farm there, herding sheep and a few goats."

"They are not wealthy people?" Stanton asked.

Grey glared at him. If he was being ironic, she didn't smile. "They are poor people. It is a very hard life. They do not have running water. For their water they fill up a tank in the back of their truck at the school five miles away. They have electricity now but no telephone." She spoke slowly, stiffly, her voice low but clearly audible.

"That was the school you attended?" he asked. "For how long?"

She nodded. "I finished my schooling there. I was one of very few to earn a high-school degree."

"Did you consider going to college?"

"I did go. I earned a scholarship from the Bureau of Indian Affairs. For one and a half semesters I attended the University of New Mexico in engineering. Then I left for New York."

"You moved to New York?" Stanton tilted his head towards the jury as if they were merely listening in and might be interested in this as well. "You left the university after all you achieved because?"

Her nostrils flared and she glanced at the floor. She looked at Stanton directly once more. "I'd grown up in a place where poor people, where Indians have nothing but injustice. It was time for me to fight to change that."

"Where did you meet Gabriel Salter?"

"It was then, in New York, at a meeting of the International Socialist Alliance."

"And tell me, Grey, what was it about Gabriel Salter that attracted you?"

I crossed my arms and settled back against the long bench.

"Well, Gabriel—he stood out from the others, from the

men. For him I was not some strange creature. The others came on to me because I was exotic or because they wanted to make a political point about how open-minded they could be. Gabriel, he had spent many years living in the Cherokee Nation with his family. He was quiet and sweet and gentle. And he was committed to working for a better world. More than anyone I'd ever met, he was able to talk to ordinary people, to persuade and make them listen and make them act. Not only by his words but by the way he worked and lived and acted too."

My face felt stiff and wooden.

"What kind of relationship do you have with Gabriel?"

"We respect each other. We never lie to each other. We are committed to the same goals."

"Do you believe there's anyone in this courtroom who knows him better than you do?"

She shook her head very slightly. "There is no one who knows Gabriel better."

Stanton drew himself up straight and, raising his voice, tried to wrestle the truth from her. "Have you ever seen any sign in Gabriel Salter, as only a wife can, that he suffers from raging sexual desires or a capacity to hurt women?"

"Never." She answered him. "Never."

For a long moment there was silence in the courtroom. Faintly, we could hear Grey breathing into the microphone.

Stanton was ready to move on. "Grey, did you know about the plans for your friends Marta and Gene Collins to spend the night of March fourth at your house?"

"I knew, yes. I'd been called for overtime—a double shift. So it was a very busy day for us all. Gabriel worked his usual shift at Consolidated. Afterwards there was a protest meeting—he'd helped organize it—about an INS raid at the plant. After all that, he had to hurry home to get food for Marta and Gene."

"Whatever your politics, you both work and work hard for a living, don't you? Thank you very much, Grey. That's all the questions I have." Stanton began to turn away.

She seemed startled that he was finished with her. "No. Wait." She lifted a hand as if to pull him back. "I have something more."

Caught unawares, the attorney hesitated.

"Mr. Stanton?" Judge Stevens demanded.

"Perhaps Ms. Navarro wishes to correct something I've stated, or answer one of my questions more fully, Your Honor," he said. "Is that correct?"

She nodded.

"Get on with it," said the judge.

"It is about Gabriel and women. I did not tell you everything. I am sorry, but I thought you would ask more. Now I must."

"Shit," I murmured under my breath. A rustle of whispers and of bodies shifting erect swept swiftly by. The tension that had been dormant through much of the day flared through the courtroom. Stanton hesitated again. He didn't know where she was going and he was wary. He'd drawn all he wanted from her, and now she was setting off on her own. Behind the lawyer, Gabriel's back had straightened and he was shaking his head at her.

"You needn't tell us any more," said Stanton, "unless it's essential to answering one of my questions."

"It is. I must tell you," she insisted.

He cocked his head doubtfully, hoping she'd get the message.

Gabriel stood. "You don't need to do this," he called to her.

"The defendant will be silent," Stevens said acidly.

Grey stared at Gabriel, her eyes narrow, her mouth grim. "You asked me whether Gabriel desires to hurt women and I said never. I did not explain." Again she halted. This was difficult for her.

"You don't have to," Gabriel said quietly, but the judge pretended not to notice.

She plunged forward. "I know it is impossible for Gabriel

Salter to hurt anyone, to hurt a woman, because of what he has been through with me. He brought me back from the dead. I was dead inside when he met me." Unconsciously, one hand tugged her hair over her shoulder, toying with it as she spoke. "The reason I came to New York was only partly the politics. I had to leave—I could not stay with my family, and I could not face the university. It seemed so futile, such an illusion after what happened." She turned a quick glance at the jury and back to Stanton.

"When I went home during that first year from the university, I was raped."

"Objection, Your Honor," Kilburn cried. "This isn't relevant or material to the case being tried here."

Stevens blinked heavily.

Stanton leapt in. "This goes to the heart of the defendant's character—we need to have this, Your Honor."

The judge breathed through his mouth. "Okay, I'm going to allow it."

Grey's head jerked nervously. "A boy I grew up with, a Laguna, he brought two White friends with him from outside the reservation. I think he wanted them to like him. Maybe he wanted to show that he could think of Indian women the same way as them. When I came to the school to fill our tank with water, they were hiding. I did not see them until I was standing with the hose. They circled round me. They grabbed me. It took three of them. One of them, one of the White boys, I broke his nose with my hand as they were pushing me to the ground." Fierce, proud of the blood, she was breathing heavily.

"He was first, bleeding on me as he did it. Then the other one did it. Then the boy I knew all my life—he was scared and he was drunk and he did it too, as if maybe that would make him forget what he did. The first one, the one with the broken nose, after he did it again, he made sure there was some of my blood to make up for his. They left me there.

"No one else came for water. I did not want my family to

find me like that. Finally, I climbed into our truck and drove home and it was never home again.

"When I came to New York, I was dead inside. You understand? I wasn't even angry. I knew with my head what I wanted to do, but I was feeling nothing. At the university I'd already become a socialist. But for the other students in New Mexico, politics was a joke. In New York I heard Gabriel Salter speak. I liked what he said—he made sense, he cared, he was willing to put himself on the line. But he was and part of me hated him too, whether he lived with Cherokee or not.

"Later, the Alliance assigned us to work together. By chance only. So I had to talk with him. And somehow he knew—he could recognize that I was wounded. He wanted nothing from me. Slowly, patiently, he talked with me because I could not talk, I could not speak of it."

Suddenly, in a quick gust, tears welled into her eyes and down her cheeks. For a moment Grey didn't realize what had happened. She pushed at the tears with her palms, furious at the show of weakness. She gasped, swallowing a sob. The rest of the courtroom had disappeared for her and she was staring only at Gabriel. Speaking of this publicly was her gift to him.

Now she swung her eyes to the jury, hunting them out one by one. "You cannot know what he did for me. He was gentle, he was patient. He talked, and the talking drew me out so I could speak of it. Telling the story brought me out of the dead." She stopped and took a deep breath. She'd taken her tale and extended it to include Gabriel, drawing a circle around the two of them. The courtroom was silent.

Then Grey's eyes lifted again: dark and quicksilver, they sought me and pierced me for a single instant. My heart shattered with surprise and yearning. For an instant I was alone in the universe with her. I hadn't expected, hadn't foreseen such an acknowledgment. How could I, after Gabriel? Could all the world see or was this invisible? I shivered. With that searching intimate glance, she'd thrown the circle farther to gather me in as well. There were the three of us now. She'd given me a gift too. But I understood it was also to be a burden.

"In your opinion, could Gabriel Salter sexually attack a young woman?" asked Stanton once more quietly.

"Never," she said again.

Stanton nodded and turned away.

Joyce Kilburn stood behind her desk without speaking for several beats, trying to deflate some of the tension by her very willingness to wait. She was well aware of how Grey's tale had charged the atmosphere. "Ms. Navarro," she said plainly and without hostility, as if she were merely inquiring about the weather, "is there anything I could put to you that would change your opinion about your husband?"

"No, there's not," Grey replied simply. She was calm and in control once more. Her stern face gave nothing away.

"Were you with him at the Jackson home on the night of March fourth?"

"I was working."

"Thank you, Ms. Navarro. That's all I have."

During lunch most of the observers went either to the small canteen in the courthouse lobby or walked to a row of restaurants a block away. I drifted outside and followed without real purpose as Gabriel's party headed towards a dingy Chinese restaurant. Through the glass I made out Gabriel and Grey heading towards a table for two. They were speaking softly, heads inclined, calm and casual. I was jealous of each of them. But I made no move to intrude. Even if Grey had drawn me into the magic circle a few moments before, now seemed not the moment to dramatize the matter. Simon was trailing faithfully behind them, along with Marta, Sara, and several other supporters. They were ushered to a larger table. Once more I was outside looking in. Someone brushed my elbow and I turned to find Hilary.

"Mind if I hang out with you?" she asked.

"Doesn't look like much room in there," I said. "Let's try the Mexican across the street."

She shrugged.

"Where's your father?" I asked after we'd ordered.

Her face darkened. "Didn't I mention this morning? He's gone. Gone home. I guess that after I left the house last night, Gabriel announced he was going through with the trial. There must have been quite a scene. Papa packed his bag and called a cab for the airport. He only phoned me once he was there." She was picking at the label on her beer bottle but not drinking. "He took Gabe's decision pretty hard. For him it felt like Gabe wasn't just rejecting advice about the trial. He was rejecting, I don't know—everything. But I don't think it's true, at least not entirely."

I tapped the soiled tablecloth with a spoon. So Joseph had slipped out of my life again. I'd vaguely hoped for another chance to confront him. Who knows?—maybe I wouldn't even have admitted what I hadn't known. Yet my feelings for Joseph had grown confused and rather muted, as if they too belonged now only to a distant past. If anything, I'd wanted to pin him down and so pin down my own parents, fitting their history into something set and stable. But they, all of them, continued to slip away as if I were clutching at a stream, my fingers grasping only water.

"You hear that Gabe and I had a scene last night too?" I asked.

A wry smile. "That was pretty obvious. Why do you think we all stayed out of the kitchen?"

"How much did you hear?"

"Nothing. Nothing I wanted to hear. Your voices got loud a couple of times, but not loud enough."

"What he told me," I said with a sour grin at my plate, "was about our parents."

She inclined her head. "Yeah. That's what I figured," Hilary said. "Something about the tone. Poor Jason. Poor, dear Jason." Her voice was barbed with irony.

"How come you never told me?"

"What could be the reason to tell? I mean, you didn't really want to know or you'd have guessed it yourself. Even your father did eventually. But it's not like both families conspired to keep it from you."

She waggled her fork with exasperation and relief to be speaking about it at last. "It exploded quietly enough when your father found out, but you were already slogging away on the other side of the planet. We were getting those tv pictures, stuff and horrors no one had ever seen before, so I was terrified for you. Everything, there and here, was going up in flames and our little family drama seemed, well, like pretty small potatoes.

"No, I remember. He never did guess—your mother finally decided to tell him. Why? Why after all those years? That I don't know. But Papa—maybe he thought her speaking was a betrayal. First I heard was a phone call to my college dorm. They were already packing for the trek out to Arkansas, and Mother thought I ought to have some idea.

"Who's going to tell you? And how, by letter? And what's the point in breaking it after you've been shipped to the VA hospital in Virginia? By then it seemed so much after the fact. I was more concerned with getting you well, with getting you home, rather than with all their failures."

I made a wry face. "These last few weeks I've been spinning my wheels trying to discover the great secret of why Joseph disappeared into the wilderness. And now it seems such a little thing." Nevertheless, an acrid sadness swelled in the hollow between my heart and breastbone.

"Yeah, well, there it is," Hilary said.

I didn't ask what else she knew.

"State your name for the record, please," Stanton asked.

"My name is Gabriel Salter." Intense, alert, he sat in the witness box in his ill-fitting suit, eager to get on with his version. Tension crackled just beyond hearing.

"Okay, Gabriel." Stanton paced thoughtfully a few steps. "I'd like you to tell us something about your childhood, so that we can all get a better sense of your background and of how you came to be so politically committed."

"Well, I have good memories from my childhood. I grew up in a college town in Pennsylvania until I was ten. Then we moved to the Cherokee Reservation, the part of it that's in Arkansas. My father is the head of a small school there." His manner was straightforward, almost chatty. He seemed oblivious to the spark of his own presence. But without doubt he was drawing every eye, focusing every breath, as his father used to do, cocking bow above cello in the instant before attack.

"How did you make the transition from a college town to the reservation? Was it tough?"

"Very tough. But it wasn't that I didn't fit in. All the kids were Cherokee, and they accepted me right off—friends I played with, built tree houses with. It's just that life was so much harsher for them. The fact my family wasn't as comfortable as in Pennsylvania, that didn't bother me much because my friends had it so much worse. Most people there were on government assistance."

"Did your father's work running the school influence you?"

"Yeah," he said. "In a big way. Truth is, I doubt he imagined what he was getting into when he accepted the job. We all thought he'd gone crazy. But once he was there, well, it took a while, but his whole attitude changed. Since then, the students have been his life. That's what I learned.

That's what I believe in today—that an individual can make a difference for others." He spoke earnestly as if admitting something for the first time. I was sorry Joseph wasn't there to hear. Like me, Gabriel had missed his opportunity.

"When did you leave Arkansas?" Stanton asked.

"Not 'til college. I'd won a scholarship out east, one of the Ivies, but I couldn't stand it there. Phony at every level. So I came back to the university in Fayetteville. I was there for two years before leaving again."

"What happened?"

"By that time I'd joined the ISA, the International Socialist Alliance. I wanted to get out, get to work, start organizing people to be strong together."

"What did your parents think of that?"

Gabriel's eyebrows arched. "They were plenty disappointed at first. A college degree matters a lot to them." He lifted his head, his wistful eyes strong. "Finally they came to understand and support what I had to do."

"Okay, but how did you earn a living?"

"I worked a number of jobs around the country—that's part of the ISA's philosophy. Members have to work, have to hold real jobs, not be cushioned in a comfortable office. So for a while I was a mechanic in a Georgia aircraft plant. Another time I did electrical jobs in Indiana. Wherever, I've always been active in local unions, grass-roots stuff, never an officer or steward. And then I was rotated for a stint in New York at the national, helping publish our newspaper, organize demonstrations, that kind of thing. That's where I met Grey Navarro."

Automatically I glanced at Grey. She seemed to be staring at something off to one side and very far away, but I could tell that she was listening intently.

"And you both came to Iowa. When was that?"

"A little over two years ago. I got a job hauling paunches at the Consolidated Packing plant."

"Hard work?" asked Stanton, rocking back on his heels.

"Hardest job I've done. Dangerous too, with the knives and the slick floors. You can go down in a second. And it's hot in the summertime—can't get any hotter. The smell—well, that's another thing."

Memories rekindled of my own visit to the plant. I saw the belly ripped from a cow. The stench woke in my nostrils as if never entirely gone.

"What are working conditions like?" Stanton asked.

"Rough," Gabriel said. "Turnover's high. Last I checked, I was twenty-fifth on my team's seniority roster. Twenty-fifth out of a hundred-fifty. And that's after only a year and a half on the job. Shows how many people are fired, are hurt, decide to quit, or just take off."

"You a trouble maker?"

"No." Gabriel's head jerked up defiantly. But slowly, out of the scowl, a wry little smile bloomed. "Yeah, actually, I guess the bosses might think I'm trouble. Like I said, I'm not a union officer. They're the one's who've sold out, mostly. They'll fuss and roar about little stuff, but nothing big, nothing that matters. Bosses make them comfortable. And being comfortable—it's like a big noose around their necks.

"My job is to convince people, the ones down on the line, it doesn't have to be as bad as it is. Like, for instance, I'll show them how the managers pit one group against another to keep them all off balance. How they'll whip up some kind of ugly scene between White workers and African Americans, or Latino and Asian. Everyone's so on edge they can't spot who's really pulling the strings."

"Objection, Your Honor," Kilburn said angrily. "You've already ruled that these outside political affairs have nothing to do with this particular case. This should all be inadmissible."

"She's right, Your Honor—you've put so much off limits that there's hardly room for me to build a case. All I'm trying to do here is establish who my client is and what he does. The jury has a right to know his character."

Judge Stevens was already shaking his head. "Sustained. Leave the politics out of it, Mr. Stanton, and get on with your defense."

Stanton ran a hand back through his hair. Frustration began to bleed through his cool. "Mr. Salter—Gabriel—do you recall an incident that occurred at the Consolidated plant on March first of this year?"

"Objection," snapped Kilburn from her chair.

"Your Honor," cried Stanton before the judge could respond. "Maybe what happened at the plant was political, maybe not. But it bears directly on what my client was doing the day of his arrest."

Stevens frowned, his eyes narrowing to slits. "I'll allow this. But tread carefully, Mr. Stanton."

The attorney nodded to his client.

"Sure I remember," Gabriel said. "That was the day the immigration storm troopers charged into Consolidated and arrested seventeen of my co-workers."

"And your reaction was?"

He snorted. "Disbelief. Outrage. It was unbelievable. But I guess in some ways it didn't surprise me at all—just more of the same. Look, the managers knew who these people were when they hired them. It was all a set up. And I'd been working with them. I knew them. These are hard workers scraping by, trying to support their families. Why shouldn't they get a chance? You think other people are begging for jobs like this? The managers need them—that's why it's all a game.

"What's worse is how the government lied—the INS broke its public word." Gabriel's eyes were alight. Even the judge was caught up enough by the story that he forgot to interrupt. "See, they had this amnesty program. They swore that if illegals registered by a certain date nothing punitive would be done. But then INS agents used that supposedly confidential information to track people down. You were asking my reaction?—I was ashamed of this government and I was angry."

"But why arrest them at the plant?" Stanton asked.

"That's the point," said Gabriel with a grim smile. "The INS is in the bosses' pocket. Arranging these busts every so often keeps workers in line. One more tool. The cops never sweep them all at once, just enough to keep fear in the air and people from trusting each other."

"So, was there any protest of these latest arrests?"

Gabriel nodded. "You bet. One of the biggest demonstrations ever in Iowa. The managers tried to stop it, but then we shut down the entire Consolidated line. That was costing them thousands of bucks a minute. Finally, they backed down." Gabriel's smile flickered. He tried to hold it back, but his enthusiasm wouldn't dampen. It filled the courtroom. I felt the faint echo of a smile on my own lips.

"When was the protest?" asked Stanton.

"After work that Friday, March fourth, down at the Mexican-American Center."

"And it was a success?"

"Was it ever. Hundreds of folk from all over the area showed up, lots of them whole families. Media covered it too. Everything we'd been working for was coming together—the solidarity and commitment. Now people were finally understanding what the company and cops were willing to do. And how standing together was the only way to block them. The ball was rolling. Of course, we were also demanding justice for those seventeen Latinos who'd been arrested—and we got that too. A judge released them a few days later. Which was maybe a lesson to the INS. More than that, we were showing the bosses they can't intimidate people that way anymore."

"After it was over, how did you feel personally?"

"Me?" Gabriel glanced directly at Stanton, surprised at the question. He flashed a grin. "I felt—I don't know—pretty terrific. After nearly two years. It was quite a day. A good day. Afterwards, some of us went over to Los Caballeros—

that's a bar—to talk about it over a beer."

"When did you leave?"

"Around eight-thirty. I'd already stayed too long, given how the rest of that night was shaping up. For one thing I had to cash both Grey's and my own paychecks. And I was supposed to be putting together a political forum for the next night at Trailblaze Books—that would take some planning. On top of it all, as you heard, Marta and Gene Collins were spending the night at our house. I figured I better get food ready too."

Stanton was pacing again with his head down. "Okay, let me get this straight. You left the bar about eight-thirty—and we have other witnesses to vouch for that. So at seven-thirty there was no possible way for you to be anywhere near the Jackson house, when Teresa Jackson says she was attacked?"

Gabriel's face went taut as if he'd just recalled what this was all about. "No way at all. I didn't attack her then. I didn't attack her ever."

"So if someone came to her house at that time, as she's sworn—"

"Objection—calls for speculation," Kilburn interrupted.

"I'll let him finish the question," the judge said bruskly.

Stanton bowed. "If someone was assaulting Teresa Jackson at seven-thirty, it couldn't be you?"

"It wasn't me," said Gabriel.

"Okay, let's go on." The lawyer paced a few steps back and forth. "You were also expecting company, your close friends, within a very little while after you left Los Caballeros. Did you have to do anything for them?"

"Well, like I said, I was planning on cooking dinner. But there wasn't enough food in the house. That's why I drove home to get Grey's check and to call Sara Oliver—she lives next door. I wanted her to keep an eye out for Marta and Gene."

"Did you make it to the market?"

Gabriel wasn't smiling. His lips were pressed together in a

thin line. "Never got there. I spent the night in jail instead."

"What happened on the way?"

"While I was stopped at a light, this young woman rushed out and started beating on my window. She was begging for help."

"Weren't you suspicious?"

"Why should I be?" he demanded. "She's upset—seemed scared out of her mind—and she's crying about how some guy is after her. Maybe I'm dumb, but I believed her. I asked whether she wanted to go to the police or get other help, but she said no way. She just wanted to get home."

"And you took her where?" Stanton was patiently working it through.

"A house on 29th, where she told me. Then she wanted me to check out the porch and make sure the boyfriend wasn't waiting for her."

"Hadn't you already played Good Samaritan enough? I mean, Gabriel, what business was it of yours?"

"What was I supposed to do?" The cry lashed out, snapping the boundaries of the story, of Stanton's careful script. But the lawyer didn't seem at all displeased.

"What was I going to do?" Gabriel demanded again. "Just drive away and leave her? She was in trouble. She was scared." He sighed and turned his head away. "At least I believed she was. And if someone's in trouble, it is my business. I don't just walk away."

Stanton coaxed him along. "What happened next?"

"So we go up inside the porch together. It's dark, no sign of anyone, but she opens the front door with a key and hustles in. I'm still waiting on the porch like she says. Next thing I know, I hear someone coming up the walk quick and then a hard rap on the screen door. I figure it's the guy she's afraid of. I was pretty scared myself just then."

"Was it him?"

Gabriel shook his head. "A cop. He busts through the door and grabs me by the arm. He calls back, I've got him. I figure it's a misunderstanding. But it only gets worse. I'm trying to explain and he won't listen. He twists my arm and shoves me through the house into one of the bedrooms. Handcuffs me, wrists behind my back. Then, well then, he jerks my pants down. What've we got here? he says."

"What did you think while this was happening?"

"It was so quick, so impossible. I don't know—I was flabbergasted. I mean, it was all so nuts." The memory wrenched Gabriel in the witness box. His face twisted with lingering disbelief.

Stanton turned and faced him head on. "Gabriel, did you ever see Teresa Jackson on March fourth?"

Gabriel set his jaw. "Never laid eyes on her until the deposition in May." He glanced at the jury and then across the way to Teresa Jackson and her family.

"Did you sexually assault Teresa Jackson on March fourth?" Stanton demanded, not letting the witness off the hook.

"Absolutely not."

"You're telling the jury you're innocent?"

"I am innocent."

Jeremy Stanton let the last remark echo in the stillness of the courtroom. I was aware of those who had remained faithful: Marta and Gene, Sara Oliver and Mary Sillito, nearly a dozen others. Each now had a different look, of seriousness, of belief in Gabriel's claim, of worry. Mary Sillito's broad face glowed ecstatically.

"Thank you, Gabriel," Stanton said.

Joyce Kilburn rose thoughtfully and studied Gabriel. She wagged her head. "I've no questions at all for the defendant, Your Honor," she said, dismissing his testimony entirely.

Gabriel left the witness box and returned to his attorney's side. If Kilburn by her lack of interest had shaken the careful rhythm they'd pursued all day, Stanton gave no sign. With a small deferential smile, he rose and buttoned his jacket. "In that case, Your Honor, the defense rests."

A rustle passed quickly through the courtroom. Judge

Stevens blinked at both counsel. "Okay," he said slowly. "It's still relatively early. Let's take a short break and then see if we can do closing arguments. I'd like to get this off to the jury."

During the recess I lingered by myself in the corridor. But when the crowd began filing back I climbed the central stair-case to the fourth floor where I was eye-level with the gold leaf on top of the corinthian columns. I had no desire to hear Kilburn and Stanton summing up. No need. Never had the two stories been clearer to me, never more irreconcilable. They were finally so different in nature, one about facts, one about faith, that they didn't exclude each other so much as collide and career off on separate trajectories. Reasonable doubt? What had that to do with these stories? My own doubts, and there were many, were all unreasonable.

Above my head loomed a series of murals. Intrigued, I walked from one end to the other, observing the sanitized epic. Bare-breasted squaws stared up contentedly as their menfolk greeted newcomers. Apparently of their own free will, the Indians were obligingly disappearing from and into history. I was embarrassed, as if I'd been sneaking a peek at the soft porno behind a shop counter. Taking a seat on a wooden bench, I stared instead at a young man with leather jacket and black greasy hair who was leaning over the rail-ing. A thin young woman was tucked into his side. Behind them the door of the Family Law Court was closed.

When I finally descended to the lobby canteen for a cup of coffee, I discovered the two parties already waiting. The Jackson family huddled, cramped into a separate glassed-in booth designated for smokers. Gabriel and Grey, Hilary and

Simon and their other friends were sitting at plastic tables as far as possible across the way, jumbled against the windows. Through the glass partition I saw Brian Phillips chatting with Leroy Jackson. He was jotting quick notes into his pad. So the case had already gone to the jury.

I put coins in a machine and sipped the weak coffee. Hilary came over and got one too, touched my arm, returned to her chair. I attempted to catch Grey's eye, but it was Gabriel who glanced up. He made no gesture, he didn't smile, but his gaze was steady and strong. Could he imagine how desperately I wanted to rush over and be accepted into the fold? But I also felt caught—as so often of late—forever within and without, a spectator torn by the process of watching.

At a quarter-to-five, the judge summoned everyone concerned. He was prepared to dismiss the jury for the night. But the foreman, his hairpiece slightly awry, asked for more time—he believed they were within striking distance of a verdict. Even as he cringed while begging the favor, I glimpsed a bullying jowl. How hard was this foreman worrying other jurors into line?

Judge Stevens hesitated. "I'll give you until six, then we'll call it quits until tomorrow."

"Your Honor," Jeremy Stanton protested, "I don't think there's reason to rush on this. The jury shouldn't feel under any time constraints."

The judge lifted his hands helplessly. "No need to convince me, Mr. Stanton. It's their request. And," he said with a significant glance over his glasses in the jury's direction, "I'm sure they will take all due time in reaching a verdict."

Both parties returned glumly to the cafeteria. To all appearance the misery of waiting might have joined them. But soon hostile murmurings from Jackson and his sons dispelled any such confusion. Simon Yoo never allowed himself to glance across the way. Again and again he removed his glasses to wipe the lenses. Naked, his eyes appeared oddly vulnerable.

Just before six, the bailiff summoned us once more. Perhaps the jury was asking to review some evidence; perhaps they were ready to admit that a quick resolution lay beyond their grasp.

Wearily, warily, the two groups climbed the stairs. At this hour the courthouse was all but deserted. In the corridor I drew aside and let the others enter. To my surprise, Gabriel stepped clear as well. He smiled, his eyes alight, and patted my shoulder as if he were an older brother both kidding and reassuring me at once.

"After all this, after everything, I'd like to think you've come to believe me," he said.

I looked at him for a moment. "I do," I murmured, surprising myself.

In speaking it, I realized there was no lie. If I could never fathom what lay in his heart, my belief was of a different kind. Whatever he'd done, whatever had been done to him, still lay beyond reach of everything except two potent stories. I'd failed after all to discover a more simple truth in the case. But Gabriel, flesh and blood, blocked my way. And I had indeed come to see that his story was twisted too intimately through my own for me, so damn pure and aloof, to deny him again. Yet neither could I deny, in my own heart, the doubts bred of simple facts. Whether he was convicted or set free, I'd have to learn to live with them as well.

Pleased, he nodded and gazed at me and then turned away into the courtroom.

The jury looked rumpled as they filed in. The toll of a two-day trial and now the first hours of deliberation had staggered them. Several sagged as if beaten down. One woman was snuffling into a ragged tissue.

"Mr. Foreman, I'm prepared to release the jury until tomorrow morning," said the judge. "Deliberations can begin again where you left off."

The foreman was already shaking his head. "But we've reached a verdict, Your Honor," he said, his slit of a mouth parsing out the words. His pale eyes were mean and triumphant as he passed a slip of paper to the bailiff.

Though apparently troubled by such haste, Judge Stevens accepted the note, studied it, nodded. "Okay. Mr. Stanton, would you and Mr. Salter please rise."

Startled by the rush of events, Stanton fumbled to respond, but found nothing to say. Buttoning his jacket, he pulled at Gabriel's sleeve to lift him. Grey stretched forward half out of her seat as well. The silence jammed about us; it rang loud.

Stevens, unable to mask his own unease, turned once more to the jury. "You have all willingly and without compulsion reached this decision?"

Sullen, most sat without responding. A few nodded timidly. "Your Honor, we have," insisted the foreman.

The judge nodded. "All right then. How find you the defendant?"

I glanced at Gabriel. He was standing stiffly, head up.

"On the charge of attempted rape, we find the defendant guilty. On the charge of burglary, guilty." The slit worked itself once or twice in silence and then sealed tight.

Gabriel's shoulders sagged, but he remained on his feet. Stanton turned from his client back to the judge, his face full of anger.

A ragged cheer broke at once from the Jackson family. They surged up from their seats.

A slow rolling groan of disbelief swept through Gabriel's camp.

The judge rapped hard with his gavel. He was speaking, but no one seemed to hear.

Gabriel turned and reached across the barrier towards Grey, brushing her cheek with his fingers as the bailiff clasped his arm. She seemed frozen in place, her eyes stricken.

"It ain't enough," Leroy Jackson called. "However long they stuff you in the can, it ain't bad enough." He was pressing forward as if to tear Gabriel loose from the guard. "I got friends inside that owe me, Salter. They be happy to do a favor on you." He was still thrusting towards Gabriel, jabbing a finger.

"Order," shouted the judge, on his feet now too, still rapping hard with the gavel, his eyes wide with alarm.

For already the blaze had spread beyond Jackson. His sons were crowding behind, desperate in the hope Simon would respond. Teresa and her mother didn't push forward but neither did they retreat. They held each other and watched, jubilation on their faces. Bodies jostled against each other in the central aisle. Someone was wailing; many voices were shouting.

I darted forward and grabbed Hilary by the arm. Her eyes were glinting with tears at the sudden verdict; her brother was already being whisked away towards the cells; she seemed almost oblivious to the conflict. "Come on," I urged. I pushed her towards the doors, and then I swung back.

Only two guards had remained on duty when the session carried beyond regular hours. The one who'd already taken charge of Gabriel, sensing the melee, pushed the prisoner ahead of him and through a separate passage, jostling the judge. The other, a reedy old man, recognized from the start that he was overmatched and fled to summon reinforcements.

Gene Collins, Marta's husband, hurled himself against two of the Jackson sons, pushing them clear so I could make out Simon grappling again with Leroy. I caught a glimpse beyond them of Grey standing still and alone, her face stern, abstracted. Then she was gone again as the small riot closed about her. Sweat poured down Simon's face as he maintained his leverage, jerking Jackson off-balance, twisting his arm. Behind his glasses, Simon's eyes shone with fury and despair.

Leroy bellowed with pain as he attempted to gather himself up, but his balance was precarious and he struggled not to topple to the ground. He was huffing and wheezing. Branford hovered perilously behind, avoiding the fray but ready to catch his brother-in-law should he fall.

I waded forward, pushing into the bodies, vaguely intending to separate the fighters but swept up too with frustrations: nothing, it came clear to me, had been settled by the jury's verdict. Nothing but a ragged dance in court, a bureaucratic necessity. Why should I have been surprised? I flailed hopelessly into the surging tangle. A stray fist slammed against my ear, sending me reeling, my ribs awakened into daggers. I gasped and fell back.

A grinding snap—so loud, too loud—froze everyone magically. Leroy groaned, slumping, all blood hurtled from his face as his arm swung grotesquely at the elbow. A keening wail went up from Caroline. Branford threw his arms about Leroy as he collapsed.

Dave, the eldest son, leapt at Simon just as the doors flew open and half-a-dozen cops charged in. Dave threw a lunging punch. Simon slipped it to the side. But the wild blow caught Grey near her eye, Dave's heavy ring clawing her cheek. Blood sprang from the wound. Helplessly, I watched her stumble with pain beyond my reach. Recovering her balance, she swung back towards the battle as if newly awakened.

The police were plunging forward. Two had already pushed Simon to the floor flat on his face, his wrists pinioned behind him. Another cop latched onto Dave's arm, but his mother and brother were clinging to the other arm, trying to tug him free.

I slipped in from behind. As a cop lunged to the left, an opening appeared. I darted through, caught Grey by the arm, and dragged her away. To my relief she didn't resist, though neither did she hurry. She seemed hardly aware of me. I held my breath, expecting to be tackled at any moment, but the guards were too occupied with what lay in front of them.

With Grey clear of the brawl, I reached for my handkerchief and pushed it against the streaming gash on her face. The fresh pain startled her. She raised a hand to the cloth and touched my hand too. Together we lurched from the courtroom.

Outside the building, rain had begun to fall in thick, warm, heavy summer drops. Far away I heard a thudding roll of thunder. The street was all but deserted at the dinner hour. We hurried now, not glancing back. Ahead, I spotted her pickup. I guided her to the passenger side and held out my hand for the key. She slumped against the seat with exhaustion or pain or grief.

As I struggled up into the other side, grunting at the stab of my ribs, her head had fallen back, eyes closed. Her hand drifted away from the wound, though still loosely clutching my handkerchief. I tugged it from her grip and carefully dabbed at the drying blood. She flinched but said nothing.

"I never pretended to be a nurse," I murmured softly. It had only been a few days since she'd said the same thing while nursing me. "I should probably get you to a hospital—this'll take some stitches."

She shook her head and struggled to sit up. "I'm okay."

I didn't force the issue.

Grey opened her dark eyes and looked at me. Rain was thumping more loudly on the roof. I leaned forward and kissed her lips softly. On them I tasted blood. When I drew back, I saw that her eyes were closed once more.

"I suppose now we'll have to raise bail for Simon," I said. "It'll mean more work for Stanton."

She nodded.

"Why don't I run you home? I'll bet Sara and the others will go back there too and make some sort of dinner. They'll convince you to get the damn stitches."

"No," Grey snapped with impatience. "Let Gabriel's friends feed themselves. I work with them. I don't need them cooking and washing for me, tending me now. I'm not an invalid. And this fight isn't over." Her eyes blazed.

"Yeah," I said, my heart sinking.

She glanced away into the early dusk of storm clouds. "Are you staying to help?" Her voice was low and hard as the drumming rain.

"If I stay, it won't be for your fight, but only for you."

Tugging both my hands into her lap, twisting them angrily, she stared at the overcast sky. "Why do you never understand? The fight is me. Everything else you know, you understand—that's what surprised me from the start."

I drew her hands to my lips. "I do know."

We didn't speak any more. Though my heart ached—a cold hard ache that had been gathering for days—I didn't feel I was simply losing her, as I'd feared. It wasn't that. One kind of intimacy had blossomed between us before. But now as we listened and held each other, that intimacy was being translated, as if without intention of our own, into another.

It seemed we'd known each other a very long time. Like an old married couple who had no need for words, we glimpsed what lay ahead and were content to face it. I did, it is true, feel a little dizzy at the pace.

I broke the silence at last. "Well, I suppose I've still got a job to get back to. My time's up."

Still she was gazing away. "Jobs," she said simply. "We have jobs to do." She hesitated, pulled back, looked at me searchingly. "Your job."

"My editor will want something from me."

She tugged at my shirt cuff. I could make out a faint smile in the darkness. "Winners and losers and stories," she murmured softly. "But Jason, remember, it's yours now."

"Yeah." I reached across, slipping my hand behind her neck and drawing her towards me. I kissed her lips gently again. I handed her the key. "See you," I said.

Hilary was checking out of the motel when I arrived. Her bags sat next to her. She looked pale, as if she'd been ill. But she also seemed impatient, relieved, eager to leave. "There's nothing else I can do out here," she said as I came up. "At least for the time being. Sentencing won't be for several weeks. And anything to do with an appeal can be managed over the phone. Jeremy Stanton has my number."

"Sure," I said. "Makes sense."

"Aren't you coming?" she asked, perplexed. Then she turned more fully to me, and her face opened, and this was the Hilary I knew, who knew me. "Is Grey waiting for you?" There was no accusation in her voice, but concern, yes, there was concern.

I shrugged. "No," I said. "I'm going home."

She brushed her hand on my sleeve. "Look, why don't you hurry? We can make Chicago in time for the red-eye."

By ten-thirty we'd settled into our seats for the short hop out of Iowa. The last flight of the day was nearly empty, and the attendant dimmed the lights. As we gathered speed on the runway, I turned to Hilary. "I'm sorry about Gabe," I shouted over the roar.

Her jaw tightened. "It's lousy," she called. "But it's not over."

"That's what Grey says."

She smiled at that and turned her head to the window to catch some sleep before Chicago.

Carnegie Mellon University Press
Series in Short Fiction

Very Much Like Desire
Diane Lefer

A Chapter From Her Upbringing
Ivy Goodlman

Narrow Beams
Kate Myers Hanson

Now You Love Me
Liesel Litzenburger

The Genius of Hunger
Diane Goodman

The Demon of Longing
Gail Gilliland

Lily in the Desert
Annie Dawid